I0761638

BREAK WIDE THE SEA

BREAK WIDE THE SEA

SARA HOLLAND

WEDNESDAY BOOKS
NEW YORK

EU Representative: Macmillan Publishers Ireland Ltd, 1st Floor, The Liffey Trust Centre, 117–126 Sheriff Street Upper, Dublin 1, DO1 YC43

First published in the United States by Wednesday Books, an imprint of St. Martin's Publishing Group

www.wednesdaybooks.com

Design by Michelle McMillian

Library of Congress Cataloging-in-Publication Data

Names: Holland, Sara author
Title: Break wide the sea / Sara Holland.
Description: First edition. | New York : Wednesday Books, 2025. | Audience term: Teenagers | Audience: Ages 13–18
Identifiers: LCCN 2025009366 | ISBN 9781250854490 hardcover | ISBN 9781250854506 ebook
Subjects: CYAC: Fantasy | Blessing and cursing—Fiction | Whaling—Fiction | Mermaids—Fiction | LCGFT: Fantasy fiction | Novels
Classification: LCC PZ7.1.H646 Br 2025 | DDC [Fic]—dc23/eng/20250421
LC record available at https://lccn.loc.gov/2025009366

First Edition: 2025

10 9 8 7 6 5 4 3 2 1

To everyone fighting to make the world a better, fairer, safer place

BREAK WIDE THE SEA

Chapter 1

Girls on the shore must guard their hearts
For the men tend to die catching whales.
Yet nothing we do for all our arts
Will keep them from their sails.

—Abbonish nursery rhyme, recorded in Kirkrell in Third Month, seventeen hundred and fifty-three years FC

The box from the dressmaker arrives just in time.

After our housekeeper carries it to my room, I kneel and sort through the contents, careful not to let my fingernails—long, sharp, reddish-black—snag the expensive fabrics. Gloves, two dozen new pairs in linen and leather, velvet and silk, of various muted colors. A gray silk pair, I think, for tonight.

I'm tugging them gingerly on, a set of movements perfected by years of practice, when a bright voice from the doorway makes me jump.

"Is that a new dress?" Lydia asks.

Glancing over my shoulder, I see my younger sister teetering in the doorway, craning to get a glimpse inside the box. Heart in my throat, I lean over it to block her view of my hands as I finish pulling the gloves on. "No," I say, letting the lid fall shut and sitting on its edge to face her. "Just some new petticoats."

She knows that I always wear gloves, but not why. And I don't want her to see the new shipment and ask again. I have enough lies to keep straight tonight.

"Oh," Lydia says, disappointed. She's ready for the shareholders' meeting in a dress the pale yellow of corn silk, her hair drawn up and her cheeks pink with excitement, or maybe rouge. "You're wearing that old thing?"

I look down, chagrined. I'm wearing a dress from a few years ago—dark blue velvet, the color of the ocean late in the evening on certain summer nights, when the sky has faded to twilight. It falls almost to the floor, skimming my body, with long sleeves and a high neck. I chose it carefully, hoping to make the shareholders see me as more than an incompetent child, as someone to be reckoned with. "This isn't a walk on the promenade, Lydia. It's a business meeting."

Double-checking that the gloves haven't snagged, I move to my bedside vanity to fix the last few buttons at my nape, the tricky ones. Maker knows I've had enough practice at this over the years, but with Lydia watching it's harder. "Our appearances are only important insofar as they inspire the shareholders to have confidence in us," I tell her reflection in the mirror.

Although I fear that inspiring confidence in the shareholders will be an impossible task. Lately nothing I do seems to impress them. Perhaps short of magically transforming into my dead father, nothing ever will.

"Did you get Kit to bed?" I ask. In the mirror, I see Lydia drift into the room, despite how often I've told her to stay out unless invited.

"Yes, though I suspect he'll be up for a while." She pauses to examine the contents of my open wardrobe. "I told him he could read for half an hour since we're making him miss the party, so I give it two hours before he's asleep."

"It's not a party," I say, pointlessly, because she's not listening. She's radiant, as always, but I can read the nervousness in her pale, set face, how she glances in the mirror and tugs at one lock of carefully curled hair.

Should teach her how to hide that, I think, *soon, before—*

"This is pretty." She reaches for the seashell on top of my writing desk, a peach-and-white conch shell nested in a black silk handkerchief.

I whirl around, almost tearing one of the buttons from my dress in my haste to fling a hand out and block her path. "Don't touch that!"

She steps back, raising her palms in a conciliatory gesture. "All right, I won't." Her brown eyes are wide, alarmed.

I take a deep breath and step back, aware that I moved too quickly. "I'm sorry." I opt for a partial truth in hopes that she'll buy it. "I'm just nervous for tonight. The shell is from August and I suppose—I suppose I'm rather protective of it." As I speak, I wrap the shell in the handkerchief—the spines sharp even through two layers of silk—and place it carefully in the top drawer of my dresser.

When I look back up, my little sister is watching me, quiet, considering. "If you say so," she says eventually. "Do you want me to do up your buttons in the back?"

"Please." I turn around so my back is to her and move my dark blonde braid over the front of my shoulder, eyes down so as not to meet my own gaze in the mirror. Lydia comes up behind me, lifting her hands. I will myself to be calm, to act like I have nothing to hide.

Because why should I be afraid? Her fingers are soft and warm and nimble, fixing the lace at the nape of my neck, where my skin is still smooth. Her smile in the mirror is sweet, placid. If she feels my pulse thudding under my skin, she says nothing.

There have been times, these past few years, when I've caught her looking at me strangely, or for too long. Times when she asked if I was all right, and when I said I was, she held my gaze like she was trying to catch me out in a lie. But those moments grew fewer and farther between, and now she never asks at all. Our conversations center around frivolous things, everyday matters. News from the docks, gossip from the neighbors.

I'm not sure if that's because I've gotten better at lying—at hiding—or if she's simply given up on hearing the truth from me.

My fingers itch in their gloves. I grip the corner of the vanity and try not to think about it.

~

"So how do we inspire the shareholders to have confidence in us?" Lydia asks as we make our way down the stairs, the sounds of the shareholder meeting getting louder and clearer as we go. Dozens of voices merge into a roaring tide, impossible to distinguish as individuals.

"August and I will be announcing the voyage of the *Heralder* to the north," I reply. "We'll be sending our best sailors on the expedition. That should win us some points." I grip the banister as I descend, polished wood smooth under my gloves, trying to remind myself of the solid ground beneath me.

There's the sound of wineglasses clinking together, the rich smell of a cooking meal mixing with the perfume of freshly cut flowers, and the string players we hired underpinning everything with a lilting, refined harmony. That was one of the lessons Papa gave me. Whenever people gather to discuss the affairs of the Fairfax Whaling Company, make it an event. Make them feel lucky to be there.

I pause at the last landing before we reach the first-floor entrance hall, suddenly gripped by a wave of dread at the thought of rounding the corner, of all those eyes on me for the whole interminable evening. "Anyway, just be your charming self," I tell Lydia, stalling. "Leave the business talk to me and August. Maybe someone has a pretty daughter you can talk to."

The curse is worse now than it's ever been. It's getting harder and harder to hide. Maybe Lydia didn't notice the new gloves upstairs; maybe she really just failed to see my too-fast movement when she reached for the shell. But so many more people will be watching me tonight. I'll have to be careful. I run through the rules in my mind.

Don't move too fast.

Don't touch anyone.

Ignore the smell of blood. At least that shouldn't be an issue here in my home—not like it is out in the streets, so many years of whaleblood and cows' blood and even human blood ground into the mud between paving stones.

A mischievous grin had flitted across Lydia's face at the mention of pretty daughters. But now it falls, her eyes growing serious. "What if someone asks about the *Orcadas*? Was it really a finfolk attack?"

My stomach sinks at the reminder. Last month, one of our ships sank in the Aegiran Ocean, hundreds of miles north of here. Though no part of me wanted to, August and I visited the hospital after the survivors returned—about half the crew—to hear their reports.

In a small room off the hospital wing, the wails and groans of the injured and dying floated through the cracks in the walls. The sailors spoke of an unnatural storm that flared up on a clear day, and some of them claimed to have seen dark figures in rowboats at the edge of their vision, watching as the ship went down. I found I could barely make eye contact as they told their stories. Meeting their gazes, it was like I was out at sea again, in the cold and the terror and the whirling fog.

I don't know how August was so composed, so at ease. I couldn't escape the feeling that any of the sailors might see in my eyes how I was like them: cursed.

One sailor refused to drink water unless the nurses forced it down his throat, crying out instead for salt water to be brought. Another spoke in a language no one recognized. A third couldn't speak at all, though at first the doctors had been able to find nothing physically amiss. It wasn't until after he died that we learned the truth, when I heard the physician's report of what they'd cut from his lungs. A still-living, still-growing bright-orange branch of coral.

I arranged for a sum to be paid out to the man's widow, enough for her to maintain herself for at least a few years. It wasn't hush money. I knew she would keep her silence. No one wants to admit that their loved one died of a finfolk curse. It means they can't be buried in the churchyard at the Seaman's Bethel.

And when the cursed go on living, well—

"Annie?" Lydia's hand finds my elbow, making me flinch. She's moved a couple of steps down the stairs, looking back up at me as if to ask what's wrong. "The *Orcadas*?"

I swallow, trying to force my rising dread back down to its customary place in my chest. It's always there, but I can't let it rule me tonight. "We're taking measures to protect our ships," I say.

"New equipment, new weapons. August will speak to it more at dinner."

"Will that be enough?" she asks, voice soft. She looks worried, and that makes my heart twist. The fleet, the whaling, everything to do with the company—it's meant to be my responsibility. If the rumblings of discontent among the sailors and shareholders have reached my siblings, I'm already failing in my duties.

I put my gloved hand lightly over hers on the banister, breaking a rule just for a moment, before letting it drop. "We have to be brave." And then I brush past her and lead the way downstairs.

After I was born, and then Lydia three years later, Papa changed the company bylaws, decreeing that women were to be allowed to sail as crew members on whaleships and even become officers. He wanted to create a more equitable company for Lydia and me to inherit. And a handful of the shareholders have always been women. I grew up attending these meetings at Papa's side. He bade me to pay attention, to remember that I would be in his place someday. But neither of us ever dreamed someday would come so soon.

The entrance hall spreads out beneath us, a sea of people in dark, muted colors traversing the parquet floor, servants in pressed white darting through like gulls. The Fairfax Whaling Company has around fifty shareholders; they will all be in attendance tonight, along with their families. Honored guests too, such as the captains who pull in the most barrels of whale blubber and whaleblood and whale meat, and the merchants we do the most business with, who buy those products and fill our company coffers. Mostly men, they wear blue and black and gray wool, ornamented with brass buttons or brooches made of whale ivory.

The captains and officers—the whalemen—are dressed similarly, but can be distinguished by their faces burnished by sun and wind; the smudges of tattoos peeking from cuffs and collars; the rolling quality to their stride, like they're unused to walking over solid ground.

Lydia's already split off from me and is moving through the crowd, her yellow dress bobbing through the dull colors like a daffodil against frozen earth. An old gray-headed captain looks at me appraisingly as I pass, not bothering with a polite smile. His eyes remind me that it's been years since I set foot on a ship that wasn't anchored in the harbor.

Tonight, the first time I'm to lead the meeting, the familiar scene feels different, overloud, the air too warm, the gazes more piercing than before. In the six years since Papa died, Grandfather led the meetings in my stead, but now that I'm eighteen and Grandfather's growing frail, it falls to me. I know the shareholders are skeptical. I hear the gossip in town when people think I'm out of earshot, read the distressed letters in the paper calling for a change of leadership. Maybe things would be different if I were older or cleverer. I can't help but think that I'm not enough.

But I have August. When a hint of copper on the other side of the room catches my eye, my heartbeat quickens, goes uneven. August holds court with half a dozen shareholders, momentarily revealed by the shifting tides of the people around him, hanging on his words.

Like he senses my gaze, he looks up and his eyes find mine across the room. Bright blue even from this distance, like chips of ice or the spring sky. Red-gold hair and a slow, easy smile, the one that feels secret just for me. His smile has never failed, not even that night six years ago—like a beacon, holding me to life.

Now he shines in the lamplight, looking like a painting in a deep blue coat that matches my dress. A united front.

He means to—

When the right moment comes, I'll—

No.

It can't be true. I shove the thought from my mind just as someone hails me. "Lady Fairfax!"

Recognizing the voice, I pull my shoulders back and smile. It's Mr. Bildad—the mayor of Kirkrell, and also one of our biggest shareholders. A man in his sixties with a white-flecked beard and rheumy eyes, dressed in a blue wool suit jacket, he hastens to catch up with me. "Lady Fairfax, Mr. Hargreave sent a report with the locations of last season's Livyati sightings, and we're concerned." He walks alongside me, bending close to my ear. His coat smells musty. "No whales at all were spotted within a hundred miles of Kirkrell, and the number seen in the Aegiran Ocean compared to last autumn is sharply lower—"

"I've reviewed the report as well, Mayor Bildad," I say with what I hope is a reassuring smile, even as I note the ticking of his pulse above his collar. I can't let the mayor leave here tonight fretting about my leadership. True, the Fairfax Whaling Company probably wields more power than the city government here in Kirkrell. But Bildad also writes reports to the governor on the mainland, which can influence everything from tax rates to where new ports are built.

But it's hard to think about tax rates when I notice he's shaved carelessly, leaving a small spot of scabbed-over blood beneath his jaw. How thin his skin must be there. *Don't think about that.*

"I don't know if you appreciate the sharpness of the decline," he presses. "We send in our reports, but when your father led the company, he sailed out himself and saw how things were on the sea."

And look where that got him. "Mr. Hargreave and I have a plan to respond," I say as blandly as possible, "which you'll hear more about at dinner."

Possibly it's the mention of August's name that makes the old man's brow smooth out. "Good. That's wonderful news. I look forward to hearing more."

"Soon," I say, still smiling. Mayor Bildad grunts and peels off to talk shop with another shareholder—and the person I see then makes my stomach drop and my smile slide away.

Pale, gray-eyed, with dark curls falling wild around his face, Silas Price carries himself like a soldier stripped of an army, straight-backed and watchful. Seeing him puts me in mind of freezing water and howling wind and storm clouds blotting out the stars. Makes my stomach turn over and my hands tremble.

I didn't know he would be here tonight; his name wasn't on the guest list. I would have stricken it if it was. His gray eyes are moving, searching. For whom?

Someone else is saying my name. My nails are pressing into my palms, too hard, my skin stinging beneath the gloves and my body rigid. I take a breath and force myself to focus on the woman in front of me—middle-aged, severe, gray hair pulled back in a tight bun.

Angelica Jennings. She's in charge of purchasing whale magic for use at the Hospital of St. Eulalia's. As usual, her mouth is turned down and her brow furrowed.

"Madam Jennings, welcome." The hospital is one of our company's biggest accounts, purchasing hundreds of barrels a year—primarily of whaleblood, with its healing properties, but also of whale oil, which applied to the skin will keep a person warm even in the dead of winter, and whale meat, which satiates after just a bite eaten. "How are things at the hospital?"

"They would be better if your prices weren't so damned high."

Straight to the point then. I keep my smile on. "Madam Jennings, I'm sure you understand that market conditions—"

"Such as?" she cuts in. "To hear your captains tell it, they're bringing in more whales than ever year over year, even if they have to range ever farther to get them."

Across the room, August and Silas are speaking. August claps Silas on the shoulder, making Silas stiffen, before they turn away from each other. What are they talking about? Why is Silas even here?

"We're preparing a new initiative that requires the use of significant resources," I say, marshaling all my concentration to hold my gaze on Jennings, not stare at my fiancé. "Once completed, it should put us in a position to bring more whale magic than ever to Kirkrell for the people's benefit."

No matter that each season brings more unnatural storms. No matter that our ships have to sail farther every year if they want to fill their holds. Talking to her is a harsh reminder of how much everyone in this city relies on whale magic. Mothers mix powdered bone of Livyati into their children's milk to make them strong. Physicians and hospitals keep stocks of powdered whaleblood. Churches hand out packets of dried whale meat to beggars to keep them satiated and tins of whale-oil balm to keep frostbite at bay. How I run the company isn't merely a matter of profit, or even of upholding my family's legacy. It's life or death for hundreds, maybe thousands.

"How long will this new initiative take?" Madam Jennings

inquires, putting a hand on my arm in what's probably meant to be a friendly gesture, but makes my muscles go rigid and sweat break out on my brow.

She won't feel anything through the dress. No one will. "Mr. Hargreave will share more details at dinner," I stammer, suddenly desperate to leave.

"Indeed I will." His voice curls around me from behind, warm and low, instantly relaxing me even as a shadow of doubt trails in its wake.

I don't know how a voice can carry a smile, but I know he's smiling, can sense it as sure as the trace of sandalwood and leather that accompanies his stealing up beside me. A hand on my shoulder, warm and solid even through the sturdy cloth of my dress, sending Madam Jennings stepping back. A quick, fierce battle ignites in the very cells of me. Half of me wants to lean into him and half wants to pull free.

I will not let lies come between us.

I turn my head toward him, meeting his blue eyes for the barest second—long enough for his secret smile to warm my chest and make me wonder how I could doubt him.

"I'll be visiting the hospital next week to discuss the accounts," I tell Madam Jennings. "We can speak further then."

Madam Jennings opens her mouth to say something else, but August cuts in.

"I beg your pardon, Madam Jennings, but I require a word with Lady Fairfax," he says, squeezing my shoulder. "If you will make your way to the parlor and find a seat"—he nods toward the door, which our housekeeper, Declan, has just opened to reveal the long table laden with crystal and silver—"I assure you that all your questions will be answered."

Madam Jennings looks, to my minor astonishment, flustered.

She looks from August to me and back to August. "V-very well then," she says after a moment. "I look forward to it."

When she's gone, I turn to August, a smile tugging at my mouth in spite of myself. "Thanks for that." His gaze stokes coals under my skin, making me feel special, important, beloved.

"As I said, I've a matter that needs your attention," he says in a low voice, pitched to reach just my ears. "It's very delicate, too private to discuss in a crowd, I'm afraid. May I escort you to the library, Lady Fairfax?"

I can't help but smile. "You may."

As he leads me away from the crowd, I glimpse Silas slipping into the dining room, the other shareholders giving him a wide berth. My mouth goes dry and my heart picks up. Images flicker in my mind.

The seashell on my dresser, twisted and sharp. A ship in a storm, sails torn and sagging. August leaning back in my father's chair, that secret smile, but not for me.

It's a trick. It has to be. He is mine and I am his. He keeps one arm around my shoulders, using the other to open the door to the library. Cool air, suffused with the smell of old paper, seeps out.

As soon as the library door closes behind us—cutting off the sound and the light from the entrance hall—his mouth is on mine, his hands on both my shoulders now. He breaks away just far enough to grin at me as he spins me around and presses my back against the door.

"Maker." His voice comes out a breathless, low laugh, close to my ear.

"No, just me," I whisper back.

"I thought I was going to have to drag you away from those shareholders."

The library is dark around us, lit only by a few oil lamps placed around the perimeter of the room. So much of the manor is essentially a public space: the entrance hall and the parlor where large groups of shareholders can gather; offices where my father would work and receive callers. But the library has always been ours alone. As well as the leather-bound books lining the walls, there are curios in glass cases scattered throughout the room. Intricate scrimshaw carvings—battle scenes or beautiful women or elaborate maps carved and inked into whale teeth and whalebone. Silver coins, smooth and irregular and tarnished green with salt water, said to be reclaimed from the finfolk. Segments of coral faded to the color of the palest rose, arranged like bridal bouquets under glass.

"You might have dragged me away sooner," I manage, his mouth moving on my throat threatening to chase all thoughts from my head. My hands respond automatically, climbing up his back, pressing him closer to me. I can't touch him how I'd like to, not with the gloves and what's under them. I have to be careful, but there's something thrilling about that too—that he wants me despite the risk, despite everything.

Yet a flicker of doubt lingers, something stopping me from closing my eyes. Instead I stare over August's shoulder at the Livyatan skull hanging from the ceiling in the center of the room. Suspended by wires, it casts barbed shadows over everything, over us, the flickering oil light making them sway like seaweed.

"Bildad asked about the declining whale numbers," I go on, a bit breathlessly, as August's teeth graze my jawline. "And Madam Jennings was complaining about prices again—"

"Don't worry about that." His voice is low, hungry. He steps closer, bringing his body into contact with mine, and a warm fog steals into my mind. Suddenly it is very easy to forget about shareholders and seashells and secrets. "We have a plan, remember?"

His hands trace up my arms and shoulders, dragging lightly up the sides of my throat. The same places where Madam Jennings laid her hand on my arm a few minutes ago, and where Lydia's fingers brushed the nape of my neck earlier when she did up my buttons.

But unlike Lydia or Madam Jennings, he knows what lies beneath.

He knows, and somehow—call it madness or love, lust or courage, or maybe just recklessness—he doesn't care. I can bring my own hands up to thread through his hair, uncaring if he notices the pointed ends of my fingers, as long as I don't hurt him.

He knows about the claws and the scales, about the poisonous energy coiled in my veins, the urge to violence that sometimes clouds my mind. He knows and he still wants me, still loves me.

He knows about my curse and my broken heart. He knows and he still wants me, still loves me.

Doesn't he?

Chapter 2

NINE YEARS AGO

Papa wakes us up, Lydia and me, when the moon outside our bedroom window is high in the sky.

The carriage that carries the three of us into town isn't the usual one, polished black with gold trimmings. It's plain wood, with no cushions on the bench. The cold winter wind reaches fingers through the cracks in the wall and makes us shiver. The coats over our nightgowns, the scarves and hats Papa wrapped us in, don't keep out the chill. Lydia and I are quiet, Papa having hushed our questions. "Wait, darlings, until we get where we're going."

He's uncharacteristically grave, in an old coat with a cap pulled over his head. He toys with his walking stick, *tap-tap-tapping* against the carriage floor, and mutters, seemingly half to himself: "You two are old enough now to understand."

So this is some sort of lesson. I frown, wishing Papa had brought me alone.

Lydia is three whole years younger than me, still little, kicking her heels against the bench because they don't reach the floor. Nor do mine, but at least I know not to fidget. The curtains are drawn, lanterns unlit; we sit in the dark. But from the downward slope and the roughness of the road beneath us, from the smells that creep in with the wind—fish, oil, burning—I can tell we're headed toward the wharf, and my heart picks up with excitement. I love to look at the ships, big as castles with their billowing sails and snapping flags. Papa's said that in a few years, when I'm bigger, I can come with him on a voyage.

Lydia, though, is scared. She clutches my hand so tight it hurts, and presses her face into Papa's coat. But I'm not scared. Or I try not to be. I'm the oldest. I'm to inherit the Fairfax Whaling Company someday, and Papa always tells me I must be brave and bold.

I am not afraid of the dark. I am not afraid of sharks or whales or any other toothed thing that lives in the sea. The only thing I'm a little afraid of is the finfolk, but that's what my iron cross necklace is for.

When we stop, it's in front of a small, squat brick building, close enough to the water that I can hear the waves. It's too dark to see much except the packed dirt beneath our feet even as Papa hoists a lantern with one hand, holding Lydia's hand with the other. He trusts me to follow, and I do as we go inside, past two men in dark uniforms who open the door for us and follow in behind.

More lanterns cast everything in greasy yellow light. There's nothing in here but a wooden bench facing a wall made up of iron bars that go all the way to the ceiling. Darkness behind them—but then something moves. Straightens up from the floor and totters toward the light.

I look up at Papa in confusion. But Lydia is the first to speak, hushed.

"Cousin Mary?"

The face that presses behind the bars is familiar, round and tearstained, with a cloud of curly blonde hair that puffs out like a halo. But the hands. The hands that wrap around the bars, the torn, ragged sleeves of her dress falling away.

Her wrists are blanketed with shiny greenish-gray scales, like the fish that Mrs. Milhouse brings home from the market and keeps in the icebox. And her fingers—they end in long, curved, mottled claws that scrape together and make a terrible noise against the bars.

And she is weeping, her words hardly audible through the sobs that rack her soft frame. I can make out only scattered words, breathless explanations. Something about it not being her fault, her husband, another woman, but she can control it, she'll stay in hiding, don't send her away.

Fear curls through me as I realize what's become of her. *A curse.*

Mama's told us that the finfolk don't like that we hunt whales, even though we need them, we need whale magic. So the finfolk punish sailors with curses, and the sailors come back broken and frightened and frightening, to beg for spare coin in Kirkrell's streets or gather outside the churchyard every Seventh Day, forbidden to touch holy ground.

Some curses are harmless, silly even—making you always smell like cabbage, or making you unable to say your own name out loud. Or they can make it so sunlight chars your skin, or so every seven years you forget everyone you know, or so food turns to dirt in your mouth and you starve. They cannot be cured—or, at least, no one knows how to cure them—and that's why when you go to sea, you must keep something sharp and iron in one hand and silver coins in the other. Sometimes, the finfolk will make a bargain, and sometimes there's no choice but to fight. Best, if you see glittering fog on the horizon, to turn around and run the other way.

But Cousin Mary's no sailor. How could she be cursed?

"Don't get close to her," Papa says, quiet but firm. He stands with one arm extended across both our shoulders, holding us against his legs. "Stay back."

When Mary calls out our names, my sister bursts into tears, breaking from Papa's hold and running to press herself against the opposite wall, as far away as possible from the bars. Papa follows and crouches down to comfort her, leaving me cold where his arm had curved protectively around me.

"She'll be taken somewhere safe," I can hear him murmuring to Lydia. "Somewhere she can't hurt anyone."

But I'm only half listening. I can't take my eyes from Cousin Mary. Just a few months ago we attended her wedding. She wore a dress of brown silk with puffed sleeves and little white flowers woven through her hair.

Now she sees me looking. She beckons me closer.

"Please, Susannah," she whispers, sliding to her knees so we're eye level as I drift nearer to the bars. "Please help me."

She looks so different, her face drawn and bloodless, and the claws glint in the lamplight. But more than that, what holds my gaze is the emptiness in her eyes. She's family. Aren't we always supposed to help family?

I shan't be afraid. I am bold and brave. I walk toward her, wanting to give some comfort. Mary cries and cries as I reach my hand through the bars. I'll wipe the tears off her cheeks, where the scales still haven't crept up.

Then—pain. I shriek as one of the scaled hands wraps around my arm, her claws breaking through the fabric of my dress sleeve and the skin underneath. I try to pull back, but she holds on. Blood spreads on the gray wool.

A hissing, grinding noise comes out of Mary's throat as her gaze falls to the blood, and all of a sudden her eyes are not empty. Very much not empty.

Hungry, is all I can think, dazed, before the silver head of Papa's cane hisses through the air over my head. *Hungry.*

He strikes Cousin Mary's shoulder with a crack that makes me flinch, and she recoils with a spat curse, dropping my arm. Papa has hold of me, and he pulls me back from the bars as she glares, snarling animal sounds. Once we're too far for Mary to reach—even as her snarls subside into sobs, even as she falls back into the shadows with a dazed look on her face—he drops to his knees and wraps his arms around me, holding me as I shake.

"It's not her anymore," he says, his voice thick with feeling. "I told you not to get close. Soon she won't be able to think or speak at all. She'll hunger only for blood."

Hot tears streak down my face; my teeth clack together as I shiver, clutching my arm to my chest. I can't tear my eyes away from Mary, crumpled and weeping on the ground, until Papa moves me behind him, out of her line of sight. The pain in my arm jumbles my thoughts, sadness and confusion and fear. Mary loves me. She always says so. Why did she hurt me? What else would she have done if Papa hadn't stopped her?

After checking my arm, Papa stands, looking grim. "Back to the carriage now."

"But what about Mary?" My voice comes out small. "Aren't we going to help her?"

"She's past help now, my love."

As he ushers us out, Papa turns back toward Mary for a moment, taking a step closer to her. In the doorway, I freeze, clutching

Lydia's hand with my good one, to look back. Papa bends to speak to Mary. Soft, so it's hard to make out the words, but I think he says, *I'm sorry, dear.*

As we trundle toward home in the same uncomfortable carriage, Papa cleans the cuts on my arm with a wetted handkerchief while I take small sips of whaleblood from the flask he always carries. It tastes horrible, sludgy and salty and rusty, but I can feel the healing warmth sinking down to my arm, until the gouges Mary left are just little pink scars.

My dress, though, is ruined, and Mama won't be pleased. For some reason that's all I can think about. Not the shimmer of the scales and claws. Not the way Mary's eyes darkened when she saw my blood, how for a moment I was sure she was going to pull my hand to her and bite it clean off.

"Why do you think I've brought you here, Annie?" Papa asks gently as he runs his handkerchief one more time across my now-healed arm, making sure the tender pink skin is free of blood before tugging my jacket sleeve back down and fastening the buttons on my cuff. "This is a lesson, a very important one. The most important lesson of all."

Blinking away the tears, I look up at him in the dimness of the carriage as Lydia sniffles quietly on my other side. Someday after he's gone, Papa often reminds me, I will be in charge of the Fairfax Whaling Company and the leader of everyone in this city who makes their livelihood from hunting Livyati. That's why he takes me with him to shareholder meetings and visits to the warehouse and the wharf to see the ships. And even when I'm frightened or confused—when I see the dead whales cut up at the warehouse, or when the sailors come back with tales of strange storms and shadow figures in rowboats—I must keep a clear head and think things through.

"Mary is cursed?" I give voice to my fears. Then, to Papa's encouraging nod, "But she's never been to sea."

"Some curses can go beyond a single sailor," Papa says gravely. "Some finfolk can cast a curse on a whole ship. Or a family."

Bumps rise on my skin at the thought. "I didn't know that."

"It's not so common now, because the finfolk are fewer and their magic weaker," Papa says. "In the old days, when their magic was stronger, they could curse an entire city. Or a bloodline, to be passed down forever, whether or not we go to sea or ever see one of the finfolk with our own eyes."

A cold understanding seeps in. "And our family has one."

Papa's face in the dark looks carved of stone. "Yes."

"But we just saw Cousin Mary," I say, not wanting it to be true. "At her wedding. She wasn't cursed."

"Some curses only appear under certain circumstances," Papa says quietly. "In Cousin Mary's case, someone she loves very much did something that surprised and hurt her, and . . . and . . ."

He turns to the window and trails off, seeming to struggle for words. The silence stretches, Mary's weeping echoing in my mind. The road slopes up beneath us, and the rough cobblestone of the tangled streets gives way to the smoothness of paving stones.

After what seems like a long time Papa turns to me. "Wake your sister," he says. "She needs to hear this too."

I hadn't even realized that Lydia had fallen asleep, her head tipped against my shoulder, her soft corn silk hair against my cheek, her hand still tucked in mine. I poke her leg until her eyes fly wide, blue and confused.

"Listen," I whisper, trying to make my voice casual, not reveal to her how scared I am of what Papa's going to say. "Papa has a lesson for us."

When we've turned to him, Papa says, "Do you two remember when your kitten died last year?"

I blink, nod, wipe my nose on the back of my sleeve. Pepper—a small gray cat I found down by the warehouse one day that I begged and pleaded with Mama to let me bring home. But he'd never grown, and lasted only a few weeks. Papa had said he must have been sick all along.

"Do you remember what it felt like when you found him?" Papa looks old somehow, the scant light from outside deepening the furrows on his face. "That hurt in your chest?"

I nod. I remember, as I remember the terrible stiffness of Pepper's little body, the strange cold of his fur. But I don't understand what Papa's getting at.

"That feeling is called heartbreak," Papa explains. His voice is quiet enough that I can hear the chirruping of crickets outside, the clatter of the horses' feet, the soft sigh of the constant breeze off the sea. "And when you're an adult, it can be worse. For instance, if a person dies and you don't understand why, or if someone you love betrays you."

I'm crying now too alongside Lydia, my mind a confusing jumble of memories, Pepper's cool shape under my hand and the terrible feeling in my chest, like thorns were growing inside me. I can't imagine anything worse than that.

"For some people, the pain and sorrow are all there is, and as terrible as they are, they can move past them," Papa says. "But some of us are cursed—for some of us that shock opens a wound in our heart that won't heal." He lets out a heavy sigh. "I carry the curse, and I'm sorry to tell you this, my daughters, but so do you."

"Does that mean this will happen to us too? Happen to you?" My voice rises; tears sting the back of my own throat as Lydia starts crying again, holding my hand so hard it hurts. *Brave, be brave,* I remind myself, but it's hard with the image of Mary's wild eyes burned into my mind.

"No." Papa shakes his head quickly. "I brought you here to show you what *can* happen. Cousin Mary gave too much of her heart to someone else. So when he hurt her, it broke her heart and let the curse in. But it need not happen if you're careful."

"Who cursed us?" I whisper.

There is a long, heavy silence before Papa answers. He twitches aside the curtain and looks out the window at the night city, his shoulders slumped. Past him, I can just see the dark shapes of the town's buildings, then the thicket of shipmasts at the docks, outlined black against the cloudy gray sky. Beyond town, beyond the wharf, the ocean lies flat and black, seeming to swallow the moonlight.

"I can't tell you," he says. "It goes farther back than I can say, than anyone can say. Maybe it was Francis Bartholomew Fairfax, who started the company two hundred years ago. What matters is, as long as there have been Fairfaxes in Kirkrell, we have been cursed." He takes a breath. "But we oughtn't blame whichever ancestor came back from the sea cursed, Annie. Remember that the finfolk cursed the Fairfaxes."

Lydia has gone quiet next to me, but I can feel her trembling, or maybe it's me. I feel stricken. "All of us? Even Kit?"

"Yes, all of us. Everyone who's born into my bloodline. I'll tell Kit too, when he's old enough." Papa fixes a heavy gaze on Lydia, then me. "Which is why you must never give anyone that power over you. Love others, but not so much that they could ever break your heart."

"But you're married to Mama," Lydia says in a small voice.

"So I am," Papa replies with a faint, fond smile. "But we Fairfaxes have to do it differently. I chose your mother not because of her pretty face or some fleeting feeling inside me, but because she is a good and trustworthy woman from a good family whose goals aligned with mine. I love her, as I love the two of you, but my heart is my own. And so yours must be, always."

He fixes us with an intent gaze. "The whaling is worth it—know that. The magic we bring to people saves lives. It is a privilege to lead the Fairfax Whaling Company, but it comes at a cost."

He reaches over and takes both our hands, gripping them tight as if to press his words into our memories.

"As you get older, you will hear stories about great romances and quickening of hearts," he tells us, words coming lower and faster, like we're running out of time. "These stories are not for you. You will see your peers courting each other, acting foolishly in the name of love and losing their senses over a pretty face or a sweet word. You must not. You must guard your heart. We're Fairfaxes, and there is only one path for us."

I promised. There, in the carriage, in the dark, with Lydia sniffling next to me and my arm still smarting, I tucked Papa's words away. Told him I would guard my heart.

But time passes. Storms descend and ships sink and hearts fracture. Boys with blue eyes and warm, slow smiles appear and promise to stitch up the cracks. Easy to say yes when you're already falling apart. To let someone else in, and cling to them as a lifeline.

Still, perhaps I should have listened.

Chapter 3

The lamplight in the library turns August's ice-blue eyes dark, the color of the sea on a late spring evening. Reflected candle flames dance in his pupils, and I have to close my own eyes against the intensity of the feeling as he kisses me again. But still my thoughts race.

"What if the shareholders don't like the *Heralder* plan?" I murmur against his lips. Bildad's and Jennings's skeptical faces float in my memory. "We need their funding to stock the ship. And we'll need at least fifty sailors, and they'll expect to be paid double for the risk—"

August's teeth nip at my lower lip, gentle but unexpected, and a laugh rumbles in his chest at how effectively it silences my words, my head emptying as blood rushes elsewhere.

"Shh," he whispers, smoothing the pad of his thumb over where his teeth pressed down. "How many hours have we spent planning? You've thought of everything, down to every last crumb of hardtack."

"They'll be afraid," I whisper around the heat flaring in my chest.

"They surely will," August says readily, voice low and melodic. I can feel the vibration of his chest when he speaks. "But you can count on whalers' ambition outweighing their fear. Or their greed, if you like." His breath on the shell of my ear makes me shiver, wrenches free what I really mean to say.

"I'll miss you." My voice trembles.

He draws back a fraction and, like he does every time we're alone, reaches down to peel my gloves off, somehow deft enough to not damage the silk. Cool air rushes over my hands and I shiver with the familiar combination of pleasure and fear.

Three times August Hargreave has saved my life. The first was the night the *Volyar* sank. The worst finfolk attack in a hundred years, but we wouldn't know that until later when the bodies were counted. Everything was darkness and chaos and terror. Yet August, only fifteen, had the courage—or maybe foolishness—not to push me off our lifeboat as sobs wrenched out of me and we watched the scales bloom in the cold starlight.

I keep my eyes on his face now, not wanting to look at my hands, the small gray-green scales creeping up over the backs of them, my long and sharp and twisted nails. "I don't know how you can bear seeing them," I whisper, shame seeping through the desire lighting me up inside. "Seeing *me*."

The second time he saved my life was in the days and weeks after we were rescued. When a physician came to examine us, he convinced the woman we were fine, we didn't need to be checked over. Then the endless rounds of questioning back in Kirkrell. He could have turned me in at any moment, he should have, but he never did.

His eyes are bright, almost greedy as he takes me in. All of me. “I like touching your bare skin,” he says, weaving his fingers through mine and pressing both my hands up against the wall behind me, where I can’t see them but he can. “I like knowing something about you no one else knows . . . well, almost no one.”

When I fell in love with him, even though I knew it was impossible, the force of feeling almost seemed to chase the curse away. So the third time wasn’t really one time at all, but a thousand small rescues over the years as gratitude turned into friendship, then love. The scales, the claws didn’t go away, but they were slow to return, easy to pluck away and file down.

I allowed myself to forget Papa’s warning about letting anyone too close. I dared to hope for the impossible, that love could mend my heart. And for a while, it seemed to—if not cure the curse, at least stop its progress.

Then the shell arrived, seeping malevolence in the back of my mind. *When the right moment comes* . . . But I’m alive because of August. How can I now doubt him? What right do I have to doubt him?

He leans down and the tip of his tongue touches the bow of my lips again. Lightly, a request, but it chases away my fears. I open my mouth and let him in. An invitation he takes greedily, tilting my head back for easier access. He tastes like apple wine, and I can feel his pulse in his fingers, just as fast as my own.

He lets go of my hands and his fingers slip around the back of my skull, pushing through the weave of the braid that Lydia constructed so carefully earlier, and the tugging sensation sends lightning down my spine.

“Don’t mess up my hair,” I gasp, a half-hearted protest as I slip my hands around his waist, careful not to let my nails snag on his coat. “People will notice.”

"No one will notice." His hand on the small of my back presses me against him, the solid planes of his body, and I want—I want—I want to give over to it and let it sweep me away.

But I can't touch him like he's touching me, not without tearing his skin. And there's the doubt I have no right to feel creeping back in. *There will be a storm—*

No, I tell myself. It's a trick, a lie.

I pull back from the kiss. My skin feels alive, alert to every touch; my body wants more but my mind chastises me to be careful, to guard my tattered heart—whatever's left of it. "We should get back to the meeting," I say, throwing on a rueful smile.

He gathers my hands up between us. I shiver as the pads of his fingers brush over the scales, my palms, my knuckles and nails.

"It's getting worse," he remarks quietly, turning my hands over in his like he's checking them for flaws. "The heartbreak. Why is that, do you think?"

I blink, trying to clear the fog in my head as the desire slowly drains from me, leaving the ever-present dread and emptiness in its place. "I forgot to pluck the scales out this week," I say, tongue heavy and voice sounding unconvincing even to myself. A year ago, I could get away with plucking them once a week. Lately it's once a day. More on bad days.

His blue eyes probe mine, face growing serious, and I wonder if he believes me, what he would say if he knew how bad it's gotten. A heartbroken heiress, a legacy of generations one weak link away from tumbling down. What if he asks me to tell him the truth?

I think I would. I think I would do anything he asked. And that frightens me even more.

A knock on the door makes us both startle, alarm shooting

through me. August steps back from me and I grab my gloves off the nearby shelf, tugging them on as fast as I can without tearing the silk.

Another knock, more insistent this time. Out of the frying pan, Mama would say; I've escaped having to explain myself to August, but now we have to go out and face the shareholders.

August lights another lantern, rendering the scene slightly more respectable, like maybe we really have been merely discussing business in here. Aside from the faint smudge of color still high in his cheeks, he is collected, master of himself. I'm sure the same isn't true for me. I'm still breathing hard, running a hand over my braid to make sure it lies flat, when he opens the door.

"Silas."

My view of the other side of the threshold is blocked by the door, but that name makes ice crystals form in my still-molten blood. I straighten my spine as August steps back to let him come inside.

I want to protest that he has no business in my father's library. Sure, he might be a ship captain at age nineteen. But Silas's ship, the *Whistler*, is the oldest and smallest in the Fairfax Company's fleet, and its task is not to hunt whales. Rather, it is to find whales that have already died, to haul them in and hack them apart and separate the salable flesh from the rotting. And secondly to report to the sites of storms and shipwrecks, pick up any survivors as well as any barrels of whale oil or meat or bone that might have been preserved. An assignment given only to those clinging by their fingertips to scraps of respectability: a salvager. A scavenger.

An enraging smirk curls around the corners of Silas's mouth as he takes August and me in, half in and half out of the library with the door propped open on his shoulder. His eyes flicker over my hair, my bruised-feeling mouth, down to my gloved hands. Heated shame rushes into me, but I push it down.

This is my home, and August is my fiancé. I can do what I will here, with him. Silas is the one who has no right to be here.

I lift my chin and glare at him as imperiously as I can. "What do you want?"

He doesn't appear stung by my harsh tone; instead he greets me with a slight incline of his head, the respectful title he addresses me with laced with subtle scorn. "Lady Fairfax. I was invited."

"By—"

"By me," August cuts in, his hand finding my arm. "My apologies for not mentioning it sooner." But he doesn't sound apologetic.

Anger makes my fingers twitch toward fists; I have to remind myself to keep them still, to remain collected. I don't want to let Silas see there's anything less than perfect accord between August and me, ever. But for a moment, my anger at them both flares equally bright.

"Well, look at us," I say. "The miracle children of the *Volyar* together again."

I want to put them off-balance, and it works. August blinks, surprised, and Silas's sardonic expression crystallizes into a cold glare. I let myself smile. August and Silas, different as they are, both move through the world with such sure-footedness. I envy that, I covet it. Yet I'm not a creature to be laughed at or pitied.

"A good portent," August declares after a long moment, glancing from Silas to me like he can see the current of rage and resentment in the air. He captures my hand in his. "Of unity and good fortune for our next ventures."

One dark brow rises. Even Silas knows he's the farthest thing from a good sign. "Can it be a portent of dinner instead?" he says. "Never having been invited to one of these functions before, I didn't realize how tedious it would be. The shareholders are waiting."

August grins and pulls me into his side. "Annie and I had important business to discuss."

"I'm sure you did," Silas says dryly, standing to the right side of the doorway to let us pass. Not close enough to touch, but close enough for the smell of petrichor and brine to make me shudder.

In the hallway, I try to paste on a smile while seething inside, ever conscious of Silas keeping pace behind us. He and August were close as boys, greenhands on whaling ships, but no longer. I know they speak, but only on business. So why did August invite him here?

Maybe that's what friendship is, mocking someone behind their back but inviting them to your dinner parties anyway. I wouldn't know—I grew up surrounded by adults, with private tutors and governesses brought in to attend to my care and keeping; there were no other young people around besides Kit and Lydia and, later, August, when he became Papa's apprentice. So I have little experience of my own to compare. Still, I can't imagine the shareholders will be happy about Silas's presence here.

August and I enter the parlor arm in arm. Despite the cozy name, it's a large room built for this express purpose—for Fairfax Whaling Company shareholders to gather and speak. At one end a huge fireplace roars merrily, and on the opposite is a raised platform with a table where August and I sit along with a handful of the most senior shareholders: Thomas Carrol, Mayor Bildad, Wilhelmina Peleg, Elias Swain. To August's right is Captain Mance—the overseer of our company's entire whaling fleet, owing to his decades of experience and familiarity with all the nooks and crannies of the five seas. He glows with the honor that's about to be bestowed on him.

He also opposed Papa's mandate to allow women as sailors and ship officers, and I suspect that much of the whispered aspersions on my capabilities as leader start with him.

The rest of the space is taken up with smaller tables where the shareholders and officers and merchants sit, staff circulating among them with plates and bottles of wine. Lydia is at the harpsichord, playing a jaunty tune, and I smile in spite of myself to see that she has indeed found someone's pretty daughter to talk to, a brown-skinned girl in a pink dress who looks vaguely familiar, though I can't think from where. She leans on the body of the instrument, looking suitably impressed. My sister has gotten herself a glass of wine somehow, despite my instructing the servants not to let her have any. She holds it with one hand, picking out a melody with the other while batting her eyelashes at the girl.

I hope as August and I take our seat at the head table, in front of the red silk banner with the Fairfax family crest, that she has also made efforts to charm the shareholders, but I can't resent her for finding a scrap of levity or happiness in tonight. Maker knows that has been hard enough to come by since our parents died.

A wave of quiet sweeps through the room as we reach the table, the shareholders looking to August and me. I clear my throat and tap a spoon against a glass to get the attention of everyone not already staring. "Good evening."

I get through the pleasantries quickly, how it's an honor to be addressing them from the same table as have my father and my grandfather and generations of Fairfaxes before that. I can hear that my words are breathy, too fast, and some of the shareholders wander to find their seats as I speak. But perhaps it's better they're not paying attention, not looking too closely at my movements, my glove-covered hands.

In the days following that visit to Cousin Mary, Papa impressed upon us the necessity of keeping secret the nature of our particular curse. The people of Kirkrell know about the heartbroken—about once-human monsters who have been cursed to roam the night, hungering for flesh. But aside from Cousin Mary, who was captured immediately once she started to turn, there hasn't been a case in generations. Over the decades, my father's family paid the right people to keep quiet any rumors. So most people know of the heartbroken only as a frightening tale for children. And no one—except for those we choose to marry—ever knows that it's unique to the Fairfax bloodline. That grief and betrayal and sorrow can turn Fairfaxes into monsters.

My family's fragile legacy rests in my hands, threatening at every second to slip through my fingers. If the shareholders saw my scales and claws, I'd be locked up or shot. But worse, everyone would surely make the connection between the Fairfaxes and the heartbroken, staining our family name forever.

"I know—I know that there have been some concerning developments lately," I continue, and smiles slip off the shareholders' faces like too much wet paint slopped onto a canvas. It's impossible to forget that I am the first woman to be here, and that even calling me a woman is generous; I'm sure most of them think me just a girl. A child, playing pretend in her mother's clothes and her father's chair. "We are aware of the Livyati's diminishing numbers, and the resulting encounters with finfolk as our ships are obliged to range farther north. But please be assured that we have not been ignoring your reports and your questions. We've been working on answers, and my adviser August Hargreave has developed a plan to share with you tonight."

There's a smattering of lackluster applause as I sink gratefully into my seat. August looks over to give me a proud smile, his hand finding my thigh and squeezing gently. It's a quick gesture, more reassuring than seductive, but still the heat of his touch takes me back to the library, his body pressed against mine, his fingers drifting over the scales. Heat rises to my face, and as he stands up in turn, I quickly duck my head and take a sip of wine, mastering myself.

Even here in front of everyone, I want to lean into him, my body drawn toward his like a magnet. But the warning hangs in my mind from so many years ago. *You must guard your heart.*

I wish Papa were here. I wish I could ask him, is my heart still worth protecting even when it's already crumbling? But since he's not here—will never be here again—I look over at Lydia, who has taken her seat at one of the tables. Even if I sometimes feel like there's a wall between my sister and me, I love her and I know she loves me. That, at least, is something I can hold on to. She catches my eye and smiles.

August looks more at home in front of the Fairfax family crest—gold thread on red silk, the shape of a hawk diving toward stylized waves—than I felt. "We aim to establish a whaling outpost in the peninsula of Kielstraat," he says, "off the northwestern tip of Solheim."

There's a tangible shift of energy in the room: shareholders lean forward in their seats; merchants look up bright-eyed with interest. "As most of you know," August goes on, "the whale species that is our special prey, the only whale with magic in its flesh and blood, the Livyati—the females return to the arctic each year to raise their young, sometimes accompanied by bulls as well."

This plan is the result of weeks of discussions, late nights sitting with him and other key officers in August's office above the warehouse. It was Captain Mance's proposal, but I couldn't deny the logic of it. Unpleasant as the man might be, I'm not in a position to shoot down any ideas that might solve my company's twin intractable problems: the declining Livyatan populations in the five seas and the finfolk's increasing attacks.

Decades ago, the finfolk had nearly destroyed the Fairfax Whaling Company. Until my great-grandfather decided instead of fleeing to fight. He gave his whalers rifles loaded with iron bullets. When the finfolk realized they too could be hunted, their appearances grew fewer and fewer. By the time my father took over the company, they were all but gone. Until the attack on the *Volyar*.

Shadowy figures in black rowboats that you see out of the corner of your eye, unnaturally still and silent. Fog that rolls in and stays for days, too dense to see through, undisturbed by the wind. Storms brewing from nothing, lightning forking down from clear skies, waves high enough to clear a ship deck, ready to drag you down to the dark and cold below the surface.

I grip the sides of my chair. *Don't think about that.* I can't afford to wallow in grief, not just tonight—because I need to be charming for the shareholders—but ever, because every surge of anger or grief causes more scales to crop up, pushes me closer to the edge of somewhere I can't come back from.

Sinking the *Volyar* seems to have emboldened the finfolk—since then, we've seen more and more attacks on our whaling ships every year. The sailors are afraid. Out for blood. They want a new weapon, like the iron bullets that saved the company in my grandfather's time.

Silas Price is a few seats down from Lydia, I realize, flanked by two young people I don't know. To his right is the girl in pink

Lydia was talking to—leaning in to speak with Silas now—and to Silas's right is a lanky boy with raven-colored hair shorn close.

Ever since Silas received his ship charter two years ago, he's been collecting a crew of young sailors bearing finfolk curses. Nothing fatal, like the man with coral in his lungs, nothing to stop them from being able to sail—I heard rumors of a man who could speak only in rhymes and a girl who found herself chased by dogs wherever she went. If these two beside him now are Cursed Crew, their afflictions aren't visible on the surface, but still the officers to either side of them give them a wide berth, scooting their chairs as far away as possible.

As for Silas, he's not looking at August, like everyone else. He's looking at me with a kind of expectant amusement. Eyes bright and challenging, mouth slightly curved into a sharp smile. Like he's waiting to see what I'll do next. I meet his gaze and pour all my animosity into my eyes.

He has the power to destroy me. But if he tries, I'll drag him down with me.

When I glance over to Lydia again, she's staring at me pointedly. *Fix your face*, she mouths, and taps a finger against her cheek before flashing an exaggerated smile.

I blink and force myself to look back up at August before anyone else notices me glowering. Uninvited or not, I will not let Silas Price swamp my composure tonight.

"To follow the whales to the far north is a taxing journey from our wharf here in Kirkrell," August is saying. "But having an outpost on the arctic's perimeter—one where ships could be repaired, blubber processed, crews refreshed, and so on—that will be worth the initial investment."

More murmurs of interest from the shareholders, and I allow

myself to feel optimistic for a second. If they'll listen to August more readily than me, so be it. He has our best interests at heart, I tell myself, ignoring the itching at the ends of my fingers. He hasn't let me down so far, has he?

One of the ship captains calls out from a few tables away. "It's not the journey to the arctic that's difficult," he says, mopping his bald forehead with a handkerchief. "It's what you find when you get there. How will our ships break through the ice?"

"Solheim is rich in metals," August points out. "Once we have our facility in Kielstraat, we will be able to install iron breakers on our prows, strong enough to sail straight into the ice."

He is breathtaking like this, washed in both the firelight from across the room and the lamps behind us, making him look gilded. It seems like an inevitable act of fate that we should marry and he should help me run the company. He is persuasive and charismatic in a way I only wish I could be. He is born to whaling, to lead.

"And the iron has another purpose." He pauses and looks around expectantly, encouragingly, and I know he's trying to bring the shareholders in, get them invested in this plan.

"To repel the finfolk," someone calls.

August nods encouragingly. But the mention of the finfolk seems to have darkened the mood in the room. There is shifting in seats, fretful whispers to match the images uncoiling at the edges of my mind.

"We've earmarked money to equip every sailor with a pistol and a stock of iron bullets," August tells the crowd, his voice pushing back the shadows in my mind. He's still smiling, unshaken by the specter of the finfolk. "Furthermore, I've secured the governor's blessing to outfit our fleet with the same cannons as the Continental Army uses, loaded with iron filings. The seas are ours. We have nothing to fear."

His hand finds my shoulder, heavy and warm, his fingers pressing in. I look up at him in surprise and confusion as he tugs me to my feet, until I'm standing next to him.

"The voyage will be led by Captain Mance," he goes on, "along with myself and a crew of our ablest sailors. And as a gesture of our confidence in this mission, joining us too—"

My stomach drops. I turn my head, stare at him. *Don't do this.* The weight of countless eyes drills into us, hungry and afraid and greedy and expectant.

"—Lady Fairfax herself," he finishes, looking directly at me. "In two weeks, we will sail north."

Chapter 4

Somehow, I manage to slip from the scene of merriment and self-congratulations that erupts in the parlor following August's speech. As soon as I get my bedroom door shut behind me, I stumble to my vanity and collapse on the stool. It's blessedly quiet up here, and dark. Kit's door is closed; hopefully he's sound asleep.

My fingers itch and burn inside their gloves, feeling like they're on fire. I scrabble to take them off, and the silk snags on my long, jagged reddish-black fingernails. The gloves fall to the floor, shortly to join the pile of other destroyed gloves piling up at the back of my wardrobe.

New scales march up my wrists, a pale, muddy greenish-gray against my irritated red skin; but I don't let myself look for longer than a second, afraid I'll see new ones sprouting up before my eyes. I can almost feel them stiffening, trying to break through my skin. My hands are shaking, my nails scratching the polished wood of my dresser as I yank open the top drawer.

Among the paints and creams and jewelry there's a corked glass vial the length of my hand, a quarter inch of rust-colored powder along the bottom. I take it out and uncork it, careful not to spill the powder even with my shaking hands and tear-blurred vision. Add a little water from the pitcher on my dresser; press my thumb over the opening and shake until a thick, muddy liquid coats the inside of the glass.

I lick the pad of my thumb, grimacing. I can't let any of the precious, healing whaleblood go to waste—it's the only thing slowing my transformation into a monster. Then I tip my head back with the vial to my lips. The taste of iron and salt floods my mouth. I force myself to swallow, letting the tepid liquid run over my tongue until the flow stops.

Stowing the vial in my pocket while suppressing the urge to gag, I lift my hand into a watery beam of moonlight through the window and watch the dark, mottled color of my nails fade to pink, their sharp ends receding. But even as the soreness and itching fades, some compulsion makes me take out the shell again from its hiding place in my drawer.

When my fingers touch its sharp edges, it shows me memories that are not mine.

The scene is blurred, the edges of things soft, but here is August, sitting in Papa's library, in Papa's chair. His boots are propped up on the desk, something he would never do around me. The suspended Livyatan skull hangs above his head like a crown or the watchful presence of some ancient god. Its empty eye sockets stare down at me, cold and accusing.

When he speaks, his voice sounds different from usual. Colder, harder, more matter-of-fact, without the softness he uses with me. Echoing, like the sound is reaching me from the other end of a long tunnel. But there is still the feeling of sharing a secret as he leans forward over steepled hands.

We will sail the Heralder *to Kielstraat. She will be with us. I'll wait for a particularly pretty sunset or a spectacular kill and then my feelings will overcome me. I'll drop to my knees, tell her I can't wait any longer. We'll marry at sea.*

And then at some point, there will be a storm. There always is. When the right moment comes, I'll . . . I'll do what must be done. People die on ships all the time. As you know.

No one will challenge me. The shareholders prefer me. She doesn't have the vision, never has, and especially not for these times.

Not for what's coming.

The shell arrived a month ago—carried in by Declan with the rest of the post, wrapped in clean rags in an innocuous white paper box addressed to me. I opened it and was met with this strange nightmare, one that threatens to push me off the ledge I've been balancing on for six years. To break my heart entirely.

Before, I had almost convinced myself that even heartbroken, even cursed, I was stronger than Cousin Mary. I knew it couldn't be stopped or reversed, but with August to comfort me, and whaleblood to heal my hands after I plucked out the scales and filed down the claws, I thought I could slow it down. Enough, at least, to last until my siblings were grown up. To know that they would be all right.

But since I first held the shell and heard and saw August plotting to kill me—even if it's not real, can't be real—the heartbreak curse has advanced faster and faster.

A strangled sob escapes me as I look at myself in the mirror, the moonlight making me pale as a ghost, my tears smearing makeup around my eyes and making them look like a skull's hollows.

We'll marry at sea. There will be a storm. I'll do what must be done.

"It's a lie," I tell myself, whispering the words out loud as if that will make them more convincing. "A trick, dark magic."

The shell holds a lie. I have no other choice but to believe that, because if I let myself believe that August means me harm, my heart will break entirely.

But it was easier to convince myself before he announced that I would go north too on the *Heralder*.

The door of my bedroom opens behind me, making me jump. I scrabble to drop the shell in the drawer, not wanting Lydia to see me staring at it—or, worse, August. But when I look up to the mirror, it's not Lydia's reflection in the doorway, or August's.

It's Silas Price.

"Do you believe me now?" he asks, low voice cutting through the room, all the air seeming to drain away.

Even as I scramble to my feet, slamming the drawer shut with the seashell inside, grief pierces me that my sister and my betrothed didn't come after me. Not that I want them to see me like this, tears streaking my face, my throat raw from the sobs I've been holding in. But not in years have I felt so alone as I do now.

"You can't be here," I hiss. "This is my family's private space." I realize too late that the gloves are still on the floor, my fingers bare. It's dark, but still I fist my hands in my skirts, wanting to hide them, even if it's pointless.

"For weeks I've been asking for an audience, Lady Fairfax." He keeps his distance, a rigid shape outlined by moonlight in the doorway. I don't doubt that he dislikes me as much as I do him. Our mutual distaste tethers us together like a rope straining between two vessels, always on the verge of breaking and taking someone's limbs off. "You've ignored every note."

"Because I have nothing to say to you."

"Don't you?" Silas's eyes fall to the dresser, the drawer that hides the shell still cracked open. "Because it seems you saw my message. He means to get rid of you on the way to Kielstraat."

I'm not surprised to hear him admit he sent the shell. I suspected as much. But it still makes every hair on my body rise with fury. "I saw a parlor trick," I say, cold as I can. "A fantasy."

"If you really believe that," he says, "why is your heartbreak getting worse?"

Fear spikes through me. Is it so obvious? If Silas has discerned that much, can others see it as well? I can still hear the sounds of the shareholders drinking and laughing, the gathering going on in my absence. And Kit's room is right across the hall. If he stayed up late reading, if he's awake to hear this—

"Come in, then, if you must," I say, voice shaking. "Shut the door."

There is a monster that sleeps coiled under my skin, a monster that hatched in the hours after my parents' deaths, when I floated in dark waters amid the wreckage of the *Volyar*, when the heartbreak curse first took hold. But for a long time, it was small, manageable, manifesting only as fleeting thoughts and impulses—an urge to take a swing at a drunkard catcalling me on the street, or when I cut myself chopping vegetables, to lick up the blood and learn what it tastes like.

But lately, seeing vulnerability in others wakes it up, as with Mayor Bildad earlier and the scab on his neck where he must have nicked himself shaving. Anger wakes it up too, and it ripples under my skin as Silas Price does as I ask, then leans against the back of the door, crossing his arms with enraging casualness.

"Why would August want to kill me?" I challenge him, seething inside. Without taking my eyes off him, I find a candle and a match, strike a flame with shaking hands. "He saved me. He saved both of us."

Because of course it wasn't just me and August on the lifeboat that terrible night. We were three.

Me, senseless with terror and grief as heartbreak set in.

Quick-thinking August, pulling me onto the boat. Holding me there even as I struggled, the new claws tearing his skin.

And Silas, silent and unreadable as the eerily calm water under our lifeboat as our crew drowned around us.

"We were children then." Silas is watching me carefully, like one would a wild animal. "Now control of the Fairfax Whaling Company is in his grasp. Lots can change in six years."

His calm, detached demeanor infuriates me. "Yes, it certainly seems so." I don't sit down. I want to stay at eye level with him. "For instance, you used to always be alone, and now your little collection of unfortunates follows you everywhere. Is it out of guilt you've taken them in? Or because no one else wants you around?"

It's the height of foolishness to antagonize a boy who could ruin me, but still something in me thrills when Silas's face darkens into a glare. Maybe if I make him angry, I'll tip his hand, learn his real game.

"Hate me all you like, but my crew are better people than you or I will ever be," he says in a voice like distant thunder. "And I've found a way to lift their curses."

I scoff. In the past six years, I've turned over the city, visited every bookstore, written to every academic, bribed every old mystic shilling folktales in alleys in hopes of saving myself from heartbreak, as Silas must well know. If such a way existed, I would have found it.

"Surely," he presses, "you've read the stories. People healed after journeys to see the finfolk."

I shouldn't even be engaging with this. This is improper on so many levels. Silas Price—Silas, whom black rumors cling to like whale-oil stains—in my room, at night, questioning me about August. I should send him away, but I need to know why he's here.

"None of it's real." I lift my chin, trying to sound uncaring. "No one in living memory has been healed no matter what they've done. It's a finfolk lie to fool us into thinking they're capable of mercy—"

"The stories are missing pieces. It's not enough to simply do a favor or two for the fae. You have to appear before them and plead your case." As he speaks, he comes off the wall and shoves his hands into his pockets, like he wants to pace. "I'm taking some of my crew to Drekja for that purpose, the ones who think they're ready."

There's a feverish light in his eyes that tells me he believes what he's saying, and that unsettles me. August and I have both dealt with the guilt of the *Volyar* in our own ways. August by throwing himself into his studies, and I by searching for ways to lift my curse—then, when I found none, by trying to forget, turning away from the sea. Silas, on the other hand, always seemed unaffected, a fact I put down to his cruel nature. But after all this time, has guilt over the *Volyar* driven him out of his senses?

"We don't even know if Drekja is real," I point out. Images of the City-beneath-the-waves from Mama's bedtime stories drift through my mind. An underwater city with buildings of coral and streets of pearl, guarded by monstrous whales. The ancestral home of the finfolk. Certainly people have tried to find it over the centuries. After all, it is said to be guarded by Livyati; the surrounding seas would surely be a treasure trove of a hunting ground. But no one has ever found it—or, at least, found it and returned.

At the word *Drekja*, Silas's mouth twitches in a faint smile, like he's pleased to hear the name from my lips. "It's real." His voice is low enough to almost be a whisper. "And I can find it. I can bring you to the queen there to ask that your curse be lifted."

"Because you're finfolk," I say. A heavy, charged silence settles between us.

I have known this, of course, for six years. August too. But none of us has ever, ever spoken of it out loud.

Because if I turned Silas in, he could just as easily reveal my heartbreak. Our secrets chain us together, a silent doomsday pact.

"Only half," Silas says at length, smiling a little, to my unease. "And this voyage is the chance I've been waiting for. The *Whistler* can't get through the ice fields, not safely. But the *Heralder* can. And my calculations show Drekja will be close to Kielstraat."

"To liaise with the finfolk is treason," I say, an automatic response while my mind races to catch up. Even though by any standard we're far past treason now.

His reply comes swiftly. "Will you turn us in, Lady Fairfax? Or will you come with us? You could be healed." The smile widens. "At least, you could try."

I clench my fists in my skirt, feeling the velvet tear under my nails as something small and bright ignites inside my chest. I've felt it before. Every time I came across one of those stories of curses being lifted, or met a swindler who claimed they could help me. A *maybe*. A spark of hope.

And I know what it will feel like when it's extinguished. I know each time hope dies, it hurts more and more. It only makes things worse.

"Has your crew swallowed this lie, then?" I say, cold and calm. The Cursed Crew, what I've seen of them, don't strike me as fools, but Silas can be persuasive. After all, he convinced August and me to keep his secret these six years. Perhaps that was a mistake.

"I'm not lying to them." Heat trickles through Silas's voice, making the monster perk its ears. It wants violence; it's attentive to anger like blood in the water. "I'm not lying to you."

I want Silas to leave and take the hope with him. I pour venom into my voice. "I know August loves me."

Something shutters behind his eyes, storm clouds turning a flat gray. "He doesn't love anything."

"Then why did you only show me that moment? If this is true—if he plans to kill me"—I swallow, the words sour on my lips—"you must have agreed, for him to invite you on this voyage. Am I in danger now?"

He goes perfectly still, unnaturally still, which is how I know I've gotten under his skin, made him forget to act human. "I told August he needn't dirty his hands," he says. "That your heartbreak would do the job sooner or later."

"Unless I go with you to Drekja." I lace my voice with sarcasm, disbelief, to hide that still-burning spark of *maybe*, *maybe* . . .

"Now you're getting it."

"And what will this cost me?" I challenge.

He smiles. "You know, most people's response to learning there's a cure to the curse that's actively killing them would be *how* or simply *yes*. Not to ask what will it cost."

"Most people are fools, then," I say. "Everything has a cost. There's a reason you came to me with this—I don't believe it was merely out of the goodness of your heart."

"Only a promise."

I exhale sharply, a half laugh. "A promise can be a heavy

thing." *I promised Papa I would look after the company. I promised Mama I would take care of Kit and Lydia while she was gone. I promised August I'd love him forever, and he promised me the same thing.* "What would you have me promise?"

"Dissolve the company," he whispers. "End whaling forever."

Shock stills everything in me; it feels like my heart skips, trembles.

Even if it were possible—and it is the farthest thing from possible—why would Silas want that?

I'm saved from having to think of a reply when, outside in the hall, footsteps fall on the stairs. Heavy. Not Lydia. August. I step back, panic flooding me.

Silas is already moving toward the door, but has to pass between me and the dresser to get there. He pauses close to me, making all the muscles in my body go tense. A faint smell of petrichor clings to him.

"Come to the Spout inn tomorrow night, after dark," he says quietly. "Down by the wharf. I'll tell you how it can be accomplished."

"Leave," I say, and hope he'll interpret the quaver in my voice as rage and not the traitorous hope that has suddenly surged through me. "Use the servant staircase at the end of the hall to the left."

He inclines his head once briefly in acknowledgment, then he's gone, leaving me in silence that seems loud with his words echoing in my ears. Healing the heartbreak. Could it truly be possible?

A minute later, the footsteps reach my door and August knocks in the way he always does, eight quick raps in the rhythm of the old song. *Girls on the shore must guard their hearts . . .*

I haven't moved, maybe haven't even breathed, since Silas exited, but the knock startles me back to reality. Catching my breath,

I spin to face the mirror. I look a little pale, but otherwise presentable. I quickly let my hair out of its braid and shed my jacket, slinging it over the back of a chair, to create the appearance that August has just caught me getting ready for bed.

"Annie?" comes his voice from the other side of the door. Another knock. I take a deep breath and open the door.

August steps inside my room without being asked, his presence sparking up a battle of love and fear in my guts. The shareholder meeting is over now, but he still smells like wine and cigar smoke. He crosses the room and looks me over with concern, hands warm on my upper arms, as the door falls shut behind us. "Annie, are you all right? You ran out of the party."

"Noticed, did you?" My voice comes out clipped. Does he really not know why I'm upset? And why did it take him so long to come after me? "I didn't feel well. I'm tired."

The crease between his brows says he doesn't believe me. Whatever his faults, he knows how important this company is to me, knows I wouldn't have run out of the shareholder meeting without a good reason. "Is it your—affliction?" he asks, meaning my heartbreak curse.

"Why did you tell everyone I was going to Kielstraat?" I'm stiff in his arms, holding my place even as he tries to move deeper into the room. "We didn't agree to that."

"Forgive me, my love." He stares down into my eyes with the expression that's melted me so many times before, that absolute, unshakable confidence, like he would bring me the world on a string if I asked. "That's why I had to do it this way. I knew you wouldn't agree otherwise. But it's right for you to be on this expedition. The leader of the Fairfax Whaling Company, breaking ground on the endeavor that will save us all."

Silas Price's words echo in my mind. *He means to get rid of you on the way to Kielstraat*. But doubt flickers. Maybe August is right and it would be proper for me to go, to be there when the outpost opens. And now that he's made the announcement, it will look even worse if I don't go. Everyone from the shareholders, the merchants, the officers, down to the greenest sailor would all know me to be a coward.

Resentment at August for putting me in this position churns in my gut, even as he brushes an open-mouthed kiss against the side of my neck, making me shiver. I pull back enough to look into his face. Even in the dark his eyes glitter and his lips curl into a familiar smile, one that says all the plans in his mind are slotting together into a vision of a perfect future. But does that vision include me? "What about Silas? Why do you want him there?"

A faint trace of irritation mars August's face for half a second before he smooths it away. "It might be useful, having someone like him on the expedition," he says. "It was before, on the *Volyar*. Useful."

My breath catches. I don't want to think about that. August presses his lips against my neck.

"Think how glorious it will be," he exhales, breath hot on my throat, chasing my thoughts away. "The whole world will hear about us breaching this new frontier together." As he speaks, he moves his hands down my arms. His fingertips brush carefully over the scales until he weaves his fingers through mine, sending warmth through my body—and, with it, guilt.

Silas Price is a scavenger. Disgraced. Why have I let his story worm so deep into me that it's making me distrust August—August, who has been at my side for six years now? Who's supported my work with the company, kept the secret of my curse when he didn't have to, loved me when anyone else would have run screaming?

August knows I'm heartbroken, knows it's getting worse. If he wanted me gone, all it would take would be a tip to the night watchmen and I'd be taken away, locked up like Cousin Mary or worse. But he's kept my deadly secret. And even like this, he still loves me. He still wants me. And I need him.

I let myself relax into August's arms, turn my face into his kiss. His thumbs move reassuringly over the backs of my hands as his tongue parts my lips, and the taste of sweet wine seeps in. The doubt is still there, a stubborn whisper in the back of my mind, but I'm not going to let it rule me, I decide as I stand on my tiptoes to press my body up against August's.

Maybe it's perverse to let August's kisses distract me from my heartbreak, fully knowing that in the morning the doubts will sweep back in and the scales will come back worse. But I've survived this long by fighting the curse with every method at my disposal, and no weapon is better than August kissing me, clutching me to him like he can't get enough, like I'm the one keeping him alive and not vice versa.

Still, my heart isn't in it. I gently detach from him and pull back. Understanding pools in August's eyes and he drops his hands to hold mine, his energy instantly shifting from hungry and aggressive to protective and tender.

He helps me out of my outer clothes, kneeling to unlace my boots, and he folds the blue dress and drapes it over the back of the chair alongside his jacket. When he's just in his shirt and trousers and I in my shift, he takes my bare hand and guides me into bed, then lies down behind me, curling his body around mine.

It's not molten and wanting and frantic like our kisses, but this too is familiar and precious. He wraps his arms around me—my own hands clasped safely against my chest—and presses his face into my hair. A mirror of how he held me on the lifeboat that night, so long ago and yet not so very long at all.

August was barely less of a child than I was. He must have been terrified, yet he held me in place as my heart broke and scales erupted and Silas watched. Held my wrists so I couldn't attack them; hooked his legs over mine so I couldn't jump into the sea.

Just like he did then, he whispers into my hair now, "Everything will be all right, Annie. I promise." And just like always, I feel like arguing that he can't know that, can't possibly make such a promise. Yet so much of me wants to accept it, to believe him.

I feel wrung out by everything that's happened. If there's any truth at all to Silas's claim that the finfolk can lift curses, I owe it to myself—and Kit and Lydia—to learn more. But I won't be blinded by hope, or let the seashell poison me against August. I can hold two opposing ideas in my mind at once. I can find out what Silas is offering while still keeping my own counsel about August.

With his steady heartbeat behind me, his breath stirring my hair, my body takes over, and despite the faint shadow of doubt still staining my thoughts, it's easy to fall asleep in his arms. But I know, even as I drift peacefully off, that I will dream of storms and freezing water and the smell of petrichor.

1 II 1836 FC

LIST OF PERSONS

Comprising the crew of the ship Volyar of Abbonheim

Whereof the Captain, Standish Price, bound for the Sea of the Crossroads

With guests Lord Richard Lawrence Fairfax and Lady Annabelle Seneca Fairfax

Hal Akamai, Greenhand

Age: 19

Place of Birth: Iron Islands

Height: 6 feet, 2 inches

Eyes: Brown

Hair: Brown

Of what Domain Citizen or Subject: Olaola

Manuel Bradford, First Mate

Age: 26

Place of Birth: Sao Martim, Izmael

Height: 5 feet, 10 inches

Eyes: Brown

Hair: Black

Of what Domain Citizen or Subject: Midlands

Grace Cadwallader, Bosun

Age: 23

Place of Birth: Carburgh, Hiberna

Height: 4 feet, 11 inches

Eyes: Blue

Hair: Yellow

Of what Domain Citizen or Subject: Abbonheim

Page 1/14

Chapter 5

In the morning, I pluck the new scales out with tweezers—more than I've seen in days—and then drink more whaleblood to heal the pinpricks of blood that remain. There is much to do if I'm to join the journey to Kielstraat.

I dress and knock on Kit's door to help him get ready for his lessons. It takes a suspiciously long time for my eleven-year-old brother to open it, and while I wait, the painting in the hall next to his door snags my attention. In it, two Livyati—one, harpooned, thrashes in a maelstrom of frothing waves, while another circles as a ship sinks, snapped in two.

I never understood why Papa—the preeminent whaler in Kirkrell, indeed along the whole north coast—only ever commissioned scenes of whales killing men. Our fortune is built on men killing whales. We render the beasts' flesh and sell it to the world: dried meat for strength, blood to heal. Yet in the artwork decorating the manor, it's always humans meeting their ends in the deep.

The small terrified faces in the white froth of waves, dark bits of shattered boat all around. I wonder if Papa would have chosen a different scene knowing that that very fate awaited him and Mama. Will it be mine too?

Finally, Kit opens the door and stares up at me with his most wide-eyed, cherubic look, trying to distract me from his crooked shirt—the buttons done up wrong—his light brown hair sticking up wildly on one side, and the book back on his bed, shoved hastily under the quilt but not quite hidden.

It's all so utterly normal that I want to laugh. "How late did you stay up reading, Kristopher?" I ask him, putting my hands on my hips exaggeratedly. He knows I'm not really angry. "And how late did you sleep in this morning?"

When I was that age, I liked roaming around the grounds, conscripting Lydia into games of make-believe where we'd crouch in a tree, pretending it was a ship, and throw imaginary harpoons at imaginary whales. Kit, though, can usually be found curled in an armchair with his latest book, or at the kitchen table, reading the *Kirkrell Maritime Gazette*.

"Not that late!" Kit says indignantly, puffing himself up. "Besides, you and Lydia stayed up later than me at the party."

"Trust me, it wasn't much of a party." I shove him gently in the direction of his wardrobe. "I would have much rather been up here reading sea stories. Now go brush your hair and fix your shirt. Be downstairs in five minutes if you want breakfast before Ms. Nilsson gets here."

In the kitchen, Lydia is picking at a bannock, dressed for her lessons, with a look of consternation on her face—one that intensifies as I enter the room. When she levels her glare at me, I freeze in the act of reaching for the plate that Mrs. Milhouse has left for us.

"What's wrong?"

"You didn't tell me you were going to Kielstraat."

My heart drops. Talking to Kit made me momentarily forget my worries, but instantaneously Lydia's words bring them back, arms prickling, Silas's and August's voices echoing in my mind and making my stomach churn.

"I didn't know," I tell her, pasting on a smile that feels false, a jester's mask. "It was a surprise. But it's a good idea, don't you think?" My voice rings false to my ears, and Lydia's eyes remain narrow, unconvinced, but I plow onward. "Kielstraat is critical to the company's future. I should be there when it goes into operation."

Lydia hunches over her food, not looking at me as I put a scoop of ground coffee into a strainer. She's only three years younger than me, and sometimes she feels almost like a woman, like last night when she floated effortlessly among the shareholders, seeming lighter and happier than I could ever be. But other times, like now—frowning fiercely, methodically stabbing her bannock like it's the cause of all our problems—she seems as much a child as Kit still is. "He should have talked to you first," she says. "And you should have talked to us."

Of course she's right, but what can I say to that? I pretend to be distracted by pouring hot water through the strainer. The smell of coffee should be comforting, but it just makes my stomach twist further, appetite suddenly gone. I grab a bannock anyway and take that and the coffee to sit down across from her at the kitchen table, the ceramic mug warming through my gloves and soothing my sore palms where I picked the scales out.

"I'll be careful on the ship," I tell her. "August will take care of me."

"You could refuse to go." She looks down at her plate while she speaks, fingers working nimbly to disassemble her breakfast.

"The shareholders would think me a coward."

"So let them." Her bannock is just a pile of crumbs now. "What does it matter what they think? You're the head of the company, not them."

I bite my lip, trying to figure out how to explain that it's not that simple, that I have only as much power as the shareholders have faith in me, and that was in short supply in the first place. But before I marshal my words, Lydia says:

"Didn't the *Volyar* go down in the arctic?"

I flinch, caught off guard by her words. Much as we might argue sometimes, Lydia never brings up what happened on the *Volyar*. Like she knows it runs the risk of shattering me. I take a deep breath, trying not to let her fear infect me—or, rather, not to let her see how deep my own fear goes, how my skin crawls and stomach churns at the words.

"In the far north, yes," I say. "But that was the Askarda. The way to Kielstraat is through the Sidhae Sea."

Not that it matters much. Like the shareholders say, the far north is the finfolks' territory. They don't abide by our borders and delineations.

Lydia looks deeply unconvinced, so I talk on, filling the silence with false-confident patter. "And the *Heralder* is a better ship. We'll have weapons and numbers we didn't have back then—"

Kit announces his arrival with a clatter, nearly tripping and falling as he races to grab a bannock from the counter, then points triumphantly at Lydia and me. "See? I'm ready in time. That means I can stay up reading again tonight."

"Not yet." I stand up, shooting Lydia a quelling glance. *We'll talk about this later.* "Only if you manage to eat that without getting crumbs all down your front. And your shoes are untied."

Half an hour later, Lydia and I are in the heart of Kirkrell's old town, the roads an illogical labyrinth of narrow byways, all etched with the deep grooves left by countless carts and carriages. The air is thick with the smells of sweat, smoke, rotting fish, horse manure, and sea brine. Declan could have taken us in the carriage, but when Papa was alive, he walked everywhere, never mind the weather, and it's a habit I've maintained. I like to keep my feet on solid earth.

Beside me, Lydia is almost too chipper, our argument over the breakfast table apparently forgotten. Tucking her notebook into her satchel, she looks every inch the heiress I ought to be, her blue flannel dress ironed crisp and her face bright. Vendors weave through the crowd, peddling their wares—fish glistening on beds of ice, blank eyes staring; pouches of powdered whaleblood and whalebone; strips of dried whale meat; candles and soaps fashioned from Livyati's rendered blubber.

As we walk, I notice the glances, the nods, the curious stares of those around us. Some offer respectful acknowledgments, a murmured *Good morning, ladies*. If any of them knew the truth of me, the itching in my nail beds, the faint metallic smells that I can detect everywhere I go, they would run screaming. And they would be right to.

Out of nowhere, Lydia says, "I've decided I'm coming on the *Heralder* too."

"What?" Surprise makes me almost stumble on the uneven ground, causing Lydia to grab my elbow to steady me and drawing curious stares from a gaggle of schoolchildren passing by. "No, you're not."

"Yes, I am." Lydia keeps hold of my arm, and it's hard not to flinch away from her touch, warm and gentle though it might be. I know she can't feel the scales through the wool of my sleeve, but it's still alarming to have her hands so close to my skin. "I'm old enough. I want to be part of it."

"You're not old enough," I say reflexively. The curse responds to the sudden jolt of adrenaline coursing through me, the skin on my arms prickling, my nail beds burning.

"The greenhands can start at thirteen," she shoots back. Her face remains bright, a smile steady on her lips for the benefit of passersby, but her voice is steely. "And that's only the official rule; lots probably lie to the dockmasters to start sooner."

"Why do you want to go?" I counter, attempting to keep my voice steady. "It's going to be dull at best and terrible at worst." We've made our way to the less respectable warehouse district, which is a mercy, as we're less likely to be recognized here—surrounded by factory girls in soot-stained dresses, washerwomen toiling under baskets heaped high with cloth, stable boys leading horses by the reins. Sailors in canvas and oilcloth, their faces weathered and bronzed by salt and sun, harpoons and bags slung over their shoulders.

Lydia's grip on my arm tightens subtly. "Because I want to be with you. Even if you're not good company lately."

Unspoken things dart in the spaces between her words—love and worry, the memory of our parents leaving on a voyage from which they would never return. But the trip to Kielstraat will be even more perilous than a typical whaling expedition—we'll be headed to the far north, the home of the finfolk.

And that's not even to speak of the secret agendas at play. Whatever Silas is after with his offer to take me to Drekja. And August . . . I don't believe he really means me harm, but there's still the whisper of doubt curled in the back of my skull, warning me to keep Lydia—keep both my siblings—away from all this.

"What about Kit?" I say.

Lydia looks troubled at that, her eyes flitting quickly to the side, but answers readily. "He'll be fine. He has Declan and Ms. Nilsson and the rest to look after him."

"None of those people are his family. If you and I are both on the voyage, and something happens . . ." I swallow down a sudden, heavy lump in my throat. "He'll be alone in the world."

"So we'll bring him too." Now Lydia sounds less certain. "He's always pestering me to read him stories about the far north. He'd be thrilled for a chance to see it for himself."

"So if the ship goes down, we can all die together?" In the distance, in the harbor, the masts of ships rise above the rooftops, their grand uprightness a contrast to the shapes of beggars huddled in doorways, many of them missing limbs. Probably whalers once who paid a heavy toll for their trade. "Absolutely not."

Lydia's smile dissipates. "Why are you going if you think it's so dangerous?" She shifts her satchel to her front and holds it like a shield. "Don't go, then. Stay here. What do they even need you for? You can't throw a harpoon. You don't know the way to Kielstraat."

My breath catches. I know she's not saying these things to be cruel, but—"You don't need to remind me of my shortcomings," I say sharply. As a whaler, a sailor, a Fairfax. "Trust me, I'm quite aware of them."

As I speak, I avert my eyes to avoid the gaze of a thin woman staring from a doorway. I don't remember there being so many beggars when I was a girl, walking these streets at Papa's side. Are there more of them, what with the whales growing fewer, or do I just notice them more readily now that I am the head of the company and everyone's fate rests on my shoulders?

Lydia huffs and lets go of my elbow. "I'm sorry, but—you seem so far away, Annie."

I turn away and focus on walking, avoiding the gazes of the passersby.

It's not uncommon for Livyati to take life and limb, even in a successful hunt. The whale's death throes are notoriously violent; the most dangerous part is the span of time between when the quarry is first hit and the end, when it bleeds out. Sometimes the whale flees with harpoons still embedded in its flesh, towing the whalers in their whaleboats along at breakneck speed. Sometimes the whale fights back, overturning the boats and sending the men into shark-clotted waves. There are even stories of whales attacking the ships themselves, staving a hole in their sides and sinking them, dooming everyone on board. That was why our maternal grandfather, a shipwright, began building ships with iron ribs, but it's not always enough.

Whalers know the risks, I remind myself. There's not a soul in this city who doesn't understand that when you step aboard a whaleship, you might not return. Papa made sure to teach us this. They know what they are signing up for. The whaling life brings danger, yes, but it also brings glory, brings fortune. The sprawling mansions in the hills surrounding Kirkrell are evidence enough of that.

When we reach the warehouse, the double-wide front doors are propped open so workers can carry materials in and out from the floor. Barrels of blood and oil, bundles of whalebone eight or nine or ten feet long and wrapped in wax cloth.

An attendant sees us in through a side door, past the four guards stationed there. They nod at me respectfully, but it doesn't register until I've already brushed past them that I ought to have summoned a smile in return. My mind feels full of noise.

There will be a storm. There always is.

Dissolve the company. End whaling forever.

Though I've been visiting the warehouses my whole life, the din and the smell and the clamor still overwhelm me when we first enter. Most of the cavernous space inside is dedicated to one working area, with the dirty skylights letting in enough light to see by, but it still feels dim and shadowy, or maybe it's just that everything is caked with a thin layer of soot and grime.

The floor is alive with activity, each quadrant devoted to one byproduct of a Livyatan. Oil and bone, flesh and blood, all brought here in barrels and bundles from the wharves. In the northeast quadrant, workers cut slabs of pinkish-gray whale meat into thin slices, salt them, and hang them in drying ovens. In the northwest, massive metal vats of whaleblood simmer and hiss as they boil down. In the southwest, workers lay out bones—massive curved ribs and heavy, knotted vertebrae, slender, oddly delicate flipper bones the shape of elongated human hands—on long stone tables, cover them with canvas, and hammer them into powder, their practiced strokes creating a harsh drumbeat underneath everything. And in the southeast quadrant, closest to me, workers lift long spirals of skin and blubber from the barrels the whalers have brought in, carefully lowering them into more vats to be boiled down to clear, fragrant oil.

The whole place smells like blood, and the workers' faces are grim from a long day, eyes red from smoke, soot caked into the lines in their faces and the creases in their clothes.

But the people of Kirkrell need whale magic. To restore the sick and wounded; make us stronger; allow us to endure the cold; satiate the worst hunger.

The supervisor, Bulkington, isn't in his office when we're first shown in; the attendant tells us to wait, another small indignity that Papa would never have been subjected to. A fire crackles low and the air is too warm, heightening the smell of blood and grime that permeates this building even past the cutting floor.

When the door closes behind the attendant, leaving us alone in the plain wood-paneled office, Lydia's posture changes as if the air has been let out of her, shoulders slumping and eyes narrowing. Not the younger Lady Fairfax any longer, but just an angry girl.

Her voice is low and controlled when she speaks. "After Mama and Papa died, it was awful, but I thought we were muddling through. I thought things were getting better. But these last few weeks . . . sometimes you look at me and it's like you don't even see me. You're somewhere else."

Even though I can tell she's upset, I feel too fragile to be patient with her. I'd hoped we were done with this conversation. "Things have been difficult," I say, clenching my fists in my jacket sleeves. "I don't know enough about the business, Lydia. Joining the expedition to Kielstraat will help me remedy that. That's all."

"I know you, Annie," she says, turning to face me. "I know there's something you're not telling me. Don't say it's just the business. We could sell the company tomorrow and move to Sant Juda and all these problems would be gone. There's something else."

I blink. She's never said anything like this to me before. "There's nothing else. The company is our family's mission. Our life's work. Papa's life's work."

"Papa's gone," Lydia says, incredulity knitting her brow, like I might have forgotten. "Wherever he is now, he's past caring. Didn't you ever want something different for your life?"

"No," I say truthfully. The sour thought crosses my mind that if Lydia were the heiress instead of me, she would be an easy mark for Silas's noble talk of ending whaling. "This is all I've ever wanted." Thorns of emotion climb the inside of my throat. "And I'm failing. Everyone is relying on us to bring them whale magic. Everyone in the city."

I keep my voice low, knowing I shouldn't be talking about this in someone else's office, but after shoving my feelings down for so long it's impossible to continue to suppress them. "Who knows how many more people we'll never meet, never even see—but they're warm, they're healed, they're strong because of our work."

I expect the reminder of our responsibilities, our impact, to overcome Lydia's protests. But she lifts her chin. "I don't care! Maybe that's terrible but I don't. I don't care about any of them. I care about you and I feel like you're going to—"

"Shh." I reach out on impulse, meaning to pat her arm comfortingly, but before I can, her hand darts out and she grabs my wrist. Grabs it beneath the cuff of my coat, where only a thin layer of cloth hides my skin and the scales. She grips tight, before I even process what's happened, then stills, her eyes widening.

"Oh."

No.

I try to pull back, heart beating in my throat, blood racing. "Lydia."

When she doesn't respond, I repeat it. "Lydia." My awareness of the curse surges, the pain in my wrists and fingertips sharpening, my senses heightening to dizzying levels until the faint sun seems too bright, the heat of the fire and the smell of stale blood and soap overwhelming, Lydia's wide, wet eyes too close, unblinking.

"Listen to me," I manage hoarsely, but then my voice dies, because what is there to say? *It's not what you think*? It is what she thinks. She knows it and I know it. That night all those years ago, Cousin Mary screaming in a jail cell, pressing her face against the iron bars—the image is surely burned into Lydia's mind as clear as it is in mine. I see the memory reflected in her eyes; I see the realization sink in as her fingers press down on my wrist through the too-thin material of my gloves.

She's still holding on. Why is she still holding on?

I pull away and she lets go without protest, her hand slowly moving to her side. Her eyes are not on my hand but on my face. And I can't read her expression. I can't identify the currents swirling there, but I can say what's absent: surprise.

"You knew."

"I guessed," she corrects me quietly.

She isn't screaming or running from me—her face is blank, her voice neutral, but surely the shock must be simply delaying her reaction. She has seen the monster I will become. "How long has it been?" she asks.

"Since Mama and Papa died," I say. "I know how to control it, mostly. If I stay calm and don't think about them, it doesn't get worse."

A half-truth at best. Because it is getting worse, not because of Mama and Papa, but because of August and Silas.

Yet I know with a deep, dark, cold instinct that I shouldn't tell her about the seashell. The memories—or at least, what Silas claims to be memories—of August plotting to kill me. Because if it's true that August means me harm, I don't want to put my sister in his path too.

"That's why you can't come on the expedition," I say, whispering because I don't trust my voice. "You need to be there for Kit." *Because, in all likelihood, I won't be.*

Her spine goes straight, her eyes steely. "Does that mean you don't intend to come back?"

"No!" I shake my head quickly. Even if I'm not optimistic

about my chances, Lydia can't think I would ever abandon them of my own free will. "I have a lead on a cure," I tell her, then immediately regret it when her eyes light up with hope.

"It's probably nothing at all," I hasten to add. Even if Silas was telling the truth about Drekja and the possibility of healing, the price he named—dissolving the company, ending whaling—is untenable. "Just . . . just a possibility."

"This just makes it more important that we be together," she says with finality. "I'm coming with you and that's that."

I'm prevented from arguing further by Bulkington's arrival. We exchange the usual pleasantries and then get down to business. Lydia's taking notes, so cheerful and diligent you would think the last five minutes never happened.

But it's difficult to sit up straight and feign interest in shipping rates and delivery schedules and the profits we can derive from a dry pound of powdered whaleblood versus in its liquid form. My eyelids droop, and I'm too hot in my long-sleeved wool dress, and the growing scales itch beneath the fabric. Worry and sleeplessness drag at my limbs and dull my mind.

To end the interaction faster, I perhaps unwisely agree to raising prices on whale magic at the turn of the season, given the increasing costs of our voyages. I have to press my fingernails into my palms beneath the gloves to stay awake, risking drawing blood.

I've arranged another errand after the warehouse, while Lydia is returning to the manor, so we part without discussing further the question of her joining the voyage to Kielstraat. But from the resolute glint in her eyes as she walks out, I have a heavy feeling the matter is resolved.

Myself, I leave Bulkington's office and climb the stairs, unlock the door to Papa's old office, and go in. Or the office that I still think of as Papa's, even though it was Grandfather's for a time after my parents died, and now August is mainly the one to use it. I work from the library at home instead. For months after my parents' ship went down, grief and an overwhelming sense of dread kept me from even entering this place. Dread that I would be inadequate to shoulder the legacy they had left. It still makes me feel small, stepping inside. I fear that I will be found wanting.

In contrast to the grit and utility of the rest of the warehouse, the office is a stately room, as long as you don't look out the window to the yard and see the vats to boil blubber, the men breaking giant bones with mallets, the rusty smears over every surface. Here, there are walls paneled in dark wood, a rich forest-green carpet, a desk with a globe atop it, and more of Papa's strange, morbid paintings. Wooden file cabinets line the far walls, each of them labeled with a tag in my father's neat handwriting. I find the one notated *Fae Encounters*, then take it to sit in Papa's chair.

I don't know quite what I'm looking for as I page through the files. Maybe just to feel close to Papa—as if by walking the places he walked, touching the objects he once touched, I could hear an echo of his voice and know what I should do.

Inside, the yellowing papers are organized by date, the files getting thicker and thicker each year. It goes far enough back that the oldest folders are labeled in Grandfather's more spidery writing, and then Papa's, for most of the length of the drawer. But then, six years ago, the writing switches over to Grandfather's again. It makes it easy to find the file I'm looking for: 14 V 1836 FC. The fourteenth day of Fifth Month, six years ago.

The crew who came upon us, who rescued August, Silas, and me, spent hours sifting through the splintered wood and scraps of sail, looking for bodies. Those still recognizable were collected and brought back to Abbonheim so that their wives and parents and children could put them in decent clothes and wash the salt from their skin.

My father and mother were not among these. They were knowable only by their possessions—Papa's red tailcoat, the one that Mama always admonished him for taking on voyages with the whalers, and his favored pistol—with the intricately carved scrimshaw handle—still clamped in his hand. Mama by her gold wedding ring and pearl-faced pocket watch. Lucky thing they hadn't been nibbled away by sharks, that these objects at least could be brought back with me, to sit in the silk-lined graveyard of my top dresser drawer.

Here is the manifest from the *Volyar*—a copy only; the original is at the bottom of the ocean with the wreckage of the ship. It feels heavy with grief and things lost. There's a map here, yellowed with age, setting out our intended route, south through the Barasi, around Cape Silver and Cavoi, and back up into the Sea of the Crossroads. A new port had opened in Sant Juda that spring. That was why Mama and Papa had been on the voyage, to meet the merchants there and make connections. Good business. Such a mundane thing to die for.

The list of the crew, though, is what I can't tear my eyes from, what I've been staring at without processing for fifteen minutes. More than forty names in alphabetical order. Second and third mates, harpooners, a cook, a blacksmith, a cooper, and a sailmaker—men and women originating from all parts of the world, many of them just a few years older than me. Mostly, I can't remember their faces. Each person, each life summed up in just a few words. It makes me feel cold. Did any of them have a feeling, stepping aboard the *Volyar*, that it would be their last voyage?

Except, of course, for three.

Susannah Fairfax, Passenger
Age: 13
Place of Birth: Kirkrell, Abbonheim
Height: 4 feet, 11 inches
Eyes: Brown
Hair: Blonde
Of what Domain Citizen or Subject: Abbonheim

August Hargreave, Apprentice to Lord Fairfax
Age: 15
Place of Birth: Kirkrell, Abbonheim
Height: 5 feet, 6 inches
Eyes: Blue
Hair: Red
Of what Domain citizen or subject: Abbonheim

Silas Price, Greenhand
Age: 14
Place of Birth: Unknown
Height: 5 feet, 5 inches
Eyes: Gray
Hair: Black
Of what Domain Citizen or Subject: Abbonheim

August and I told everyone we met that the finfolk had attacked us. Called down a storm that sank the ship. But no one wanted to believe it at first. Finfolk attacks were a relic of old times, they said. The fae couldn't sink a ship, not in our age of iron.

Then details started coming out. Papa's gun was empty of its iron bullets. The barrels of oil and whaleblood and meat that the *Volyar* had already collected were found bobbing empty, neat round holes carved in their sides, the precious magic inside long since seeped back into the sea.

Silas wouldn't speak at all for weeks after. So long that the adults who looked after us thought he'd been hit on the head in the wreck, lost his speech. But I knew better. Knew that the finfolk hadn't harmed him. Wouldn't harm him.

Sitting there in my father's chair, I want so badly to hear Papa's voice in my memory. But instead it's my own voice, a child's voice, warped and trembling with rage.

Silas had come to the funeral for Mama and Papa. I hadn't realized he was there at first. I stayed in the sanctuary long after everyone else filed out, not wanting them to see me cry. I thought I was alone. But when I finally got up, he was there in the backmost pew. Alone too.

"Annie," he said, voice rasping like that was the first word he had spoken since the *Volyar*. Maybe it was. "I'm—"

The words came out without my meaning them to, shocking me with their venom, so acidic they practically burned on my tongue:

"You should have died with the rest of them."

Silas Price looked right through me, face pale and hollow, like his body was in the church with me but his mind was still out at sea. Still drowning.

Chapter 6

It's early evening, the shadows lengthening in the narrow, damp alleys of the wharf district, by the time my sister and I make it to the Spout and duck inside, out of the cold wind coming off the ocean. Surveying the objectively lackluster interior—ale-damp sawdust heaped over an uneven dirt floor, grim-about-the-mouth old men drinking in the corners, dirty tankards left scattered haphazardly over sticky tabletops—I begin to doubt my impulsive decision to bring Lydia here with me.

Having told her at the warehouse that I had a lead on a cure to the heartbreak curse, once I got home there was no avoiding giving her the details—though not the whole story. I told her about Silas's plan to heal the Cursed Crew, his offer to take me to Drekja to be healed—but not about the shell or Silas being finfolk. As far as she knows, Silas is just an ordinary sailor who has come across stories of Drekja on his travels. As far as she knows, my heartbreak is due only to the loss of Mama and Papa. And she doesn't know it's getting worse.

Nor did I tell her about the cost Silas has named: ending whaling. Because even if that were possible, I'll never destroy our legacy by agreeing to it. Yet maybe I can find a way to outmaneuver Silas here—to be healed without paying the price.

We've borrowed plain dresses and cloaks from Ms. Nilsson, so no one pays us any mind as we walk in until a familiar face tilts up from a table near the fireplace. The tall, dark-haired boy who was with Silas at the meeting last night. He catches my eye, unsmiling, and beckons.

"Lady Fairfax," he says coolly when I'm close enough for other patrons not to hear. Then he sees Lydia and his eyes widen. "Ladies Fairfax."

The girl from the meeting is there too, playing cards with another young man and woman I don't recognize. But she looks up, her motions quick and economic like a bird's, and breaks into a smile when she sees Lydia. The others notice too and turn to look at me. An apple-cheeked young man with curly brown hair, and a muscular girl with a crooked smile and shiny black hair pulled back from her face. Dressed in unassuming sailor clothes, linen and battered leather and worn boots and oilcloth jackets, the four of them push cards and drinks aside to make room for Lydia and me to sit down.

Silas isn't among them, which suits my purposes just fine. Maybe I can get some answers talking to them without their captain present. I sit down, pushing my hood back but not taking off my coat. I can't help but wonder again what their curses might be.

The girl from the party smiles and looks between the two of us. "Introductions!" she declares brightly. "Everyone, this is Susannah and Lydia. Susannah and Lydia, this is everyone. I'm Josephine Haskins, first mate." Her words come in a rapid patter as she points to the tall boy. "Ezra McNaughton, second mate.

And these are Zimri and Teuila, our harpooners on the *Whistler*." The boys nod as Josephine introduces them, and the harpooner girl, Teuila, waves, as if this is any ordinary night. Maybe it is for them. "Silas is doing a walk-through of the *Heralder*," Josephine adds as an afterthought. "But he should be here soon."

"Annie," I manage to say around the nervous dry weight of my tongue. Even though they all know who I am. "Call me Annie. This is your whole crew?"

Ezra shakes his head. "No, we usually take fifteen or twenty when we sail on the *Whistler*. But we'll be the ones on the *Heralder* for the voyage to Kielstraat."

"Oh good." Lydia slumps in relief. "You can teach me how to sail, won't you? I don't want to be shouted at by Mance."

I shoot her a sharp look, aghast that she would admit such a deficiency to near-strangers, but already everyone is laughing, and I feel wrong-footed. Lydia has always made friends easily, but it just makes me feel like more of a foreign species by comparison.

After we've all shaken hands and Zimri has poured two more glasses of questionable ale for us from a ceramic pitcher, Lydia leans forward on her elbows. "So are you the Cursed Crew? What are your curses?"

"Lydia!" This must be impolite to ask. But the others don't seem fazed. I get the sense that they've gotten this question a thousand times before and have their answers down pat.

"I burn everything I try to cook," Teuila offers. She has a slight Embran accent and a quality to her voice and smile that makes it seem she's always on the verge of bursting out laughing. "It doesn't matter what it is. Even if it doesn't involve fire. I could put something in a jar to ferment and it would come out burned."

"Plants die around me," Josephine says. "Makes you unpopular on land."

Ezra says, sounding slightly reluctant: "I can't cross running water. No streams or rivers or creeks. When it's raining, I can't go anywhere at all on land."

I realize as they're speaking that they all wear a similar necklace, a pendant of ivory or polished whalebone about the size of the pad of a man's thumb. Each bears a design in red ink—scrimshaw?—but I can't make out the details.

"My family's curse started with my grandfather," Zimri says. "I don't know the whole story, but he crossed a finfolk and ever since we've been cursed always to lose any money we might have." He laughs ruefully. "Not really conducive to life on land. I was born on a ship, grew up on one. And when Silas came around looking for new crew, I figured why not try to fix things?" His laugh booms around the bar, but then his next words come out quiet, just for this table. "What about you two?" He looks from me to Lydia. "Are you cursed too?"

Lydia blinks and meets my eye. I cut in before she can answer. "That's private."

I'm conscious of the fact that the others have shared their curses, but heartbreak is different. Would that my curse were only burning food or losing money. I think I could live with something like that forever and happily. But heartbreak is deadly, not just to me, but to others if I'm not very careful. If they knew what curse I suffered from, they could chase me from the bar or even turn me in to the authorities. Yes, the Abbonish government is a friend to the Fairfax Whaling Company. But not so much so that they would let me live carrying this curse.

"Fair enough." Zimri raises his glass in a sympathetic salute. "Here's hoping the finfolk let us into Drekja."

Drekja. It's a small shock to hear the word spoken aloud by someone other than Silas Price—it makes it feel more real to know that these people have bought into his claims. Can these four really believe Silas can take them to the finfolk city and lift their curses?

I take a sip of the ale to buy myself a moment—it tastes as bad as it looks, but it's good to have something to do with my hands as I figure out how to ask what I need to ask. "Why is it just you four going? Why not your whole crew?"

This quiets everyone; Teuila and the others exchange glances before she speaks. "We volunteered," she says. "It's going to be dangerous, and Silas can't promise that it will work. But we wanted to try."

There's quiet conviction in her voice, but the mention of danger sends chills through me. "How do you know he's telling the—"

The tavern door opens, letting in a cold draft, and I look up to see Silas in the flesh. The others greet him with waves and easy smiles, but my mouth goes dry and my heart jumps into my throat. After months of fruitless searching and years of reconciling myself to my own death or exile, is it really possible that an answer exists and I'll learn it here tonight?

Dressed in a long oilcloth coat that looks like it's seen many voyages, with color high in his cheeks and frost streaking his dark hair, Silas looks much more himself than the tense, buttoned-up boy from the shareholder meeting did. He's Captain Price in his own right now. He pulls up to the table but doesn't sit down, registering Lydia's presence with a raised eyebrow. "Lady Fairfax. Little sister."

I would have snapped at him to address us properly, but my sister just says, "Lydia," and reaches across to shake his hand. If she finds Silas unnerving, she doesn't show it; only looks a little wary as she settles back in her seat.

Silas's eyes find mine, questioning. I stand up, anxiety rising as I realize I should have conferred with him before bringing Lydia here. I need to tell him not to say anything about August in front of Lydia. "Can I have a word?"

He shrugs. "In there," he says, pointing to a short door set into the tavern's far wall. He strides away, not looking back to see if I follow.

"Nice meeting you," Josephine chirps, maybe a touch too brightly, as I get up to join Silas, mouth dry. Lydia catches my eye for a moment too. Hers glitter with excitement and hope, and it just makes the anxiety that I'm going to let her down grow. *Be careful*, I think at her. *Guard your heart.*

The door doesn't lead to a back room like I expect, but to a landing atop a narrow, uneven set of stone stairs. A few steps down, Silas is lifting a lantern from a wall. "Lady Fairfax," he says with a faint smile, looking up at me as yellow light washes over his face. "I didn't think you'd come."

"Well, here I am." With those strange pale eyes boring into me, the distrust surges back to the surface. I take a deep breath in through my nose, out through my mouth. I feel sick, but I have to stay calm. Calm is the only thing that will keep the scales and claws at bay.

"What does your sister know?" he asks, tilting his head in Lydia's direction. Then the door to the tavern falls shut, leaving me in the dark with only Silas, his lantern, and my own quickening heart. He doesn't offer an explanation, just starts climbing down, and I have to stay close on his heels to remain in the sphere of the lamplight.

"She knows about my heartbreak." I keep one hand on the wall for balance, and the stone is rough and damp through my glove. "She knows you're proffering a cure. Not about August and . . . the shell." I glare at the back of Silas's head. "And she can't find out."

"That should be easy enough, since you don't believe it anyway." His voice is laced with scorn, inviting me to denounce August, but I won't.

I feel certain that Silas is braiding lies and truth together, hoping I'll buy it all. I'll hear him out—maybe that will help me untangle what's real. But I won't—I can't—believe that August wants to hurt me.

Cold air seeps up from below, and the lantern light extends only a few feet ahead, and I can see nothing but darkness beyond, but Silas's tread is sure and steady as he goes down. Whatever this place is, he has come here many times before.

"You told me you want to end whaling—why?" Even to ask the question feels blasphemous. "You're a whaler. This is your livelihood."

"Have you ever actually seen a whale hunt, Lady Fairfax?" Silas asks. His voice sounds distant somehow, swallowed up by the dark. I grit my teeth. He must know full well that I haven't, at least up close. On the *Volyar*, Papa made me stay behind during hunts while the crew rowed after the whales, and everyone knows I haven't been on a voyage since.

"It's a bloody business," Silas continues into the silence. "Stick a Livyatan with harpoons until he rolls over and spouts blood. Tow him back to the ship and cut off his head and hack off the blubber with spades and strip his bones of flesh. By the end of it, the sea's more sharks than water. The smell of blood never leaves your clothes."

"I know how the hunt works," I retort. Maybe I've never seen it close-up, but I've spent years studying the equipment, technique, weapons, every aspect of the hunt. "You don't strike me as the squeamish type. Where are we going?"

"Have you ever visited the tunnels beneath the city?"

"I haven't had the pleasure." I've heard of the tunnels, but always thought them just a schoolyard story, or something out of Mama's fae tales. The legends say that the landmass of the north coast, or sometimes all of Abbonheim, is made up of the corpses of giant beasts. Beasts as big as continents crawled out of the primordial sea and then died, and their eye sockets became lakes, and their vertebrae became mountains, and their calcified veins still make branching paths deep in the earth: underground passages where seawater flows far inland.

My thoughts are getting away from me. Just because one tale—of Drekja, of healed curses—might be true—*might*—doesn't mean they all are. Maybe there are tunnels, but if so, they were dug by human hands, for human ends. Smuggling, maybe, or thievery.

"Some of us care for things beyond our own skins," Silas says, picking up the conversation I tried to derail. A ripple of anger runs beneath the placid surface of his voice. The lantern bobs in his hand, casting strange shadows on the rough-hewn wall. "You said it yourself last night. Livyati are disappearing. Your father knew that, you know that. But instead of doing anything to change it, you just send our crews farther and farther afield, push us harder to kill more and more."

"People need whale magic," I say. Silas Price knows this; everyone knows this.

"It doesn't matter," he says, implacable. "Like you said. Everything has a cost. We have to stop whaling, or the cost will be unimaginable."

These last words have the feel of recitation, of words he heard long ago that have hung around his heart ever since. Memories of the night the *Volyar* sank intrude—teeth chattering, icy water lapping at my ankles, heart tearing in two—and I will them away with a shudder.

"So you're just doing the finfolk's bidding," I hiss. "Were you doing the same on the *Volyar*? Are you on their side?"

He stiffens, almost stumbling in his climb down, my words landing. I don't doubt Silas remembers just as well as I do what I said to him after the funeral, what I'm still ashamed of sometimes, in my nobler moments. *You should have died with the rest of them.*

"I'm not on anyone's side," he says coldly. "But I'm a sailor, Lady Fairfax; it's not in my nature to ignore how the wind is blowing. You can try to sail through a storm or you can turn and run from it. But pretending you don't see it, that's a sure way to find yourself on the sea bottom."

He stops walking. The staircase stretches away beneath him who knows how far, but the light from his lantern illuminates a small doorway set into the wall. It's unremarkable, damp, questionable-looking wood, except for its placement.

And except for what I see when Silas opens it. The door is blocked by what I first think is a wall of dirty glass. But then I step closer to look, and I see the moisture beading on its surface, and feel the chill emanating from it.

It's ice.

A shiver—not from the cold—runs over my skin. It's cold down here, but not cold enough to allow for a wall of ice. Something is at work here, something unnatural.

Silas, a few steps below me on the stairs, has turned around and is watching me carefully. The lantern washes the color from him, painting him in black and white and silver, his eyes bright as coins. "Take off your gloves."

I don't know why, but I do as he asks, tucking the gloves into my pockets. It's strange to feel the air on my bare skin. The oily light of the lantern catches on the scales, and I look away, hoping Silas didn't notice.

"Do you want to be healed?" he asks, face unreadable in the dark.

I take care to keep my voice level and my posture casual, not to show any signs of the terrible fear suddenly pooling in me. "What kind of a question is that?"

"A genuine one."

"Yes, of course I want to be healed." My wrists and fingertips itch, a constant reminder of the ugliness there, of the curse infecting my blood, even if I don't look. "But the only good and true magic is the kind we get from the whales." It's a childish maxim, and my voice sounds childish to my own ears, high and uncertain. "Other kinds might be real, but they lead into darkness . . ."

Silas waits for my words to trail off, then says, "And here I thought you were already in darkness."

He reaches out with one hand and touches the ice wall. A faint hissing noise starts up around us; there's the strange note of petrichor in the air again. And the ice—the ice is melting rapidly beneath his hand, his fingers sinking deeper, water trickling down his wrist. A concavity appears around his outstretched fingers, growing wider and wider. Like his hand is radiating heat, or like he's commanding the ice itself.

He drops his hand and it continues to spread, continues to melt, until a stream of water is running down the stairs around his feet and there's a hole in the ice to the darkness beyond.

"You don't have to believe me." His voice is inflectionless, his gaze and his hand steady. It feels as though we've stepped out of time, like the rest of the world has faded away and this is all there is, the staircase and the lantern and Silas. "Not yet. But when August tells you he loves you, do you believe it? Put aside whether you want to believe it. Does it feel true?"

I swallow, a memory-ghost of August's fingers brushing down the side of my neck, his intention clear—*You're mine.*

Silas doesn't wait for me to answer. He ducks inside, and even though every cell in my body is sounding the alarm—that I have gotten mixed up in something beyond my understanding, that I should run and not look back—I follow him, stepping over the dripping remnants of the ice wall. Silas reaches back behind me and closes the wooden door, the one that was only concealing the ice, and turns a rusted latch.

We're in a small oval room, maybe ten paces long and half as wide at its center. Strangely, the air inside is warm. The walls and ceiling are the same rough stone as the staircase, though less grimy and soot-stained. But the floor is flat and smooth, and something glitters in between the flagstones. Silver etchings, symbols I don't recognize as part of any human language. And at the opposite end, something shines.

A pool is set into the floor, its edge perfectly straight, the water in it black and mirror-smooth, its surface slightly below the level of the stone. It takes up half the room, going right up to the walls. As Silas hangs the lamp on a hook on the wall, our eerie reflections mirror us below.

"What is this place?" I ask.

"Somewhere magic is close to the surface." He leaves the lamp hanging and walks to the pool's edge, kneels down. "This water is from the ocean. It comes in through a tunnel below us."

Silas looks at me and then at the lantern—and it goes out. Darkness falls, so heavy and thick it almost feels material. My voice comes out choked, every sense instantly on high alert. "What—"

I sense Silas move in the small space and press myself back against the wall. But there's just the sound of disturbed water, and then an eerie green light illuminates him. He's on his knees by the pool, reaching in; the water glows where he's touched it. There's the smell of petrichor again, and as I watch, fog begins to rise from the water's surface and curl away from the damp walls.

It climbs the slope of the floor, flowing around Silas where he kneels, creeping around my own feet. The air takes on a charged feel. Mist kisses my face and wets my clothes, too heavy and cold and sudden to be natural, and electricity lifts the ends of my hair. Silas stands up, glowing water dripping from his fingertips.

He's just a tangle-haired boy with chapped, bitten lips and wide earnest eyes. Yet as I stare at him in the unnatural green light of the pool, it sinks in like it never quite has before that he is *not human*. Not fully. The fog swirling around my knees whispers his true nature; the wind tugs at my clothes even though we're deep underground. Even the ice wall is rebuilding itself of its own accord, strands of water climbing over one another toward the top of the door frame and then freezing, branching over with frost.

The sight of the ice blocking my way out fills me with a sudden, wild panic. It's like falling into freezing water, the realization that I'm down here alone with someone who has his own agenda and magic I can't begin to understand.

"Stop this," I command, cold and authoritative as I can, aware that the gap of the doorway is shrinking. I unclench my fists and start a silent countdown. *Three*. "Stop it now."

"Please, Annie." His voice comes out low, almost desperate, like he needs me and not the other way around.

Two. I tense my muscles.

"There's a way out," he goes on, words coming faster. *One*. "Let me show you."

I raise my hands and launch myself at him.

I have never attacked anyone in my life—even when I bickered with Lydia as a child, we traded insults, not blows. So I wonder if it's the curse in my blood steering me, sending me surging forward. That's the last lucid thought in my head before something else takes over. The something I saw in Cousin Mary's eyes through the bars all those years ago. A red haze, a hunger for screams and the smell of iron and flesh parting beneath my nails.

It's so loud in my head, so all-encompassing, but the other voice—soft but strong, it sounds like my sister—still cuts through.

No.

This isn't you. Not yet.

I gasp, awareness flooding back into me slowly. First my hearing—I can hear my own ragged breathing, but someone else's too, harsh and fast and scared. Then sight. Wide gray eyes, a halo of iridescent green. Then touch. A body trembling under mine. His chest under my knee. His throat under my fingers, his hands wrapped loosely around my wrists.

I've pinned Silas down by the edge of the pool, his head hanging over the ledge. The ends of his hair trail in the water, sparking enough green glow to illuminate my right hand wrapped around his neck, nails digging into the sides, my left hand holding my knife to his throat. Both the nails and the blade draw trickles of blood that look black in the strange light, and dark veins creep out from the place where the blade nicks his skin.

His pulse hammers beneath my fingers, throat bobbing as he swallows, and his breath is rapid as he stares up at me, shivering. He's afraid, and the monster under my skin revels in that. It fills my head with images of pushing his head underwater or dragging my nails across his throat.

It's not me, I think desperately. The monster might be lurking inside me, the curse growing stronger in my blood, but it is not me, not yet. I don't want to revel in his pain and fear, even if he's finfolk. I don't want his death on my hands.

His throat moves under my hands. I blink and realize that he's smiling. Faintly, and clearly still afraid, but smiling. "So much for not dangerous."

I'd been considering letting him go, but his mockery makes me want to tighten my grip. "Only to liars and devils."

"Strong words for someone who needs my help."

Blood streaks down my fingers, drips into the pool, each drop sparking a flare of green, and the monster wants more. "I don't need anything from you," I growl.

"Go back to your manor then, and let heartbreak take you." Pain roughens his words, but they're still clear, each syllable distinct. "Or give in to it now and tear me open. As you like." A ragged breath. "But I'm your best chance to lift the curse, Lady Fairfax, and you know it."

A wave of disgust both for him and for myself breaks over me. I let go and roll off him, sheathing my knife and scuttling backward as he sits up slowly, wiping the blood from himself with a sleeve pulled over his hand. "Touch the water," he says.

"What?"

"Look—" Before I can draw back, he catches my wrist—fingers closing warm over the scales—and tugs our hands down toward the surface of the water.

The vision comes suddenly, in the way lightning in the sky at night for an instant paints the world silver, brighter and stranger than day. Leaning over the side of a boat, gray water beneath me. A massive shape in the water, rumbling as it rolls, a giant eye blinking at me out of the dim.

A small, dark space with walls of weathered wood. A kneeling figure with eyes that are jade green from corner to corner, no iris, no pupil. If I had form, I'd scream, but I'm nothing but fog, nothing but smoke, swept on a fierce wind to somewhere else. I see a body in whaler's clothes sprawled on a ship deck at night, face down, body contorted. I see a spiral seashell, its spines stained red with still-wet blood.

Other images flash by, there and gone as quick as a blink. An upside-down map of the world. The whale skull in Papa's library, smashing against his desk. A cave big enough to fit a castle. The wharf at Kirkrell burning. A room with ceiling, walls, floor all carved of glittering crystal. An undulating shape moving just below the sea's surface.

Then everything goes dark again, but for the green light leaking in around the edges of my eyelids. I come back to my body slowly, awareness returning of my breath; the fog; Silas, sitting a yard away, watching me intently. The images stay sharp in my mind, like they've been burned into me.

"What do they mean?" I ask Silas quietly, frightened enough by the visions that I momentarily forget to hate him. "Is that—was that the future?"

"More like possibilities," he says cryptically. "Things that could be. Not necessarily what will be. They don't have to mean anything." He reaches down and plucks something floating on the surface of the water. A flat whitish oval about as long as my pinky finger. He holds it out toward me, luminescent water dripping as he places it on my palm, the tips of his fingers just brushing my skin.

My breath catches as I hold my flattened hand up to look closer, realizing it's a stone—or bone?—like the ones the Cursed Crew wear upstairs. It's smooth, heavy, the yellow-white of what looks like whalebone, with holes worn through at the edges. Not something that by rights should float. But I can feel the magic in it, seeping down through my fingers. Sparkling pinpricks of static that make me think of fog and dark waves.

"Put this on a chain and carry this with you," he says as I close my hand around it. "Whenever you have an opportunity to do a favor for the finfolk—anything you think they'd appreciate—put a drop of blood on its surface. That will earn you their blessing."

"Blood?" I echo. "What kind of blood?"

"Cuttlefish blood," he snaps. "What do you think? Your blood."

I suppose I can't begrudge him being surly after nearly dying at my hands. I slip the stone into my breast pocket and it sits warm over my heart. "How will I know when I've done enough favors to be healed?"

"You don't; that's the beauty of it." Silas gets up gingerly and brushes himself off, but there'll be no saving his shirt; a fresh red stain seeps down the collar. "From what I can tell from the stories, you just have to approach the queen with the pendant when you feel you've done enough, when you feel worthy. And hope for the best."

He holds his hand out in what feels like a peace offering, or at least a truce. I wait for my anger to surface, but it doesn't appear. My mind and heart feel crowded and heavy with everything I've learned, everything I've seen here. Maybe there's no room for anger right now. I put my gloves back on before taking his hand and letting him help me to my feet.

There's a beat of strained silence that I try to break by fishing in my coat pocket for a vial of whaleblood—I carry one everywhere I go. I hold it out to Silas. "For your neck?" Truce or no truce, that's the closest thing I'll give him to an apology.

He grimaces, seems to waver, but in the end accepts the vial. "Trying to get an early start on the favors?"

I try not to stare at his throat bobbing as he drinks the whaleblood, at the small gouges my claws left closing up, the blood flaking away. His words dislodge my thoughts and I try it, pricking my thumb with my knife and letting the bead of blood fall on the pendant's surface. It rolls off and *plinks* to the ground.

I blink. "What's meant to happen?"

"Not that." Silas shrugs. "Sorry."

I try not to feel disappointed. Probably it doesn't count as a favor to heal a wound I inflicted. "Maybe if I bring you a cup of coffee every so often on the voyage?"

His lips—traces of red whaleblood clinging to them—twitch upward as he caps the now-empty vial and hands it back to me. "Could be worth a try. But that won't be enough to win the queen's favor."

Climbing the stairs back up to the tavern, I ask: "What makes you think I can even end whaling?" Bitterness tinges my voice. "The shareholders don't respect me."

"Maybe not, but you don't have to convince them," he replies without turning around. "You are your father's daughter. The company is yours. Give an order and they'll be honor bound to obey. Will you try?"

Just like Lydia, he sees things as more simple than they truly are. Silas may think the company belongs to me, but it's the other way around. I belong to the company. I belong to the legacy built by my father and grandfather and all the Fairfaxes before them, stretching past memory into myth. I will not be the one to let it crumble. I cannot.

But I can't protect the company—or, more important, my brother and sister—if I'm heartbroken. I almost killed Silas tonight with my bare hands. I can no longer convince myself that I'll somehow manage to escape the curse when no one else ever has. Sooner or later I'll die, or turn into something unrecognizable.

Yet if it's true that I can be healed, if the visions from the water mean something, I can have my life back. All Silas needs is my word. And once I'm healed, he will have no power over me. All I have to do is say:

"Yes."

Chapter 7

On Seventh Day morning, the cursed always start gathering at the church before sunrise. By the time I get there at eight bells, an hour before services, the sky is pearly gray and a dozen people huddle around the edges of the square of green grass that the Sailor's Bethel presides over. The entrance to the churchyard is fashioned from a Livyatan jawbone, twelve feet tall, stripped of its teeth and polished smooth and inscribed with scripture verses. It stands against the gray morning like a sentry, casting a long shadow over the cursed.

Kit and Lydia will come later, in time for the nine-bells service, but I like arriving early, helping in this small way, how quiet and peaceful it feels without the town's eyes on me. And though I feel guilty being away from Kit with so little time left until the *Heralder* sets sail, it's nice to get a break from Lydia's questions too. Since I told her about the heartbreak and going to Drekja for a possible cure, they've been nonstop, the partial truths I've been giving not satisfying her.

Now that she's apparently going on the voyage as well, she's already started making arrangements, ordering new sailors' clothes and a crate of her favorite coffee to be packed in the hold. She knows Silas has promised to help me, but I don't want her to know about the promise he extracted in return, or the fact that I don't intend to keep that promise. We'll both be living in close quarters with Silas for months—and August, and Mance, and so many others—and I don't want to burden her with my secrets, nor worry about her accidentally spilling them.

The eyes of the cursed follow me as I stride toward the church entrance. Hiding my affliction under neatly pressed clothes and an erect bearing, I walk toward the archway with my back straight and head held high, greeting the others as I pass. There's nothing in our scriptures about finfolk curses, nothing to say that their victims can't tread on holy ground. But sometime in the centuries since whalers came to Kirkrell, it seems to have been established as a rule. None of the cursed set so much as a toe onto the church grass.

None but me.

Some of the faces are familiar: the old man who can only speak in a series of clicks that no one has ever been able to decipher; a woman whose eyes are red and swollen always because, she says, her tears are seawater. Today there's a man I haven't seen before, huddled a few yards off from the entrance, staring fiercely up at the steeple. He's middle-aged, with a craggy face but no visible ailments, and I wonder what his curse might be. I know all too well not all the finfolk's vengeful punishments are visible to the outside world.

The clicking man returns my greeting with a nod, but the others don't acknowledge me, their gazes fixed instead on the church, lips moving in silent prayers and pleas. I suppress a shudder as I pass through the archway, walk up the path, slip through the wooden doors. It's not lost on me that however the people outside got their curses, whatever they did to incur the wrath of the finfolk, they likely did it in service to the Fairfax Whaling Company.

Papa said it was good for the people of Kirkrell to see us at church, handing out battered leather hymnals or brewing coffee or lighting candles. But I think he wanted me to see them too, and remember that our business is not without cost.

He always said we were here to serve the people of Abbonheim, not the other way around. Heal them, protect them, make them strong. And I've kept up the tradition since my parents died, even as I suspect it's a kind of blasphemy for me to set foot inside.

In the vestibule off to the side of the sanctuary, the scent of strong brewed coffee enriches the cool, dusty air. Harriet Prescott, a round middle-aged woman with a brisk manner, bustles about, stacking hymnals and donation baskets along a side table for the service. "Lady Fairfax! How long now until your journey?" She smiles warmly at me.

I force a smile as I hang my jacket on a hook on the wall. "Three days." The voyage to Kielstraat has been the talk of the town this past week, everyone buzzing with excitement over the prosperity the expedition will surely bring. All of it has an undercurrent of desperation. With the declining whale numbers, people are looking to August's plan for the arctic port as a last hope.

Once, that would have made me glow with pride, that my beloved was going to save the company and the city. But now my heart is heavy with doubt, suspicion, resentment. If he truly means to kill me and take over the company, what better time to do it than now? The people of Kirkrell don't love me as they loved my father. If August ushers in a new era of prosperity and I disappear somewhere along the way, I can't imagine anyone will look too closely at the *how*.

"I'll surely miss having your help here when you're on your grand adventure," Harriet is saying. "But don't stray from the right path when you're at sea." She pulls a face. "Drinking, carousing. I'm not sure a whaling ship is any place for a young lady."

If only she knew how very far I plan to stray. I suspect that consorting with finfolk, making bargains with them, and wearing their enchanted pendants are all far worse in the Maker's eyes than drinking and carousing. "I'll behave," I say anyway. "Say some extra prayers here for our smooth sailing."

A few minutes later, I let myself into the sanctuary, holding a lit candle to light the others that line the aisle. Dim and empty, the sanctuary is as spare as the church's outside. Papa used to show me drawings from his travel sketchbook of ornate temples and towering cathedrals he'd seen. Not for whaling people, these. The Sailor's Bethel is a stark, simple building, whitewashed wood walls broken up by stripes of dark stained glass, a stone floor worn smooth by age, pews unadorned with cushions. The most striking feature are the grave plates—plaques of iron and copper and silver of all different sizes nailed to the walls beneath the stained glass, engraved with hundreds of names and messages.

In memory of Hugh Tilley. He loved the sea and will now rest in its arms for ever.

In memory of Koto, lost to a Livyatan's wrath on 21 VIII 1796, along with the rest of his crew on the good ship the Commerce.

In memory of our beloved Philip Clement. The finfolk have taken you from us but we know you live in glory above.

They stretch across the whole walls of the church on both sides. More than a hundred years they encompass, and the letters on some of the oldest ones in the front have worn smooth from decades and decades of existence. Familiar as an old song, they glitter in the light of the new flames as I move up the aisle, carefully tipping my candle against each unlit wick. Harriet's words echo in my head. *Don't stray from the right path when you're at sea.*

I left the straight and narrow path a long time ago, I know that, when I felt my heart break and hid the curse rather than turn myself in. Farther and farther I've wandered into lies and secrecy and rot, and now it feels like Silas Price of all people is offering a lifeline, a chance to get back to the light. But to take the chance, I have to lie to my family and everyone around me and make bargains with finfolk, do them favors even. Can I be forgiven if I sin in order to hold on to my life?

Then a sound from up ahead makes me realize I'm not alone in the sanctuary. A whisper of ragged breath. I freeze in the act of lighting a candle, scanning the pews I had thought empty.

Strange how heightened awareness can make the world more frightening. Sometimes in quiet moments I can almost forget that I'm cursed, as doomed as the unfortunates clustered around the churchyard perimeter outside. Then a pulse, the sound of someone else's blood, catches my attention before I remember that's wrong, unnatural, reminding me of all the threats both in the world and inside me.

It takes me a long moment to find him, kneeling in a pew a few rows up, head bowed low so that only his shoulders and a glimpse of wild dark curls rise over the top of the benches. My heart picks up and I take a few silent steps forward to see better.

Silas must be praying, but his posture isn't prayerful; rather it's as if some great weight is heaped upon him, his head hanging down and sweat dampening his shirt between his shoulder blades. His hands aren't clasped together, but grip the back of the bench in front of him, knuckles white.

Inside me something shifts, sensing vulnerability and becoming suddenly attentive, interested. Like a wolf in the woods coming across the blood-spotted trail of a wounded deer. I swallow and try to push the monster down, but I can't stop the sound of his ragged breath in my ears or the flow of saliva across my tongue.

He realizes my presence and turns, springing to his feet. His face is pale and sweat-slicked and something is wrong with his eyes: white sclera and gray iris and black pupil all veiled in a shimmering rainbow sheen like a mirage, or an oil spill. The kind that happens on the floor of the whale processing warehouse and must be mopped up quickly lest a stray spark from someone's pipe send the whole enterprise up in flames.

Then he blinks and it's gone, leaving his eyes gray and clear and watchful. "Lady Fairfax," he says, voice hoarse.

I blink too, wondering if something has gone wrong with my vision. Did I imagine the sheen over his eyes? An image hangs momentarily in my mind. Silas as a child in the lifeboat, his eyes blotted out white then too. But when I try to focus, to recall the memory, it swims away, and I can't decide if it's real or not.

For a stretching moment we regard each other across the pews. Two creatures not quite human. His face is still pale, and seeing his weakness makes me feel cold and vengeful.

But—Lydia's voice in my head. *This isn't who you are.*

I swallow against a dry throat. Push the monster down as best I can and find my voice. "Are you all right?" My voice seems overloud in the silence all around us.

Silas wipes his brow with his sleeve and runs a hand through his hair, self-consciousness in his movements. "Fine," he says in a clipped tone. "A migraine. I get them sometimes."

That doesn't explain the sheen over his eyes, if it was ever there, but I decide not to care. Whatever ails him, it doesn't affect me; it's not my business. "I thought finfolk can't tread on holy ground," I say instead.

I've seen Silas in church before—at my parents' funeral, here and there at services—and always wondered about that, but I never asked since we weren't acknowledging our secrets out loud until now. The stories say finfolk despise all things holy. Iron and crosses, prayers and church bells.

"Holy is what people say is holy," Silas says, shortly. He walks to join me in the aisle. "A church is just a building; a cross is just a shape. The finfolk existed before any of this was built. Why would it hurt them?"

What to make of the fact that when he speaks of the finfolk, he says *them*, not *us*? "But you were praying, weren't you? Why, if you think holiness is just a construction?"

His gaze slides from mine; he glances over his shoulder, up at the stained glass windows casting us in jeweled light. "I always pray before a voyage. To the Maker. To Thala and Haelgrim and the Sollish god-lights. To anyone else I can think of."

"That seems sacrilegious," I say, though Maker knows I've blasphemed too much in the privacy of my own head to judge anyone else for it. "Which ones do you believe in?"

"I believe in what I can see. In storms and shipwrecks. I believe that my crew is relying on me and now you are too."

As he speaks, his eyes dip down my throat and catch on something, and I realize the bone pendant I received in the chamber beneath the Spout—I put it on a chain like he said, like the Cursed

Crew do—has slipped from my dress's high collar. Heat washes up my neck as I hastily tuck it back beneath the cloth. I must be more careful.

Silas doesn't miss any of this. His eyes glitter with an expression I can't read. "We've a lot of sea ahead of us," he says. "If there are blessings to be had, whatever the source, I would be a fool and a poor sailor to disdain them."

Hot wax trickles over my fingers, making me flinch even though the fabric of my gloves keeps it from burning my skin. I half turn from him to finish lighting the candles, but the unpleasant reminder of our imminent voyage has ignited worry in my chest.

"On the *Heralder* we'll be taking a straight shot northeast," I say, affecting casualness as I raise the candle to light another. "Aside from maybe a resupply or two. What if we don't cross paths with any finfolk? What are the odds that I'll just happen upon the chance to do them favors?"

"You're thinking about this like a human, Lady Fairfax, mathematically. But that's not how it works. It's not about odds." Silas walks to a candle across the aisle, raising a hand to cup the wick. "The finfolk are writing a story with us. The story requires favors, so the chances will come."

"Writing a story with us?" I look sharply toward him. "We're not—"

Then my words die in my throat as I realize two things: firstly that Silas has no candle of his own, and secondly that the air has taken on a strange, charged feeling like sometimes happens before a thunderstorm. There's a minute *snap*, a spark flickering between his fingers like bottled lightning.

When he moves his hand away, the candle is lit and his gaze rises to mine, a challenge in it, daring me to say something.

My mouth dries up in the face of this finfolk magic. Three

times now I've seen him do something unnatural—the shell, the ice, and now the flame. It feels even more wrong under the eaves of the church. Strange that the truths about each other we always pretended not to know are out in the open.

I make my voice flat and unbothered as I finish my thought. "We're not tools for them."

"Believe that if you like," he says, moving to the next candle. "But why do you think they let us live?"

My answer comes readily without having to think about it. "Because you asked them to."

The memories crash in. Most of the crew of the *Volyar* had gone out after a whale when the storm came. The only ones still on the ship were me, my mother, and a handful of the crew, including the two other children on the ship—August Hargreave, Papa's bright-eyed apprentice, and the captain's son, Silas Price, strange and always alone.

Mama and I stood at the railing, passing a spyglass back and forth between us. The crew in their whaleboats had rowed so far after their quarry that they were as small as ants on the horizon. I wanted to see them kill the whale; Mama had little appetite for such things but hoped only to keep an eye on Papa, make sure he was being safe.

Mama saw them first. I still remember how her body went rigid and her face paled.

Don't move an inch, she'd said, then turned and ran flat out for the mainmast.

My mother never ran. Everything she did was graceful and dignified. But she ran now, seizing a rope off the mainmast in her delicate hands and pulling it with all her strength. The bell halfway up the mast began a frantic, rhythmic cry to call the boats back to the ship.

She'd dropped the spyglass; I picked it up and put it to my eye to search out what she had seen. Everything in me went cold. Past the rowboats and the whale, on the horizon all around us, dark figures crept up out of the gloom. Tall and thin, they stood in strange longboats, wrapped in shadows that could be cloaks or fins. They advanced on us without the benefit of sail or oar, faster than anything natural can move, and overhead, dense greenish clouds raced in even faster.

Lady Fairfax—

Unprotected by the ship and exhausted from the chase, the crew in the whaleboats didn't stand a chance. I watched through the spyglass as waves tall as houses formed behind them, formed out of nothing, rising from the sea like living things before converging on the whaleboats. Thin screams reached us over the water, drowned out by the alarm bell and the sudden boom of thunder. My mother had joined the skeleton crew as they scrambled to adjust the sails, desperate to reach the whaleboats before the waves did.

But then—lightning, forking down from the clear evening sky, igniting our mainmast in a plume of flame. The ship shuddered and lurched like a shot beast as the ensuing thunderclap drove me to my knees, spyglass rolling away.

Lady Fairfax—

With hands over my ears and eyes squeezed shut, I didn't realize I was directly in the path of the falling mainmast until it was too late. I felt the heat at the crown of my head, then hands on my chest, shoving me out of the way. I opened my eyes and saw Mama's face, full of love and grief, in the second before the flaming mast came down.

Sometimes in my darker moments I can still feel the scream climbing my throat, like I didn't get it all out that night. Like shreds of the scream still linger, rotting, in my lungs, and I'll never get them out.

"Annie!"

The voice jolts me back to the sanctuary, back to the skin on my arms crawling as scales threaten to burst through, back to aching fingertips and a chest that feels split open. Silas is right in front of me, hands gripping my upper arms, shaking me slightly.

"Not here," he hisses. His eyes are wide and fearful as they fly from my face to the door of the sanctuary. "Listen to me. *Not here.*"

But I can't hold on to the present, not with his storm-cloud eyes on me just like they were that night, the electric smell of finfolk magic in my nose. Distantly, I can feel him adjust his grip on my arms, bodily propelling me somewhere. But most of my mind is in a lifeboat as it lowered toward the water, the *Volyar* creaking ponderously over my head as bolt after bolt of unnatural lightning pummeled it. The smell of petrichor and burning flesh. Debris from shattered whaleboats spinning past us in the water. August locking his limbs around me, ignoring how I battered at him with my small fists, as we saw Papa's body float by, empty eyes turned to the clouds.

All at once the finfolk were there around us, ringing our lifeboat. So many of them. Motionless figures of shadow, steady even as the wind howled and their dark garments rippled around them, inhumanly tall and still. Only their eyes showed, pale and glistening in the sudden dark.

In the present, a door closes; darkness falls. In memory, the thunder and crackling flames and waves crashing and the alarm bell still clanging—it all faded like someone had dropped a great glass cloche over our boat. The torrent of heartbreak was momentarily quieted by some deep-seated prey instinct to be still and silent beneath the gaze of a predator. Even without seeing the finfolks' faces, I could tell their attention was trained on Silas. August and I watched as he stood up in the lifeboat prow, shaking all over.

In no language that I could understand, but unmistakably a language, they spoke to Silas.

And he spoke back.

And then the finfolk let us go.

"Stay with me," he says now, voice low and urgent. His fingers sink into my arms, dragging me back to the present.

We're in one of the vestibules off the sanctuary, a tiny room barely wider than the doorway we came through, and maybe six paces long. Dimly I realize it's the church's memorial to the lost of the *Volyar*. Panels of carved scrimshaw inscribed with scripture verses, depictions of ships and flowers and birds and beasts and the hawk from the Fairfax family crest; no candles are lit, but there's just enough light to outline the plaque set into the far wall, commemorating the lost captain and crew, so very many names and dates, and its passengers Lord Richard Fairfax and Lady Annabelle Fairfax.

Two small windows to either side overlook the churchyard. If I looked outside I would see my parents' tombstones marking the spot where two empty coffins lie beneath the grass. Papa's strong hands and Mama's kind eyes and all the rest of them rot somewhere at the bottom of the ocean. Because of the finfolk.

"You're all right," Silas says, eyes drilling into mine. "Pull it together. The churchgoers are arriving."

"You asked the finfolk to let us live," I say again, groggily, trying to stay in the moment. Why does his gaze threaten to pull me under? I yank back from Silas and retreat as far as the tiny room will allow, pressing my hands to the wall to ground myself. I squeeze my eyes shut, trying to reclaim my thoughts.

The bone pendant feels heavy around my neck. The favors—that's what Silas and I were speaking about. The favors I have to do for the finfolk in order to be healed. His conviction that my chances will come because fate dictates it. No, not fate—the finfolk.

"Yes." In the dim light of the vestibule—the only illumination the slanted, weak rays coming in through the small windows—Silas looks haunted, ghostly. "I asked them to let us live. But they wouldn't have agreed without a purpose. They gave me a message I was meant to carry back to shore."

"A message?" So many years of trying to block out the memories of the finfolk make it difficult to remember the particulars—a general sense of terror and grief swamps the details. The sounds they had made, surrounding us, were composed of echoing, rhythmic clicks rather than words. "What was the message?"

Silas is silent a long moment, regarding me as if evaluating whether I can be trusted. It makes my skin itch, because he shouldn't trust me. What just happened out in the sanctuary was too close a call. That makes three times in less than two weeks that the heartbreak has nearly gotten the better of me, that I've felt like I was losing my grip on myself.

"Why I asked you to end whaling," he says finally. "Because if whaling doesn't end, the finfolk will make war on us."

My nails scrape against the wall as my hands twitch, the claws threatening to push through the fabric of my gloves as my mind attempts to wrap itself around the words. I want to think it a joke, but Silas's face—pale, eyes burning with surely the same memories that haunt my mind—undercuts any possibility.

"Why haven't you said anything all this time?" I manage. My voice comes out hoarse, somewhere between a whisper and a wheeze. By contrast, his is barely audible.

"Would anyone have believed me? Do you believe me now?"

There's something pleading, almost childlike in the question, the way his shoulders hunch. Like he wants me to absolve him. But I won't. These past few days, it's been him pulling the strings. Showing up in my room, summoning me to the Spout, feeding out what he knows—the knowledge that could save my life—in small, controlled segments, like I'm a fish on a line he's reeling in. Time to take back control.

"We were all half dead," I hiss. "Whatever they said to you could have been a hallucination."

"That doesn't explain why they let us go." He slumps back against the door, looking like he regrets everything about this exchange.

"A lie, then. The finfolk manipulating you." I know the fury rising in me is only slightly less dangerous than the memories that gripped me a moment ago. That it can accelerate heartbreak too. But anger *feels* so much better than grief. "We're already at war with the finfolk. Every year they sink our ships—what is that if not an act of war?"

"Those are skirmishes." Now anger threads into Silas's voice too. "It could be so much worse. They could make the sea impassable and cut us off from the mainland. Or come ashore like in the old days."

"Why now, then?" I press. "If the finfolk wanted to attack us, they've had centuries to do it. Centuries when we were weaker and fewer than we are now. Why would they choose now, when we have gunpowder and iron bullets?"

Throughout all human history they have kept to the shadows. Picking us off in storms and sneaking into villages by the light of the moon. If the finfolk were capable of exacting a cost greater than they already did every year—wrecked ships, dead sailors, countless souls lost to the sea—why wouldn't they have done it already?

"Because the whales are disappearing," he says. "That's what's changed. The finfolk won't let the Livyati die out. They'll go to war to stop whaling, even if a war will be their own ruin."

The words—and the utter resigned conviction with which he says them—send a chill through me. "You should have said something sooner."

He looks sorry, but not sorry enough. "Nothing would have come of it. Except maybe I'd have been driven out of the city."

"But now you think it can be done because . . ." I wait for him to reply, but then realize the answer myself. "Because you have leverage over me. You can take me to Drekja, or so you say."

His answering shrug makes my rage flare hotter than ever. To my eyes he has all the freedom in the world to do as he wills. And yet he acts like the finfolk have bound him in chains. Like he has no other choice but to play foot soldier in their efforts to end whaling. "You might have accepted that you're a—a tool, or a messenger, or however it is you see yourself," I tell Silas, pitching my voice low. "But this isn't a fae tale for me. It's my life. I'm doing this for my family and the Fairfax Company. Don't forget that."

"I don't think you'd let me, even for a second, Lady Fairfax."

"Maybe a war would be justified," I add recklessly. "The finfolk killed my parents. They killed your father."

He stiffens. "I was there. I remember." His voice warns me that I'm nearing a threshold I oughtn't cross. "I don't expect you to trust me. You don't have to. But you do have to keep your promise. End whaling. Or the war will cost us dearly."

Chapter 8

I stay in the vestibule for as long as I can after Silas leaves, breathing deeply and trying to get myself under control. Sitting on the ground with my back against the door, so no one can walk in on me, I take out the vial of whaleblood and the nail file I always carry with me. Drink the whaleblood and file down the claws, biting my lip against the pain. The idea of sitting through a church service now sounds torturous. All I want to do is go home and lie down, but my siblings will miss me if I slip away. And something Silas said comes back to me. *If there are blessings to be had, I'd be a fool to disdain them.*

I can't bring myself to consider the rest of it, the message, the war with the finfolk. The implications are too huge, too overwhelming. But he might be right about blessings, at least. I get up, straighten my clothes, and double-check my gloves are in place, then take a deep breath before slipping out.

The sanctuary is mostly full, all the candles lit—did Harriet come in and finish the job, I wonder, or did Silas light the remainder with his magic? Well-dressed men and women, officers and merchants and their children, file into the front pews, while the sailors tend to sit in the back in battered oilcloth and faded linen, wearing iron knives and iron necklaces, their throats and wrists and waists ornamented by strings of yellow-white bone beads carved with tiny crosses.

Our people, Mama called them when she was here. She never wanted us to forget that our true allegiance wasn't to the shareholders but to the sailors on our ships and the lowly of Kirkrell. The men and women who toil on ships to bring in whales, and those back on land who rely on whale magic to stay alive. Seeing them, slumped and tired but still here, usually fires me up with determination to fix what's gone wrong. Cure my heartbreak not just for me and my siblings but so I can carry on the work of bringing whaleblood and oil and bone to everyone who needs them.

If what Silas says is true, I'm putting them all in danger by carrying on whaling. But to do otherwise would be to tear away their lifeblood.

I find Kit and Lydia in our usual pew and plop down next to them, pressing a kiss to Kit's combed hair, and smile hesitantly at Lydia. At least she can't ask me more questions about heartbreak and the voyage, not in church surrounded by strangers, not to mention Kit's sharp ears.

Kit fidgets. When he was younger, I would sometimes let him bring a book to church to keep him quiet, but recently I've forbidden it, conscious of avoiding any seeming impropriety with the eyes of the city on us. I know he's not happy about it, but he tries to be good, though he can't help but fiddle with the hem of his shirt. I put an arm around him, and he leans into me, making my heart twist.

"Will August be joining us?" Lydia asks, her tone neutral.

"Not today. He's down at the docks to oversee the preparations of the *Heralder.*" I glance over at her, trying to read her expression, but her eyes are slanted away from me, wandering over the stained glass windows like she hasn't seen them most every week of her entire life.

I've never been able to quite parse out whether Lydia approves of August. She tends to make herself scarce when he visits our house, but I never gave it much thought before. Now, though, knowing that she and he and I will all be living in close proximity on the *Heralder*, worry gnaws at me. I didn't tell her about the seashell, about the possibility that August may have designs on my life. I let her think that my heartbreak is merely over our parents. But has she guessed that something else is at play?

I send up a little prayer that she hasn't. If the unthinkable is true—if Silas is telling the truth and August means me harm—I want Lydia to know as little as possible, to protect her.

The service begins, its rhythms familiar, and for a while, I can get lost in the recitation asking the Maker to guide us through the rough waters of life. I let my attention wander to the windows, splashing panels of bright-colored light over the congregation.

The nearest window to me tells one of Mama's favorite stories. Ivar Kirkrell was half human, the son of a finfolk woman who tricked a human man into marriage. She agreed to join her husband onshore for seven years, on the condition that at the end of it he and the boy Ivar go with her to her home, which the husband didn't realize meant Drekja. Yet the man's mother, a wise old woman, saw the finwife for what she was. Tasked with watching her grandson one day, she secretly burned the shape of a cross onto Ivar's skin—a ward, so that when the bargain came due and his mother came to carry the babe into the sea, she couldn't touch him.

In the story of Ivar Kirkrell, the finwoman gnashed her teeth and wailed, but she couldn't touch Ivar, and he stayed with his grandmother on land. He was strong and brave, grew up to be a hero, founding the city that would come to be the whaling capital of the world. Which would imply that human blood is stronger. Is it so with Silas? Is he really on our side?

The time slips by, so I'm caught off guard when Lydia pokes at my arm. "It's time."

I blink, coming back to the moment.

"If any among you are planning to go to sea this week," the minister is calling from the pulpit, "please approach for a special blessing to protect you on your voyage."

Kit slumps in the pew, crossing his arms as I lean across to speak to Lydia. "You want to go up?"

"We're going to sea, aren't we?"

We stand and join the tide, heading for the front of the church to be blessed. I keep my eyes forward, but I can feel the gazes of others on me, on us, as we move to the front. Again Silas's claims echo at the edges of my mind. All these people rely on the Fairfax Whaling Company in direct and indirect ways. But if there really is to be a war . . .

The bottom of the bowl the minister holds is carved with a cross, the bowl itself is forged with iron, and the water has been prayed over before the service. Three layers of protection against the sea, its storms and sharks and finfolk.

The minister doesn't look surprised to see me and Lydia in front of him, just smiles kindly. Probably word of the Kielstraat expedition has already reached him. My heart beats faster as I reach the front, clasping my hands in front of me as I step up to the minister. I've no choice but to tilt my head up, baring my throat, but his eyes just skim benevolently over my face.

"Remember there are no waters in the world where the Maker does not reign," he says gravely. "May your voyage be blessed."

He thumbs briskly between my collarbones, two crossed lines, leaving my skin chill in his wake.

Chapter 9

The morning we're to depart, I find Kit in the kitchen, fully dressed in shirt, trousers, and boots. He's sitting at the table, bent over a handful of newspaper clippings—book advertisements he's cut out of the pages.

"Have you chosen what you're going to get?" I ask brightly. I told him that Ms. Nilsson would take him to the bookstore after the *Heralder* leaves and he could put in an order for three books. If he finishes those while Lydia and I are on the journey to Kielstraat, his governess will help him order more.

He looks up at me, frowning uncharacteristically. "I'd rather come with you."

It's too dangerous. Not in a thousand years. "You need to focus on your lessons."

"Ms. Nilsson can come too."

"Ms. Nilsson hates the ocean. She'd get seasick and then she wouldn't be a very good teacher, now would she?"

He pouts. "How long will you be gone?"

"It depends on the weather," I say, trying to sound casual. "Three months maybe."

If I return.

The thought sends faint pain rippling across my wrists and hands, a tiny surge of heartbreak. If I fail in this, if I die, will this curse afflict him and Lydia too? Will their hearts break?

Even if their hearts don't break, their problems will not vanish with me. The shareholders who view me with such skepticism, even though I was educated to take over—how will they view Lydia, who lacks even the bit of training Papa gave me when he was alive?

"I'll *definitely* finish three books in three months," Kit pronounces. He's crossed his arms, looking a little affronted that I've underestimated his reading prowess. "Can I get more?"

"Maybe if you ask nicely." To distract him and myself from thoughts of the voyage and the possibility of not returning, I sit down beside him and ask again, "What books have you chosen?"

This time the question works. He perks up, shuffling the newspaper clippings with careful consideration and pulling three from the pile. "*A Compendium of Enchanted Fauna* by Edmund Thornton," he reads. "He thinks that long ago, other animals besides whales had magic too. Second, *A Study of Cartilagyga, Marisquilae, and Other Denizens of the Deep* by Kohei Ito."

"What are Cartil-aj-yee-ga and Maris-kwee-lay?" I echo, stumbling over the unfamiliar words.

"Sharks and giant squid," he replies cheerfully. "Their scientific names."

I swallow a groan, the thought sending a surge of anxiety through me, making the scales hidden beneath my jacket sleeves prickle. "Great."

He pulls out the clipping from the bottom of his chosen three.

"And *The Romance of Thala and Haelgrim* by Sigrida Thorvalsdottir," he concludes, pronouncing the lengthy Hibernese name with confidence.

"Oh, a love story?" I tease, pushing away images of grasping tentacles and flat black eyes. "I'm not sure you're old enough for that, brother mine."

"It's not a love story!" he protests, tipping forward in his seat to pass the clipping over to me. "Thala and Haelgrim are the sea gods, remember? The ones who made the finfolk, who the finfolk worship. During the summer, Thala sends fair winds and keeps Haelgrim locked in a cage at the bottom of the sea. But every winter Haelgrim escapes and locks Thala in the cage, and sends snow and ice."

"Yes," I say slowly. His words, the names of the old gods, call to mind what it was like as a little girl tucked in my bed, feeling the mattress dip beside me and the warm flicker of candlelight wash over me as my mother sat down next to me. "Mama liked that story."

Kit tilts his head slightly, his brow furrowing, and I can tell from his expression that he doesn't remember. His knowledge of the fae tales comes from his own reading, not Mama's tellings. The realization brings a lump to my throat and I swallow it down.

"Just make sure to always remember the difference between what's true and what isn't," I remind him.

"We don't know they're not real," Kit says. "I wish I were coming to Kielstraat." He sighs and flops back in his seat. "I'd watch off the side of the ship at night and see the storms for myself."

I ruffle his hair with exasperated affection. "I'll be back before the storms." *Maker, I hope.* I'll have to tell him to tamp down his interest when he's older, or if I'm not around, hopefully Lydia will.

Because it's all right for a child to speak of sea gods and finfolk legends, but it won't be when he's older, with the scrutiny that comes from being a Fairfax. In the simultaneously hard-minded and superstitious culture of Kirkrell, it's viewed as unseemly, even ungodly, to take too great an interest in finfolk stories—at least in anything more than the bare facts: where they have been sighted, how to kill them. Like thinking too much about them might draw their attention.

A sniffle sounds from beside me, and I startle to register that Kit's eyes are red with tears. He leans in and wraps his thin arms around my waist, holding tight enough to knock the breath from me in a surprised huff. My arms come up automatically, and I carefully cup the back of his head with my gloved hands, swallowing back the tears that threaten to rise in my throat.

"We'll be back before you know it," I say softly. But I disbelieve the words even as I speak them, and Kit doesn't look up, so I can't tell if he buys them either. "Will you be good while we're away? You're the man of the house; you'll need to look after things. Make sure the doors are locked at night, and that the gardens stay watered." Of course Kit doesn't need to do any of these things, strictly speaking. Declan would die sooner than let the lawn go brown.

But I know from experience that it's a powerful anchor, knowing others are relying on you. A heavy weight, to be sure, but I'm fairly certain it's all that's kept me from drifting off entirely and being lost in the curse. Maybe a sense of responsibility will help Kit too.

I pull back a little, enough to see his face. I'm surprised by his expression—beneath the tear-swollen eyes he looks almost . . . guilty? Then he blinks and gives me a watery smile.

"I'll be good."

"I love you, Kit," I say around the lump in my throat. The words feel strange and awkward, insufficient. We're not, we've never been, the type of family to be constantly declaring our love for one another, instead showing our care in other ways. But it feels important to say now.

"I love you too," Kit whispers, but he won't quite meet my eyes.

What seems like half the city comes to the docks to see the *Heralder* off. August and I stand by the railing on the stern deck of the ship, hand in hand, smiling and waving as we look out at them.

The force of their hope sickens me—or maybe that's just being on the water. On a ship this large, and with only the harbor's placid waves beneath us, one can't really perceive the movement of the ship. But it's like my gut still knows I'm not on land. Holding the smile makes my cheeks ache and my hands itch in their cotton gloves.

The *Volyar* was a large ship too.

"The whole city is with us," August says, his eyes bright and his arm tight around my shoulders. "They believe in us."

I force a smile and a nod of assent, eyes skimming over the crowd. So many faces, pressed so close together, so many eyes on us, gazes sharp with need and excitement. I see children watching with awe-wide eyes, women wiping away happy tears, men baring their teeth in envious grins. August seems to feel their faith, their expectations, like a wind at his back, but for me it's a weight around my neck. How quickly will they turn on us—on me—if we fail to find more whales, if we don't fix things? Yet if what Silas says is true and we're heading toward war with the finfolk, will the city blame the Fairfaxes for that too?

"Cast off stern lines!" I hear Silas cry from the forecastle, and I have to stop myself from turning around to look as the dockhands move to obey, loosing the *Heralder* from land. He's been busy about the ship this morning, up in the rigging to check the sails, striding the deck directing the crew, his face turned to the horizon and the wind ruffling his hair. I haven't seen him like this before, in his element. He's always seemed faintly ill at ease on land, but he cuts, even I have to admit, a dashing figure at sea.

There are thirty-four souls on board this ship—Mance, August, Lydia, and myself; Silas and the four *Whistler* crew; and twenty-five of Mance's men. The two crews have been uneasily folded into one, with Mance as captain, August as first mate, and Silas as second, with Mance's associate Hammond next in line.

Mance's men seem resentful about answering to Silas—I've seen sidelong sneers, heard low-pitched comments about *the scavenger*—but they do as he bids them. The rest of the *Whistler* crew have proven more successful than their captain at fitting in. Glancing over my shoulder, I spot Josephine and Lydia coiling lines for the whaleboats; Teuila is up in the rigging, doing complicated-looking adjustments to the sails alongside a handful of *Heralder* men. The rest of the combined crew are belowdecks, organizing and tying down the supplies. I'm a little impressed to see my sister working—not that I thought she wouldn't be able to, but I envy how easily she seems to have settled in here.

Everything has been planned out, every day and every hungry mouth accounted for, the ship inspected for flaws, spare harpoons and fabric for sails stowed away. Yet the same must have been true for countless voyages over the centuries that ended at the seafloor. A heavy sense forms in my gut that all this carefully orchestrated activity is just a charade, a game of pretend that we are doing anything other than throwing ourselves on the mercy of the sea.

"I can hear your brain whirring," August says with a low chuckle. His arm moves to my waist, pulling me to him. "What are you thinking, my love?"

Mostly I'm just trying my best not to look at the water, which feels very far away and yet entirely too close. I return my gaze to the docks and the crowd, their cheers getting fainter as we move through the harbor. Beyond the crowd, the city rises; the buildings that feel so familiar when I'm among them are rendered strange and toylike by even this short stretch of water. The squat countinghouse where sailors charter to ships and collect their wages after returning home, the soot-stained masses of the factories and warehouses, the white spire of the Bethel, the tree-covered hills swelling beyond the city, a world of its own against the forested smudge of the mainland.

The island of Kirkrell is my life, my whole world, and suddenly it seems so very small.

"It's strange to think it will be months till we see the city again," I say. "We'll miss summer." This hasn't occurred to me until just now somehow, and my throat seizes with longing for my city in the summer: the hills and valleys all blanketed with wildflowers, the cool, damp mornings, the brilliant blue of the sea under the blinding sky.

"But think how glorious summer in Kielstraat will be," August says. He dips his head to speak into my ear and goose bumps spring up at his breath on my skin, the warm air sparking memories of tongue and teeth traveling those same paths last night.

"The sun never fully sets, even at midnight," he says. "The air is so clean you can see for miles and miles. I'm told that sometimes you can see the god-lights in the sky at night, hear them even. The Sollish say it's their gods singing in the heavens."

I let out a shaky breath. I know he doesn't believe in such things. Know that there are scientific explanations for the Sollish god-lights and the midnight sun. August is painting a picture for me with words, inviting me to be swept up in his vision. But much as I want to let myself get lost in it, my mind leaps ahead to the squat, smoke-belching factories we'll raise on the glorious arctic landscape, how we'll shear the trees from the mountainsides, smear the sky with oily smoke.

Nothing is without cost, I tell myself. Precious magic can't be bought with spun sugar and songs like in the fae tales. Humans have always had to strip the seas for our livelihood, paying for what we wrest from the water with sweat and smoke and blood.

"We'll be part of something bigger than ourselves," August says, and his voice chases the uneasy thoughts away. Right now, today, he is not the slick, ambitious leader he's become but the boy I met all those years ago, orphaned and alone but still with the stars in his eyes. "Something that outlasts us."

On impulse I turn my head to the side and press my lips to his. It's not proper out on the deck where anyone can see us, but August doesn't seem to care, pulling me into him, tilting my face up to his with a finger beneath my jaw. A wind kicks up then and I feel the ship respond to it like something alive, shifting subtly beneath my feet, and I don't know whether it's that or August's tongue dancing over my lips that makes a wild thrill shoot through me.

"Thank you for coming with me, Annie," he murmurs against my mouth.

"Not like you gave me much of a choice," I retort, half a jest and half not. But his hands trace up my throat, frame my cheeks, and I can't help letting my lips fall open beneath his. Can't help letting him breathe bravery into me, stoking the fire of hope slowly building in my chest.

One of the men catcalls, and it breaks the spell. August breaks off the kiss, pivoting to scan the crew, and it's eerie how quickly his face can go from flushed and happy to cold and murderous. Behind him, it's a shock to see that the distance between us and the shore has tripled, the small craft that always bustle around the waters of Abbonheim rocking softly in our wake. The crowd on the dock could be so many blades of grass swaying in the wind, their cheers a cicada buzz.

August takes a step from me, like he means to go find the sailor and reprimand them or worse. I tug him back; I don't want to be alone at the moment when we lose sight of the city. "It's fine. Leave it." Maybe I shouldn't have kissed him out here. I notice with a prickle of unease that several of Mance's men are watching us with expressions ranging from amusement to distaste.

August frees his arm from my grip. "I'll speak to Mance later, after we pick the whaleboat crews. Make sure his crew shows you the proper respect."

Whaleboat crews. I haven't given that a thought, but of course it needs to be sorted out. Each of the three boats—hanging now from davits over our heads, swaying slightly in the breeze—will hold six people when the time comes to strike out to hunt a whale. Each will be helmed by one of the officers—Mance, August, or Silas. "You'll have me as an oarswoman on your boat, of course?"

As soon as the words are out, I regret them a little, but not enough to take them back. They hang in the air as August stills and looks back at me.

"You want to crew a whaleboat?" he asks, sounding a little astonished.

I lift my chin. "What else am I meant to do here? Just drift around the deck and look pretty?"

A harsh laugh escapes August, and I hate that I can't tell if he's laughing with me or at me. "It's difficult, Annie." He comes back to my side, lowers his voice. "It's dangerous."

"I know that," I say, stung but trying not to show it. I know sailors treat their boat crews as a matter of life and death, because it *can* be in the chaos of the whale hunt. "But I can learn. I want to understand what it's like." What the Fairfax Whaling Company asks of everyone who sails under its flag, every day.

He stares at me, eyes unreadable, and a small voice inside me whispers that I've made a mistake. That if Silas is right that he means to kill me, I'm handing him the opportunity on a silver platter—a frantic chase, sharp lances, harpoons, taut ropes, and blood and water flying every which way.

But I can't think like that. Maybe that was why the request spilled out of me. A way to prove—to everyone, to Silas, to myself—that August can be trusted.

"During the chase, everyone's focus has to be on the kill," August says finally. "Not on keeping each other safe. It would compromise both of us."

"Don't you think I can do it?" My face feels hot.

"Annie, it's not that." He trails a hand over the small of my back, tries to pull me into him, but I don't let him. "It's not dignified. And it's dangerous. You'd be better off staying with the ship."

"I told you I want to be on a crew." Anger heats the inside of my chest like live coals. I am still the head of the company. Technically, I outrank everyone on this ship except Mance, since the captain is always the ultimate master when aboard a ship. But August cannot order me.

"We can talk about it later." August's eyes flit side to side. I can tell he doesn't want to argue with me out here where people are watching. He takes my hand over the gloves. "Let's take a stroll around the ship, shall we, get you acquainted with things?"

He's not wrong that we should present ourselves to the crew as a united front. I nod and push down my anger, shaping my face into a smile. "Fine." But I feel nothing but dread. As we turn from the railing, the cold wind rushes past my face, smelling like salt and brine and the unseen world.

Chapter 10

The next day, by the time the sun reaches its noon apex, not just Kirkrell but the entire north shore, the whole continent, is out of sight even with a spyglass—nothing but open ocean on all sides.

Twice over the course of the last day has another vessel passed us in the other direction—the first a merchant ship with Hibernic flags, the second a returning whaler whose crew lined up at the railing and cheered us as we passed by, their shouts tinny and faint over the some two hundred yards between us.

I wish I were with them, homebound instead of outbound. The roll of the ship beneath my feet has me queasy, and the expanse of the sea, the horizon unbroken by anything save for the dipping specks of seagulls, is unnerving. It's like we're alone in the world. It's been only a day since we left Kirkrell, but already the idea of home almost feels like a dream. Like if we turned around and sailed in the direction from which we came, we might find nothing at all, the city dissolving like a mirage.

When the galley bell rings for the midday meal, I make my way belowdecks to the galley kitchen with the rest of the crew, most of whom ignore me or acknowledge my presence with a bare nod, even as they chatter familiarly with one another. I look for my sister, but Lydia is nowhere to be seen as I get in a slow-moving line that threads half the length of the ship. Worry prickles the back of my neck and I try to push it down. Even Lydia can't have managed to fall over the railing two days into the voyage. But where in Maker's name has she gotten to on this ship that's the largest of our fleet yet somehow feels so small?

The creaky stairs from the upper deck let out into a narrow hallway, off which are the closed doors to the officers' cabins. Then there's the blubber room, a long, wide space that takes up most of the space of the mid-level; a few long tables without chairs stand throughout. If we catch a whale, this is where we'll set about the work of cutting it up and storing the oil, blood, meat, and bone. All of it is sparely lit with skylights of thick frosted glass, set into the deck above. Beyond that is the bunkroom, where the crew sleeps—dozens of too-small bunk beds crammed into every possible space. One corner is generously walled off for the women, with bunks for Lydia, Josephine, Teuila, and Willa, the *Heralder* cook.

With bunks set apart just for them, they're lucky. The men have to sleep in shifts or wrapped in blankets up on deck.

The galley kitchen sits in between the blubber room and the bunkroom. Willa, an older woman with a lined, long-suffering face, doles out tin plates with bowls of stew and a brown rye roll and a mug of ale each.

After I get my food, I search the blubber room, where everyone is settling in to eat. The *Heralder* men group up easily at the long tables, but there's not a familiar face among them, not my sister or the *Whistler* crew. It's an enormous relief when Lydia materializes at my elbow. "Where have you been all day?" I ask her.

She shrugs. "Helping out in the kitchen. I'm eating above deck with the *Whistler* crew," she says, offhanded. "Join us if you want."

Just like that, the worry is back. It doesn't seem like Silas's crew, the Cursed Crew, is particularly well-liked. The *Heralder* men tend to ignore them around the ship unless forced to work together on some chore. If Lydia and I are seen as befriending them, how will that reflect on us?

But I also don't want to eat with strangers or, Maker forbid, Mance. And I don't see August anywhere. So I sigh and follow my sister upstairs.

Above, a few of the *Heralder* men have the same idea, scattered around the deck in twos and threes, but it's much less claustrophobic than the press belowdecks, maybe because of the stiff evening breeze that has kicked up. Lydia leads me to a spot by the port railing where Josephine is sitting along with the gathered *Whistler* crew—Ezra, Teuila, and Zimri sit on the ground with plates in their laps. Silas isn't there.

My sister looks right at home among the others, catching my eye and grinning. Maybe her sailor clothes are a little more crisp, the whites brighter, but aside from that she could have been on the *Whistler* crew for years with how her hair is braided tightly back from her face, how she's adopted the slouching devil-may-care posture of a sailor, how she plops down and tucks in to her stew and stale roll with no indication that they're anything different from what she's used to.

"Why do sailors always call ships 'she'?" she asks the group, with an air of picking up a conversation recently left off, and I hope she hasn't been bothering the others with a flood of questions.

But the crew laughs heartily. "They're beautiful, for one thing," Josephine pipes up, swinging her legs.

"And complicated," Zimri adds. He has a patchy attempt at a beard and a warm Midlands accent. "They require a keen eye and a steady hand to navigate. Just like some ladies I know." This causes Teuila to playfully swat his arm before turning to Ezra, eyebrows raised.

Ezra swallows a mouthful of stew and shrugs. "No comment," he says, just as Josephine flashes a bright smile that seems especially for Lydia.

"We're being rude," Teuila says chidingly, and turns to me. "Lady Fairfax, welcome. How have you found your first day at sea?"

"Please, call me Annie." It feels strange to be Lady Fairfax here—yet another layer of separation between me and everyone else. "It's been fine. At least I haven't lost my breakfast over the railing yet." My words are coming out too fast. I don't know why I said that, when I should be projecting an image of competence and confidence. "Where's Silas?" I say to change the subject.

"In his cabin." Teuila frowns sympathetically. "Headache."

I feel a strange mix of relief and disappointment not to see him, but before I can think too much about it, Lydia is off again. "I think I saw a dolphin jumping earlier," she says. "Off to the south. Could that be?"

"Sure," Ezra says with the barest hint of a smile. "That's a sign of good luck, you know, especially at the start of a voyage."

"What about whales?" Lydia asks eagerly. "When will we start seeing them?"

"Maybe in a week or two," he says. "Maybe longer, maybe shorter, though that's less likely these days. It's hard to say for sure."

"When can I go in the crow's nest to look out?" Lydia asks.

I choke on a noodle, so I can't intervene right away when Teuila says, "Whenever you like. It's not a coveted shift; the other sailors'll be glad to be shot of it. As long as you have good eyes and a loud voice—"

"Not whenever you like," I cut in once I've managed to swallow. "Practice climbing the lower riggings first before you worry about the crow's nest." I see the corner of Josephine's lips quirk; she meets my eyes and shrugs slightly as if in apology.

"There are hoops attached to the mast," Lydia argues, like I wouldn't know, like we haven't spent years side by side studying the ship diagrams with our tutors. "You stand inside them so you *can't* fall."

"And you still have to climb up there," I say with finality. "Give it a few days."

Zimri puts in, "It's perfect if you want to freeze your ass off and get the worst sunburn of your life at the same time."

Soon a debate is raging about the pros and cons of a shift in the crow's nest. "That's why they invented sweaters and hats," Teuila retorts, while Ezra says, "It's the only way to get some peace and quiet."

"Enough, all of you!" Josephine's voice is sharp, but there's a laugh in it too. "I didn't corral you all here to bicker. I need your support with something." She checks over her shoulder like she's making sure no one's watching, then lifts something from around her neck and holds it in cupped palms. My heart jumps in recognition. It's a bone pendant, like the one I'm wearing now.

Around Josephine, Ezra, Teuila, and Zimri grow somber, looking on with understanding. Zimri touches his own shirt collar. They must all have the pendants. Silas is taking them to Drekja to hopefully have their curses lifted—if they do enough favors for the finfolk, and if these favors are deemed sufficient.

Josephine speaks in hushed tones. "Back in Kirkrell, I stole a pouch of finfolk silver from a sailor in the Spout. It never should have left the sea. I went out that night and dropped it into the harbor. But I wanted to wait for you all to be here before I did this."

She opens her hands and reveals the pendant. There are five or six small red spots scattered across its pale surface, whereas mine is pure ivory. She pulls a dress pin out of her pocket and uses it to carefully, delicately prick her finger.

Lydia tenses as a small drop of blood wells up, but Josephine is calm. "If the blood rolls off the bone, the favor wasn't good enough," she explains softly. "But if it sticks . . ."

Everyone looks on with an air of tense hope as Josephine holds her finger above the pendant, allowing one drop of blood to fall onto its polished surface.

When the droplet doesn't roll off but sinks into the bone and makes another perfect red dot, the four Cursed Crew let out a breath all at once.

Teuila swears appreciatively, Ezra leans over and gives Josephine a one-armed hug, and Zimri claps her back. As Josephine looks up at me, her face glowing, I realize with a jolt she is one step closer to being healed.

I realize, too, that this was likely for my benefit, her waiting until she was on the *Heralder* to test if the favor would be accepted. She's trying to show me how it's done.

"Do you really believe Silas about Drekja?" I ask, slightly choked up, to my chagrin. "Do you believe you can be healed?"

The implicit question, of course, being, *Do you think I can be healed?* Because no matter how I try to convince myself I have the heartbreak under control, a deep-down part of me knows there's no stopping it. Yet these four are the picture of vitality, happiness even. It makes treacherous hope spring in me.

"None of us believed him at first," Josephine says quietly. "And we might still be proven wrong. But I don't think we will be."

Lydia follows the back-and-forth with her eyes, looking quiet and thoughtful.

"And if that should happen," Zimri puts in, "I'm no worse off than I was before. Still penniless. Coin burns a hole in my pocket, literally."

He turns out one of his jacket pockets to show me that, indeed, the linen lining has a hole through its bottom, the cloth around it singed but the hole perfectly round and even. As if someone cut it out with scissors, held a match to the edge, and ironed the whole thing.

A startled laugh escapes me, heart beating fast. "How do you know what favors to do?"

Now Ezra picks up the conversation, all of them seeming to finish one another's thoughts so easily. "You think," Ezra says, "what would the finfolk want me to do? For instance, last month I was fishing in the bay and found a dolphin that had gotten fishing net tangled around it."

My stomach flips at the strangeness of it. Asked what the finfolk wanted, I would have said *To sink ships and end lives*, not *To save helpless sea creatures*. "Aren't you afraid of them?" I ask in a whisper.

Zimri shrugs. "For a while before this, I crewed a merchant ship. Transporting furs, sugar, and the like all around Hainei, Tarasca, Nulusk. In all that time, the finfolk never bothered our ship. Made me think maybe it's not them, it's us." His voice is gentle, but his eyes, steady on mine, hold a challenge. "It's the whaling."

A bell rings down the deck, three short peals, making Lydia and me jump, though not the others. They all start to get to their feet with resigned expressions as men emerge from belowdecks. "It means to gather at the forecastle," Ezra tells my sister and me, tilting his chin toward the raised deck at the front of the ship. "Some sort of announcement."

As I get up, my skirt catches on Lydia's satchel and it tips over, two bread rolls spilling out. Lightning fast, she grabs them and stuffs them back inside. "In case I get hungry later," she says, not meeting my eyes.

"You know you can just ask Willa in the galley if you get hungry." Zimri offers a hand to help me to my feet. I pretend not to see it and push myself up. I'm not sure if Silas has told them about my heartbreak, but I don't want him to feel the scales through the gloves.

"She was the cook on the ship I sailed with before the *Whistler*," he goes on. "Lovely woman—she'll give you leftovers if you make sure to ask nicely."

"Great," Lydia says brightly.

I'll need to talk to her later about being more judicious. It's not a good look for a Fairfax to be hoarding extra food or getting special treatment from the cook, not when the captain and crew are already skeptical of our presence. But there's no time to address it now as we move toward the forecastle, parting ways with the *Whistler* crew in the crowd.

Captain Mance stands six feet up on the upper deck, surveying his little kingdom as the crew gathers below. He gives Lydia and me a magnanimous smile as we take up spots side by side near the back of the group, and irritation curls in my stomach.

I was a small child, and Lydia only just born, when Papa ordered that women were to be allowed to crew whaleships. While I don't remember it, I've read through his correspondence from that time, and I know Obadiah Mance was one of the loudest voices opposing the edict. He claimed it would distract the crews, that women were meant to be sitting pretty in their houses in Kirkrell, not doing the ugly and dangerous work of killing whales. I make myself return his smile without baring my teeth, though I long to drop the Lady Fairfax facade, to show him that beneath my gloves I'm the ugliest and most dangerous thing on this ship.

I feel a warm presence to my right a moment before August's hand finds the back of my neck, fingertips idly toying with the soft short hairs coming loose beneath my braid. "Don't mind Mance," he whispers, warm in my ear. "He'll get used to you."

August. The mix of feelings that has recently become so familiar, relief and want and uncertainty all tangled together, flows through me like liquor. I nod and lean into him as the gathered crew quiets, waiting for something to happen.

For what seems like a long time, Mance just stands there and looks at us, cigarette smoke curling around his head, a dingy halo. Men exchange glances, shift on their feet, uncertain. Mance's eyes, watery blue beneath a tanned, leathery brow, travel from sailor to sailor seemingly at random, lingering on each person, taking their measure.

"A good crew, I think," he says finally. "A brave crew. But then again, Fairfax Company men always have been. And still we find ourselves here. Chasing the beasts farther and farther from our home harbor, spending months under the sun and in the ice, while our loved ones keep watch for our sails on the horizon."

Murmurs of assent throughout the crew, long-suffering sighs. I press my lips together and keep my head high. No one's looking at me—all eyes are fixed on Mance—so I try to push down the hot self-consciousness I feel. The harsh conditions of whaling aren't my fault. It's always been thus—even if the whales have gotten scarcer, the journeys harder, in my lifetime. I thread my hand through August's for support. He gives mine a reassuring squeeze.

"Most of your faces are known to me," Mance says, beginning to pace. "But this journey will be different from any you've undertaken before. The port in the arctic will allow us at last to gain the edge on the whales and their fae protectors."

I don't mean to do it, but my eyes flit to Silas, who has emerged from his room for Mance's speech. Nor are mine the only eyes—I see several faces turn subtly his way at the mention of the finfolk. If he notices, and I'm quite sure he does, he pretends not to, standing tall and straight with his eyes on Mance. There's just the slightest hint of defiance in the tilt of his jaw, the way his arms are crossed over his chest.

"You all know Livyati go north to mate and raise their calves," Mance goes on, "but how many of ye have seen it with your own eyes?" Back and forth across the forecastle he paces, slow and natural like he's an extension of the ship itself, powered by the wind just like the swelling sails over our heads or the Fairfax Company flag rippling in the breeze.

Silence among the crew. Most of the men seem riveted; they're utterly silent and still, giving the feeling of a collectively held breath. When I steal a glance at August, even his constant habitual smile has slipped away, as it sometimes does when he's lost in thought or listening intently. His face is open and serious as he listens.

"I won't promise smooth sailing, mind." Mance's tone is gentler than I'm used to hearing from him, almost fatherly. "None of ye are greenhands here. You know what waits in the north, the cold, the icebergs, the fae with their storms and curses." He lifts his face to the horizon, casting a long shadow out over the deck. "But anything tries to stop us, we'll break them with our iron hull and our iron will. And when we reach the north—it's something to behold, sailors. The sun never dips beneath the horizon. I tell you if you look over the prow, you'll see more whales than water. The spouts coming up like a field of flowers."

He laughs, loud and free and unexpected, a sound that fills the ship from prow to stern and rings out over the sea; and the crew joins in, low laughter and slow smiles, lips split to show teeth. It puts me in mind of a pack of wolves, the leader's howl taken up by all. But as goose bumps spring up the backs of my arms and August's low chuckle sounds beside me, I realize I don't want to run from it. I want to join the chorus.

"Gloriously easy pickings it will be, men," Mance goes on, dropping his voice almost to a whisper, and like puppets everyone falls silent to catch his words. "Like that same field of wildflowers if the blossoms were jewels and every blade of grass was gold. All you have to do is reach out and pluck them. All these years, we've done little more than hold the line against the whales and the waves. Now, here is where we gain ground. Here is where we turn the tide."

A small smile tugs at his weathered face as cheers rise up all around, and much as I dislike Mance, even though I can see how his words are calculated to appeal to our bravery and sense of duty, I can still feel the stirring of ambition in my chest, the feeling that triumph is within reach if I were but to stretch out my arm. I look up at August, wanting to share this moment with him, but his eyes are still pinned to Mance, bright in thought.

A beat, and he blinks, glances down at me and smiles as Mance says, "Now to choose the whaleboat crews."

Another ripple of excitement goes through the crowd, but my stomach drops as August gently detaches his hand from mine. I thought . . . I don't know why I thought the selection of the whaleboat crews would be a private affair, perhaps a list of names tacked up outside the captain's cabin door. Not like this, selected in front of everyone.

August moves away from me, through the crowd and up the stairs to the forecastle, and across the deck I see Silas is doing the same thing. They take up positions on either side of Mance. August's face is bold and confident, eyes roaming the crowd; Silas is very still, eyes fixed on the horizon.

Mance doesn't waste any time, barking out six men's names I don't recognize—but each name falls like a blessing in the crowd; I see the sailors he's chosen straighten their backs, chins lifting as the captain's esteem settles like a mantle on their shoulders. Then August steps up. His blue eyes roam the crowd, never quite landing. "Thomas Gardner," he calls out. "Abel Noham. Amos Tucker. Gideon Pierce."

My mouth is dry. We spoke about this earlier. How I wanted to be in his boat. He won't forget.

"Noa de Silva," he goes on, and maybe I imagine the infinitesimal pause, the way his eyes skate over me before he finishes, "And Caleb Brewster."

Numbness spreads through me as the men turn to congratulate one another again, puffed and beaming. And they are all men. I can feel my cheeks heat with anger and embarrassment, but I'm not worried about anyone seeing it, because no one's looking. The crew brushes past me to clap one another on the shoulder, *Good man, good luck*, and it's like I'm not here. I don't exist. I breathe deep, willing down the tears that threaten to prick at my eyes.

"Ezra McNaughton. Josephine Haskins." Silas's voice cuts through the crowd, clear and commanding even as the *Heralder* men don't hush for him. I scarcely hear him myself, my blood pounding in my ears as August descends the stairs to convene with his chosen crew. "Zimri Pires. Teuila Roha. And Annie Fairfax."

I almost don't register it at first—Silas's words float over my head. Then come the snorts of surprise, the scoffs hastily turned into feigned coughs, sailors' eyes landing on me before they're quickly averted again. Only then does it sink in. Silas picked me for his whaleboat crew. Not August, not my fiancé. Silas Price.

I can't process it. It's all I can do to stay calm, taking deep breaths to cut through the rising anger in me, my wrists and fingertips itching as scales and claws threaten to break through. As Mance calls out for the crew to get back to their duties, Silas descends the staircase but doesn't go into the crowd, rather turning toward the staircase and his cabin. What's his game? Does he pity me?

Someone calls out my name—Lydia?—but it feels as though the sound is coming from very far away. I can see August's red-gold head dipping among the crowd, but I don't want to talk to him. I don't want to hear his apology, or likelier, his explanation. My skin itches all over and suddenly I feel desperate to be anywhere but here, here where everyone could see I'm unwanted, if they ever bothered to turn in my direction.

So in the end, I'm the one to turn on my heel and flee for belowdecks.

Chapter 11

My feet carry me down the narrow staircase, past the officers' staterooms and into the blubber room, but it's not far enough. Men are already all around me, loud and oblivious. I don't want to be among them, but nor do I want to be alone in my cabin. My cabin, boxy and odd, squatting on the deck of the ship like a flea on a dog's back. Just like me, clearly out of place.

Instead, I go down the next set of stairs, stairs I've never taken before, into the hold.

It's dark down here, and cold. It feels like the air itself changes in the time it takes me to stumble down the steep, ladderlike stairs, going cold and damp, my very skin telling me I've descended beneath the water level.

I emerge into a vast, cave-like space, divided into narrow aisles by rows of barrels stacked higher than my head. It smells like tar and sawdust, and the chill seeps through my clothes into my skin. Here is where all the supplies for the voyage are stored, food and extra clothes for the crew, furs and tall boots for when we reach the arctic. Nails and boards and hammers, lances and harpoons, all of it shrouded in pitch-black but for the small circle illuminated by the lamp at the base of the staircase.

This I take out of its sconce and carry with me, not knowing where I'm going, just that I need movement to keep the swirl of dark thoughts at bay. I walk far enough, turning and weaving among the barrels, that I doubt the light will be visible from the staircase.

But even as I glance over my shoulder, I know no one is going to come after me. August didn't even notice me leaving. We talked about the whaleboats. I told him I wanted to be on his crew. He smiled and nodded and like a fool I took that for a promise.

Footsteps on the staircase. I freeze amid the maze of barrels and shrink against their bulk, swiping at my cheeks—wet now—with the back of my sleeve. But they aren't August's footsteps—they're light, uncertain almost, not his bold, confident tread.

I consider putting out the lantern, but that seems silly, childish. I'm not doing anything wrong; this ship belongs to my family. So when Silas rounds the corner, I'm just standing there with the lantern dangling from my fingers, trying not to cry.

The lamplight casts his pale face in strange shadows as he stops a few feet away, making his gray eyes look dark, almost black, unreadable. I blink and swallow, furious that he's seeing me so vulnerable once again. The shareholder meeting. The room beneath the Spout. The shrine at the Seaman's Bethel. And now this. He must think me so fragile.

"Lady Fairfax," he says quietly. "Are you all right?"

I lower the lamp slightly, hoping the light doesn't glint off the tear tracks. "You don't have to keep me on your crew," I say, aiming for briskness. "That was kind of you to name me, but not necessary."

"I didn't do it out of kindness," he says cautiously, hands in his pockets. The light brings out the hollows in his cheeks, shadows under his eyes. "But if you don't want to be on a crew, I can speak to Mance and rearrange things."

"I did—I do want to be on a crew. I want to learn. But . . ." I swallow and shake my head. "August was right. I have no experience. I'll just be a liability to you." My muscles twitch with the desire to pace. "I won't hold it against you if you want someone else."

I turn on my heel and set off down the aisle again. I don't expect Silas to follow—indeed the aisles are too narrow for two people to walk side by side without brushing shoulders—but he falls into step slightly behind me, pace matching mine.

"I wouldn't have named you if I didn't want you on my crew," he says from behind me. Our shadows pool together at my feet. "I thought you knew this, Lady Fairfax, but I'm not particularly selfless or brave. I'm not in the habit of putting myself and my crew in danger unnecessarily. I don't think you'll be a liability. Quite the opposite."

Each word makes my cheeks burn and I'm glad my back is to him. His words are brusque, not silky like August's would be, but he's the one who stood on the forecastle in front of everyone and called out my name. Not August. "Thank you."

"One thing you should know about being on my crew," he adds. "It won't make you any friends among the *Heralder* men to be associated with me."

I glance over my shoulder to see that the words are delivered with a wry smile, but a dullness haunts his eyes that makes me think maybe guilt nips at his heels same as it does mine. "But they don't know you're finfolk," I say.

"They suspect. I lead the Cursed Crew, after all. And I have a cross scar, like in the story of Ivar Kirkrell. Someone saw it once and rumors spread."

"A scar?" I turn, confused, remembering the old story told to every child in Kirkrell, reproduced in stained glass in the windows at Seaman's Bethel. The story of a human fisherman and his finfolk wife and their son, whose grandmother burned a cross onto his skin to prevent him being taken away by the finwife. "Who gave it to you?"

"My father. Who else?" In the story, Ivar Kirkrell's scar was a badge of honor, of humanity. But the bitterness in Silas's voice makes it clear he doesn't see it that way. More and more stories are turning out to be not what they seemed.

"But I thought—" I stumble over my words, trying to choose them carefully. "In church you told me that holy things didn't really affect finfolk. So why . . ."

"They don't," he says, meeting my eyes quickly before glancing away. "My father wasn't exactly thinking clearly the day my mother left. She wanted to take me too, but he wasn't going to let her." His throat works as he swallows. "He locked me in the cellar and told my mother I'd hid from her. That I didn't want to go with her. The scar was just a precaution."

"I'm sorry." It's hard to get the words out; my tongue feels heavy and uncooperative. "I don't care what the *Heralder* men think. I'll join your crew."

Our words fade into the silence, leaving only the light drumbeat of our footsteps. It's an unsettling thing, feeling empathy for Silas Price, someone I've hated for so long.

But even as that thought floats across my mind, I realize that hatred isn't quite the right word anymore. Maybe it never was. The heavy weight in my chest when I look at him feels vinegar-bitter, like guilt.

If he survived something he shouldn't have, I did too. And furthermore, he's been taking to the ocean all these years, when I turned away from it. He's a living reminder of all the ways I fall short.

"I think you're brave," I add reluctantly. Credit where it's due. "You've survived a lot. I . . ." I take a deep breath, half hoping he'll interrupt and save me from having to say this, but he doesn't. There's just the heat of his gaze on my shoulders. "I'm sorry for what I said when we were children," I finally say in a rush. "At my parents' funeral. I know it wasn't your fault what happened."

He stops walking. It takes me a few seconds to realize it and turn.

I don't know how I expected Silas to react, but it's like he's drawn in on himself. His light-dark gaze skates away from mine; his shoulders hunch in, uncomfortable. Then he seems to shake it off and start walking again. "Surviving the *Volyar* doesn't make us brave," he says quietly. "It just means the finfolk decided to let us live."

"But you're still here." We turn the corner into another aisle, darkness and silence all around. The sounds of the ship over our heads, heavy feet on floorboards and muffled laughter and shouts, feel very far away. "You still came on this voyage, even though everyone on this ship would hate you if they knew the truth."

He flinches, making me wish I hadn't phrased it so harshly, but I'm not wrong. Silas seems human enough most of the time, but I remember the strange sheen in his eyes when he prayed at Seaman's Bethel, the too-fluid way he moves sometimes when he thinks no one's looking. If Mance's men knew for sure he was finfolk, beyond just rumors, I fear they'd run him off this ship, or worse.

"I don't mean to be argumentative, Lady Fairfax, but that's not bravery either," he says after a moment. "I'm here because if we don't succeed, the alternative will be worse."

"You mean succeed in ending whaling?" Anger flickers in me. I tried to extend a peace offering, only for him to press his agenda. "The alternative being a war between humans and finfolk if the whales die out?"

Maybe it's the dark eeriness of the hold; maybe it's because we're at sea now and the bulk of the *Heralder* is still so small next to the vastness of the water and the creatures in it. But his intimations of war frighten me more here than they did when he first told me about them at the Spout. They seem more possible.

I jump when his hand finds my shoulder, turning me around. His skin is warm through the fabric of my shirt, trailing prickles of electricity even after he's dropped his hand. "I'm not trying to frighten you," he says, a strained plea in his voice. "Please understand that. If there was another way, I'd take it."

It's strange—the desperation in his words makes it seem like he's asking for forgiveness, when if anything he's the one helping me by taking me to Drekja, with nothing in return except my promise to end whaling, a promise I don't intend to keep. "It's okay," I say, shrinking back from him in fear that my sudden guilt will show on my face.

He blinks. "We should get back above," he says, echoing my thoughts. "Your fiancé will be looking for you."

I scoff. *Doubtful.* For a few minutes, I'd forgotten about August passing me over for the whaleboat crew. But the anger stokes back to life quickly, the skin on my wrists prickling along with it, new scales I'll have to pluck out tonight. I take a deep breath, trying to calm myself, and make an effort not to stomp after Silas as he turns toward the staircase.

Then halfway across the length of the hold, something stops

me. Sends a bolt of mixed revulsion and excitement through me, the monster under my skin stirring. I stop walking without quite meaning to.

Silas pauses too, turning back toward me. "What is it?"

Something in the air, making my heart beat fast, something that doesn't make sense. I blink, take a shallow breath. "Nothing."

"Lady Fairfax?" comes another voice from the direction of the staircase, making us both jump. It takes me a moment to place it as Teuila. "You're needed above. Bit of a problem."

There's urgency in her voice, prompting me to hurry to the staircase. My head clears as I approach the entrance to the upper deck, and I brush past Silas without looking at him, though he's clearly trying to meet my eye.

Because I don't want to explain what made me halt just now.

I don't want him to know how very attuned I am to the smell of fresh blood.

Chapter 12

Teuila and Zimri wait at the top of the stairs in the blubber room, wearing nearly identical expressions of faint concern despite their very different appearances. It would be funny if I weren't so shaken.

"What's going on?" I ask as Silas brushes past on his way to his cabin.

"Nothing to worry about," Zimri says at the same time Teuila says, "I'm sure everything will be fine, but you're requested in the captain's stateroom."

I frown. What does Mance want? I've never had a private audience with him before, never wanted to. August has always been there to mediate, but he's nowhere in sight. Probably still on deck bonding with his whaleboat crew.

And who, or what, was bleeding down in the hold? The heartbreak bloodthirst shifts restlessly deep inside me, wanting to return and investigate. Of course, it's no strange thing for a whaleship to smell like blood. Most ships are soaked with it, the unavoidable result of doing the cutting-in of dead whales on deck.

But the *Heralder* is a new ship; this is her maiden voyage.

The stateroom—the captain's quarters—is less grand than its name would suggest, though still a generous size for a room belowdecks on a ship. A curtained-off bunk on the far side, a dresser, a writing desk, maps tacked up over the walls, all of it smelling of sweat and cigarettes. And in the middle, an aged oak dining table where sit Mance, Lydia—and Kit. My little brother.

My spine stiffens with shock as they both shoot to their feet, Lydia holding Kit's hand and dragging him upright. Kit is ragged and rumpled, wearing sailor's clothes much too big for him, and he's trembling with what must be nervousness, but his eyes are bright.

"Mama and Papa always told us we had to stick together," Lydia says, her voice quiet but resolved, shoulders squared. "They said—"

"Silence yourself," Mance barks at her before whirling on me. "My quartermaster found the boy stuffed in a cabinet in the galley. The girl was sneaking food to him."

What were they thinking? I can't catch my breath, panic rising in me. The two bread rolls spilling out of Lydia's satchel flash through my mind. Her shifty gaze when she said she was helping out in the kitchen. It was bad enough for her to be on this voyage I know will be dangerous. But Kit—as much as I knew I'd miss him, never in a thousand years would I have wanted him along. Not to Kielstraat. Not to Drekja.

"They said that the world would try to split us apart, but we couldn't let it." Lydia's words spill out fast, her eyes hard. "That's why, Annie."

I can't keep them safe here. The fear spirals up in me, pain pricking my arms and the tips of my fingers, sensing a threat to the remains of my heart. I try to breathe, curling my gloved hands into fists. "How did you get on board?" I ask stupidly, the only question I can think of.

Kit brightens—something he knows the answer to—but before he says anything, Mance practically spits at them, "Out, both of you. We need to have a little discussion. Your sister will come to you after."

Lydia starts to object, but I level her with a furious gaze, and something in her seems to wilt. She grabs Kit's hand and shepherds him from the room. I want nothing more as they pass but to reach out and hug them, but I know I can't, even if I didn't feel rooted to the ground.

"Well?" Mance barks as soon as the door falls shut behind them. "What do you have to say?"

"I apologize on behalf of my siblings," I say with as much authority as I can, which isn't much; my voice trembles with surprise. I have to resist the urge to stuff my hands in my pockets. "Clearly, I didn't know about this. I don't know how my brother got on board."

"Save your apologies," Mance says. "What I want to know, Lady Fairfax, is what do we do with them? It's bad enough to have women on my ship. I didn't sign up to have children too."

Anger will only make everything worse, will only accelerate the scales pricking at the underside of my skin, so I breathe deep and force myself not to react to how my name drips with his scorn. "We're barely two days out of Kirkrell. Can't we just turn around and take them home?"

Mance scoffs, like I'm a pitiable fool for even suggesting it. "That would lose us at least five days and likely more. We'd be sailing against the wind. I wouldn't expect you to understand, girl, but these voyages are carefully timed to make the most of the winds and the tides. Turning back now will throw the whole plan off course and shorten our time in Kielstraat, not to mention making it more likely we'd run afoul of the spring storms."

"I know our time is dearly bought," I say, low and cold, reminding him that while he may be captain, he is not to treat me like a servant or a child. "What do you propose, then, Mr. Mance? A sailor of your caliber, I'd expect to have a solution to any problem."

He scowls, the expression carving the lines in his reddened, weatherworn face deeper. "Unloading them when we restock at Nunaqvik."

"And how would they get home from Nunaqvik?" I inquire icily.

"Plenty of ships going south. Trains, even." He leans back on the table, produces a cigarette, and lights it.

"A fifteen-year-old and an eleven-year-old can't take an international journey alone."

"They won't have to. You'll be disembarking with them."

"That's not an option," I say, forcing myself not to clench my fists any tighter, afraid that I'll break the skin and then have to explain torn, bloody gloves.

"Well, I can't spare any of my men to babysit them on the way back to Kirkrell." Foul smoke wafts toward my face. "Maybe one of the ladies from the scavenger crew."

I bite back what I really want to say—that though I've only known Josephine and Teuila a short while, I'd lay our family fortune down that they're as capable sailors as any of the *Heralder* men. "Then we'll just have to keep them with us. I'll see to it that they stay out of trouble."

I can tell Mance wants to shout more by how his scowl stays etched on his face, but evidently he's remembered his position vis-à-vis mine. "See to it that you do," he says sourly, then turns on his heel and seats himself at the writing desk, a clear dismissal. "Send Hargreave in here if you see him; we have matters to discuss."

I respond with a curt nod and leave the room as quickly as I can.

Out in the hallway, Kit and Lydia turn to me, two anxious faces that look so much like my own. A mixture of love and anger twists at my heart. They are my reason for living, but it's difficult enough to get Mance and the others to take me seriously without them humiliating me by their deception. "My cabin," I say, jerking my chin at the stairs.

Just as we're about the climb the narrow staircase to above deck, August emerges from it. News must have traveled quickly, because he doesn't look surprised to see Kit, instead greeting my brother with a clap on the shoulder. "Mr. Fairfax." Then he looks up and trains his warm smile on me.

"August!" Kit practically glows. He adores August, always has, mostly since August will listen to his long treatises about the books he's read.

Usually it charms me, but I'm still furious about my fiancé passing me over for the whaleboat crews. I meet his smile with a stony gaze. "Captain wants to speak with you."

His smile flickers. He nods and goes to pass me, but pauses to bend and speak into my ear, warm air stirring the hair at my temple. "My cabin after?"

Warmth blooms automatically in me, but I keep my face blank. He won't be able to assuage me that easily. "Maybe," I say and brush past him.

A moment later, I catch up with Kit and Lydia in my cabin. The instant the door is closed, a small body collides with mine. My breath goes out of me in an *oof* as Kit's arms come up around me, holding tight as he presses his face into my shoulder.

"I'm sorry, Annie," he mumbles into my shirt. "I didn't want to be alone."

It's not a decision to bring my arms up to wrap around him, careful not to hold too tight. I lay my cheek on the top of his head, and for just a moment my anger and fear recede; I could be home again, everything could be all right. Then I open my eyes to see Lydia looking stonily at me, something clearly on her mind. As if I'm the one at fault here. I disentangle from Kit. "Just what in Maker's name were you two thinking?"

The little room is crowded with three of us in it. Kit bounces nervously on his toes, taking a deep breath, but Lydia silences him with a gesture before he can start talking. She's imperious, with a lifted chin and her arms crossed over her chest. Sometimes in moments like these I think she should have been firstborn.

"I was thinking," she says, somehow both hotly and deliberately, "that you're heartbroken—"

My breath catches and my eyes flit to Kit, expecting to see confusion. But his expression stays the same. With a shock, I realize Lydia must have told him everything. About the heartbreak curse, about me.

"—that you're sailing into dangerous waters," Lydia is saying, "the place where Mama and Papa died, with a harebrained plan to find the finfolk and convince them somehow to cure you. I was thinking there's a thousand, a million things that could go wrong, even if you've deluded yourself into thinking otherwise."

"I'm not delusional," I retort. "Do you think I don't know how far-fetched it all sounds? I know anything could go wrong. That's why I wanted you both to stay home." My hands worry at my sleeves. "But without going to Drekja, I have no chance at all to save myself from the heartbreak. A chance is better than no chance."

"I'm not saying you shouldn't try. But we deserve the chance to be with you." *In case it doesn't work out*, is the unspoken second half of the sentence. "Besides, what if we can help? Kit knows more about the finfolk than practically anyone." Lydia nods at Kit, who brightens at the praise.

"It's not in any of the books, that they'll lift curses," he offers up. "So how do you know they'll do it for you?"

I bite my lip as Lydia raises her brows expectantly. Before, I didn't tell her about my side of the bargain with Silas, and in the hectic swirl of adding her to the voyage at the last minute, I was able to brush her questions about the particulars aside. But now it seems I won't get off the hook so easily.

I glance over my shoulder to make sure the door is closed and then take a step closer to my brother and sister, finding a small measure of comfort when they don't back away. "Remember how Father told us that sometimes you must do things that are difficult or even frightening for the greater good?"

Kit bites his lip and nods.

"Silas Price is half finfolk," I tell them quietly, causing Kit to perk up with interest and Lydia to go pale. "He said he could make sure I'm healed if I go to Drekja."

Silence for a stretching moment, then Lydia says, "And you believe him?" Her eyebrows are so far up now they disappear into her bangs. She huffs a sigh and plops down to sit on the bed, arms still crossed.

I shrug, suddenly feeling very tired, and slide down to sit cross-legged on the floor. Kit does too, and I have a flash of memory of being a child—Mama curled in the armchair in the sitting room and reading us a story, the three of us sitting on the floor around her feet.

"It's a fair question," I admit to Lydia. Maker knows it's a fair question. "But what choice do I have? Heartbreak is a finfolk curse, so it makes sense that the finfolk could cure it."

"And what have you promised him in return?" Her gaze pins me in place. "The finfolk always want something in return."

I look down at the floor, tracing the knots and whorls in the rough-hewn floorboards. "He asked me to dissolve the company and stop killing whales."

Kit's eyes widen and Lydia's face hardens into a glare. "And what did you say?"

"What do you think?" I hiss quietly, the words edging close to a snap. "Of course I agreed. It doesn't mean I actually plan to do it. I intend to get to Drekja, be healed by the fae queen, and figure out what to do from there. But this family, and the company, is my first priority."

"What makes you think Price will keep his word?" she presses, her eyes boring into mine. "Don't you remember Mama's stories? The finfolk are full of tricks."

I can hear the uncertainty in her voice beneath the brittle surface. I know that Papa taught her, just like he taught me, to hide fear at all costs, that it was better to appear harsh or even domineering than to reveal doubt. So I understand why she's acting like this, but that doesn't make it any easier on the receiving end. It feels like my chest has cracked open, like icy air is trickling between my ribs.

"I do remember," I say. "But I've researched this for years, I've asked everywhere, and there's no other cure, not one made by human hands. It's either trust Silas or give up and turn monster. Would you prefer I do that?"

"When Papa told us sometimes we would have to do hard things, I don't think he meant allying with our oldest enemy," Lydia says loftily.

My heart twists when she doesn't answer my last question; my arms prickle with the promise of scales. It's going to be a miserable time plucking them out tomorrow. Of course she has a right to be upset with me, angry even, after all the secrets I've kept.

But she's looking at me like I've failed her utterly.

I decide here and now: if there's no way to get them safely home, protecting them during this voyage will be my first priority. Higher even than healing my heartbreak. I will not fail my siblings again.

Still, their disappointment stings like salt water in a wound, the feeling that I've done everything wrong. Every choice I've made since our parents died has been for them. To try to shield them from danger. And this is when Lydia decides to take matters into her own hands? Now all of us are in danger on this ship heading to the cold north, the domain of the finfolk, with the line between ally and enemy so thin as to be invisible.

Chapter 13

Somewhat to my chagrin, Kit seems to fall into place on the ship even more easily than Lydia has. Easier than me, certainly. He helps Willa in the kitchen; he persists in asking me if he can climb to the crow's nest and keep watch for whales. The *Heralder* men mostly ignore him, but the *Whistler* crew is kind to him, as they have been to me and Lydia. Even Silas—I'll see him showing Lydia how to adjust a sail up in the rigging, or bent over a map with Kit, his long fingers tracing a route as he tells stories about past voyages. At first I worried I'd made a mistake telling my siblings he was finfolk, but they both seem able to keep his secret.

And then there's August. Even living in such close quarters, I can't shake the sense of distance that has sprung up between us. He spends much of his time with the captain, he and Mance conferring in low voices. No matter how handsome he looks with the wind tugging at his coat, outlined in golden sun, the memories from Silas's seashell echo in my mind when I look at him. *There will be a storm. I'll do what must be done.*

As a distraction, I throw myself into the rhythm of the ship, learning how to do various tasks, getting used to the feeling of the sea rolling far beneath my feet. I start trading my dresses for shirts, trousers, and oilcloth jackets, and my cotton gloves for wool and leather. It's a relief to be less worried that the scales and claws will tear through, and I stick out less and less amid the rest of the crew. But I still feel set apart from everyone else; I feel the gazes of the crew following me, and I'm not sure if it's curiosity about the heiress to the Fairfax Whaling Company in their midst, or if they can tell that something deeper is wrong with me.

In the commotion of finding Kit, getting him settled, and placating Mance, the blood scent in the hold slips from my mind for a couple of days. One afternoon when the wind feels less vicious than usual, I feel brave enough to take a shift in the crow's nest when the noon bell rings—brave enough, even, to let Kit come up with me when he asks. We bundle ourselves in scarves and hats and gloves, which make us overwarm on deck, but which I know we'll need up so high. My heart lives in my throat as we climb the rigging, Kit ahead of me so I can catch him if he slips. But I don't need to worry. My brother is a natural; I'm just trying to keep up.

The top of the mast is fitted with a steel hoop, meant for one sailor to stand in while he keeps watch. But it's built to fit a large man, so both Kit and I can squeeze inside. He folds his arms over the hoop and leans out, for all the world as if he's just leaning out the parlor window watching for birds in the garden. Meanwhile, I can't help keeping one hand looped protectively over his chest and one hand with a death grip on the hoop, even as the cold seeps in through my glove.

Still, I can't deny that it's beautiful up here, the afternoon sun painting everything in washed-out shades of gray and blue and white, even though the sun burns my skin and eyes. The ocean, stretched out as far as I can see in every direction, ripples like silk on a clothesline, and the rest of the crew look like dolls going about their business on deck. I search for familiar figures: Ezra fishes off the side of the ship, Josephine and Lydia repair nets, Zimri coils ropes. August is at the prow, watching our progress, hair shining in the pale sun. He looks like a prince in a storybook. Then there's the sea, looking calm and docile at this distance, the waves like ripples in a mug of tea. I don't see Silas, and wonder where he is. Another headache, or is he simply working on something belowdecks?

There's something else we might see too. "Remember what to do if there's a spout?" I ask Kit, my stomach tightening in mixed anticipation and nervousness at the thought.

"Sing out for him!" Kit chirps, just like every schoolboy and schoolgirl in Kirkrell is taught.

"Good man," I tell him, affection warming me from inside. "You'll have to shout loud for the crew to hear you down there."

He stands on his tiptoes, like that will help him see just a little farther. "When we're done with this voyage, can I join Captain Silas's crew on the *Whistler*?" he asks, shouting slightly to be heard over the wind.

Now, that would be a scandal, a Fairfax sailing under the flag of a scavenger. "Wouldn't you rather crew a real ship?" I call back. "Chase living whales?"

I feel his shoulders stiffen under all the layers. "I don't want to kill whales," he says.

My throat goes tight. "We can talk about it back home," I say once I find my voice. Guilt trickles in, Kit's words reminding me of my lies to Silas. Silas thinks I'm going to end whaling entirely. I know that's impossible—*all of Kirkrell relies on whale magic*—but the knowledge sits heavier than it used to. The thought of betraying Silas doesn't feel quite so easy anymore.

After an hour or two up the crow's nest, a commotion on deck draws us back down. The fishermen have brought in a haul of herring and a dolphin is caught in the net. Kit, Lydia, and I join the gathering crowd out of curiosity, never having seen a dolphin before. "They have babies, not eggs," Kit informs us, looking torn between distress and fascination as we all watch the fishermen pull the creature from the net, its thrashing weakening moment by moment. "They have red blood like us."

When someone produces a club, I realize what's going to happen and order Lydia to take Kit to my cabin. None too soon. In a few minutes that red blood is smeared across the deck and the *Heralder* men are discussing how Willa might cook the animal up for dinner. And I'm staring in a sickly kind of trance, the memory of the smell in the hold slamming back into me. As the blades come out, I turn away, a little dizzy and uneasy about what someone else would see if they looked at my face. Disgust or hunger.

I'm not sure if it's my conscious mind or the monster under my skin that carries me back toward the hold, brushing past the sailors with my eyes on the ground. But neither I nor the monster is much pleased when Ezra, Silas's taciturn second in command, detaches from the crowd and falls into step beside me. "Lady Fairfax," he says, clipped. "Where are you off to?"

Annoyance flares and I grit my teeth. "Is it such a tall order to have a moment alone on a whaling ship?"

A rueful smile crosses Ezra's face, the first time I think he's smiled in my presence. "It is, actually, yes."

I stifle a groan as the gravity of this settles on me. Back in Kirkrell, I spent a great deal of time alone—too much—and it never occurred to me how taxing it would be, living packed in with so many others.

"You get used to it," Ezra adds, which is little comfort.

When we near the entrance to the hold, I expect to part ways, but instead Ezra hesitates only slightly at the top of the stairs before following me down. Which presents a problem. I can't investigate the blood smell with him there, but I don't have any other reason to be in the hold. I pause on the staircase and look over my shoulder at him.

"That was a hint, in case you couldn't tell," I say pointedly, rudely, but I don't know how else to get him to leave. Yet Ezra doesn't seem fazed as he takes a lantern off the wall and hands it to me.

"Oh, I could tell," he replies amiably. "But my captain asked us to keep an eye on you if you started wandering around the ship alone."

So Silas is having me tailed now and not even bothering to hide it? "I'm not going to fall over the railing," I snap. It occurs to me that sailors, especially the Cursed Crew, might have different standards for rudeness than the high society I'm used to. That I might have to try harder if I mean to cause offense.

"Not by accident." The reply is low and serious. "That's not what Silas is worried about."

I swivel to look back at Ezra and almost end up in a heap at the bottom of the stairs, caught off guard by the implication of Ezra's words. Silas must have told his crew about August and the supposed plot to murder me.

It isn't so surprising in and of itself. Silas and the Cursed Crew are clearly close. But that makes it worse. Because if Silas told them that August means me harm, that diminishes the likelihood he was lying to me, like I've been telling myself.

It would be one thing for Silas to lie to me, to try to drive a wedge between August and me. But why would he tell the same lie to his crew?

"How much do you know about all this?" I ask Ezra once I've found my feet at the bottom of the staircase. The voices of the crew are dim and distant above us, the lantern illuminating little.

"More than I'd like." Ezra crosses his arms, waiting for me to lead the way, but I don't move yet.

"He told you about my curse," I venture, and I can tell from the way Ezra's eyes flick down to my gloved hands that it's true. I scoff and turn to stride deeper into the hold, trying to hide my hurt and anger.

No matter what I felt toward Silas, I kept his secret—that he's finfolk—all these years, right up until telling Kit and Lydia a few days ago, and that was out of necessity. But he didn't keep mine.

"Only the four of us know," Ezra says, the soft tread of his footsteps starting up behind me. "Silas wanted us to make an informed decision about this voyage. He doesn't send us blindly into danger."

It's not lost on me that this is more respect than my own fiancé has accorded to me. "Are you not afraid of me?" I ask bitterly, without turning around.

A beat passes before Ezra's reply comes. "Silas says you can succeed in this, so I'm choosing to believe him." A skeptical note runs through his voice, an unspoken *for now*. "But send me away if you like—just don't blame me if you get murdered."

Suddenly I find that I don't really want him to leave. I don't want to be alone down here, though I'd jump in the sea before admitting it. "Well, when you put it like that, I suppose I could use an extra pair of eyes."

"And what exactly are we looking for?"

Seeing as Ezra seems impossible to rattle, I don't see the harm in telling him the truth. "I smelled blood down here earlier. Which doesn't make sense because—"

"The *Heralder* is a new ship," he finishes in a murmur. "Troublesome."

A few yards in, I catch the trail again. The faintest hint of a scent, yet it stands out from the smells of tar and sawdust and smoke that otherwise dominate. It doesn't smell like human blood or whale blood, not precisely. There's a similar metallic tinge, but it's brinier, with a sharp edge of something like charcoal.

"You were cursed by the finfolk, weren't you?" I say to Ezra as I retrace my steps back and forth, trying to determine where the scent is the strongest. "So why follow Silas? He's one of them."

According to Silas, his crew follows him because he's promised to help them. But that doesn't seem to explain how fiercely defensive of Silas Ezra seems to be. Young though he is—maybe in his early twenties—he strikes me as an experienced sailor. Most whaling men would scorn to answer to a nineteen-year-old captain at all, much less a half finfolk one or a scavenger.

"No other captain will have a cursed sailor," Ezra says with a touch of irritation. "You must know this."

"You said your curse was that you couldn't cross running water?" He nods. "You could hide that easily by not going far inland. Stop at the wharf, collect your pay, and sign up on another ship the next day. Lots of whalers do."

"I don't want to be on the sea forever," he replies, quieter.

I feel a pang of sympathy at that, even though his curse to me still sounds like something to be envied. "And you really think," I press, "he can take you to Drekja? And that the queen will heal you?"

Ezra starts to answer, but just then, the next breath I take is full of the blood scent and I stiffen, my feet moving automatically to follow the trail. It gets stronger and stronger as I weave through the barrels, the metallic edge as strong as a coin laid on my tongue. But then—

I stop inches from a wooden wall, so distracted by the blood smell that I barely stop myself from running straight into it. There's nothing there. Just barrels on either side of us labeled *Nails* and *Bolts*, and a wall in front. I back away, looking down as though I might find a trail of blood there, but there's nothing. Disappointment churns.

Yet Ezra is examining the wall, biting his lip. One long light brown hand rises to trace the curve of the planks. "This was constructed more recently than the rest of the ship," he says quietly. "Look, the tar is still sticky."

My mouth goes dry. "A false bulkhead," I realize, pulling up the ship schematics in my head. No wall is meant to be here; there should be another row of barrels.

Ezra glances at me, eyes wide, then raps on the wall with his knuckles, once, twice. It rings out, clearly hollow behind.

My mouth is dry, my throat thick with the smell of blood as I run my hands over the wall, searching for some kind of entrance. There's nothing that I can find, except for a place where the wall joins with the true wall of the ship and a board is loose, sloppily nailed in. Wordlessly I pass the lantern to Ezra and strip off my gloves, fitting claws into the grooves of the wood.

It wouldn't be all that strange for a hold to have a storage room here. But why add one after the ship's construction and not put it on the schematics? What would need to be held in a secret compartment rather than in the hundreds of barrels all around us? Why is there no door?

Knock, knock.

I rear back in shock, shoving a knuckle in my mouth to stifle a scream as Ezra swears under his breath. The rapping came from inside the compartment.

Someone or something is in there. Something bleeding. We both stay where we are for a long moment.

Then—"Let me," Ezra whispers, taking my place crouching before the wall as he pulls out a large pocketknife, flips it open. I fall back to let him work at the plank until a section of it comes away, leaving a gap as big as my hand. He stoops to look into the gap.

Then his body goes rigid, and he swears creatively, tipping backward. When he looks back at me, his face is pale, shocked. Not so unflappable after all. Everything rational in me urges me to stay back, but morbid curiosity and the smell of blood together are too strong. I crouch down too and my stomach drops precipitously.

It's pitch-dark in the secret room with my face up against the gap, blocking the lantern light. Yet I can still see two jade green lights across the space, glowing in the black. Something deep in my gut recognizes them before my conscious mind does, jerking me back with an icy rush of dread.

Caught between a hungry sea and merciless stars, those lights once floated all around me, unblinking.

There's the *ch* of a match striking. Ezra crouches next to me with a long lit match in his slightly shaking hand, ready to look, but instead I take the match from him and put it through the gap myself. The smell of blood is so strong, even though it's like no blood I've ever smelled, inescapable.

Everything in me seems to turn to lead as the firelight fills the small space, as the green lights angle away from the candle.

The compartment is built around a thick wooden pillar that

extends from floor to ceiling, which from its positioning must be the bottom part of the mainmast. Bound to the pillar in a kneeling position is one of the finfolk.

It takes me a minute to make sense of what I'm seeing, so different is he from the creatures that surrounded us on the open water the night the *Volyar* sank. Here away from wind and moonlight, he seems diminished compared to the ethereal beings I saw, and perhaps even more terrifying. Out on the sea, the finfolks' garments concealed their faces, but now the dark clothes have been pinned down by chains, rippling weakly as if in an anemic breeze. He is taller and thinner than a man, yet his face is more or less like a human's except for a gray tint to his skin and those bright green eyes.

That face turns down toward me slowly. Pupils appear out of nothing and grow in his eyes, like something rising out of deep water, and focus on me. I can't breathe. The chains seem not to be wrapped around the mainmast, but rather feed through holes in the wood before wrapping around the finfolk's limbs, his torso, his throat. It must be iron. I can smell it and see the metal cutting into flesh, drawing green-black blood.

The finman's lips part, revealing pointed white teeth, and a faint series of clicks emanates out. The same sound that for six years has formed the backdrop of my nightmares. I flinch back, almost dropping the match.

As I back slowly away, stunned, Ezra grips my elbow. "I'll go find Silas."

Terror sweeps through me at the prospect of being left alone down here with the finman. Ezra must see it on my face, his own softening slightly, though still pale with shock. "You go, then," he says. "I'll stay here."

Part of me wants to protest—it feels wrong to leave Ezra here alone. A bigger part wants to put the board back in place and forget I've seen anything at all, but I know I can't. Something malevolent is happening on the *Heralder*. *My family's ship*, I think with a surge of possessive anger. I need to find out who's behind this, and why.

I rush upstairs, taking the long way to avoid having to pass by the stateroom, where I imagine August will be having dinner with Mance. On the upper deck, Silas is eating dinner with the rest of the Cursed Crew and my siblings. Kit has a book open under his plate in his lap—of course he took his books with him even as a stowaway—and is eagerly telling Teuila and Zimri about giant squid sightings in the Aegira while Lydia and Josephine laugh at some private joke. Silas sees me coming before the others do and seems to register something wrong on my face.

He gets up and paces to meet me before I reach the group, eyes alert. "What is it? What's wrong?"

My tongue feels heavy in my mouth. How to even begin to explain? And Silas's people aren't the only ones on deck; *Heralder* men are all around eating their dinners. "Ezra and I found something in the hold," I manage. "Something you need to see."

He blinks, concerned, and pivots to head toward the staircase. I move to follow him, then freeze as someone calls my name from the other direction. August.

Silas hears it too; his mouth thins. "Go to him if you like. I'll find Ezra." And he's gone down the deck.

I turn to August, pulling on a smile that strains my already stretched nerves. The smell of blood from the hold still lingers in my throat, and I'm reminded that Silas told his crew to look out for me, told them about August.

If Silas *isn't* lying and the memories in the shell are true—if August really did say those things—where does that leave me?

It's possible that August said those words and didn't mean them. He could have been bluffing. Trying to manipulate Silas, win him over, knowing that Silas hates the Fairfaxes.

But believing in August is becoming more and more of a balancing act.

"I've been looking for you," he says when we converge, reaching out to trace my face with the back of one finger. "Are you all right? You look ill."

I let my smile fall away, since apparently it wasn't convincing to begin with. "Just a little seasick, maybe."

"Well, eating the crew's food won't help you there," August says. "Come have dinner with me and the captain. It's not fitting, you hanging around out here like a common sailor."

I might have dined with them before Kit was caught stowing away, but now it's the last thing I want to do. I can't help but eye August, measuring him up. He planned this voyage; he decreed exactly what supplies in what amounts should be brought with us from Kirkrell. Does he know about the secret compartment and what's inside?

"I hope Mance didn't give you too hard a time about Kit," August says, interpreting my glare as displeasure about the captain. "He's used to being in charge of everything that goes on on his ship. Doesn't like surprises."

I want to remind August that the *Heralder* isn't *his* ship. It's the company's. But then it occurs to me I should be playing nice with Mance. August too. Maybe if I'm clever, I can find out what they both know about the finman in the hold. I reach out and take August's hand, squeezing slightly, feeling the heat of his skin through my gloves. "Let me change clothes and I'll meet you there."

Going into the stateroom, smoothing down the front of my dress, I feel rattled, jumpy. I knew that the old guard of the Fairfax

Whaling Company, the shareholders and officers and many of the sailors, didn't necessarily respect me. But the finfolk prisoner in the hold is evidence of outright deception and subversion.

Mance must know about it. Does August know too? And if he does, what else might he be lying to me about?

There's fear of the finfolk there too, deep and instinctive, to know I am sharing this vessel with one of *them*. The same beings that slaughtered Mama and Papa and so many others, their unnatural storms serving as weapons as surely as swords or cannons would. Trapped and diminished as the finman in the hold seemed, those green eyes spoke of hunger and defiance, of danger.

Mance looks consternated to be playing host as we sit down. A meal for three has been laid out already—fresh bread and salt fish and soup, all on ceramic dishes, rather than the battered tin bowls the rest of the crew uses. August seems comfortable with the situation, even as our stabs at small talk grow increasingly contrived. I am too on edge to be charming, and Mance clearly has no interest in humoring my attempts.

"Do you expect we'll encounter finfolk on this voyage?" I ask finally, directing my question at Mance. "Where are they most commonly seen?" I don't want to reveal what I've found, not without knowing who's keeping the prisoner below, and for what purpose. But I do need to learn more.

August glances at me—he knows I'm familiar with the maps of finfolk sightings that Fairfax Company officers have put together. But let them think I'm simply seeking reassurance. It's not hard to let a note of fear trickle into my voice.

Mance takes another leisurely bite of fish before he deigns to respond. "They rarely venture south of the seas off Nulusk," he says shortly. "I'd be surprised if we see them at all, considering. They'd be smart to stay away with the weaponry we have on board." He nods at August, who allows a small smile of pride at the weapons he's designed.

"But how would the finfolk know what weapons we have or don't have?" I choose my words carefully. "I always thought of them as a force of nature. Not rational. Not afraid of us."

This is more or less true in my experience—back in Abbonheim, people speak about finfolk without curiosity, only fear, the way one might speak of hurricanes. And even the heroes and heroines of Mama's fae tales never concerned themselves overmuch with the finfolk's fears or desires, just how to outwit them. But I wonder, now, if sailors understand them differently. Or if Mance is hoping to learn more by capturing one.

"Who's to say," the captain says with a grunt after a moment. "I always supposed they could smell iron." Mance's eyes flit to August. "Would be good to find out."

My skin prickles. Does August know something? He takes a long sip of wine and says, "Perhaps that's something we could look into." He's looking at Mance, but his eyes go to me as he speaks.

I try to keep my voice neutral. "It would be difficult to get close enough to study them."

"Difficult, yes." His face turns to me, head tilting and a faint smile appearing on his lips. "But the knowledge may be worth the risk."

⁂

"Take a turn about the deck with me?" I ask August after dinner. I want to keep him occupied for as long as possible, knowing that as we conversed with Mance, Silas was going down to the hold, where Ezra waited with the prisoner. I haven't seen them since, and I have a sinking feeling that I've tipped my hand with my questions. If August does know about the prisoner and if he can guess that I know too, I don't want him descending to the hold to check on things.

When we walk across the deck hand in hand, I see Silas and Ezra sharpening lance blades over a worktable. Ezra catches my eye as we pass, shooting me a look of grim acknowledgment, but Silas doesn't lift his gaze from his work, knuckles white as he passes a blade over and over again across a grindstone. I can feel the fury coming off him in waves, tangible as heat off coals, and it puts me even more on edge—fearing that August will feel it too and wonder as to its origins.

August doesn't say anything, though, just wraps an arm around me as a cool breeze lifts off the sea, pulling me into the warmth of him.

I try to tell myself that it doesn't matter if August and Mance learn what we've seen. This ship belongs to my family's company. I have a right to look around, to know what's happening aboard. But that doesn't quiet the deep instinct that tells me to play innocent. Tells me something is wrong. I'm still not ready to believe that August means to kill me. But I don't think I fully trust him either.

Not anymore.

Chapter 14

It's not until the next afternoon that I have a chance to speak to Silas, when August heads to the stateroom to review navigational charts with Mance and I claim a headache. August kisses me goodbye, even though he's just going belowdecks, and I wait until he's disappeared down the staircase before heading to where Silas is pacing the forecastle. He looks up as I approach, and again my breath evaporates at the cold anger on Silas's face. It makes sense he'd be angry, but why does it feel like it's directed at me?

"The thing in the hold," I say after checking no one else is close enough to hear. "What did you—"

His mouth twists and I wish I could bite my tongue. I only meant to broach the topic in a manner that wouldn't attract undue attention—not to call the finfolk prisoner a *thing*—but I can hear how it sounded. Being around Silas, talking to him like this, is disorienting. Words spill out of me unconsidered, or won't come out at all.

Maybe it's because I hated him so fiercely for so long. Now—I understand him a little better after meeting his crew and hearing about the finfolk's message of war. I think he believes himself to be doing the right thing for the Cursed Crew and for Kirkrell. But I am not convinced that he has *my* best interests at heart, not with the way he's looking at me.

"The *thing* in the hold," he echoes my words in a hiss. "Did you know about it?"

"No!" Shock reverberates through me. "I'd never—"

But he's already striding away. I start to go after him, but Ezra materializes from belowdecks and takes my arm, gently stopping me. From the sympathetic expression on his face, he's heard our exchange.

"Sorry about him," he mutters.

"I didn't know," I say defensively, anger twisting through me that Silas could think such a thing. "Really, I—"

"I believe you. I saw you almost fall on your ass when you heard the knock." Ezra considers me. "Shall I tell Silas as much?"

"I guess so." Though the thought makes my cheeks heat, I'd rather Silas think I'm a coward than a monster. "Thanks for that."

The indignance seeps out of me slowly. Taking a breath, I turn around and lean against the railing, looking out over the deck so I can see if anyone's in earshot, and Ezra does the same. "Did you learn anything yesterday after I left?" I ask, pointing with my chin at Silas's retreating form. "Did he . . . talk to the prisoner?"

Ezra nods, dark eyes following Silas as he darts up into the rigging. "Yes. The finman's name is Io. He was captured on another voyage some time ago, hard to say how long. Been down there since before we left Kirkrell."

Io. I try out the strange name silently. It hadn't occurred to me that finfolk had names. At least the ones out on the sea, the ones without human blood. But of course they do.

"Mance is feeding him," Ezra goes on quietly. "Checking in on him."

It's awful to admit even to myself, but I feel relieved not to hear August's name. Though that doesn't mean he's ignorant of this. "To what end? Does the . . . the prisoner know what Mance wants?"

Ezra's mouth twists in a grimace. "From what he would say, from what Silas could understand—somehow his weather magic is being siphoned. To keep up the wind and keep storms away."

My breath catches as I think back on our sailing so far. We've had fine weather, nearly a week of sun, of blue skies and calm seas and wind in the exact direction and speed needed for ideal sailing conditions.

Ezra shudders. "It felt wrong to leave him there, but we heard Mance coming down and . . ."

Across the deck Silas climbs the ropes to the crow's nest, too fast surely to be safe. His shadow shrinks away at our feet.

"What should we do?" I whisper.

Ezra leans back against the railing, appearing casual, but I can sense the tension in him. "I'm not sure there's anything to be done," he says quietly. "We must get to Drekja."

"To heal everyone's curses."

Ezra hesitates a beat too long, his eyes darting to my gloves, before replying, "Right."

And I realize—none of their curses are life-threatening. The most urgent reason to get to Drekja is me.

Before I can feel too guilty about this, Ezra goes on. "If we interfere with whatever scheme Mance is running here, he could force us to leave the ship or worse."

His voice is brisk, practical, but my mind spins at what *or worse* could mean. Prior to this voyage, I thought Mance crude and grasping, more enamored with the hunt than was tasteful—but not dangerous. And even if I'd known what he was capable of, back in Kirkrell, maybe I'd have thought it no sin to wrest every possible advantage in our struggle against the finfolk, even if the methods seemed brutal.

"What do you think?" Ezra adds, eyeing my face with a note of surprise. "Do you want to do something about it?"

I shake my head, stomach churning. "I don't know."

Ezra's right; I don't know how it would be possible to free the prisoner without consequences. And a selfish, scared part of me—the part that's conscious of every new scale, that suspects my time before the heartbreak takes over is running out—is glad for the wind that fills our sails and lets us sweep quickly across the sea.

But everything about this feels deeply wrong, knowing that somewhere not so far below my feet a living creature is bound and bleeding in the dark.

Our fair skies hold. A few days later, there's a stir among the crew when something is spotted on the horizon in the early afternoon.

I'm mending nets with Teuila, but when I hear the cry of "Whale spotted!" and the crew starts shouting, a queasy mix of anxiety and excitement quickens my heart. Half the crew is gathered at the portside railing, the air thrumming with anticipation. It's early afternoon, a cloudy day. I spot August looking out with a spyglass and make my way over to him.

He hands me the spyglass, eyes flat with disappointment. "No hunt today."

When I look out with the spyglass, there is no movement from the shape in the water, no mist of breath from a blowhole. It is a whale, a Livyatan, but it's already dead, a mound of gray-black flesh bobbing in the waves like a small, bleak island.

The mood on deck changes, like a spring breeze given way to a damp wind. Mutters from the crew. A dead thing at sea is a bad omen. Even so, a whale is a whale, and we have the questionable fortune, on this voyage, to count a crew of salvagers among our sailors. It would be foolish not to go see if anything could be salvaged from the corpse. A few yards away down the deck, I hear Mance shout for one of the whaleboats to be lowered and the scavengers to strike out for the whale, and my stomach turns just as it has every time I've seen or heard the captain these last few days.

Ezra, Josephine, Zimri, and Teuila separate from the larger crew, coming forward as Silas himself checks over the boat with a grim set to his mouth. The *Heralder* men have already gone back to their various activities, but there's an uneasy twinge in my gut. I assume Ezra was true to his word and vouched for me to Silas—that I was just as shocked as Ezra was to discover the finman prisoner in the hold. But I haven't spoken to Silas myself since then.

"I'm going to go with them," I tell August, trying to sound more certain than I feel.

He cocks an eyebrow at me. "It won't be pleasant."

"When is whaling ever? Besides," I add with a touch of bitterness, "don't forget I'm on Silas's crew now." *No thanks to you.*

"Then I'd recommend you change your clothes." His eyes trace down my body, my blue wool dress, in a way that would normally send a desirous shiver through me, but there's no room right now for anything but nerves.

I change quickly in my cabin, trading my dress for a long-sleeved shirt and pants of rough-spun cotton, hands covered in thin leather gloves. The small space is more crowded now; I have to step around Lydia's trunk as well as my own, plus the sleeping mat and blanket I've rolled out on the floor. That first night after he was discovered, I sent Kit to sleep in the bunkroom with the rest of the crew, but then my own guilt kept me from sleeping myself until I went and fetched them both from the bunkroom. These last few nights, Kit and Lydia have slept in the bed in my cabin while I bunked down on the floor, the peace of mind making up for the physical discomfort.

The whaleboat is lowered when I come out, with most of the *Whistler* crew already waiting below. Silas stands at the railing, his eyes dark as he looks out at the dead whale. But as I make my way over, Kit materializes and zooms up to Silas. "Can I come too?"

I tense, expecting Silas to chastise him, but he just says seriously, "I need your help here." As I walk up, Silas produces a spyglass from his oilcloth jacket and hands it to Kit. "Someone needs to keep eyes on us and make sure the *Heralder* doesn't leave us behind. Can you do that?"

Kit beams and darts off, gone before I can call after him to stay away from the railings. Silas's mouth quirks, though it doesn't reach his eyes as he turns to me. "Lady Fairfax."

"You're patient with him," I say. I mean to add a *thank you*, but it gets stuck in my throat. It's difficult to observe polite niceties around Silas. With those strange eyes, sometimes it feels like he can see right through me, and it makes me want to hoard my words, as though I could protect my secrets that way.

"You sound surprised," he says dryly, tugging at the rope ladder attached to the gunwale to check that it's secure.

"Well, he's a Fairfax too." I keep my tone neutral, letting the rest be implicit. *And you hate me for it.*

Something goes shadowed in his expression. "They're innocent," he says shortly, before swinging over the railing and disappearing over the rope ladder, leaving me to wonder when I became *not* innocent.

Yes, I am head of the company he despises, but it's not as if I decided to inherit. Does he understand that I never had a choice in this? And why do I care if he understands or not?

I've been dreading looking over the side of the ship, down at the water, but there's nothing else for it. I give Silas a minute to climb down before I clamber over the railing. Even with Silas weighing the ladder down below, it sways and thuds against the side of the ship, making it hard to let go of each rung. I look down and wish I hadn't.

Silas jumps easily into the boat where Ezra, Josephine, Teuila, and Zimri are already waiting, all of them seeming very far away. The water seems violently alive in a way it doesn't when one is standing on the ship deck, looking out at the flat horizon. The waves beat like drums against the side of the ship, sending up sprays of foam that dampen my clothes and mist my face when I finally climb down. The boat looks small amid the waves, the sea the color of gunmetal beneath.

A whaleboat is bigger than a lifeboat, but not so very much bigger.

Josephine and Zimri hold the ladder steady for me at the bottom, but I still manage to trip stepping off. For a second, I'm off-balance, water rushing up toward me, and panic blooms.

Then Silas catches me around the waist and sets me down with my feet on a bench. "Careful." His hands press into me, heating through the old cotton, then he lets go just as quickly, drawing back like I'm the one whose skin is too hot.

He's turned away before I can draw breath and moves to take up his position at the boat stern, quick and steady as if we were on flat land. But the waves that look small and peaceful from the *Heralder*'s deck are heaving against the whaleboat; it rocks beneath my feet. I gather my wits enough to sit down on the bench next to Zimri, who smiles at me though his eyes are grim. “You ready?”

I shrug, which is going to have to be enough answer for now. My stomach is churning suddenly and I want to keep my mouth closed.

We set off rowing, leaving the anchored *Heralder* behind. The movement helps my queasiness a little. I can see August watching from the railing, a column of bright color against the dark ship and dingy sky in his blue coat.

But soon the rowing requires my full attention. I thought being on the *Heralder* was already too close to the water, but here I could reach out and touch it if my grip on the oar weren’t white-knuckle tight; drops of freezing salt water fly up with each stroke and fleck my cheeks, my eyes.

The others are clearly practiced at this; they fall into a rhythm right away, rowing in sync like they share one mind. I try my best to match their movements, and the boat rotates so that we’re rowing backward, facing away from the dead whale, yet moving toward it. It’s unnerving, rowing in a direction I can’t see. Silas is the only one with eyes on the whale, acting as the boatsteerer as the rest of us face him. He braces himself in the whaleboat’s stern, using the steering oar to make small adjustments to our course. His gaze is pinned to the horizon, his jaw set.

The smell when we near the dead whale isn’t what I expected. It’s copper and iron and petrichor and smoke, with an electrical tinge that burns my throat. Not the nauseating sick-sweet smell of most dead things. Even more strangely, the rhythm of the wind and the water seems to change the closer we get to the creature—the wind becoming stronger and colder, the waves more choppy, like the very weather is in mourning. The very world.

We pull alongside the carcass and stop rowing. I pull my shirt up over my nose and turn to look alongside the others, then quickly avert my eyes. The carcass hangs low in the water, only a stretch of a few yards of flesh showing above the surface, a torn dorsal fin. Something—sharks, likely, though I don't want to think about that—has taken bites out of the whale, and most of the skin and blubber and some of the muscle are gone, exposing grayish-pink flesh. Birds circle overhead, maybe frightened off by our presence.

"How do you think it died?" Ezra asks Silas, sounding grave.

A line has appeared between Silas's brows. He shakes his head, shrugging his shoulders slightly. "I'm going to go in and take a look." He addresses us as a group, eyes still on the whale. "Get the rope ready. We'll have to tow it back to the *Heralder*."

He crouches to unlace his boots, then pulls his shirt over his head. I blink, taken off guard, though I don't know why. It's not uncommon to see male sailors and dockworkers going around shirtless. Not Silas, though. Lean muscles flex beneath freckled shoulders as he kicks his boots off. I'm about to look back at the whale just to have somewhere to put my eyes when something else snags my gaze.

A scar in the shape of a cross stretches over his breastbone, bigger than my hand and faded with age. Though he told me about it in the hold that first night of the expedition, it's still shocking to see, brutal in its clear deliberation, its right angles and straight edges.

He wears something around his neck; now he pulls it off and tosses it over his shoulder in the direction of his crew without looking. "Someone hold this for me."

I'm the one to catch it, my hand shooting up automatically. And suddenly in my palm is an oval pendant carved of bone, strung on a leather cord. Like the one now hidden under my own collar. The pendant that floated to me in the chamber beneath the Spout.

He's cursed too? I glance around to see the reactions of the others, but none of them seem surprised or are even paying attention. They must already know—the captain of the Cursed Crew, cursed himself.

Yet why would the finfolk curse one of their own? Questions churn in my mind, but I don't have time to put the words in the right order before he dives neatly over the side of our boat.

My heart clutches, but I remind myself that not everyone fears the ocean like I do. Silas is finfolk, after all, a creature of the sea. Maybe that's why no one seems concerned when he doesn't resurface right away, even as the seconds stretch on. Zimri starts to pull rope from the line tub, looping it around his arm.

I don't realize I'm counting in my head until I hit thirty. When I hit a minute—"Um." My voice sounds high and strained. "Should we be worried?"

"Not yet," Teuila says cheerfully. "He does this a lot."

"I wish he'd hurry, though," Josephine grumbles. "All my clothes are going to smell like dead whale."

Just then, Silas's head pops up on the far side of the whale carcass. He pushes wet hair out of his eyes, and I try not to notice the relief that fills me at his resurfacing. His hand waves from the water, and Zimri tosses him the end of the rope.

While Silas laps the carcass, tying it up so we can bring it back to the *Heralder*, I look down at his pendant. Its shape is slightly different from mine, its color darker, but otherwise they look the same, like two stones on the same beach. No red spots like the others have. He hasn't completed any favors to the finfolk. Or maybe he's tried and they haven't been enough.

When he comes back to the whaleboat and mercifully puts his shirt back on, I don't give the pendant back just yet, acting like I've forgotten about where it's coiled in my jacket pocket. I want a reason to speak with him alone when we're back on the ship.

On the *Heralder*, the rest of the crew is gathered at the gunwale when we finally pull up, evaluating the whale carcass with critical eyes. They conjecture about how many barrels of meat it will yield as we come back up, and no one thanks the Cursed Crew. As they start fastening the whale to the side of the ship to salvage what they can, I duck out of the crowd and follow Silas.

I catch up with him at the door to his stateroom. Belowdecks is empty in a way it almost never is; everyone else is above deck attending to the whale. He turns and his eyes widen to see me.

"Sorry," I say too brightly, taking the pendant from my pocket. "Forgot to give you this back."

His shirt sticks to his chest with seawater or sweat; his curls cling to his neck. He blinks in surprise, like he'd forgotten all about it too, and I consider the casual way he tossed it over his shoulder beforehand, hardly seeming to care about the chance it would sail past our hands into the sea. Either he has immense trust in the reflexes of his crew, or he is strangely careless about his chances of lifting his curse. Whatever it is.

"So you're cursed too," I say to him as I drop the pendant into his outstretched hand. I mean to make the words light and curious, but they come out accusatory, stung. "What is it?"

All this time, from our strange first conversation in my room at Fairfax Manor, he's known about my heartbreak. He's known about my curse, and all its attendant ugliness and terror and desperation. He took me to the enchanted pool beneath the Spout, he told me tales about Drekja and the cure I could find there, without ever mentioning that he shared the experience.

He looks at me for a long moment, as if debating whether to

tell me. "It's about the war with the finfolk," he says eventually, quietly. "After the *Volyar* sank, the finfolk didn't just tell me the message. They showed me. I saw it."

My stomach drops as memories creep up at the edges of my mind and I realize something. It escapes out loud before I can think better of it. "Your eyes. The white . . ."

Fogged over with white when I stumbled upon him praying in church. Blotted out as the finfolk spoke to him amid the wreck of the *Volyar*. His breath catches and he inclines his head in the barest nod. I wasn't imagining it.

"It's happening more and more lately." He lets out a strained breath. "When the visions come on, they take over. I can't see anything else."

"What do you see?" I don't really want to know, but I can't stop myself from asking.

"What you would expect to see in a war. Blood in the streets. Storms wiping out the shoreline. Dead men, dead women, dead finfolk, dead children."

I swallow. "Are you also hoping to lift the curse in Drekja, then?"

"I wanted that, once," he says softly. "I went to the chamber beneath the Spout like you. But . . . I don't think it's going to happen. I've tried doing favors. Nothing's ever worked."

I remember how worried I was when I first got the pendant about how I'd know when I was being called upon to do one of my favors. How casually Silas assured me—*The finfolk are writing a story with us,* he'd said. *The story requires favors, so the chances will come.*

"I'm not as bad off as you, curse-wise," he says after a spell. "It won't kill me. Unless the visions come on when I'm climbing the rigging or crossing the street, I suppose."

Or in a whale hunt, I think. He sounds so resigned to his fate. Again I wonder—he's one of the finfolk; why would they curse him with no chance to free himself? "There must be something you can do. Won't you appeal to the finfolk when we go to Drekja?"

An even longer pause. "It would feel wrong," he says, voice heavy. "I'm the only human who knows what's going to happen. I can see what's coming, I can try to warn people. It feels wrong to cast that off just so I can sleep better at night." He shakes his head slightly, as if shaking off the melancholy.

He turns to go into his cabin, but I blurt out, "Something else too."

"What?" His hand rests on the door frame. He doesn't sound angry so much as exhausted.

I glance over my shoulder to make sure we're alone, then push the words out before I can think better of them. "I've been thinking about . . . the hold."

I don't say *the finfolk prisoner*, but I know Silas knows what I mean. He's just been standing and listening, but now somehow goes even more still.

"We'll reach Nunaqvik soon," I rush, keeping my voice low. "August says we'll stay ashore two nights. We should break the finman out while the *Heralder* is harbored."

Silas's breath catches. Then he opens the door to his cabin. Hurt balloons in my chest, thinking he's going to fully ignore what I just said—but instead he stands back, holding the door for me. "You'd better come in."

It's not until the door has closed behind us both that it registers that his cabin is tiny, small enough that I could reach out my arms and touch both walls with my fingertips. A narrow bunk runs along the opposite wall; there's a writing desk that's more of a writing surface, a stool, and a washbasin. A blanket is crumpled and hangs half off the bed. Silas gestures for me to take the stool, but realizing that that would put me roughly eye level with his chest, I lean against the desk instead.

"Ezra told me you hadn't known what was down there." He sits down on the bunk and quickly pushes the blanket to the back corner, out of sight. Almost like he's self-conscious. "But I wasn't sure. I thought a Fairfax would do anything for her trade."

I tense and correct the tack of my thoughts. He's not self-conscious; he hates everything I stand for and is helping me only out of absolute necessity. Probably counting down the seconds until I leave. "I swear to you I didn't know about this. I . . ."

I was going to say *I would have never allowed it*, but something makes the words stick in my throat. I don't know if that's true. If August or even Mance had approached me about the prisoner—spun some good reason for it, something that would help the company—what would I have done?

This conversation is already offtrack. I clear my throat and try not to think about how close Silas is, close enough for me to smell salt water, sweat, petrichor. "Right. The harbor in Nunaqvik. The ship will be empty, or near enough. And Mance won't know it was us who freed the finman; we'll have plausible deniability at least. And," I add, "we can get your whole crew in on it. Then everyone will get a chance to do a favor for the finfolk." *Including me. Including you, apparently.*

Silas considers this, one hand tightening on the pendant he still holds as if his thoughts echo mine. "It's practical," he says finally, with a faint smile. "I like it. But we could still be caught."

"Then I'll tell Mance it was my idea and I ordered you all to help me," I say, heated. "What could Mance do? He has no right to be running dangerous experiments on a company ship."

Silas holds my gaze. "Do you really think it's Mance behind this?"

My breath catches, and I'm trying to form a response when Silas shakes his head suddenly.

"Never mind," he says, his eyes cutting away to the porthole window. "Have you considered that if we succeed, it will take us longer to reach Drekja?"

I'm relieved to move the topic away from August. "I've made it six years," I say. "I can handle a few more weeks."

Probably.

Chapter 15

We make landfall in Nulusk at midmorning three days after recovering the whale carcass. The terrain is more vertical and rugged than Abbonheim. Instead of the wide, sweeping shoreline of home, here land and sea tangle together in a maze of peninsulas, small islands, and inlets ringed by low brown cliffs that drop directly into the sea. As if the gods have carved up the land with a crooked knife. Yet the waters are deep, and Mance steers the *Heralder* between the flanks of land with ease until the city of Nunaqvik appears before us.

"Wow," I hear Kit breathe next to me at the railing.

"It's pretty." Lydia, on my other side, snatches the spyglass from me to examine the shore. "Why don't we paint houses like this in Kirkrell?"

Washed in the bright, pale sun, the landscape is gray and brown even in spring, with only a few scrubby trees to speak of, but the buildings are painted vivid reds and blues beneath mossy roofs—many of the houses being carved partly out of the sloping earth, with doors and windows facing the sea. Thin streams of smoke issue from chimneys. It's much smaller than Kirkrell—if this place was in Abbonheim, I'd call it a town rather than a city. Yet here, in a landscape so harsh, there's something triumphant about the collection of buildings and people and society. So that you can't call it anything but a city.

Though it makes no difference at all, I find myself rising on my toes to get a little closer. The last few days on the ship have felt like sitting in an open trap, waiting for it to snap shut. I couldn't stop thinking about the finfolk prisoner belowdecks, and the whole ship stank of burning whale blubber as the crew performed the cutting-in—processing what was left of the Livyatan carcass. Now I feel a bubble of joy expanding in my chest. It's childish, maybe, to feel joy when the danger hasn't dissipated in the slightest. But still, to see another shore makes me feel lighter. I have never seen another country before.

Something glitters on the cliffsides beneath the city, casting sparkling reflections over the *Heralder*'s sails. I shade my eyes and squint over the railing, trying to see what it is that shines so. Minerals in the stone? No; whatever it is moves with the wind. I ask for a turn with the spyglass and adjust the aperture until the cliffsides come into focus.

Silver. The cliffs are fairly covered with bits of silver, hammered into medallion shapes, hanging from scraps of leather cord so they shift and catch the wind and the sun. "What are they for?" I ask Kit, handing the glass over to him to have a look.

Kit peers out through the spyglass, screwing his other eye shut, then answers readily, eager to share a tidbit of knowledge from his books. "It's for the finfolk, so if they come up on shore, they'll find the silver and leave before they get to the houses."

His voice is chipper. Even here at sea, the finfolk are only a theoretical to him, creatures of ink and paper. He scarcely remembers Mama's and Papa's deaths. I think again of the being in the secret hold and suppress a shudder, good mood momentarily punctured by the reminder of what we must do later.

The *Heralder* is the biggest ship in the harbor by far, but the other vessels bear flags from all over the world, snapping proudly in the chill breeze. Smaller rowboats and fishing boats dart between them and the docks. We drop anchor in the harbor where the water is deep, and I take the first rowboat to shore with August, Mance, and a few other *Heralder* men. As we approach, I can hear the silver pieces decorating the cliffs clinking softly in the breeze. The sound and the smell of the wharf—absent the scent of sooty, burned whale oil, but with the stink of old fish and waterlogged wooden docks—remind me powerfully of home.

A woman waits for us at the end of the dock, in her fifties, stout and strong with graying dark braids. She wears a long-sleeved wool dress and pearlescent bracelets and earrings, as well as a richly patterned red shawl draped around her shoulders. I rise to my feet, suddenly more nervous, because I recognize her from the shawl as Lady Kata. The head of this city.

No ship docks at Nunaqvik without her approval, and it's crucial that the Fairfax Whaling Company maintain friendly relations in order to keep resupplying here. Months ago, as August and I planned the voyage to Kielstraat, I commissioned the shawl from one of Kirkrell's finest weavers and had it sent to Kata as a gift, to show our appreciation.

I also wrote a letter before I knew I'd be joining the voyage, introducing myself and asking if she might meet with August on my behalf during the *Heralder*'s stop here, but this went unanswered.

Yet she steps up to the edge of the dock as our boat draws close, catching the rope Mance throws and winding it around a post to anchor us in place, with an ease suggesting she's used to handling boats. August goes to stand up, but I beat him to it and step to the front of the boat. She looks us over, dark eyes impassive.

"You must have had fair winds," she says in Abbonish, words inflected with a faint accent. "We did not expect you for another week."

That makes my stomach drop. "We have been fortunate," I say, looking up at her from the boat. "Thank you for allowing us to make port here, Lady Kata. I'm Susannah Fairfax, head of the Fairfax Whaling Company."

She nods—she knows who I am—and stands back to let us all clamber onto the dock. August goes first, then turns and offers his hand to me.

"Careful," he says softly, with a hint of the secret smile. "You're a sailor now; watch those sea legs."

I scoff quietly for his ears only as I put my gloved hand in his—a few weeks at sea does not a sailor make—but sure enough, when my feet are on the aged wood of the dock, I sway as the world seems to undulate beneath me. August pulls me close before setting me on my feet, and I can't help but stiffen. Thinking, even as his breath stirs my hair, of what secrets might be hiding behind those blue eyes.

Lady Kata's eyes stay on me as August introduces himself and Mance. She greets them politely, but then turns back to me. "Walk with me, Susannah?"

My heart rises into my throat as I nod. Lady Kata is doing what so few people back home do—actually treating me as the leader of the Fairfax Whaling Company. But that also means there's more pressure not to make any mistakes.

"I'll catch up with you at the inn," I murmur, detaching myself from August, and step forward. I can feel his eyes on my shoulders, but I don't look back.

I walk with Lady Kata down the dock and up wooden stairs onto a cobblestone path that stands a little above the rest of the wharf. With the lack of trees along Nulusk's coast, the Nunak tend to build with stone instead where possible, and the path under our feet is worn smooth with the passage of centuries. The silver decorating the cliffs casts bits of shimmer over the stone. Below us, people go haggle for fish or furs or baskets of vegetables; lean over overturned boats, sanding and painting the hulls; cook food and weave nets and mend sails. It's so much like home, only there's no smell of soot or burning oil on the air, no smokestacks from warehouses or factories; only small fires where people smoke fish or warm their hands.

"How shall I address you?" I ask Kata, keeping pace at her side, trying to make my walk stately.

"Just Kata is fine," she says, her tone cordial but reserved. "You look very like your father, you know."

A flush of pride suffuses me. "Really?" That's not something I've heard often. I've always thought I resembled Mama more, sharing her wheat-colored hair and brown eyes. She was beautiful, but I was always my father's creature, yearning for his acknowledgment and approval, which was harder won than my mother's.

"It's the way you stand and how you meet one's eye." She fingers the fringed end of the shawl. "Thank you for this gift. It is finely made."

"A token of our gratitude," I say, smiling. "Thank you for meeting me here. I appreciate your taking the time to speak to me." Even if I didn't expect it.

People in Abbonheim speak with scorn about how the Nunak treat with the finfolk, taking a strategy of appeasement rather than aggression—like these offerings on the cliffs, how they eschew iron, and of course the fact they don't hunt whales in the same way we do. They kill Livyati only, Papa taught me, when there is a great need.

But I never understood that. The need for whale magic at home is endless. People are always cold, always sick, always hungry. Is the same not true here? When is there *not* great need?

Kata's eyes drift out over the harbor toward the ship, where I can see the small figures of the rest of the crew taking turns rowing to the shore. I think it's Silas rowing, his dark curls and lean shoulders bowed over the oar, movements rhythmic and strong.

"The *Heralder*," Kata says contemplatively. "Why have you named it so? What does it herald?"

I force my attention back to her. I didn't in fact name the *Heralder*—August did—but it matters little. "I hope an era of prosperity for the people we serve. And continued peace between our nations."

"You wrote to me about your ship's mission," she says, her face and voice carefully neutral. "A new whaling town in the far north."

"Yes."

Of course, Kata likely doesn't approve of the Kielstraat plan. Most Nunak look with judgment upon our kind of whaling, just as we're suspicious of them for their dealings with the finfolk, though diplomacy prevents either country from outright opposition.

"Back home in Kirkrell, our needs are growing," I go on when the stretching silence starts to feel too long. "We must find new hunting grounds if we are to sustain them."

"I don't wish to relitigate here the discussions I have had with your father," Lady Kata says, and I dearly wish I could ask Papa what those discussions entailed. Her voice isn't harsh, but serious, and I can tell that each word is carefully chosen. "But for the good of your people, I urge you to take a hard look at the difference between your people's needs and their wants." Her eyes move from the *Heralder* to me. "Or indeed, between the people's wants and those of the Fairfax Whaling Company, and finally between the company's wants and your own."

Discomfort pricks at me. I shift my gaze from the sea to the city, sloping up above us. It's sleepier than the wharf. The roads appear too rough for horses and carriages; people walk and lead donkeys here and there. Children play in the streets and dart between the small, low-slung buildings. "How do your people survive winters here without whale magic?" I ask Kata.

"It's a lean time," she says, "to be sure. But we gather together; we don't leave anyone out in the cold or let them go hungry. It's when people get lost, when they venture farther than they ought in the wilderness, that things become dangerous." She casts a meaningful glance at the *Heralder*.

"You think we're venturing farther than we ought." I keep my voice neutral to mimic hers. I want to know what she thinks, this leader who chose to speak to me over August. Months ago, working with August to plan the journey of the *Heralder*, I believed in its mission just as much as he did. But my faith has been fractured again and again.

"Even our finest oarsmen do not venture into the northernmost waters of the Sidhae for the hunt," Kata says. "Just as you and I desire a safe home to retreat to at the end of the day, shielded against the dangers of the world, so too do the Livyati and the Folk. Breach that sanctuary and they will lash out."

"We've taken measures against that," I say, echoing the familiar talking points. "Iron reinforcing our ship, weapons for the crew."

That's not the point. Kata knows it and I know it. But she lets me finish speaking. "Just so," she replies at length. "I know that the Fairfaxes of Kirkrell will do as they see fit. I am not trying to dissuade you from your path. But as our peoples are friends, I warn you as a friend that things may not go as you expect."

My stomach clenches. "Can we continue to count on your friendship?" Commercial relations with Nulusk have not been at the top of my mind with everything else happening. But they're still something I must attend to in case I survive this voyage.

"The people of Nulusk are not against you," Kata says, bestowing a smile on me that though faint feels warm and real. But then it slips away. "But we will not cross the finfolk. We have survived this long only by respecting the Folk and the deities of the sea. If they require it of us, we'll have no choice but to close our ports to Fairfax Company whalers."

A shiver runs beneath my skin as I'm struck by how her words comport with Silas's warnings. *War with the finfolk.* "I understand." If such a war were to come to pass, closed Nunak ports would be the least of our concerns.

"What do you call your sea gods?" Kata asks. "Your warring lord and lady of the waves?"

"Oh—" They're not really my gods, but I know to whom she refers. The sea gods from Mama's stories, the ones Kit likes reading about. "Thala and Haelgrim, that's what we call them in Abbonish."

"Then," she says, too seriously for my liking, "may Thala and Haelgrim look kindly upon you."

This far north, the changing season seems to wage a daily battle with the unending cold. It was only chilly when we arrived this afternoon, the ice and snow still on the ground but melting in the springtime sun.

But the sun finally set, and now it's eleven bells and hard to forget we're most of the way to the arctic when every time the tavern door opens, a gust of cold wind whips through. Maybe that's why everyone seems so eager to get drunk, to keep warm.

I'm nursing a tankard of berry cider as slow as I can, leather gloves shielding my hands from the cold glass, sitting at a table with my siblings and the *Whistler* crew while keeping one eye on the table across the room. There, Mance sits surrounded by a coterie of *Heralder* men. August went to bed half an hour ago. All I have to do is outlast Mance and the *Heralder* crew, and then Lydia and the *Whistler* crew and I can sneak out to the docks and onto the *Heralder* to free the prisoner.

I'm only half paying attention to the conversation at this table until I realize that the *Whistler* crew seems to have invited my brother along with them for some unspecified future voyage.

"What are you good at?" Silas asks my brother seriously, like he's interviewing a new sailor at the countinghouse.

Kit, with a mug of hot chocolate leaving a brown mustache on his upper lip, beams at the question. "Lots of things. Reading, and arithmetic, and jacks, and singing, and recitation . . ." He trails off and ducks his head, apparently out of ideas.

"Those are all important skills," Silas says gravely. "Especially singing. It gets morose on the *Whistler* sometimes. We could use someone to lead us in shanties and keep our spirits high. What songs do you know?"

I meet Lydia's eyes and fight down a cough as she smirks, both of us knowing that Kit's favorite songs, inexplicably, are the slow, solemn, and stern hymns from church, the ones meant to remind us of our sinful nature and the brevity of this life.

Sure enough—"'Pity the Afflicted, for Thou Too Are Mortal,'" my brother ventures.

Silas blinks. "A good song, but whalers don't have to be reminded that we're mortal. Do you know anything more . . . optimistic?"

Kit thinks about it for a moment. "'Our Joy Lies Beyond the Grave'?"

Silas blinks. "Great." He looks at Teuila to my right. "Your job is to teach him more songs. Nothing bawdy."

"What does *bawdy* mean?" Kit asks keenly, eager for Silas's approval.

Silas coughs, a sound suspiciously like a suppressed snort, and turns to Lydia. "What about you? Do you dream of sailing?"

Lydia looks up. When she first learned Silas was finfolk, she was angry. *When Papa said we'd have to do hard things, I don't think he meant allying with our oldest enemy.*

But she was still angrier when I told her about the prisoner in the hold. It seems I'm not the only one whose sympathies are shifting.

She looks at the others, and then her gaze lands on me. "Maybe," she says contemplatively. "The sea life is growing on me. Though the food leaves something to be desired."

"You'd like the *Whistler* better then," Teuila assures her. "Our cook, Hector, can make even stew and hardtack taste good—"

The conversation dies out as across the room, a bench scrapes back, and Mance excuses himself from his table to a chorus of drunken cheers. "Bright and early tomorrow, boys," he drawls to them with a wink. "Don't get in too much trouble."

My heart beats fast and I meet Lydia's eye. *Time to go.*

She nods slightly and feigns a yawn. "Well, we three better be off to bed." She reaches behind her for her bag.

I lean down to whisper in Kit's ear. "Remember your job?"

His eyes go serious and he nods. "Stay awake and if anyone knocks on our door asking for you, say you're asleep."

"Good man." I give him a brief side hug, then look to Silas for a moment, a silent understanding passing between us before I excuse myself and leave the barroom with my siblings. We walk together toward the back stairs, but only Kit goes up to the room; Lydia and I steal instead out the back door to the street.

The wind tugs at my clothes as Lydia and I walk from the inn, wrapped in hoods and scarves both to keep warm and to hide our faces. The streets here are narrower than in Kirkrell, windier, but cleaner. Not a city built for horses and carts and carriages; people walk—sailors of all stripes and shades, merchants selling fish or warm clothes—even at this time of night. The crowd lets us blend in, and Lydia and I walk without speaking. I'm guessing her mind, like mine, is on the ship and the prisoner. Silas, Ezra, and Josephine will be following a few minutes behind us.

The docks, unlike the streets, are dark and quiet and mostly empty. The harbor is maybe half the size of Kirkrell's; small ice floes drift through the water, white ghosts in the dark ocean. Silas, Ezra, and Josephine catch up with us there and we stand silently in the shelter of some fisherman's shed, taking in the vista. Even in the dark it's not hard to distinguish the *Heralder*; it's the biggest ship in the harbor by far.

Nor is it deserted. Of course we knew it wouldn't be—Mance would never leave the jewel of his fleet unattended. Two of the *Heralder* men have stayed behind and are on watch on deck; I can see their small figures on the platform, lit by the lantern they've hung on the mainmast.

But we planned for this. Ezra and Josephine split off and walk south, while Silas, Lydia, and I locate the small rowboat that Zimri arranged for us earlier, tucked unassumingly behind a pile of old broken boats and boat parts, its rust and dirt hiding its seaworthiness.

In a moment of uncharacteristic chivalry, Silas wades to his shins in the freezing water, holding the boat steady so Lydia and I can climb in, then pushing it off and jumping in after us. Lydia in front, then me in the middle, then Silas. We don't have a lantern; the only light comes from the thin sliver of a crescent moon half hidden by clouds, plus the lanterns that glow from most of the ship decks. It's eerie to be drifting in the dark with the bulks of ships all around us. They groan and sigh like giant sleeping animals we have to tiptoe around not to wake.

The boat has an oar tucked away at the bottom, but when I reach for it, Silas stops me with a touch to the shoulder. "No need," he whispers. Instead, he bends down, reaching to dip his hand in the water. I half turn in my seat to watch, fascinated and unnerved when I realize what he's doing. Weather magic, tide magic. Finfolk magic.

It's subtle; I don't think Lydia even notices from up front, her head on a swivel to make sure we stay unobserved. It's just the faint smell of petrichor and electricity on the breeze, and I feel the tide respond underneath us, gently and silently carrying us where we need to go. We skirt the edge of the harbor, passing in and out of shadows cast by the ships, and approach the *Heralder* from the port side, the prow looming over us.

As we glide closer, Silas speaks quietly. "I told Ezra and Josephine this earlier, but if anything goes wrong—if we're caught—you two should hide if you can, or say it was my idea. I found the prisoner, I tricked you into coming here."

Lydia scoffs. "Why would we do that? You don't have to be here. You're the one helping us."

"Helping me," I correct. Freeing the prisoner is my task, my favor to the finfolk.

Lydia shoots me an irritated look and repeats, "Helping us."

My heart thaws out a little to hear her refer to us like that, as a unit. A team. Even if she says it with a glare.

"I appreciate that, but it just makes sense." Silas speaks low and fast. Beyond him, out in the harbor just past the ends of the ships, a light winks into existence—a flame rising seemingly out of nothing. "August knows I'm finfolk. Probably Mance too. As far as they know, I'm the only one on the *Heralder* with any reason to help one of the fae."

Another flame joins the first, and this one burns bright green. They must be burning driftwood. Even though I know it's just Ezra and Josephine's handiwork—stacking kindling in old leaky boats, shoving them off and striking a match—it still sends a chill down my spine.

"And you two have access to information," Silas goes on. "You can find out what their game is even if everyone's keeping an eye on me. But if the *Heralder* men link you to the missing prisoner, they'll go further to hide what they're doing."

"They're already hiding it," I point out.

"Case in point, we're out here in the dead of night freezing our asses off," Lydia mutters.

Silas meets my eyes. "They can always do worse."

More flames spring up in the harbor, and finally someone notices. I hear a shout from above, and footsteps as the two *Heralder* men keeping watch run to the stern. Similar shouts rise up from watchmen around the harbor. As Silas rises to standing, a repurposed whaling hook in his dripping hands, I look past him at the lights.

Several columns of flame in different colors dance on the water's surface, red and orange but also blue and green and white. Their hiss and crackle echo over the water. The watchmen's confused shouts mask the thud as Silas lands an expert throw over the side of the ship, the hook—meant to fasten itself in a Livyatan's hide and hold the creature fast—serving just as well as a grappling hook on the railing. Silas pulls himself up, the boat rocking gently as his weight vanishes from it, and a moment later the rope ladder drops for us. I catch it before it can clatter against the *Heralder*'s hull, heart in my throat.

Lydia climbs up, then me. It was her idea to wrap the tools at our belts—each of us carries a cooper's wrench, a crowbar, and a knife—in cloth so they don't clink together.

The deck is empty; no one wanted to waste an opportunity to go ashore. The watchmen at the far end are oblivious to us as we steal our way to the staircase leading belowdecks and creep carefully down, wary of the creaky floorboards, Silas ducking down so he doesn't hit his head on the low ceiling. At the bottom, he pauses and lights a match, looking out for any movement on the middle deck, before flashing a thumbs-up at us. We go through the hallway toward the blubber room, but immediately I see what Lydia and Silas didn't.

A light on in August's cabin. I thought he was in bed at the inn, but a thin line of light glows beneath his closed door.

Silas and Lydia are both past the hall and into the blubber room; it would do no good to say something out loud. I make myself keep moving past my fiancé's door as Silas disappears down the second staircase into the hold, then Lydia. I'm almost there too when the door creaks open and his voice floats out, soft and surprised.

"Annie?"

I freeze just as I'm about to step down the first stair, time slowing down to a molasses crawl. Below me on the staircase, Lydia freezes too, her frightened face turning up to mine, a pale oval floating in the pitch-darkness of the hold.

Behind me, I hear August walk toward me. "What are you doing?" His voice is conversational, surprised, not angry.

I don't think he saw Lydia or Silas pass by. But if I speak to her, if I gesture to her, he'll know they're there. If I run down to the hold and hide, August will come looking and find all three of us.

My mind spins, a new plan taking shape like clay on a wheel. They don't need me to free the prisoner. Lydia has her wrench and crowbar and knife; Silas has magic. He can get Lydia back to the inn if they escape notice. I know he'll keep her safe.

And I have tools too. Not ones I ever wanted to use like this. But tools perfectly suited to keeping August Hargreave's attention on me.

All these thoughts whirl through my mind in the space of an instant, before I turn to August and smile.

August is backlit against the warm yellow glow coming from his cabin, so I can only see the outline of him. Not his expression, not his eyes.

"Looking for you," I say, my voice coming out tinny, too bright. "You weren't in your room at the inn."

"Then what are you doing going into the hold?" His voice is almost gentle, with a trace of laughter flickering along its edges. Like a flame held to paper, the long second before it all goes up.

My face burns and my mouth is dry as I snatch my hand off the railing. "I'm not. Just pacing."

I can't stop myself from looking down the stairs just once more—and my stomach drops to see that Silas now stands beside Lydia, both of them staring up at me. Even at this distance, even though he stands in darkness, I can see the tension in him, his clenched fists, flat mouth, burning black eyes.

I blink and try to communicate everything I need with my eyes alone. *Keep going. I'll manage.*

Then I move toward August, feeling as though I've lost every memory of ever walking before in my life. I don't know how to move my limbs in a natural way. What they're meant to feel like.

"Will you come in?" He stands aside, waiting for me to pass before following me into his room. The rest of the ship is silent.

Please let Lydia and Silas succeed, I think faintly as I turn into August's cabin. *Please let them make it out unnoticed. Please let the finfolk still see fit to count this as a favor, even if I don't release the prisoner with my own hands.*

The moment the door closes, August is on me, spinning me gently around with hands on my shoulders and pinning me against the door. My breath catches and my muscles stiffen in shock as he leans his body against mine, pressing me into place.

It's a familiar move, and despite everything it starts the familiar trickles of heat through my insides. He likes to do this, kiss me against closed doors. Only he isn't kissing me now. His blue, blue eyes search my face, close enough I can feel his breath on my parted lips. His hands roam, tracing my jaw, my throat, my sides, fingertips questing at my waist like he's searching for a button to unsnap.

I only realize what he's after when my belt latch clicks free and it comes away in his hands—the belt, and all the tools on it.

He steps back slightly so we can both see them, the cloth wrappings doing little to disguise their purpose. He tilts his head, letting the silence stretch, waiting for an explanation.

I take a slow breath. I have to be very careful. August knows me—maybe not as well as I once thought, but he knows me. And I've always been a poor liar.

"I found the finfolk down there," I say. "The prisoner."

August doesn't blink. "When?"

"After we killed the dolphin." I pitch my voice as a whisper, knowing that otherwise it will shake. "I heard something in the walls."

"Why did you come here tonight?" His voice is soft as silk. "Did you mean to let the prisoner go free?" When I stay silent, he laughs softly and flattens a hand on my chest, fingers spread wide. "That tender heart."

"August." I don't breathe. But I can't stop my heart, and I know he can feel it, how it flings itself into my ribs like a wild bird caught. "Why is he here?" I know the answer Ezra relayed to me—ensuring good sailing weather—but I want to hear August say it, I want to understand.

He drops his hand and steps backward, setting the tools carelessly on a side table and sitting on the bed, leaving space for me. "To give us fair skies," he says simply.

A hollow, numb kind of shock sinks in. So it really is that simple.

He hasn't pulled me with him to the bed or even asked me to join him. He just watches me steadily, waiting to see what I'll do.

I could leave, but to what end? August might go to the hold and find Silas and Lydia. And I do want to know the truth about the prisoner. Silas's words from earlier echo in my head.

You have access to information. You can find out what their game is.

The more brave I appear, the safer I will be, and the more I will learn.

I go and sit next to August, the thin mattress dipping under my weight. He turns his head and presses his face into my hair, breathes in, like I'm what gives him strength.

"I was thinking about the *Volyar*," he says, hushed, slipping an arm behind my back to wrap around my waist. "About all the ships and all the lives that have been lost to the finfolks' storms. Come here."

He tugs at my waist, and understanding what he wants, I shift so I'm sitting between his legs, my back against his chest. As he wraps his arms around me and rests his chin on my shoulder, I can feel my heart start to slow, the fear that had been skittering through my blood metabolizing into a different kind of energy. I let my body go soft, allowing myself to lean against him. He must have a reason for all this. Maybe if I just hear him out . . .

"What a wonder, to be able to control the wind and the rain," he goes on. "And I thought—why not use that to our advantage?" Even though he's only murmuring quietly, his words start to take on the same thrilling expansiveness he gets in front of a crowd that has won over the shareholders and bewitched the merchants of Kirkrell. The tone of voice that makes you believe a straight, wide path to everything you ever wanted is laid out before you. That August knows the way, and that he can lead you there, and all you have to do is follow. "Nothing like what happened to us would ever happen again."

Still, my stomach turns, thinking of the smell of fresh blood in the hold. How is the finman convinced to call down the wind to fill our sails?

"It seems cruel," I whisper, internally bracing myself. "Keeping someone in the dark, keeping them bound in iron."

"Someone?" August echoes, a hint of surprised laughter in the word. "Annie, a finfolk isn't *someone*. And cruelty—cruelty is the finfolk killing our families. Cruelty is them cursing our sailors and blighting our city, sentencing you to death for the crime of loving your parents and grieving their loss." Conviction strengthens his voice as he traces my hands tenderly over my jacket cuffs. "This is hardly a drop in the sea of bloodshed they've unleashed on us. A feather on the scale."

The ache of missing my parents mixes into the tempest of emotions swirling in my chest. How I wish I could speak to Mama and Papa now. Maybe they could help me understand what is true, what is necessary, what is right. "Who else knows about this?" I ask, nervously plucking at the fingers of my leather gloves. "The crew?"

"Only Mance." August captures my hands between his own and peels the gloves off, left and then right. They fall discarded to the floor as he turns my palms up, tracing idle patterns from my fingers, across my palms, up my wrists. I was careless in my routine this morning. Scattered scales wink in the low light; my nails extend out past my fingertips, reddish-black and sharp. But August doesn't seem to care.

"This is only the first test," he says. "Imagine the yield, Annie, if every ship in the fleet could sail twice as fast as it does now. We'd never lose a whale again." His lips brush the shell of my ear, breath cascading hot down the side of my neck. "But I am sorry. I should have told you. You shouldn't have had to find out like that."

"And I'm sorry I didn't ask you about it sooner," I say between stuttering breaths of my own. I'm not sorry, but it feels like what I should say—what he expects me to say.

He turns my face up toward his with two fingers, kisses me softly at first. Then the kiss deepens; he catches my lower lip between his teeth and tugs gently, scattering the remnants of my thoughts.

Breaking away slightly, he murmurs, "You have nothing to apologize for." Another kiss, the tip of his tongue flickering over my lips. "It will take more than a little misunderstanding to frighten me from you, my love." He lifts me up to sit on his thigh, so he can kiss my neck. "I have to admit, though, I thought you'd be upset."

"I was at first," I say, twisting to get my arms around his shoulders. "But I understand. We need every advantage we can get." I hesitate. "But how did you capture . . . this one? How will you find more?"

"That's my girl. Every inch a Fairfax." I feel him smile open-mouthed against my throat, teeth grazing my skin. "I have some plans up my sleeve still."

"Flatterer," I say breathlessly. His hands are almost too tight against my waist, but I want them tighter. My own hands, resting carefully on his back, twitch with the desire to touch him like he's touching me, firm and decisive. But I can't. Not without hurting him or, at the very least, ruining his clothes.

"I'm not," he protests. "You're stronger than I ever knew, to have fought back the curse. Brave, to accompany me on this expedition." The tip of his tongue leaves a trail of embers down the side of my neck. "And clever to have found the prisoner. Even if you had to go behind my back to do it."

If there's the barest hint of threat in his words, I'm too far gone to register it the way I should. The awareness dances across my mind like a skipped stone and is gone as one hand slips under the hem of my shirt, fingers skimming the bare skin above my hip. I kiss him again, my muscles turning soft as his tongue dances with mine.

In the scene from the seashell, August said he would marry me at sea, then find a way to end my life. But none of that has happened so far. Maybe Silas misunderstood his words, or misremembered.

"I wish I could touch you," I whisper when we break off to breathe. I have one hand braced on August's back, the other cupping the back of his head carefully, so carefully. The scales on my skin glitter in the low light; I close my eyes so I don't have to see them. The words escape me, grieved and plaintive. "How can you want me like this?"

He doesn't know I'm looking for a cure. As far as he knows, this is all he'll ever have of me—heartbroken, beating back the tide of the curse, unable to put my hands on his skin for fear of breaking it.

The words float unbidden into my mind. *I'll drop to my knees, tell her I can't wait any longer. We'll marry at sea.*

"Touching you is pleasure enough." His voice is midnight dark, velvet dark, as he hauls me closer against him. "Keep your hands there. Let me take care of you." His hand climbs my ribs, seeking upward.

And then at some point, there will be a storm. There always is.

But his ragged breath in my ear, the hungry, greedy way his hands range over me—that doesn't seem like a lie. His fingertips are drawing circles over my skin, making me whimper and squirm against him, my head tipping back onto his shoulder as everything in me turns to water. It's impossible to think the sound he makes at that, satisfied and hungry all at once, is anything but sincere.

His body is tense beneath mine, his pulse raging. He closes his teeth almost too hard on the side of my throat, making me jolt in his arms, every movement stoking the fire higher and higher. His desire echoing mine. That has to mean something.

I am not the same blinkered, weak-willed girl I was in Kirkrell. Maybe August sees that in me, that this voyage has forged me into something better. He said I'm stronger than he knew. Maybe I've proved my worth to him.

Maybe, just for tonight, I can believe that.

Chapter 16

As much as I'd been looking forward to a real bed at the inn in Nunaqvik, I can't quite bring myself to regret where I ended up instead. Bright, cold light splashes into August's cabin through the porthole window, lent a glittering quality by the ice and snow blanketing the shore. August is still asleep, blanket bunched up around his waist, his face smooth and young-looking in sleep. It strikes up a strange ache in me. Like remembering something I lost long ago. It makes me want to avert my eyes.

When I go to retrieve my clothes, it's a shock when my bare feet touch the freezing floorboards. I dress quick as I can, shivering. The elation that clung to me upon first waking up ebbs quickly, to be replaced by worry as all the memories of last night trickle back in.

Drifting off next to August, tangled together on the too-narrow bunk. His arm around my waist, pulling me to him after he blew out the lamp. The mixture of contentment and low-simmering desire in my veins, marveling over what we had done and hoping—

more than I've hoped in weeks—that there might be opportunities to do more things on other nights soon.

I glance at myself in August's mirror—bright eyes, flushed cheeks—braid my hair quickly, then check my arms in the morning light. There are just a couple of stray new scales this morning, not enough to even bother plucking out. A sign of being happy, at peace.

But beneath the glow, I'm worried about Lydia and Josephine and Ezra and Silas, whether they made it out of the harbor and back to the inn. About the prisoner. About August and whether it was right to come to him like this.

Yes, I wanted him. I still do. But there's a queasy undertone mixed into how I feel when I glance back at his sleeping form in the bunk. Knowing that it's just as well most of me enjoyed last night, because I couldn't have walked away, not without consequences.

I find the bone pendant tangled up in my shirt, and when I lift it up to put it back around my neck, it glitters in the morning light. My breath catches with the memory of what I'm meant to do.

I find a letter opener on August's desk, prick my finger, and very carefully let one drop of blood fall onto the pendant, like I watched Josephine do early in the voyage. For a long moment nothing happens. Heart in my throat, I brace myself for the blood to slide uselessly off.

Then it sinks through the pendant's hard surface and remains, a bright, bold spot of ruby. I let out a breath as understanding sinks in. With the freeing of the finfolk prisoner, one of my favors is complete. I am one step closer to being healed.

But the thought is little comfort. Because there's no way to tell if it will be enough in the eyes of the finfolk. And that's if I even make it to Drekja at all.

Suddenly, there's a swell of voices from somewhere over my head, filtering indistinctly through the ceiling. I can't make out their words, but they sound angry. My stomach drops and I finish dressing as quickly as I can.

By the time my feet hit the deck, Nunaqvik is a small shape behind us. The main deck is crowded with most of the *Heralder* crew, clustered around something or someone near the forecastle.

"Our hold was broken into while in the harbor." Mance's gravelly voice rises over the noise, harsh and commanding. "Must have happened while we were ashore in Nunaqvik. Something of great value was stolen."

My stomach drops, and I take a deep breath as mutters rise from the crew all around. I knew, of course, that setting the prisoner free likely wouldn't go unnoticed forever. But there should be no way for Mance to know *who* did it, I reassure myself as I make my way across the deck.

Then for a minute the crowd shifts and my stomach drops as I see what everyone is looking at. Silas stands pinioned between two burly *Heralder* men, who grasp his upper arms. I don't make out his face before the crowd shifts and blocks my line of sight.

The *Whistler* crew, along with Kit and Lydia, are clustered by the starboard railing, bodies tense, and I rush to them. Josephine watches the proceedings at the forecastle with her brow furrowed with concern, and Ezra's face is dark with anger, whereas Lydia's is dead white.

"What happened?" I hiss as soon as I'm close enough not to be heard by anyone else. I turn to Lydia. "Did anyone see you last night?"

"We weren't caught." Lydia sounds distraught. "Silas and Ezra and Josephine and I all made it back to the inn. You were the one I was worried about." She turns wide eyes on me. "But one of the sailors says he saw Silas walking to the docks last night. Mance accused Silas of breaking into the hold."

"How can Mance prove it if no one saw you down there?" My mouth feels dry.

"He can't prove it." Ezra tugs at a nearby bit of rigging, knuckles white. "He's just guessing because of who Silas is."

"We already tried to speak to Mance on his account," Josephine adds, "but Silas is determined to take the fall. He's saying he did it." Her arms are crossed over her chest, brow furrowed with worry.

Staring into the shifting wall of bodies that blocks Silas from view, I feel sick, heart beating too fast. What now?

"Silas asked us to keep quiet," Lydia mutters beside me. "I don't remember the part where we agreed." Abruptly, she spins on her heel and starts to shove through the crowd, ignoring the men when they curse and glare at her. My heart jumps into my throat and I follow her as she stops in front of Mance and Silas.

Silas stands ramrod straight between the men holding him, his face blank, his eyes closed. Like he's somewhere else in his mind. He keeps them that way even with Mance looming over him. "Open your eyes, boy," Mance is hissing. "Look at me when I'm speaking to you."

"Captain!" Lydia's voice rings out.

Silence falls among the crew as Mance pivots to face us, an unpleasant smile spreading across his face. Silas, too, turns his face toward Lydia and me, eyes still closed. But his mouth presses flat, and he shakes his head slightly, his meaning clear. *Don't say anything.*

I stare at him, stomach churning as I remember what he said about Lydia and me having access to information. He was right—as evidenced by August telling me his plans last night, just because I asked. We have a better chance of learning more if Lydia and I remain guiltless. But it feels wrong in every cell of my body.

Lydia steps right up to Mance. "What evidence do you have to accuse one of your officers of theft?" Her voice is icy and harsh, authoritative. She's the one who's a Fairfax through and through.

But Mance laughs in her face. The smell of stale breath and old cigarette smoke hits me too as I come up next to her.

"The boy confessed to the theft," he says. "This isn't your concern, Ladies Fairfax. Why don't you retire for a spell and let me run my own ship?"

"This is a Fairfax Company ship," I say. Behind him, I see Silas flinch at the sound of my voice. My arms itch, my fingers twitch as adrenaline streams through me. "Everything that happens aboard is our concern. What is it you said was stolen?"

He won't want to let the whole crew know about the prisoner. Surely we can use that to our advantage somehow.

He sneers. "Finfolk relics. Bone carvings and curiosities."

Behind him, August appears at the front of the crowd, making my breath catch. His eyes rove over the scene, taking everything in, his expression faintly curious. I wait for him to come to us, but he stays where he is, outside the circle of attention burning around Mance and Lydia and Silas and me. I swallow and redirect my attention back to Mance.

"Why were such things locked up in the hold, Captain?" I hold his gaze, trying hard not to look at Silas. Why won't he open his eyes? "Surely we could use that space for food or supplies."

"A real sailor would know it's no waste of space to carry a good luck charm or two. That it's customary on jaunts like this." His lip curls. "An honest sailor would know better than to touch them, but this one's no honest sailor, is he? He's *something* else."

There's an upswing in the noise of the crowd behind us, discontented and accusatory mutters, as Mance rounds on Silas again. "Open your eyes!" he snarls, so close that his breath blows back Silas's hair. "Or are you afraid we'll see the treachery there?"

Chills break out over my skin and I step forward. "What you're referring to, that's nothing but a rumor, Mr. Mance. I would have thought you above such petty gossip." It's one thing for people to whisper about *the scavenger*, one thing for rumors to swirl. Another thing for the captain himself to bolster people's suspicions about Silas. My heart screams at me to step in front of him and shield him from all this hatred. But my feet won't obey.

"Rumors always come from somewhere, Lady Fairfax," Mance says with a sickly sweet smile, not turning from Silas. "One last time, boy. *Open your eyes.*"

I plant my feet. "You have no proof—"

"OPEN YOUR EYES!" Mance roars and backhands Silas across the face, knocking his head to the side. Shock hollows me out as Mance grabs Silas's jaw and wrenches his face back to forward.

Silas's eyes are open and they have gone white. No—not white, not one color at all, but every color swimming together. The war visions overtaking him, I remember. It looks like nothing so much as an oil spill, covering his eyes from corner to corner. Like greasy tears might be about to run down his cheeks. His jaw is clenched, blood dripping from a split lip.

"Unnatural," Mance spits, dropping his hand and shaking it like he touched something revolting. My pulse roars in my ears as the shock wave travels through the men, as they jostle one another to see better. I catch scattered bits of the shouts that float up.

"—never seen the like . . ."

"—all this time alongside us—"

"—ill fortune—"

Desperation rises. I turn to August, asking him with my eyes to please help me. He meets my gaze and steps forward, to my relief. He has power over these men; they listen to him. If anyone can dissipate the ugly tension that's heavy in the air, he can.

But he brushes past me without meeting my gaze and whispers something in Mance's ear. Something that makes Mance's eyes glitter with malice.

"Fetch the tails from the galley," the captain instructs a nearby sailor, then calls over my shoulder to the men holding Silas. "Take his shirt off."

Nausea climbs up my throat as jeers rise from the crowd. Lydia is saying something, clutching my arm, but I can't make sense of her words. August steps back, face grave. What did he tell Mance?

Cloth tears. Something skitters to my feet. Silas's bone pendant with a broken cord, the one I saw the day we found the whale carcass, the one he carries even with no hopes of his curse being lifted—of ridding himself of the visions of war.

Like before, the pendant is still blank white, none of his favors to the finfolk complete.

When I look up again, Mance's order has been accomplished. Silas, eyes still blotted out by those strange slick colors, stands stripped to the waist, bloody teeth bared. Muscles rigid with suppressed fury shift beneath pale skin. And there's the cross scar, visible to everyone.

The reaction ripples through the crowd, a violent wave, angry shouts rising in every direction.

Everyone in Kirkrell grew up hearing the same stories, passed down from our parents and their parents before them. We all go to church at Seaman's Bethel and gaze up at the same stained glass windows. Everyone remembers Ivar Kirkrell, the son of a fisherman and a finwife, branded with a cross so that his mother couldn't take him back to the sea. To them, this is confirmation.

"*Finfolk*," someone shouts, the word echoing through the crew. Their faces seem to merge together in my vision, becoming one many-headed beast, seething and hungry. A gesture from Mance, and the men holding Silas haul him toward the mainmast.

He helped me free the prisoner, complete a favor of my own, and he's going to be whipped for it.

I can't let this happen.

The words rise up in my throat. "I did it." But it comes out a whisper. No one hears but Lydia, who shoots me a frantic glare. I draw breath, readying myself to shout.

"I did it!" Lydia yells, loud enough for every nearby face to turn our way. "I broke into the hold."

I seize her arm. "*Don't*," I hiss. "Let me."

But her face is pure defiance. "No," she retorts under her breath, so only I hear. "They'll see your curse and that can't happen. Besides, August was with you last night, he knows it wasn't—" She bites off her words as August himself approaches, frowning, Mance a few steps behind him, gesturing for the crew to stay back.

"Is this true?" August asks my sister and me, quietly.

"Yes," Lydia says calmly at the same time as I exclaim, "No. It was me."

Mance brays out a laugh. "So one of you children got past my watchmen and took it upon yourself to unleash—" He seems to catch himself and bites off his words. "My stateroom, now."

August wordlessly accompanies us to Mance's cabin. He was with me all night; he knows it can't have been me who freed the prisoner. But he did find me at the entrance to the hold, carrying the tools to break a chain.

I realize what I have to do and drop my hand to Lydia's,

squeezing it, silently apologizing and begging her to follow my lead. Straighten my spine and lift my chin, faking confidence.

"My sister is fifteen and can be hotheaded," I say to Mance and August, holding their gazes. "She and I came across the finman in the hold, and when we docked in Nunaqvik she decided to free him. When I realized, I went to the *Heralder* to stop her, but she had already released the prisoner. Mr. Price had nothing to do with it."

Across the room, August tilts his head, blue eyes glinting in the way that means calculations are happening behind them. I'm changing my story; last night I told him I came to the *Heralder* alone. But let him think I was covering for Lydia then.

Lydia squeezes my hand back, even though her eyes are scared. I take a deep breath, trying to channel the strength and authority of Mama and Papa and all the Fairfaxes before me.

"She was wrong to do it," I go on, "but I would remind you, Mr. Mance, Mr. Hargreave"—I cut my eyes to August—"that all of you are in my family's employ. Let this pass and I may choose to overlook that you were running a dangerous experiment on a company ship without my knowledge. Lay a hand on my sister, and I'll see to it that not a man on this ship ever works in Kirkrell again."

Chapter 17

In the end, absent any proof, Mance has no choice but to accept my sister's confession. He can't put the whip to a Fairfax, so instead he orders her to take deck-swabbing duties for a week. Nor does he flog Silas but orders him to be locked in the brig, claiming it's for his own protection now that the men know what he is.

I can't object—Mance might be despicable, but I don't think he's wrong in this instance. Not with the venomous looks that follow Silas as he's led belowdecks. Soon after, Ezra slips away too, and I suspect he will be serving as self-appointed guard outside the brig.

All the while, I have Silas's bone pendant in my pocket. Its blankness still makes no sense. How is it that my paltry attempt at a favor was acceptable, but never anything he's done?

Days pass, the *Heralder* men giving me and my sister a wide berth. They think Lydia stole artifacts from the hold and used her status as a Fairfax to weasel out of a punishment. It's not ideal. My skin itches with the growth of new scales, pushed up by anger and fear; I can feel them snagging the inside of my gloves. Ezra and Zimri take turns keeping watch in the hold, and Teuila and Josephine look after Kit, allowing Lydia and I to stay away. The distance from our brother hurts, but I don't want the suspicion now cast on me and Lydia to fall on him too.

One morning, we can see the shoreline of Solheim to the northeast through a spyglass—dark, low, jagged hills crowned in snow—and soon they disappear in a cloak of fog. Mance announces that if the wind holds, we should make landfall at Kielstraat in another day or two.

I hand August back his spyglass with a bitter taste in my mouth. We've barely spoken since the other day's commotion. I can't get the image out of my head, August bending to speak in Mance's ear. I think he knew about Silas's cross scar. I think he told Mance about it. It was only after he whispered something to Mance that the captain ordered Silas be whipped.

August wanted everyone to know Silas is finfolk.

At around three bells, a cry from the crow's nest. "There she blows!"

My breath stops. I look up—everyone looks up. Up in the mast, the sailor points excitedly past the *Heralder*'s prow. "A spout!" His call sounds tinny from so far away. "A spout to the northwest!"

There's a general stampede to the railing, all the sailors trying to catch a glimpse, but I hang back. Catch August's arm as he passes by. "Tell Mance to let Silas out," I say.

August looks down at me, eyes glittering. Excitement for the hunt? Questions about me? I can't tell. I used to be able to read his face so well. Or I thought I could.

"Why?" he asks at length, plucking my hand from his arm and holding it between us. He's donned gloves now too, against the cold. But even through two layers of wool his fingers cinch tight around mine, almost too tight.

"He's a fine whaler, you said so yourself." My heart beats fast as I stare at my fiancé, as the crew streams around us to get a look at the whale. "He's done nothing wrong, and it's been days. Let him prove his loyalty."

"I thought you hated him." August's tone is conversational, but he shifts so that he's between me and the crew, blocking everyone else from view. His eyes have gone cold. "What is he to you, Annie?"

As his other hand tilts my chin up, I try not to swallow, to blink, to give anything away. "A friend." Part of me wants to downplay it even more than that, say *A subordinate*, say *Nothing at all.* But that's not true, and I can be braver than that. I have to be.

The last few days have shaken my faith in August. Still, my stubborn, cracked-open heart clings to his tender words from the night we shared. *Brave. Clever. Stronger than I ever knew.* Maybe he spoke to Silas about getting rid of me, but never meant it at all.

If I'm right about August, if he does love me, I can tell him the truth. Because if my plan somehow works, I'll have to tell him how and why I'm not heartbroken any longer. It's past time I start being honest with him. If only with small truths at first, to practice.

August's lips curl up, but no light touches his eyes. "A friend? You know what he is."

"And we know he's been in Kirkrell his whole life, just like us, and he's never hurt anyone. He hasn't betrayed us." I take a deep breath. "You said when we set out he could be useful. What did you mean?"

"As the captain said." August doesn't look at me as he speaks;

his eyes stay fixed on the horizon, on the promise of the spout. "It's no waste of space to carry a good luck charm. Or two."

It takes a moment to string together the implication in his words. Then my stomach drops. "You wouldn't do that."

"Lucky thing the wind returned, so we didn't have to, not today." August pulls me against him, rotating me so my back is to his chest, and speaks in my ear. "But this business is full of hard choices, Annie. You know that."

I push out of his arms and whirl around as August blinks in mild surprise. "He's as much human as he is finfolk," I hiss.

"How very enlightened of you." August steps back from me, that mirthless smile still pasted on, and retrieves a key ring from his coat pocket. He detaches a key—old, iron—and flips it to me. "Go fetch him then. But hurry. You won't want to miss this."

I'd never had occasion to visit the brig before—a cell meant to hold drunk or mutinous sailors. It's down in the hold, squeezed into the rear corner of the hull, a tiny room with a tinier barred window set into the door around knee level, maybe to pass food through.

Ezra lurks outside the door. He and Zimri have been trading off shifts down here ever since they locked Silas up; I've seen them sneaking away down the stairs. Ezra has his hands shoved in his coat pockets against the chill of the hold—and I wonder if he doesn't have a weapon in there too. He tenses when I approach, but his shoulders slump again when he sees it's me.

I explain quickly, flashing the key. "The lookout saw a spout. They want us all in the boats."

"Our lucky day," he says flatly.

"Can I talk to him?"

Ezra gives me a tense nod and retreats above deck. I pad the rest of the way to the hold, dread dragging at my limbs. "Silas?" I whisper at the door, setting my lantern down.

It's freezing down here; we're below the water level, after all. The chill from the wall leaches through my coat and shirt and I try not to think about how nothing but a relatively thin wall of wood and metal separates us from the crush of the sea. About how cold Silas must be, inside.

A moment passes before the reply comes, terse and unhappy. "Annie. I told you to let me take the fall."

I try to mask my emotions with humor, the relief and regret swelling my throat. "Then you'd have landed on Willa's table, getting sewn up with a dirty needle. No one wants blood in their hardtack." Mance might not mind, actually, but that's beside the point.

"Instead I get to sit here in the dark thinking about how you spent the night with August to keep me safe." The coldness in Silas's voice takes me aback, deeper and darker than the chill in the air. "Lucky me."

The anger in his voice casts everything in a different light. One that makes my stomach twist with confusion. "That was days ago. It doesn't matter."

"It matters to me." His voice sounds rough, shredded. "You shouldn't have had to do it."

Does he think less of me for spending the night with August? I wouldn't have thought him that kind of person, judgmental, but maybe August isn't the only person I've read wrong. "It was to keep Lydia safe, not just you." I make my voice cold, a warning. "Besides, it's fine. It's nothing I haven't done before."

Not quite true, what I'm letting him think, but also none of his business. I'm rewarded with a long, tense silence.

"He wants you dead." Silas finally speaks, enunciates each

word. I can picture his storm-cloud eyes fixed on the back of the brig door. I imagine that if I put a hand to the door it would be hot to the touch.

"I don't believe that," I say softly, trying to decide if I believe the words as I say them. "Maybe he did once, but things are different now. He sees me now in—in a way he didn't before. He called me strong. Called me clever."

It sounds hollow down here in the dark. I clench my fists, and only then, when the key cuts into my palm through my gloves, remember why I came down here. I curse myself, fumble with the key, telling him as I do, "They spotted a whale up above. They want you in the boats."

When I get the door open he's standing directly on the other side. His crew has brought him some clothes, at least, but his hair is dull and lank, a bruise fading on his jaw. Yet his posture is alert, ready; his eyes on mine are fierce, pupils blown wide, before he brings a hand up to shield his eyes from the lamplight.

I open my mouth to say something about the whale, the hunt, but Silas cuts me off. "Is that how you want to live?" he asks from behind his hand, a current of some emotion I can't name raging just below the frozen surface of his voice. "Falling asleep every night knowing that only if you've sufficiently proven your strength and cleverness will you see another sunrise?"

He must think me such a fool for staying with August. And maybe I am. I know it's a possibility—just not one I'm ready to accept. Silas doesn't understand what August is to me. How he kept me from heartbreak all these years.

And I am not the same girl I was in Kirkrell, weak and avoidant and fragile. August sees that; I've shown him that I'm worthy. To let myself believe otherwise might shatter me. It would mean so many years wasted, so many lies swallowed.

I hand Silas's pendant back to him and he accepts it wordlessly. "Isn't all of life like that, if you think about it?" I say with false lightness. "Especially at sea."

He drops his hand, blinks down at me. "It doesn't have to be."

My chest feels tight, brittle. He's a mess, unwashed, locked up, jeered at by the crew. But the way he's looking at me, I feel like I'm the one who's broken.

I can't abide it. I turn my back. "Come on," I tell him. "They'll be waiting for us in the whaleboats."

We split up once out of the hold—Silas heads to his cabin to get his lance, while I continue above alone. The deck is a clamor as the *Heralder* crew shove past one another in an effort to be first into the boats. The bell clangs are overloud, stabbing my eardrums. Men haul at pulleys to extend the davits, which creak laboriously as they swing the whaleboats—laden with tubs of rope, buckets, oars, hatchets—out over the sea. Mance's shouted commands rise over the din. "Stow line tubs! Check the grapnel!"

Something beyond the prow catches my eye. The spout. Close enough now to see with the naked eye.

It hangs on the air for a fleeting second before dissipating on the wind. A slope of gray and shining flesh crests the water, just for a moment, before rolling back down.

Livyatan.

I am not the only one to have seen it. Shouts and a tangible feeling of queasy excitement fill the air, marked by the sharp smiles across the faces of most of the crew. Despite myself, I can feel it infect me too, a thrill beneath my skin, my senses sharpening with the instinct of the hunt. Maybe it's the heartbreak curse, the bloodthirstiness in me stirring to life. Or maybe I just really am a whaler, and the sense memory of it lives in my blood despite my lack of experience. Even at this distance, I swear I can see the vapor from the whale's plume glitter. I think I can smell its humid breath, warm and musty as it gusts from cave-sized lungs.

I halt by the mast as sailors rush by in every direction, their feet a fierce drumbeat on deck. Harpoons and lances pass from hand to hand, both old-fashioned straight weapons and the new harpoon guns, cruel tips shining under the sun. Most of the crew will strike out after the whale, with only ten or so sailors left back to man the *Heralder*—enough to send another boat if one of ours gets broken.

Kit and Lydia will be among these ten. My siblings stand by the port gunwale watching everything with wide eyes, Lydia's arm looped over Kit's chest protectively. They'll be waiting here on deck. Just like Mama and I were when the storm came that brought the *Volyar* down.

My eyes snag on the place down the deck where August stands watching one of the whaleboats being lowered—the boat he will lead with the men he chose as his crew. Despite the cold, he's left off his blue coat, his crisp white shirtsleeves rolled up and his hair blowing in the wind. He's striking as ever, but the sight of him leaves me cold.

"Come on then, crewmate." A low voice in my ear as Silas himself brushes past me, dressed again in his oilcloth jacket, Ezra on his other side. Silas's hair is combed back, face pale but determined. I follow, heart pounding, as he cuts a path toward one of the whaleboats being lowered over the side. The *Heralder* men draw out of his way when they see him.

Josephine, Teuila, and Zimri work the ropes to lower our whaleboat, while Kit and Lydia are at the gunwale, tugging at the knots to release the rope ladder. The sight of my siblings helping makes it sink in. This is really happening. The hunt is upon us.

I step up beside Kit and take his place at the ladder. "Go below-decks," I order him. "You need to stay out of the sailors' way."

It's harsher than I'd usually speak to him, and I can see his face go scrunched and hurt at my tone. Lydia casts me a reproachful look, but I don't care. I'm hyperaware of the swinging equipment and the ropes snapping taut all around us, the sharpened points of the harpoons and lances the sailors casually toss to one another. We haven't even shoved off yet and already the scene crawls with danger. I fix Kit with a hard look; he ducks his head and turns for the staircase.

The boat hits the water below, and Lydia and I hold the ladder steady as the *Whistler* crew vault over the gunwale one by one and climb down to the boat, quick as spiders. Ezra, Zimri, Teuila, Josephine. I catch Lydia's eye, pulling her attention away from Josephine's descending form. "Look after Kit," I say. "Don't let him see the kill."

Her mouth is pressed tight, her eyes glinting unhappily. But she nods. Then Silas appears, jerking his chin for me to precede him down the ladder.

I dearly wish I had practiced this more than the once, when we rowed out to retrieve the whale carcass a few weeks ago. The ladder feels less sturdy when I'm on it, the rope and wood straining under my weight. The wind—what was a stiff breeze on deck feels like a gale with each step down—snaps at my face, tugs at my limbs.

This time at least I manage to get myself in the boat without nearly going overboard. I drop into place next to Ezra, who hands me an oar. Teuila is in the front testing the point of her harpoon with the pad of her thumb, face serious. Zimri behind her. The sea is the color of iron broken up by white-capped waves, choppier than the last time we rowed out. August's boat glides past us. He stands in the stern with his hands around the steering oar as his men row.

His face is tipped up into the wind, eyes fixed on the line between sea and sky, on the whale, which seems very far away, a gray bump on the horizon breathing out mist. Then, like he feels my eyes on him, he looks over at me where I sit. His face breaks into his secret smile, the one he's always saved just for me, wide and unguarded. A glimmer of desire in his eyes.

But I can't return the smile. It leaves me feeling hollow as his boat slips past, then Mance's. The closeness we shared that night in his cabin seems like years ago.

"Eyes forward, Annie."

My face burns hot as I turn forward and Silas drops nimbly into the boat and takes up his own spot at the stern. His eyes, too, are fixed in the distance, on our quarry. The order comes low and cold. "Shove off."

It's eerie, how sudden and complete the shift is among the crew at those words. I knew most of them were whalers before joining Silas's crew, but suddenly there's none of the smiles and laughter I've become accustomed to. As we lurch away from the *Heralder*'s hull, Silas raises his voice just enough to be heard by the five of us. "You've trained for this. You know what to do. Participate just enough not to draw suspicion. Be good, but not too good. And look after yourselves above all else. Understood?"

A soft chorus of ayes all around. I mumble it too, feeling like an impostor. For all the barbs about scavengers from August and Mance and even me, Silas looks as much a captain as any of them, towering over us. The wind blowing his hair back from his face makes him look older, severe.

"It's okay if you don't feel ready," Ezra says quietly, surprising me. "No one's ever ready. Just row hard and stay out of the way of anything pointy. The ropes too; those can take your head off if you're in the way when they snap to."

His unexpected consideration doesn't quite ameliorate my fear. "Is that meant to be reassuring?" I whisper, trying to sound lighthearted despite the general mood of grim determination thickening the air.

"Apologies." Ezra's mouth twitches in a joyless smile. "I should have just said, *Don't screw this up*."

"I'll try my best," I say through gritted teeth. Sailing alongside the other boats as we are, I've left my gloves on, making it harder to keep a grip on the oar. When I lower it into the water, it feels like the waves are trying to tug it out of my hands.

I row, my mouth dry and my heart pounding. It's still unnerving to cut through the waves facing backward, straining at the oars without seeing where our efforts are taking us. The *Heralder* shrinks in my vision and a living Livyatan waits somewhere behind me, out of sight. In contrast to the cacophony on deck, now all three crews are silent, or at least as silent as possible—we can't stop the rhythmic smack of our oars hitting the water.

But the quiet only lasts until we get closer, and then I can hear the whale breathing—great wet sighs, gusts of hurricane wind accompanied by the hiss of vapor.

"Quickly now." Silas's voice cuts under the great creature's breath. "Catch up. If we can reach the whale and frighten it off before anyone lands a harpoon, so much the better."

Everyone's breath huffs out in rhythm. The *Heralder* looks like a toy ship, the kind Papa once built in bottles, and time passes strangely, fast and slow all at once. We're fighting the wind, and it's not long before my arms and back and legs all start to ache. But it's a faint ache, muted by the adrenaline coursing through me. Then—

A strange, deep clicking sound, muffled, traveling upward through very deep water. It gets into my bones, radiating through my body. It sounds somehow like it's coming from all around us. It makes me want to drop the oar and cover my ears, put my head between my knees,

Fear grips me. Suddenly it seems the worst kind of hubris to be out here with nothing but a few planks of wood and a bit of tar between us and the vast cold dark of the sea, and all the sharp-toothed and hungry things in it. To row to the point of exhaustion toward a creature so much more vast and ancient than we are.

I try to calm myself by remembering my lessons. Even though I've never done this before, I know how it goes, what will come next. When struck with a harpoon, the Livyatan will either take off across the sea's surface—pulling the now-attached whaleboat and its crew on a bloody, dangerous sleigh ride—or dive in an attempt to escape. But whales have lungs like us; they breathe air; they have to come back up.

Silas's face looks carved out of stone, set and expressionless even as every other part of him is in motion—his hands gripping the steering oar, straining with the effort of bracing it against the wind, his hair and jacket swaying. The waves slap our boat like they're trying to climb our sides. White froth springs up, outlining Silas in glittering spray. Traces of fog cling to his ankles, and the smell of petrichor hangs around him, a faint metallic edge in the air.

He drops his eyes to fix on me for just a moment, and there's no emotion there that I can find, no fear, no compassion, nothing at all.

"Row, Annie," he commands. Then he raises his voice to address everyone else. "Faster!"

Chapter 18

I row. Everyone rows. And if the wind seems to curve and shift so that it's suddenly not fighting us back but urging us onward, if the waves seem almost to rearrange themselves around Silas, propelling us onward, I can't think too hard about it.

We are close. The water grows choppier. The clicking and groaning are so loud now I can feel my teeth vibrating. I risk a glance over my shoulder as I row, just as a spout trumpets up from the whale's back, not thirty yards away now. Chills ripple through me, skin tightening with anticipation.

The other boats have pulled into position ahead of us, fanning out around where the Livyatan—its gray bulk like a small island arcing out of the water—floats and breathes, each breath sending a mist of white water high over our heads. The wind blows the vapor into my face, and it's warm, smelling like musk and salt, unmistakably the breath of something alive.

I understand suddenly why whalers go out to sea again and again in all seasons, leaving behind their families and all the comforts of life on land. The adrenaline crowds every thought out of my head, leaving no room for grief or fear or responsibility or anything at all but the task set out for us: *Catch the whale. Kill the whale.* Faced with such a massive creature, I feel a bond of kinship connecting me with every soul on our three little boats, even the ones who just days ago were howling for Silas's blood. We have a common purpose now.

The harpooners at the stern of each boat rise slowly, metal shining in their hands. The tide pushes us faster. But it doesn't drown out Mance's scream of "Now!" or the bang of the harpoon guns or the whistle of weapons through the air or the thud of metal into flesh.

And it certainly doesn't drown out the cheers that rise up from the *Heralder*'s men, or the simultaneous deep, inhuman groan that radiates from the whale—a sound that, although I've never heard anything like it before, I recognize as pure, terrible pain.

It punctures through the thrill of the chase. Dashes coldness into my heart.

I'm panting, my muscles screaming, by the time our boat pulls into formation with the other two and everyone jams oars in the water, bringing us to a stop. I turn in my seat, gripping the sides of the boat to keep my balance against the choppy water, mouth dry.

August's harpooner missed and is hauling the rope back now. Mance's harpooner, though, has struck the target; a rope trails from their boat to the whale's flank. Zimri pulls his arm back, harpoon pointed down, but before anyone can get off another blow, the whale dives. Waves ripple out from where it disappeared, and I clutch the side of the boat, instinctively leaning into the wave that drenches my clothes.

"Let out the rope!" Mance barks. The men in his boat lean out of the way as the whale's clicks and groans grow dimmer, replaced by the hiss and clatter of rope being let rapidly out of its tub, the line stretching down into the water.

As the waves die down, a strange quiet settles, everyone waiting to see how deep the whale will go. My heart beats in my throat. Mance's men throw buckets of seawater on the rope as it feeds out, wetting it so it doesn't catch fire. A towheaded man seated in the back by the line tub counts the distance. "A hundred feet. A hundred fifty." His voice gets higher and more nervous with every declaration. "Two hundred."

Each of the line tubs holds three hundred feet of rope. If the whale dives deeper than that, the crew will be forced to cut the line or be pulled under, unless they can extend it. Teuila grabs a coil of rope from our boat and tosses it over to them; August does the same, eyes focused. Mance's men get to work trying to tie off the ends, but—

"Two fifty!" The prow of Mance's boat dips, the rope going taut. It's spooling out too fast for them to tie it. The men glance to one another frantically and my stomach drops. Little though I like Mance or his men, I don't want to watch them drown.

"Two seventy-five!" The man shouting the numbers pulls out a machete, ready to slash the rope, but Mance shouts, "Hold! It's slowing down."

He's half crouched at the back of the boat, which is tilted thirty degrees downward. His men lean back in their seats, faces twisted in fear as every coming wave risks swamping them. But Mance is right; the rope stops tugging, and for a stretching moment all is still. Like the whole world is holding its breath.

Then—"It's going slack," the blond man shouts. "She's coming up!"

As the nose of Mance's boat rocks upward, his crew begin to

frantically crank the line tub, pulling the rope back in as fast as they can, but the whale is coming up faster.

"Take up oars," Silas orders, and the others and I obey, loath though I am to let go of the boat as the sea seethes beneath us. I'm seized by a sense of how very small we all are out here in the waves, even with our boats and ropes and killing tools, and of how the sky and the sea and even the whale are only playing a game with us. Humoring us for a little while until it's time to swallow us whole.

Then a burning at my collarbone makes me gasp. The pendant beneath my shirt has gone hot. I clap my hand to my throat, scrabbling to pull it away from my skin. Everyone's attention is on the water; no one notices but Silas. He looks down at me, eyes wide with understanding. The pendant appears the same as ever, but the surface is hot even through my gloves.

Yet there's no room to think about it. I sense the whale's approach more than hear it, at first. A disruption in the pattern of waves, a clicking that feels more like something inside my body than outside it, traveling up from the soles of my feet to my limbs, to my chest, my teeth, the top of my skull. A dark shape in the water.

It sounds angry. It sounds enraged.

It's right beneath us.

"Down!" Silas's cry cuts through the air, above the sudden clamor of swearing and shouting. He drops into a crouch, and the rest of us grip the gunwales just in time.

A hundred things happen at once. The whale breaches, its entire body erupting like a volcano directly between our three whaleboats, Mance's rope still hanging from the harpoon fastened in its side.

None of my lessons could have prepared me for its mass. Not the diagrams in my books, not the skull hanging in Papa's library or the massive vertebrae I've seen in the warehouses. Vertical in the air, the whale towers over us—as tall as a house, as long as a ship, outlined in red and white spray. Its thunderous clicks rattle my insides.

My senses are crystalline sharp with adrenaline, or maybe it's the heartbreak curse kicking in, the monster part of me surfacing when shock and fear have chased all else away. In slow motion I realize the whale is twisting, falling in our direction. I see it coming down, blocking out the sun. Awe fills me. Like seeing the Maker's hand coming down from the sky. For a second, I forget to be afraid.

Then Ezra grabs me and hauls me over the side with him, pushing off from the boat with his feet, and I catch a glimpse of the rest of the *Whistler* crew doing the same, even as Mance's and August's crews throw more harpoons and lances.

Our just-vacated boat shatters. The boom of the whale hitting the water sounds like a thousand cannons, like the end of the world, as water swallows me. The shock wave seizes me—seizes everyone—and the current tears me away from the others, our crew flying in all directions. Bubbles stream from my mouth in a silent scream.

When I open my eyes, the light from above—broken by the battling masses of the whale and the two remaining boats—is far away and getting farther. I flail, but my clothes pull me down; I frantically kick off my boots, wrestle out of my coat and gloves, letting it all sink. I can't see the *Whistler* crew anywhere. Panic blooms as my air dwindles. All the while, the pendant burns and burns against my skin, even as the chill of the ocean consumes the rest of me.

Then my heart skips. Another whale swims toward me from below. This one is still huge, but not as massive as the one overhead, the one we harpooned, the one that breached.

I make myself not scream, not give up any more precious air. Pedal my arms and legs, but then realize it's not aiming for me—it's angled toward the surface, the fight. Its flesh is smooth and light gray, not puckered and scarred. A juvenile. A calf.

It swims past me, my entire field of vision filling up with a toothed jaw, a glittering eye, a frantic fin. And suddenly, with a surge of adrenaline, I know what I have to do.

I kick forward, seizing hold of the whale calf's fin as it passes by. It feels smooth and alien under my hand, but I force myself to kick, to wrap my other arm around its body, my legs too, so I'm lying flat to its back as my chest aches for air.

The whale wheels in shock, emitting a series of higher, shorter clicks. Its flesh is slick and featureless, nothing to grab onto. But my claws are exposed, longer and sharper than they've been in weeks, and I sink them into the calf's hide, clinging to its back, one objective fixed in my mind as if dropped there by a higher power:

Don't let it reach the surface. Don't let this one be killed too.

The young whale twists and thrashes, but swims still toward the surface, toward the adult whale I know instinctively must be its mother. The clicks from both whales ping back and forth; I can feel them in my teeth—one high and one deep, a frantic exchange I can understand all too well. Shouts and yelps from the men, the legs of other crew members dangling in the water. A cloud of red blooms out from around the mother whale. When she twists, I see more harpoons, more ropes tangling her fins, a wide rolling eye.

I'm running out of oxygen, my body weakening, but I beat at the calf with all my strength, kicking, tearing at it with my hands.

My scratches don't go deep enough to draw blood, but I must make it understand that hope is lost. Its clicks speed up into something like a scream, and it whirls beneath me, eye turning up to meet mine. I scream too with my last scrap of air, the bubbles trickling out weakly, as our gazes meet, creature to creature.

A great semitranslucent lid sinks down, then rises up again over the dark, liquid eye. Its pain and confusion and sorrow fill me to overflowing. I feel what it feels. After all, my parents were taken from me too.

Go, I think, my vision going black at the edges. *I'm sorry. Go.*

It goes, disappearing into the depths. I hang there in its wake, stunned, my oxygen-starved brain slow to process the certainty spilling through.

This is unconscionable.

This must end.

Air. I remember—I need air. My chest feels like it's on fire. My vision is dimming.

I kick upward, but suddenly the light isn't where I thought it was. I look around, but I can't see anything. I must have sunk farther down without realizing it. My limbs feel numb, and I can't tell if my eyes are open or not. It's so cold—when did it get so cold?

Hope dissipates as Lydia's voice sounds in my head. *Good job, Annie. Your whole life dedicated to killing whales and now you've killed yourself saving one.*

Then he's in front of me, close enough to see through the murky water and my fading vision. Silas, eyes wide, dark hair floating around his face like seaweed.

He grabs me around the waist, kicks for the surface, but I've sunk too far. I won't make it. I open my mouth to tell him I'm sorry. That I would end whaling, I would, but he'll have to find someone else. I try to speak, but water rushes in instead.

We stop moving. His hands frame my face, pulling me closer. I'm strangely at peace knowing his storm-cloud eyes are the last thing I'll ever see.

My own flutter closed as he presses his mouth to mine.

At first I think it's a hallucination, my dying mind trying to distract me from my aching limbs and screaming lungs, replacing them with Silas's hands framing my face, his body pressed against mine, warding off the icy immensity of the sea.

But then, the smell of petrichor. Air rushing into me, oxygen. The pain in my chest lifts as I gasp. My limbs come back to life and my hands find Silas's waist, cling to him, as his chest rises and falls beneath mine.

Not a kiss. He's breathing air into me, the sharp tinge of enchantment filling my lungs, my veins, every cell of me. Finfolk magic, keeping me alive as the battle rages on far above us, as the mother whale thrashes and the men scream.

Our chests move together as time stretches and life comes back into my limbs. An almost painful warmth, like holding my hands in front of a fire in winter. A feeling of the world coming unfastened around me, light and air pouring in through broken seams.

Finally, he breaks away, loops an arm around me, and swims us up toward the surface.

We emerge into chaos, the sun blinding after the dark of the sea. Air burns as it pours into me. I splutter and choke, spitting up water over Silas's shoulder. He's pulled me against him with one arm while he swims, my legs wrapped around his waist and my arms over his shoulders, my cheek pressed to his wet hair.

I dimly register the impropriety of it all, but I don't have the strength to move, my limbs still numb and lead-heavy. As my senses recover, the chaos around me organizes itself into recognizable shapes. More sailors from the *Heralder* have arrived with a spare boat to replace our shattered one, and Ezra, Josephine, Teuila, and Zimri huddle inside, but other men have spilled into the water; meanwhile, *Heralder* men a few yards away have landed more harpoons in the Livyatan, tangling her in a net of ropes and bloody iron. She has stopped clicking, and distantly I wonder if it's because the young one has fled.

"Annie!" August's distraught cry hooks my attention. He kneels at the side of his boat with four other men. The others are gripping the rope from their line tub with all their strength, trying to prevent it from swamping them as the whale bucks at the other end, but August ignores the chaos to reach out to me. His blue eyes skim over Silas and search my face, but I can't read his expression as Silas swims us over and grabs the side of the boat so my fiancé can grip me beneath the arms and haul me in.

Bracing one hand on the back of my head to keep it clear of the snapping rope, August settles us on a bench and wraps his arms around me while Silas crawls into the prow. August takes in my bare hands and feet, and I think of my gloves, boots, and coat settling on the seafloor, crabs and fish making homes of them.

"I thought you were gone," he whispers as he pulls a damp blanket from the bottom of the boat and hurriedly wraps it around me. The other men are too occupied with the rope to notice, but I see his eyes flick to Silas and back to me as I shiver. He sees what I see. The rips in Silas's soaked shirt between his shoulder blades, ten small points of blood seeping through in the shape of my clutched hands.

I'm freezing all over, except for the spot on my chest where the pendant burned me and my mouth with the memory of Silas's lips pressed to mine. It wasn't a kiss, and there's no way August could know about the not-kiss anyway. But I feel like it must be written all over my face, this current of mingled shame and electricity lighting up my veins.

A wave from the whale's tail rocks the whaleboat, then another, tilting us sideways, and August holds me tight to him. Men swear and water splashes into the boat as the whale thrashes, its tail striking the water again and again like a hand of a god.

But it's flagging, its movements slowing. Its breaths come fast now, the plumes of white from its blowhole stunted and piteous. The screaming—because that's all I can think to call it, a scream, even though it's lower than any human voice could ever be—feels like it's going to shatter all my bones as Mance in the other boat readies another harpoon.

"Aim for the heart!" Silas cries, standing in the prow with his fists clenched. Wind whips at his wet hair, his clothes.

But if Mance hears him, he doesn't acknowledge it. The captain's harpoon pierces beneath the whale's eye; blood flies. The waves push us away from the whale, then yank us closer, like gravity has vacated the earth and now resides in the whale's massive body. She gnashes her jaw and groans thunderously. The froth from her blowhole comes out tinged red.

"Aim for the heart!" Silas screams again at Mance, voice rising with the wind. "Damn you all! The heart!"

Then something seems to change in him. Even with his back to me I can see it in his posture, how he goes still, the horror draining away and an icy determination flowing through him in its place. He turns back toward me, our eyes meeting, and my blood goes cool and slow.

"A lance," he says with cold authority, and I pull out of August's arms. My hand moves seemingly of its own accord, freeing one from a nearby bundle. The metal is cold under my wet hands, and the arrowhead tip glitters in the sun as I pass it up to Silas.

The heartbreak scales glitter too, but no one is looking at me. Silas holds all eyes like gravity as he plucks the lance from my fingers.

August pulls me back as Silas strides across the benches of our pitching whaleboat, steady and deliberate. "Silas," August says with a scornful laugh, but I can hear the fear beneath the brittle surface. "What are you—"

But Silas is already moving, launching himself out of our boat onto the new one from the *Heralder*, the one holding his crew. His weight rocks the boat and shouts of protest rise up, but before anyone can tip into the sea, he's moving again, running the length of the whaleboat and flying onto the next, Mance's boat, the one fastened to the whale.

He lifts the lance as he moves, up to a ready position. The crew's faces are tilted up to him in shock—all except for Mance himself hunched at the prow, stabbing mindlessly at the whale. For a moment, I'm sure Silas is going to bury his lance in Mance's back.

But instead he launches himself off the prow and into the sea. He catches himself on the whale's side and scales it, using the snapped and straining harpoons as grips, and rises to his feet on the whale's heaving back.

Each of the beast's choking breaths outline him in pink water. His eyes are wide and inhuman as he raises the lance over his head. As he brings it down.

The next and last breath from the whale's blowhole paints him in a fountain of blood.

Chapter 19

When I was very young, after I first learned what the Fairfax Whaling Company was and how we made our money, I hated it. Later, Mama would tell me it is a phase every child goes through. But I didn't understand why we had to kill innocent creatures in such a violent way.

For the next two days, Mama took me on two outings. First, we took a carriage out into the country, to a farm, like the one Mama herself grew up on before her father found success as a shipwright. There, Mama paid the farmer a handsome price for a cow and asked that it be slaughtered there and then, while we watched.

The next day, she took me to the city hospital. A few coins changing hands and we were allowed to walk through the sick ward, watching doctors use vials of whaleblood stoppered with the Fairfax Company wax seal to bring sick and injured patients back to health.

"Do you understand?" she asked me after, when we were in the carriage home. My head was full of all manner of confusing thoughts, blood and cries of pain, the sounds of the cow being slaughtered eerily similar to those of the injured patients at the hospital.

"It's how life works, my darling," she said to me. "Just as a fox in the woods might kill a rabbit to feed its babies, and a farmer kills a cow to support his family, so we Fairfaxes have to kill whales to give the world the magic it so desperately needs."

And I did understand. It took a few days for everything to sink in, but I never questioned the company's mission again.

It's almost dark when we get back to the *Heralder*, towing the whale carcass behind our three boats. The sun has slipped beneath the horizon and the wide-open sky is gold in the west, indigo in the east, and a dull purple in the middle like a bruise. I've been excused from rowing on account of my spill into the sea; instead I huddle against August's legs as he mans the steering oar. Zimri charitably gave me his jacket, and I have the blanket on top of that, but the cold has settled into my bones. I think it might stay there forever.

The men sing shanties as they row, pleased after a successful hunt. Josephine has a twisted ankle from when we had to jump overboard, and one of Mance's men has a deep slash in his arm from a lance gone astray. But aside from those minor injuries and our one broken boat, everyone made it out unscathed. A minor miracle. Still, despite the cheery melodies echoing across the water, the sense of kinship I felt earlier has dissipated. These men feel more alien to me than the whales did. I clutch the blanket tight around me and try not to look at Silas where he stands in the stern of the next boat over. Still covered in blood from head to foot, he cuts a grim figure against the twilight.

Exhaustion covers me like a heavy fog, keeping my thoughts more or less at bay, which is a mercy. Even so, they lurk under the surface, clawing at my veneer of calm. Silas breathing life into me, pulling me to the surface. The frantic clicking of the mother and calf as they communicated with each other. The feeling that I knew exactly what they were saying—the same thing I told Kit on the *Heralder* this afternoon. *Stay away. Stay safe.*

Lanterns shine on the ship's deck above; I can see as we pull up alongside it the small figures of Kit and Lydia at the railing, letting the ladders down for us. "Fasten the catch alongside," Mance calls. "We're only a few hours from Kielstraat. We'll sail there tonight and start the cutting-in tomorrow after we make landfall."

At August's direction, I go up first, and even that is a challenge, my muscles screaming from overuse and my eyelids heavy. I have to leave the blanket behind, but the dark gives me enough cover, I hope, that no one will see my scales as I climb. After heaving my body over the railing, I tuck my hands into my armpits as my brother and sister race up to me.

"Annie!" Kit cries while Lydia demands, "Are you all right?" They fall into step beside me as I rush toward my cabin, but their words float over my head.

"I'm fine," I mutter. I'm sure I look as bad as I feel, half-dry and shivering in someone else's coat, with no shoes. But for some reason I feel ashamed to look in their faces. If Kit and Lydia had seen what I'd seen, the violence, the grief, what would they think? "Everyone is fine. Go get blankets and water for the sailors."

When the door to my cabin finally closes behind me, I drop to a crouch and put my head between my knees, trying to quell the rush of dizziness that swarms up. I'm shivering and my hair is crispy with dried salt; I smell like sweat and salt water and whaleblood. Part of me, a large part, wants to collapse into bed and not come out until we reach Kielstraat, but I can't. I'm a Fairfax and we have just concluded a successful whale hunt. I can't let the crew see how much it's shaken me.

As I quickly file down my nails—they've grown half an inch past my fingertips over the course of the day—it occurs to me that I completed another favor for the finfolk when I frightened off the young Livyatan. Mechanically, I prick a finger and sprinkle the blood onto the pendant, watch it sink in and remain, two red spots now. Two favors done. But I don't feel proud. I don't feel anything.

What kind of existence will the calf have now? Will a pod take it in, or is it old enough to survive on its own? For all we know about whales' insides—centuries of accrued knowledge regarding how to take them apart and render their flesh into usable, profitable materials—we know precious little about their behavior or how they interact with one another.

As I'm opening my clothes chest, the door to my cabin opens. I look up, surprised, as Lydia barges in—never having knocked, naturally—and crosses her arms. "Are you really all right?" she asks again.

My heart squeezes, my movements slow as I rifle around for the thickest wool gloves I can find. Try to think of something to say that will appease her, but find I'm too tired to lie. It's an effort just to stay upright.

"This can't go on," I say, my voice coming out small. "Whaling. We have to stop it."

Lydia's face softens as I speak. She crosses the room to crouch beside me, lays a hand on my shoulder, even though I'm still damp and probably smell like blood. "I know."

I blink. "You know?" She seemed so angry before, when I told her what I'd agreed to so Silas would take me to Drekja.

"It took me a while to accept it, but numbers are numbers." She elbows me out of the way, rummaging in my trunk. "Josephine told me that normally by this point of a voyage, a crew might have killed a half dozen Livyati. But we've only even seen two, and one already dead."

"That's why we're setting up the outpost at Kielstraat." I don't quite know why I'm saying this when I've already decided, or at least I thought I had. Maybe there's a part of me that needs to test Lydia, or myself, like I could inoculate us against every counterargument. "Because the whales come here to calf. There will be plenty to hunt."

"For now." She finds a wool shirt and trousers, throws them my way. "But what happens when there are no more whales in the arctic either?"

"That won't happen for a long time, not within our lifetimes." There's still a part of me that wants to cling to the old ways. To take the easy out. I tug my wet, salt-crusted shirt over my head, glad to be rid of it, and throw it over the back of my chair. If Lydia agrees, if she says there's a way to keep on whaling, can I forget what I saw underwater?

"But it will happen," Lydia says doggedly. I think of Kit in the crow's nest. *I don't want to kill whales.*

"Someone will have to deal with it," Lydia goes on, helping me with my shirt. "Our children or our children's children. Something has to change."

It's a terrible sort of relief to hear it from her. Before now, whenever I thought about ending whaling, I thought that would mean betraying my family. But that's not true, has never been true. The betrayal would be letting things stay the same.

I hid the heartbreak curse from Lydia for so long; I hid my worries about the company, my doubts about August. But I shouldn't have. She might be the one person I can trust entirely. Silas and August have agendas of their own; Kit is still too young for some truths. But Lydia—I should have realized earlier—is stronger than I gave her credit for. Braver.

She has a pair of thick wool gloves and holds them open so I can slide my hands in, left then right. "Why not get ahead of it?" she says more gently, brown eyes holding mine. "Why wait until our hand is forced?"

"People will hate us," I say shakily, giving voice to the problem I've barely let myself consider. "They'll say we're betraying Papa's legacy."

"So what?" She doesn't blink; her jaw is set, fierce. "He was our father, not anyone else's. If he were here, I think he would understand."

My eyes burn, a few scant tears forming at their edges, even though I haven't drunk anything but salt water in hours. "I should have talked to you about this sooner."

"Obviously," she says. Her voice is harsh and annoyed, but her movements are gentle as she helps me pull on a fresh jacket, my movements still clumsy. "Just don't wait so long next time."

"I won't," I promise, wiping my eyes on my clean sleeve.

The last of the crew is still climbing up from the whaleboats when we emerge from my cabin. Ezra, Teuila, Zimri, and Josephine have just disembarked and are stripping out of their wet things on the far side of the deck. Kit flits between the sailors, carrying a stack of blankets half as tall as he is. Willa distributes vials of whaleblood to the wounded while the third mate bandages the injured man's arm as he swigs from a bottle of whiskey.

August is among the last to come aboard. He's scanning the deck even as he swings over the gunwale, and when he sees me, he strides straight for me. I stiffen. I haven't forgotten his words earlier. *Lucky thing the wind returned*. But then I register with astonishment that his eyes gleam with tears, flooded with real relief, in the instant before he sweeps me off my feet.

He's already kissing me as he carries me toward the nearest object—the capstan—and seats me on top of it, stepping between my legs and tilting my face up to his. He still smells like the sea: salt water and sweat. "I thought I'd lost you," he murmurs in the space between kisses, eyes molten. "Annie."

He kisses me like we're in a locked bedroom, not out on deck with everyone busy around us. His kisses take me under like a riptide, making me forget my exhaustion, forget where we are, forget the seeping suspicion between us. His lips know mine, his hands know me, and he knows exactly how to chase every thought from my mind and leave it melting soft. My hands find his sides as his lips part mine, tongue seeking mine out. His body presses against mine, heavy and solid, while his tongue traces a question onto mine.

Are you still mine?

We break apart to a chorus of wolf whistles. The deck is packed and busy around us, sailors putting up the whaleboats and wiping down their weapons, but I hardly care, captured in his eyes. He kisses me once more, softer, slow, as he lifts me off the capstan and sets me on my feet. Whispers in my ear.

"You should get some rest," he says, low and regretful, like he can hardly bear to part with me but knows it's for the best. "By the time you wake up in the morning we'll be at Kielstraat. I can't wait to show you everything."

Then he's gone, leaving my mind wiped blank for a long moment until thoughts start to trickle in.

I need to tell him about my decision to end whaling. But somewhere in the back of my mind, under the melting, languid desire, a voice reminds me that just like the night we freed the prisoner, he has me in a corner. The *Heralder* is a large corner indeed, but I have no way off it, not for me or my siblings, not until we make landfall.

I'll tell him everything in Kielstraat. I'll tell him and he'll understand. He has to.

Someone clears her throat. I blink to realize my siblings have materialized in front of me. Lydia's scowl tells me just how much they saw.

"Do you need directions back to our cabin?" she says grumpily.

"Oh, it's *our* cabin now, is it?" I mutter, avoiding her eyes. I blink more until the fog clears and then push off the capstan in the direction of the cabin. But a tug on my sleeve stops me.

Kit. His little face looks haunted. I had hoped that we chased the whale far enough away that he wouldn't see or hear too much of what followed, but I think of the way the creature's clicks and screams settled into my bones and know that was too much to ask.

"Is Captain Silas hurt?" he asks.

My heart stills as I follow Kit's pointed hand with my gaze. To where Silas stands by the mainmast, a pillar of stillness amid the bustling activity.

There's not an inch of him that's not covered in blood, the lamplight stretching his shadow and making him into a creature out of a nightmare. But his eyes are all too human; he looks stricken. Our eyes meet and it's like the rope from a whaleboat going taut, ready to snap or catch fire or take off a limb. How long has he been staring? Why does he look like he's watching his home crumble into the sea?

Then the spell breaks. He turns away, every line of his body tense and rigid.

"Annie?" Kit pokes my stomach, voice high with worry.

"That's not his blood," I manage hoarsely, tearing my eyes

away too. Except for the scratches I left on his back as he carried me to safety. Or maybe it happened underwater. I scarcely remember what my hands were doing—only how gently his cradled my face, the relief as he breathed air into me.

I detach Kit's hand from my sleeve. "I'll go check on him. But I'm sure he's fine."

Yet as Silas stalks off in the opposite direction, as my feet carry me in his wake, I'm not at all sure that's true.

Chapter 20

Belowdecks, a few men are leaving the kitchen with crates of ale. I lurk in the hallway waiting for them to leave before I knock at Silas's door.

No answer. I try again. "Silas?"

Nothing but a choked kind of gasp.

Oh Maker, maybe he really is hurt. I could have failed to notice in all the chaos of the hunt; he could have hidden it as we rowed back to the ship. There were so many sharp edges, so much blood, who could say what was whaleblood and what was his? My heart bobs to my throat and my hands move to open the door.

Stepping inside, I recoil at the sight of something soft and sodden smeared across the floor. A dead animal, I think, like the carriage-struck rats in the streets of Kirkrell.

But no—it's Silas's discarded shirt, seeping blood and seawater over the floorboards.

He kneels beside his bunk across the cabin, back to me, gripping the side, head down. A lantern on the nightstand casts everything in low yellow light. The relative cleanness of his bare back makes the red everywhere else all the more grotesque. His arms are stained to the elbow and more blood mottles his neck, muscles jumping beneath his skin as he gags over a bucket, but nothing comes out.

Everything in me wants to look away, my own stomach turning at the gore and the sounds. But he saved me out in the water. What kind of coward would I be to leave him to it now? My feet still feel outside my control. They carry me to crouch next to him.

"Silas," I say, touching his shoulder. His bare shoulder, the pale expanse of his back damp with sweat. His breath hitches, spine shifting under his skin, and I have to stop myself from the impulse to trace my fingers down the ladder of his vertebrae. My mouth burns with the memory of his. Not a kiss. Just air, just him saving my life.

He flinches away; his voice, when it comes, is scarcely audible. "I'm fine." He leans his head on his forearms, hair falling around like a curtain. "I'll be fine."

And here I thought I was a poor liar. "Really?" I demand, worry making my voice high and strident, my words spilling out fast. "When was the last time you slept? Or ate something? I can get something from the kitchen—"

Silas's breath escapes in a half-hearted mockery of a laugh. "Please leave, Annie." The words come colder now. "You can't help me."

Hurt pricks at my chest. I drop my hand but stay where I am, kneeling next to him. "You saved my life out there."

"And ended another," he says, quieter. "My ledger isn't looking very good."

My stomach twists. I know what it's like to feel the weight of lives lost like stones in your pocket. "The whale was suffering. You gave it mercy."

"I could have stopped the hunt. Called a storm."

"They'd have killed you for that."

He stays quiet, fingers twisting themselves into the bedsheets and leaving red smears on the linen. I get the horrible feeling that in the moment, maybe even now, he wouldn't have cared if they'd killed him.

"I saw you with the whale calf," he says at length. "You almost drowned scaring it off."

My throat tightens at the memory. "It wasn't selfless." I'm not that altruistic, tempting though it might be to let him think so. "I want to break my curse."

"Two favors down now?" The ghost of a smile in his voice.

"Two," I confirm. We sit with that for a moment, anxiety building up in my gut. We're nearly to Kielstraat and I still don't know if that will be enough. I swallow it down and turn my thoughts back to Silas. "Do you want to clean up?" I suggest, going for a mix of briskness and gentleness. "You'll feel better."

He turns his head, showing me his face still streaked with dried blood. The oil-slick film over his eyes that tells me he's not seeing this room at all but visions of war.

"It'll pass," he says, voice small, strained. "Just need a minute."

I let out a slow breath, willing my own hand not to shake. I feel unsteady, like we're still out in the whaleboat, buffeted by waves, but I need to be a steady presence for him. Colors roil in his eyes, irises and pupils invisible beneath the unnatural sheen.

But seconds, then minutes tick by and his breaths come faster, his pulse races. I know I can't snap him out of the visions, but I can do something.

"Can you turn around?" I ask finally. "Turn around and sit against the bed."

I expect him to argue, but after a moment, he moves to sit cross-legged with his back against the side of the bed, eyes still filled with the colors. The contrast between his pale bare chest and the reddish-brown stains covering the rest of him, everything up from his collarbone and down from his elbows, is still startling. I'm already moving to the dresser, finding a washcloth, and filling a bowl with water from a pitcher.

After a moment's consideration, I take off my gloves too and lay them beside the basin. I feel strangely calm, like within the space of this cabin only, I can forget everything else because Silas needs me. Here, I've outrun all my fears, if only momentarily.

There are different kinds of fear, I suppose. The adrenaline-soaked kind when you're surrounded by pummeling waves and broken boats and screaming men, and the deeper kind that lives in your bones and whispers to you that you're not fit to draw breath. That kind has had its claws in me for months, but strangely, at this moment, it's nowhere to be found as I wet the cloth and wring it out.

When I come back, kneeling in front of Silas and setting the bowl beside us, he turns his face up toward me, but I know he doesn't see me. I take a deep breath, letting it out as quietly as I can, and raise the wet cloth to his face, touching it against his cheek.

He flinches, then seems to master himself and settles back against the side of the bed, his eyes fluttering shut. As I run the cloth along his cheekbone, his eyes still dart around beneath his lids.

"What do you see?" The words spill out without my expecting

them to. I don't really want to know, but I feel like I have to. "What are you thinking?"

"I don't know if we can stop it," he says quietly as I move the cloth to his ear, wiping away a spot of blood there. "What if the shareholders won't accept an end to whaling? What if it's too late?"

I've never heard him talk like this, doubting the one thing he's always been dead set on. He looks more like himself with a clean face, but it also makes it harder to ignore the dark shadows under his eyes, the anguish twisting his mouth. I settle back on my heels and take his left wrist, tugging gently to get him to extend his arm. "What can we do besides try?"

His pulse races beneath my hand. Each pass of the cloth down his arm reveals skin so unlike mine—smooth and soft, no scales or claws, just constellations of freckles, small scars here and there, the price of life on the sea. "We could run," he says. "Take your siblings and the crew. Leave the war behind."

I scoff softly. "And go where?"

"Anywhere. Anywhere you want."

His words dissipate into charged silence. The idea feels like the north star, cold and glittering and impossible. Running away from all this. The idea has its appeal, but . . .

"I'm still heartbroken," I remind him. Rinse the cloth and reach for his other arm. "And even if the finfolk queen heals me, I can't just wash my hands of Kirkrell and leave it behind."

A shadow of pain crosses his face, an expression I can't quite interpret. "You're right. Of course you're right. It's just a day-dream."

His eyes have stopped darting around beneath his eyelids, and I wonder if he's stopped seeing the war visions, if he just doesn't want to look at me. An ache grows in my chest as I cradle his hand between both of mine, trying to wipe away every place where dried blood has settled—around his nails, in the creases of his knuckles, the lines of his palm.

I understand how it feels to be overwhelmed by a reality that feels insurmountable. But I want—I want him to believe in me, that I can end whaling, that I *will.* He seemed to trust me so readily even as I lied to him about my intentions. And now his faith is faltering just when I've finally made up my mind, when I thought we'd be standing together.

"You could leave," I point out. I keep my tone level. "You could have left Kirkrell years ago. Why didn't you?"

"I had to pass along the finfolks' message." His breathing hitches as the cloth moves between his splayed fingers, and something in me answers, an ember flaring in my middle.

Unease prickles. Maybe I should leave, let him finish washing up if he's no longer blinded by the visions. But it feels like stopping now would be an admission of guilt, proof that his closeness and vulnerability are affecting me. If I finish the job, clean up the blood and walk away, I'm just doing a favor for a friend in need. That's all.

"You could have left still, given us the message and gone somewhere else. Anywhere else." I keep my eyes down, focusing on his hand, hot in mine. My mind flickers back to that day at my parents' funeral, and I wonder if Silas's does too, if he's listening to me tell him *You should have died with the rest of them.*

But Silas never held that against me, I realize. Not then and not now. "You could go anywhere," I say again when he doesn't reply. "Why did you stay?" Why stay on the bloody, vicious, grease-choked, possibly doomed island that is Kirkrell?

"Because of you."

He speaks simply, plainly, like it's the most obvious thing in the world. A quiet shock wave ripples through me. "What do you mean?"

"I knew you were heartbroken. I thought you'd turn soon." His voice is ragged, like cloth that's fraying as he drags it out from under the accumulated years. "I was sick over it. Another life lost to the finfolk. Another person gone because I couldn't save the *Volyar*."

"It wouldn't have been your fault."

"I know that. Most of the time anyway." A rueful flicker of a smile. "But time went on and you didn't turn. I saw you at church, around town, at the docks. You were stronger than your curse. You made me want to be stronger than mine." His voice drops to a whisper. "I felt like you would be important in all of this."

"I thought you hated me." A strange mix of self-consciousness and shame has immobilized me with our hands still tangled together. To the extent I thought of Silas after the *Volyar* sank, I thought of him with loathing. "You acted like you hated me."

"I did," he said with a joyless chuckle. "I thought I did. I felt so helpless, so out of control, and here you were and not even heartbreak could slow you down as you carried on whaling. I didn't understand why you did it." His eyes open and land on me as he speaks, no longer curse-blank. Only scraps of oil-slick rainbow seem to cling at the corners of his eyes, pooling like tears.

My mouth goes dry, trapped in his gaze. "But you stayed."

Silas swallows, throat bobbing beneath flaking red-brown. I didn't clean the blood off there. He searches my eyes. "Was it a mistake?"

I don't know the answer to that, and I'm afraid of what will come out if I open my mouth, so instead I extricate my hands from his. Silas blinks in surprise as I brace his face with my left hand, but he lets me tilt his head back, eyes half closing.

His breath catches when I bring the cloth to his throat with my right hand. The pad of my thumb rests less than an inch from his lips; I could slip it into his mouth if I wanted. His skin feels like live embers burn beneath the surface; I'm half surprised the water doesn't turn to steam. As I move the cloth down the side of his neck, I realize very clearly that this—*this* is a mistake, and also that I'm not going to stop. At least not yet.

He leans his face into my hand, the movement so slight I'm not sure he means to do it. His eyes have gone lidded, and his pulse races under my fingers. My hands tremble with the effort of staying on course as excess water trickles over his collarbone, between his ribs.

I want to follow it down, to wipe the cloth down his chest, his back. I want to run wet fingers through his hair until it's clean. I want to touch his skin without the intermediary of gloves or cloth, I want, I want—

"Annie," he says, voice unsteady. His hands come up to wrap loosely around my wrists, not restricting me, just anchoring me as gravity threatens to crash us together.

Strange how I usually think of Silas as so mysterious and enigmatic, but now his body gives the game away. Breath coming fast, a flush climbing his chest. It makes me feel powerful and terrified at the same time. In control and utterly out of it.

I hear what he's asking.

But I can still feel the jagged edges inside myself where my heart is broken. To give in, to sink into him—it would let me forget for a while, but I know how this works now. Know that would make the heartbreak all the worse when something goes wrong.

"You deserve someone's whole heart," I tell him. The words hurt coming out. "Not broken scraps."

His eyes glisten, wounded yet unsurprised, when I pull away, sit back on my heels. "Deserve," he echoes, the word a soft, questioning exhalation. "Most days I think I deserve to be on the ocean floor with the others from the *Volyar*."

My throat goes tight. "That's not true." I take the bowl and cloth back to the dresser, stumbling slightly because my legs went to sleep without me realizing it. Try not to watch in the mirror as Silas rises, finds a shirt somewhere, and pulls it on. Graceful, somehow, even now as the silence stretches.

Then he goes still, all at once, face turned toward the porthole. His breath draws in sharply, the atmosphere in the room suddenly brittle.

I freeze in the act of pulling my gloves on. "What is it?"

He's moved to the porthole in three silent strides. "Put out the lantern."

My stomach turns over at the controlled tension in his voice. I flip the lantern cap down and move to his side as the flame shrinks and dims. In the moment before it sputters out, I see Silas's and my reflections in the porthole, faces floating side by side. The thick glass warps our reflections, turning our eyes into dark pits; then we vanish.

It takes a moment for my eyes to adjust after the light dies. The moon is a plump near-circle in the sky, reflecting off the great black surface of the sea. But then more colors start to bleed in. The deep purple undertones to the waves; their whitecaps and the greenish tint to the sky.

And in the distance, the gray shapes of three rowboats. The tall, dark figures standing inside.

Chapter 21

As Mance promised, we reach Kielstraat during the night. I can feel it as soon as I open my eyes, before I even leave my cabin—that we're docked. The ship is quiet, absent the usual distant bellow of the wind in the sails. Unease fills me even before I remember last night. Silas's cabin. The finfolk tailing us.

Quiet so as to not wake Kit, I get up and dress in sailor clothes, pluck a few stray scales before splashing water on my face, pulling on my gloves, and rolling up my bedroll. When I finally ducked into my cabin last night, Lydia and Kit were asleep already, crammed in the bunk as usual. But Lydia's not here now; Kit snores softly, having taken advantage of the extra space by throwing his skinny limbs in all directions.

As I step into a cold gray morning, there's a bad smell in the air, greasy, rancid smoke like bad meat burning. The deck is empty of people, and above me the sails are furled, tied up against the rigging. Half the sky is a pallid blue, but half of it is stained dark with a column of smoke. Under the smoke is land. Kielstraat. We've finally made it.

My breath catches as I drift to the prow to see. It's a bleak land, like an icebound desert. Not soft with green forests and rolling hills like Kirkrell, nor beautiful in its wildness like Nunaqvik. The low, rocky peaks I saw from the sea earlier thrust up in the distance; between here and there is a featureless stretch of scrubby brown earth, unbroken but for the buildings: two warehouses, marked by chimneys belching smoke and great furnaces out front, surrounded by low-slung shanties that look like they're cowering against the harsh landscape. In the center of it all, the foundation for a half-finished fort rises up, its raw beams thrusting from the highest point in the settlement.

But if the buildings are unimpressive, the smoke seems to be the way we truly assert our dominance over the land. It rises black and startling from the buildings, from lookout fires out in the hills, and, most of all, from the cutting-in taking place in front of me.

A spit of rocky land extends out from the mainland, maybe sixty yards long and twenty wide, creating a natural harbor. Docks have been built outward from it, all leading to a wide, sloped beach of gray and black stones. There, the whale we killed yesterday hangs suspended between four wooden cranes as crew swarm around it, cutting off slabs of blubber and pitching them into the sizzling try-pots.

The creature that was so fearsome and graceful in the water is grotesque out of it. Its jaw gapes open, the tail that shattered our boat so easily drooping limply. Chains indent its fleshy sides. Blood and offal trickle down the beach to be lapped up by the tide. My fingers dig into the railing, so tight my freshly scale-plucked skin smarts in protest. Nausea turns my stomach as I search the faces of the crew for Lydia or Silas or August.

But I can't make out details of faces, obscured with blood and smoke. Some crew work on the carcass with pitchforks and spades, pulling strips of blubber and slinging them onto long tables that have been set up along the beach. More stand at the tables, chopping the blubber into thin pieces before scraping it into the great metal try-pots from which the foul smoke bellows.

I find myself walking down the gangplank to the docks without really wanting to. Two other, smaller ships are docked here alongside the *Heralder*—a weathered schooner and a nimble-looking sloop. We're not the first people to arrive at Kielstraat; there's a crew from Kirkrell that we sent out months ago to start building, plus hired crews from Solheim and Nunaqvik. Besides the two ships, maybe ten whaleboats rest on the docks, covered in oilcloth. Mance said that often whales appear close enough to the shore here that the men can simply row out from the beach and collect them.

As I glance over at the various boats, I see something pass beneath them—a sharp gray fin rising out of the water. Again fear swoops in my stomach and I place my feet very carefully until I'm on the beach. The smell is a physical assault; the smoke blocks out the morning light so that it feels like walking up the beach is entering a dark labyrinth.

Men and a handful of women work all around. I'm pretty sure it's a mix of *Heralder* crew and the work crews who preceded our arrival here, but everyone is so covered with soot and blood that I can't make out anyone's faces, just flashes of eyes and teeth. They speak little—if they did, it would be swallowed up in the creak of the burdened cranes and the thud of metal in flesh and the hiss of the try-pots as stoked fires beneath render the solid whale blubber into shimmering liquid oil. No one pays me any mind as I scuttle through.

I recognize Lydia by silhouette more than anything else, the smallest person here. She's at one of the long tables, back to me, straining to cut through a thick slab of grayish-white blubber with a long flensing blade. Walking up behind her, I call her name, but she doesn't respond, doesn't hear me, just keeps raising and bringing down the blade with mechanical determination. She jumps when I touch her shoulder, and when she turns, her face is pale beneath streaks of grime.

"Annie," she says. "I didn't know it would be like this. This is . . . this is . . ."

"I know," I reply after she trails off. I know what she means.

This is awful. This is barbaric. *This is wrong.*

Right now, choked by the smoke and the smell of gore, it's hard to remember why I ever thought whaling could be right.

A man looks over from the other side of the table with a sooty grin. I recognize Mance by his teeth and gravelly voice. "Here for a shift, Lady Fairfax?"

I swallow, trying to steel myself, and pull Lydia to the side so I can take her place. "Yes," I say, projecting my voice to be heard. "Here to relieve my sister."

We killed this whale. I should see the process through to the end.

"Go look after Kit," I tell Lydia, expecting her to argue. But she doesn't. Just stands there, shell-shocked, for a moment before turning and trudging off. A few yards away, she pauses, bends over, and is sick on the beach before straightening and continuing calmly on her way back to the ship.

Maker. What was I thinking, bringing her into this?

Mance, his clothes dripping and reeking with oil, pays it no mind. He puts a cutting spade in my hand and shows me how to use it. It's a metal oval with a sharp bottom edge and handles at both ends; I am to grip the handles and use it to saw through the slab of blubber. Mance demonstrates, easily cutting off a thin slab, which another man scrapes from the table and dumps into the nearest try-pot. A sizzle and a tongue of flame and a belch of smoke, and it starts melting along with the rest, one step closer to being filtered, bottled, and sold.

I take the spade and bring it down on the blubber. It isn't soft like I expect; it's tough as gristle. It takes all my strength just to work the blade down a couple of inches. Mance's mouth curls with vindicated amusement as he watches me struggle.

"Thin sheaves, so they melt clean in the pots," he tells me cheerily. "Thin as the pages of your holy book."

Nothing about this is holy, I think but don't say. As I work, eventually I start to recognize some of the others around me, more by their shapes and the way they move than by their faces.

Silas is beneath the whale, cloaked in its shadow. Working alongside the *Heralder* men to peel long strips of blubber from the carcass, which they slowly rotate, like peeling the rind from an orange. They were screaming for his blood just days ago, but seem happy enough to accept him back into their midst now that there's work to be done.

Time passes slowly. Shifts change. Some of the crew cycle out and go up the beach to Kielstraat; others come in. Never Silas, who stays and stays. I try not to look at him, but as the motion with the cutting spade becomes rote, my eyes keep dragging back up. Hooked blade in hand, he moves like a machine, spearing flesh then pulling, pulling, his natural grace giving way to brutal efficiency.

I might as well not have bothered with the washing-up in his cabin. His face, like everyone else's, is hidden beneath a coat of grime. If he knows I'm here, he doesn't acknowledge it, which stings more than it should.

I'm not naive; I know what happened last night—the fishnet woven of heat and unspoken questions, one Silas and I were both caught in, contracting and pulling us closer together. I know what lust is. It's alarming to be feeling it for someone other than August. And of all the people in this wide blue world, for Silas Price. Scavenger. Finfolk. Enemy—at least, he should be.

But I know, too, it doesn't have to mean anything. Maybe I can't control what I feel, but I can control my actions. I am still promised to August.

It's like my guilty thoughts conjure him, a flash of red-gold among the smoke and the filth. August materializes out of the smoke from the east, coming from inland. He scans the crowd and finds me easily—even now, I think bitterly, I still stick out from the rest of the crew.

He comes up behind me, reaching over my shoulders to disengage my gloved hands from the cutting spade handles. They cramp and spasm and come away in the shape of claws, I've been at it for so long. "Maker, Annie," he says, low in my ear. "I've been looking for you everywhere. You weren't on the ship."

"I've been here all morning." My voice scrapes out, raw from a smoke-seared throat. I turn to face him as he draws me a few paces up the beach, upwind where the air is clearer. After hours at the cutting-in, his bare face and clean clothes seem alien, as if I've forgotten that to be covered in blood and filth is not humans' natural state.

He once spoke of marrying me at sea and then ending my life. Now our sea voyage is over, with no proposal. Maybe he never meant what he said to Silas back then, or maybe he just never found the right moment.

His expression is gently curious as he looks me over, making my skin prick with shame. Even though at some point I was supplied a heavy canvas apron that I left behind on the table, my clothes, my hair, my skin are still sticky with blood and smelling of rancid smoke. My stomach churns and my hands shake. August takes them and draws them to his chest, not seeming to mind about the grease and blood.

"You don't have to do this," he says gently. "Let me show you where you'll be staying."

His hands massage mine softly, tugging my fingers from their clenched pose. But all I can think about is Silas. Silas last night in his cabin, the shadows his eyelashes cast over his cheeks. Silas plunging the lance down into the whale, Silas with curse-blank eyes and bloody lips. *Lucky thing the wind returned*.

"I'm head of the company," I say. "I should understand what it means to be a whaler, every part of it."

It hurts to say out loud. My memories of Papa and the reality of all this gore and violence and greed couldn't be more divergent. But it's true all the same.

A strange mix of emotions plays over August's face like light and shadow through dappled leaves, mirroring my own complicated feelings. "And now you do." His voice is lullaby-soft. "But as the head of the company, you have a higher responsibility here. Come away, Annie."

Though I desperately want to do just that, beg off the rest of the cutting-in and wash until my skin is raw, something makes me straighten my spine and lift my chin. I don't want the crews to see me walking away. No—the truth is, I don't want *Silas* to see me walking away. Even now the skin on the back of my neck prickles, and I know if I turned around, I would find storm-cloud eyes on mine.

But August's words also remind me of the resolution I made last night after he kissed me on the capstan. It's increasingly hard to imagine any kind of future with August anymore, but I promised to tell him the truth when we reached Kielstraat. Here we are.

And so I let August lead me up the beach, dread gathering in my chest.

Chapter 22

I expect to feel something, walking up the beach into Kielstraat as the midday sun shines weakly above. This moment so long in coming. But I don't feel anything except empty, numb, like my insides have been scooped out too and fed to the sharks that have patrolled the tides all morning.

Despite the vastness of the landscape around us, the buildings of the settlement are set close together as if they are flesh and blood and need to huddle together for warmth. They all look the same, rectangular, unadorned structures of raw wood topped with shallowly pitched roofs varying only in size. August points them out as we pass—a storehouse, a kitchen, an infirmary, bunkhouses—and I half listen, drained with physical exhaustion and a formless, foggy kind of fear. The cold doesn't bother me much now after the exhausting labor of cutting-in, but I feel the the edge of its teeth and know it will be biting at nightfall.

The pathways between the buildings have drainage gullies dug out alongside so we can walk without our feet sinking into the spongy, half-frozen earth. Men and women move among the buildings carrying lumber or barrels or sacks clattering with whalebone. Some I vaguely recognize from back in Kirkrell; more are strangers. Pale, stocky Sollish; dark-eyed and dark-haired Nunak; grim-mouthed Abbonish. Even so, the place feels empty, depopulated. Kielstraat feels like nothing more than it is, a hastily constructed skeleton of a port town, gaping open for people to swarm in and money to pour out.

August shows me to the small shanty I'm to share with my siblings, Josephine, and Teuila, suggesting I wash my face and change my clothes, then he has something to show me. Too tired to argue, I trudge in, leaving him waiting outside.

The shanty is plain inside, with bunk beds, a small washroom, chests of drawers. I see that all our trunks have been brought in, and Kit's books are strewn over one bed, Lydia's clothes over another. In the midst of the clothes—like they were putting them away before getting distracted—Lydia and Josephine are kissing, giggling as their hands wander.

They jump and break apart at the sound of the door closing, turning to face me. Josephine grins ruefully, and a furious blush spreads over Lydia's face. "Annie," she splutters.

"Hi. Sorry." I cough, looking around as if this spartan room is the most fascinating place I've ever been. "Um, where's Kit?"

"In the dining hall with Teuila and Zimri," Josephine says, overly chipper.

"He's fine. Everything's fine." Lydia's brow has drawn down, like I might have something to say about her taking up with one of the *Whistler* crew. She doesn't know I have precious little ground to stand on there.

She holds Josephine's hand, and it makes my throat tight. I'm happy for them, but it throws into sharp relief the shambolic mess of my own love life. August is waiting outside and all I want is to be away from him. I loved him so much—part of me still does—but I don't trust him anymore.

And where do I go from such a place? How can we have any sort of life together without trust?

I bustle over to my trunk and open it. "Maybe you could lock the door next time," I suggest as I check to make sure that my gloves and stock of whaleblood are accounted for.

"Or you could knock." But there's the curl of a laugh in Lydia's voice now that she knows I'm not angry.

"Lydia," Josephine says, affectionately reproving. "We'll be more careful. Annie, are you okay after the cutting-in?"

I glance up at her as I grab a change of clothes. Her dark eyes are full of concern and sincerity. She came off the shift at the beach maybe an hour before I left. She and Lydia are both scrubbed clean, every trace of the cutting-in gone. All I want to do is the same. Wash until every speck of blood is forgotten and fall into bed.

"Don't worry about me," I say brightly as I retreat to the washroom and pull the privacy screen around myself. "I'm not staying."

A ponderous silence from the main room, then Lydia's footsteps approach the washroom. "You don't have to leave on our account, Annie," she says with no trace of sarcasm, only concern. "You must be tired."

Just as well there's no mirror in here. I must look terrible for Lydia to be so sincere. "August is waiting. He's going to show me around the settlement."

"Is that a good idea, do you think?"

Unease fills me at her tone, cautious and cool. I haven't told her everything about August, certainly not about him having designs on my life. But she could have heard something from Josephine or another member of the *Whistler* crew. Or she can just read the tension in me.

I know Lydia is strong, capable; I know she wants me to confide in her. But the understanding I've been pushing down for so long, that August is dangerous, is surfacing.

He makes me feel like I'm alone in a whaleboat, floating toward a bank of fog. There's still a part of me that believes something beautiful might lie beyond it. That I can navigate whatever waves come, whatever weather. But I know that's not true. And I don't want to bring my sister in with me. The less she knows, the better.

When I emerge from the washroom, Josephine is tactfully pretending to be absorbed in one of Kit's books. It gives me the opportunity to grab Lydia's arm and whisper in her ear, "Remember what Papa said. Guard your heart."

Lydia's face falls. "Oh, Annie, don't you understand? Papa got it backward." Suddenly she looks inexpressibly sad. "Love isn't what breaks your heart. Love is the only way we survive any of this."

Outside, August doesn't lead me back to his own cabin as I half expect. Instead we walk inland, away from the settlement and the smoke.

"Where are we going?" I ask after what feels like ten minutes, though I can't be sure. The midday sky shines a delicate blue-white, and the low black mountains rise up before us, tundra stretching out endlessly to our left and right. Without the packed-earth paths and meager shelter of the buildings, my boots sink into the half-frozen earth and the wind nips at my face.

Lydia's words echo in my head, the almost-desperation in her tone. *Love is the only way we survive any of this.*

More and more with every step, I think she might be right. For years I grappled with the curse, and my love for Lydia, for Kit—and, yes, for August—kept me alive. Maybe he never loved me back, not truly, but it doesn't matter. I loved them and that was my lifeline. My love gave me just enough to hold on to.

And not just my love, but others' for me. Silas's voice echoes in my head. *I stayed because of you.*

I don't know if that's love, exactly. But I do know that Silas has put my well-being ahead of his own, again and again. He's told me the truth at every turn.

"Somewhere I've wanted to show you ever since we left home." August maintains pace a half step ahead of me, somehow managing to avoid the mud. "I know the main part of Kielstraat can seem unprepossessing, but there is beauty here."

He's not wrong. The landscape isn't featureless, as I first thought. There is beauty to it, if a harsh, ascetic kind of beauty. Colors emerge in the scrubby grass, streaks of rust red and dull green. Veins of snow running down the black mountains gleam in the sun. But for all that, the anxiety in me only grows as we approach the foothills, the ground getting steeper, less marshy and more rocky.

I've never been alone with him like this. On the *Heralder* and back in Kirkrell, even when it was just him and me behind a closed door, there were others around—watchmen on deck, siblings in other rooms. Then, we had to be quiet so as to not be overheard by others. Here, I could shout as loud as my lungs would allow me and no one else would hear.

"I have to talk to you about something," I say, feeling like there are rocks in my stomach. Up ahead, curls of what look like smoke rise from the earth. Not thick and black like the smoke from the try-pots but white and wispy. Another part of the settlement?

August looks back over his shoulder at me, blue eyes keen. "Oh?" With his voice raised above the wind, he sounds younger than usual, boyish almost.

I've delayed long enough. Nothing to do but get it out. "We need to end whaling."

The spring wind whistles; my heart thumps. But August just keeps walking. I stand there for a second, then scramble after him. "August, did you hear me?"

I don't know what reaction I expected, but this wasn't it. I swallow and plant my feet carefully with each step. We come to the top of a slope and my breath catches as what must be our destination comes into view.

A pool of water, irregular in shape, splays out at the base of the hills. Long grass and bushes sway at its edges, more green than anywhere else in Kielstraat. Strange colors shimmer within as steam curls from its surface. Turquoise and rust red and oil black.

"What is this?" I ask, for a moment forgetting our conversation.

His smile strikes me like lightning, like the first time I ever saw it. "Just one of Kielstraat's many secrets." He takes my hand, his glove around mine, and pulls me down toward its surface. "I thought you could use a break after the hunt. The cutting-in."

My chest goes tight as we pick our way down toward the water's edge. I can feel the warmth of it carried on the breeze, smell it, strange and sulfuric but not unpleasant. Idyllic, almost. Like there should be birdsong. But there's just the wind and, in the distance, the smoke of the settlement smudging the horizon.

It's beautiful, but what I just said hangs in the air like a bad odor. Is he simply going to pretend he didn't hear me? Or is he calculating what to say next, weighing every word?

August drops my hand and, like nothing at all is wrong between us, removes his jacket and lays it over a boulder. His shirt next, skin almost glowing under the sun. Then he crouches and unlaces his boots. He straightens and watches me as I slowly come up next to him and do the same thing, stripping down to my shift. His expression is a mix of fondness and hunger.

We wade into the water hand in hand; as ever, August seems not to notice the claws, the scales. The water is pleasantly warm, not hot, and feels thick with salt and minerals. Like if I tipped back, it would be easy to float. After the whirlwind of the last day and all the routine deprivations of life on a ship, it feels like heaven. The stones beneath my bare feet are smooth and warm.

We're up to our waists when he finally asks, his voice level, neutral: "Why do we need to end whaling?"

I take a deep breath, still unsettled, but starting to feel a flicker of hope. "Because the whales are dying out," I say, striving to keep my voice even, calm, reasonable. "The lower numbers aren't just a blip. We have to stop soon or they'll be gone."

August tilts his head slightly. "Well, yes." One hand holds mine; the other floats on top of the water, fingertips skimming idly over the bright surface. "I thought that was obvious."

Shock steals my breath. I blink, close my mouth and open it again. "You did?" My voice comes out small.

"I don't know about stopping entirely," he says. "But certainly we won't be able to rely on it like we used to."

"But this settlement . . ." I feel off-balance, and shuffle my feet beneath the water to search out footholds in the rocks below. "Kielstraat, you planned it all."

"Yes." This observation seems to please him. He smiles faintly, gaze ranging out over the horizon. "We'll need this place for what comes next."

Tongue heavy, I ask what I know he wants me to ask. "What comes next?"

"Do you remember the fae stories?" he says. "The finfolk's City-beneath-the-waves is said to be in the far north. The place they call Drekja."

"Oh?" My voice sounds tinny. My pulse races; I know he must be able to feel it in my hand.

"I read about it back in Kirkrell," he goes on. "And not just the fae stories—all the historical accounts, the explorers' journals. I compiled all the references I could find. I can't determine its exact location, but I know it's close by."

"August." I remember the skepticism I felt back in Kirkrell what seems like an age ago, discussing this very same thing with Silas. Try to channel it into my words now. "Those are children's stories."

He gives me a sly look, letting go of my hand to caress my cheek briefly, a gesture that says he knows I'm lying but he's not going to call me out on it.

Warm, metallic water trickles from his fingers, past my lips, dissipates under my tongue. "Even if it were real," I go on, "shouldn't we try to avoid it? Avoid the finfolk?"

"No. We've run from them for long enough." He slips backward into the water and floats, hair making a red-gold halo around his face. He is beautiful and every word darts dread into me. "It's time to turn and face them. All the rest of nature we bend to our own purposes. Why not them?"

"Like with the prisoner?" I remember his words from the night we spent together in his room while Silas and Lydia freed the finfolk in the hold. *Imagine the yield, Annie, if every ship in the fleet could sail twice as fast as it does now. We'd never lose a whale again. . . . What a wonder, to be able to control the wind and the rain.*

"I want to do more than that," August says calmly. "I think they're touched with the same magic as Livyati. I think their blood can heal us. Maybe other properties too; time will tell."

I take a step back, causing August's eyes to dart toward me. The colors of the water shift, and for a moment, it matches his irises precisely. The effect is eerie, like he's just a mask floating atop the water, like the sea and sky look out through his eyes.

Then the water shifts to greenish-black and I find my voice. "That's impossible." But it's an automatic reply and I hear the falseness of it.

"Why else would they fight us so bitterly for so many centuries?" August keeps his eyes on me as he speaks. "They want us to fear them and stay away. But we don't have to anymore. We have guns, we have iron. They should fear us."

"What exactly are you proposing?" I take another step back, cold all over, even with most of me under the warm water. "That we hunt them? Cut them up and—" My voice dies abruptly, throat clogged with rising panic. August comes to his feet slowly as I scramble out of the water. Teeth sharp enough to slice through dried whale meat flash in a smile.

"We already kill them in self-defense when we must," he says as I grab for my clothes and start yanking them on. "Why would hunting them be worse than hunting whales? Because they have arms and legs?" He comes out of the water with the silent menace of a crocodile. "Because they're intelligent? Livyatan is too. More than us, I'm certain of it."

He dresses as he speaks, leisurely, stretching before he shrugs back into his shirt. "All that means is that we need to press what advantages we have."

The world chills and slows around me as I watch him pull on his coat, my wrists and fingertips itching with the sudden sense of danger. The hope drains away slowly. I know now, I think I have known for some time, that there is no way we can fix things between us. For so long I've lain awake at night wondering if he wants me dead. But that hardly seems to matter now; what he's proposing is so much worse.

"Who else have you spoken to about this plan?" I ask, choosing my words carefully. Mance likely knows; he did about the finfolk prisoner. How far has the poison spread?

"Annie." He takes a step forward and I take a step back, which seems to amuse him. He smiles faintly and it makes fear and rage curdle together in me. "When you fell overboard during the whale hunt, I started counting."

My gloves are still on the ground. I crouch to retrieve them without taking my eyes off August and cram them into my pockets. My muscles scream at me to either fight or run, but I force myself not to do either, just keep slowly backing away.

"No one could survive that long without breathing," he goes on. "But then you came up with Silas. Finfolk magic saved you. Don't you want to share that with everyone?" Again there's that boyish, optimistic ring in his voice. It makes my chest ache as I stumble over a rock and catch myself.

"We will never hunt finfolk," I say once I catch my breath, near spitting each word. "Never. Put the idea from your mind."

"You can't stop it," August says, almost gently.

"The Fairfax Company is mine." Pain shoots through my arms, skin prickling, rage coiling around my heart. "I thought I could share it with you, but if that's not possible, so be it."

"Easy," August says with a smile, climbing the slope after me, and the double meaning of the word hangs in the air. *Be easy*. *Rest*. *Relent*. "I know you feel the weight of your father's legacy."

The impulse to lash out makes my limbs twitch, but somehow I stay rooted to the ground as he comes up to me, hands settling loosely on my shoulders. Thumbs on my collarbone, long fingers curved around the nape of my neck. In another world it could be reassuring, the warmth and the weight of them. But I'm aware of how quickly he could bring them up around my throat.

"We can talk more about it back at the settlement," he says, tone conversational. "Mance and the other officers may have some wisdom to offer."

I hear what he's saying. Reminding me that most of the whalers stand with him, from the crew up to the shareholders back in Kirkrell. I might be the head of the company, but August's vision is so much bigger than a surname. Even if I dissolve the company, he could just start another one.

"Why did you bring me here, August?" The enormity of my disadvantage presses down on me and steals my breath.

"To talk. To be alone with you. It's been too long." His eyes flicker over me, head to foot and back again. "You've changed, Annie, but I don't mind it. Whaler Annie . . . I like her."

"You didn't expect me to last this long." Possibilities unspool in my head, each more absurd and impossible than the last. I could attack him. Try to subdue him. But even with the scales and claws, I don't know that I could overcome him. Could I bear to hurt him? Even knowing his intentions. His hands are warm, his smell as familiar as my own heartbeat beneath the lingering sulfur trace of the hot spring. I have held his body with such tenderness and he mine.

A smile touches his lips. "I promise I won't underestimate you again. Come on." He steps back. "There's going to be a celebration on the beach tonight for our arrival. Not to be missed."

Even if I could hurt him, what then? Return to camp alone and bloody and expect no one to ask questions? There's no way I win this. No world where I come out with everything I want. Only, if I'm lucky, get out alive with the others.

Because I'm not the only one in danger here in Kielstraat, I realize as I fall into step next to August, my jaw tight. I never was.

Kit and Lydia, the *Whistler* crew, Silas—they all are too. All the more now that I've tipped my hand.

"Fine," I say through gritted teeth. "We'll discuss it more later."

We walk back to the settlement in silence but I never put the gloves on. I want him to see the claws. To remember that I'm dangerous too.

Chapter 23

When the sun finally sets after nine bells, dark brings a strange scene on the beach. By now the whale carcass has been lowered to the ground, stripped of its blubber and muscle; only the skeleton remains.

It looks horribly diminished, scarce believable as something once living even though scraps of blood and flesh still linger in the hollows of the bones. A heavy-jawed skull bigger than the one that hangs in Papa's library back home. An impossibly long, thick spine tapering off to that once-powerful tail. A rib cage big enough for three people to sleep side by side within, except for the great bonfire that has been built there. As I walk down from the dining hall in a stream of sailors, it casts flickering, striped shadows across the beach to be swallowed by the black tide.

Between the full moon, the bonfire, the still-glowing fires beneath the try-pots, and the light reflecting off the snow on the distant hills, the beach stays frozen in a sickly kind of twilight even as the minutes tick into night. Tomorrow the crew will break the skeleton apart, disassemble the bones. Soon the Livyatan will be gone, taken apart and preserved and stowed away, all its precious parts packed into barrels in Kielstraat's warehouses. I don't intend to be here for any of that.

By the time August and I got back from the foothills, it was almost time for the evening celebration planned for tonight. August waited outside while I washed up, alone in the shanty. The only thing I could think to do was leave a note for Lydia, tucked under her pillow. *You and Kit and the crew, stick together tonight. Be ready to move.*

If I can just find Silas, just talk to him, we can leave tonight. Where is he?

On the beach, the combined crews are already drinking, loud and loose, and the atmosphere is festive. Food has been brought out from somewhere and set up on the tables—roasted goat and chicken, fresh bread, raisin pudding, and far more beer and wine and whiskey than seems advisable splashing out of everyone's tin mugs. I dodge the clinking mugs, running over in my head what to tell Silas when I find him, what we have to do.

Steal a boat. Go to Drekja. Throw ourselves on the finfolks' mercy.

Every instinct in me quails at the idea. I think of the *Volyar* and the fog and the names of the lost inscribed in metal and stone all along the walls of the sanctuary at church. I think of my parents' empty graves and the fear that racks Silas when he has the war visions. I've done only two paltry favors and I've no idea if it will be enough, but I try not to think about that. It's not important anymore. My fate, whether or not the fae queen heals my heartbreak, is secondary to getting out of Kielstraat—at least, getting Kit and Lydia and the *Whistler* crew out.

I didn't realize we had musicians among the crew, but four

Heralder men—two fiddlers, a drummer, a piper—are playing a rendition of "Round Cape Silver." As a crowd of sailors masses around the skeleton, clinking tin mugs and singing shanties and shouting congratulations, I weave through the crowd, an untouched mug of ale clutched in my hand, a smile hoisted on as people call my name and clap my shoulder, drink making them forget their suspicion toward me.

Then the crowd parts and I see Silas dancing with Teuila. When she sees me her lips quirk and she mysteriously vanishes. Silas sees me and his eyes darken, the air in between us growing charged with electric, unspoken possibility. He holds a hand out to me.

My breath catches. I briefly worry that someone will see, then I look around and realize everyone is dancing with everyone. Mance with Willa the cook. August with a pretty Sollish woman. The crews mingling together. No one is watching me except to greet me as they pass by. No one will care. I walk up and accept Silas's hand, hot through my thin wool gloves.

All evening, I've been chewing on plans in my mind, running through every obstacle and outcome I could think of. But I didn't think of the one infuriatingly simple problem that makes itself apparent now as Silas draws me close: he's been drinking. I can smell the wine on his breath, feel it in the languidness of his movements, the boldness with which he grabs my waist and draws me close for a moment before stepping back to a respectful arm's length.

Irritation and fear and wistful desire zip through me all mixed together as he laces his fingers through mine, swaying to the beat of the song. "Where have you been?" I demand in a whisper.

He blinks, slow. "Finishing up the cutting-in. I wanted this over with." Without looking, he waves a hand in the general direction of the Livyatan skeleton, nearly taking out an unsuspecting Nunak man in the process.

I grab his hand and pull it down before he can make any more enemies. "Let's get you some food."

Silas resists my tugging him in that direction, bends his head close to mine. "They're waiting for something," he murmurs, eyes roving around the combined crews. "I heard them talking about it."

"Probably for another cask to be opened." I let out a long breath as I grab his elbow and pull him toward the food table. The same table on which I chopped up slabs of whale blubber this morning, though I try not to think about that as I make up a plate for him, not trusting him to do it himself.

We retreat down the beach, away from the crowd and the light, and lean on the table, where I glare at Silas until he eats. But the harshness is for show, the prickly feelings fading. He doesn't know about the events of the past few hours, doesn't know I needed him sober tonight. These past few days have been even more of a relentless nightmare for him than for me. I understand wanting to forget for a few hours. It might even be charming, seeing him like this, guard down and tapping his foot to the music, if the stakes weren't so high.

I let out a breath and tell myself not to catastrophize. So it's not the right moment to tell him about August's plans to hunt finfolk. So we won't escape to Drekja tonight. I can tell August I've come around, buy us more time. I can talk to Kit and Lydia and the *Whistler* crew, tell them not to go anywhere alone for the time being.

It'll be all right. It has to be.

"You said you heard the crews talking about something," I say, echoing his earlier words. "About what?" It does feel like there's something in the air, a crackling vein of anticipation, but maybe it's just that Silas put the idea in my head. I scan the beach, keeping tabs as best I can. Checking that Kit, Lydia, and the *Whistler* crew are warming themselves by the bonfire. That August is still making the rounds among the revelers.

Silas shrugs. The food seems to have sobered him up some; the watchfulness is back in his eyes as he scans the crowd, and I privately mourn the short-lived carefree version of him. "It was one of the Sollish crew," he says. "Something about a full moon."

"You speak Sollish?" I say in surprise.

He shrugs, all humility. "You pick up bits and pieces at sea. But it might be a mistranslation."

The musicians start up a new song and a cheer goes up. A favorite, "The Ladies of Embra." One of the men sings—

Goodbye, goodbye, fair ladies of Embra;
To the verdant green land and the sun on the main.

Silas sets his plate aside, pushes off the table, and holds his hand out to me. "You promised me a dance, Lady Fairfax."

"Did I?" I don't seem to recall that. But against my better judgment I reach out and take his hand.

It's unwise to be so close to Silas for any length of time. August is still somewhere in the crowd and I'm sure he has eyes on me. Since there will be no flight to Drekja, I should go dance with him instead. I should try to walk back what I said this afternoon. I should make him think I'm on his side.

All the *I should*s leave me cold. I'm so tired of acting out of fear.

The crews are well into their cups now, dancing close to one another or weaving drunkenly. I don't want my toes stepped on. I tell myself that's why I steer Silas not toward the crowds but into the relative dark and privacy of the empty buildings.

We end up behind the far wall of the dining hall, the music now a little quieter. The way we're standing, he can see the beach, see if anyone's coming. But all I see is him.

Our king he has set us a course for to westward
And nevermore shall I see you again.

Neither of us makes a move to dance, though his hands drop to my waist. I look back at Silas, drawing breath to say something, but the look on his face steals my words.

Somehow we have gotten very close. His eyes are dark in the moonlight, filled with such transparent longing it sends a jolt down my spine. Yet there's something desolate in his eyes too. For a moment, the world seems to stop spinning around us, an unsteady feeling like stepping from land to sea. "What's wrong?" I ask.

Silas blinks slowly, draws an uncertain breath. He's sobered up some, but not entirely.

"This," he whispers, gestures to the space between our chests. "Cards on the table, Annie. Tell me it's not just my imagination."

He sounds so earnest, almost pained, as if he's bracing himself for a blow, and it makes my breath catch. I thought he would have known this from the way I touched him after the whale hunt—not exactly innocuous. Thought he might have guessed that I want him.

But looking into his face, it's clear he's talking about more than that, more than lust, and it makes me feel like a gust of wind is welling up in my chest. I feel electric, alive and acutely vulnerable, like all my nerve endings are exposed, left open to either great pleasure or terrible pain.

"It's not your imagination," I say, my throat tight. "But what happens next?"

I've deliberately stopped myself from thinking too much about after my curse is lifted; since that's always been such a big *if* to begin with, it would be an exercise in masochism to consider the future.

His eyes skate away from mine for a moment. "August?"

"That will end as soon as it's safe." The words surprise me—I've never said as much out loud before, not even articulated it to myself. But I know as I say it that it's true. I feel a kind of distant, muted grief for the girl I was and how wrong she was about everything. "Still, I have to go back to Kirkrell and end whaling. Remember? And you . . ."

I blink, trying to force out the words that have suddenly become heavy and cumbersome. "You could go anywhere." Why would he stay in Kirkrell any longer? If I end whaling and avert the war with the finfolk, he'll have done what he set out to do.

His throat moves as he swallows. "I told you I stayed because of you." His body shifts minutely closer to mine; I can feel the heat of him against my skin and I want, I want. "I'll stay still, if you tell me to."

My heart is thundering, an answer forming on my lips, just as soon as I can catch my breath.

But I never have the chance to give it. Because shouts surge suddenly from down by the water, a wave of words.

"There she blows!"

"Spouts! Spouts!"

Silas is already facing the ocean, me with my back to it, looking up at him. So I see the dread creep over his face first, a mirror reflecting the sea. His eyes go to the horizon and the color leaves his cheeks, the smile dropping away, eyes going wide and glassy.

I turn to see what looks like a field of white wheat erupting throughout the bay. Spouts appear all across the horizon, flag, reappear, and multiply, and the hiss of the vapor and the creak of enormous lungs are carried on the wind.

"Every full moon they come," Mance cries rapturously down the beach. "What did I tell you, men? Easy pickings."

Without thinking, I start running toward the water to look closer, Silas at my heels. The sailors' exclamations die down quickly as they turn to one another to quiet the shouts. For a long, impossibly peaceful moment, every soul on the beach is still, watching the horizon sparkle, each person thinking their own private thoughts.

But there's movement on the far side of the beach. I turn my head and gasp in shock when I see a knot of *Heralder* men have corralled the *Whistler* crew along with my siblings and are leading them all back up to the settlement with their arms pinioned behind them. As if she feels my gaze, Lydia turns her head and meets my eyes across the beach. Her mouth opens soundlessly; her eyes blink out a warning. I reach for Silas, to tell him.

Then I become aware of two things at once: the scent of sandalwood, a footfall behind me. August's arms wrap around me from behind and a blade comes to rest gently against my throat. My mouth goes dry, every beat of my heart pulsing my skin against the sharp edge.

Silas turns a second too late, the color draining from his face even further as he grasps the situation. He takes an aborted step toward us, then falters as August adjusts his grip on the knife. No one else sees, turned as they are toward the water and the whales.

"To the docks now," August says quietly. "Time to see how far this little dalliance goes."

Chapter 24

In the end, for all August's grand ambitions, all he needed to bend finfolk magic to his will was a knife.

He and I sit in the back of a whaleboat while Silas stands in the stern, forced to manipulate the tides to carry us soundlessly out into the bay. My back is to August, his knees on either side of me. His knifepoint is pressed gently against my spine, hidden under my jacket so nobody sees. Beneath us, a multitude of whales—dozens and dozens of them—socialize close to the surface.

Under other circumstances it would be beautiful. They bob gently in and out of the water, which is clear enough to see them beneath the surface, nuzzling one another familiarly. I could reach out and touch them if my hands weren't tied in front of me. Instead I watch them and try to breathe through the rising tide of rage and terror. Think of Kit and Lydia and the others, who August has assured us are locked safely in one of the Kielstraat outbuildings until all this is over. *All this.* Two words containing the promise of so much blood.

The whalers have lined up along the beach, weapons at the ready; a few at a time, they push rowboats out into the water. Silas's tides pull them out into the bay without the need for noisy rowing; they simply trail oars in the water to steer. Thus we can surround the whales, hem them in, all in near-silence. August has sent around the instruction not to strike until everyone is on the water. Which will allow us to kill as many whales as possible as they try to flee.

Silas is pale, jaw set in concentration as he helps the small army of whalers get into place. His hands tremble as he raises them to either side, beckoning the tides. *This will be a massacre*, I think numbly. He will never forgive himself for it. But he didn't hesitate to do as August said. Not with my life in the balance.

The whales breathe and click to one another all around, paying no mind to the little creatures in their little boats on the surface, at least not now. Whaleboats fill the water around us, cutting through the forest of spouts. The men hoist harpoons and lances, wordlessly testing their heft.

My heart stutters when I notice a bank of fog forming out on the ocean, out to the northwest. It's subtle, just a smudge of gray on the water in the distance. No one else notices. The men's eyes are on the water, tracking the progress of our prey. A cry of alarm builds up in my throat; I ignore every scrap of instinct and swallow it down.

Then something seems to shift in the bay. Maybe the whales notice us, because their clicks swing up and then fade, the spouts flagging as the whales turn beneath the water. The men tighten their grips and raise harpoons.

All the whaleboats are out here now. August stands and raises a hand, counts down on his fingers. Boats creak as men lean forward, arms drawn back, weapons ready. *Five.*

Silas's body goes rigid as he watches the water.

Four.

What does he see?

Three.

He drops into a crouch, gripping the sides of the boat.

Two—

It happens so fast.

A great scaled hand shoots from the water and pulls down a nearby boat. Waves slosh angrily into the vacuum left behind.

The men inside don't have time to scream before the water closes over their heads. For a stretching moment, no one else does either.

Then the wind picks up, the fog rolls in, and everyone starts screaming at once.

August's hand, still raised for the countdown, falls slowly. He's slack-jawed, face pale, entirely dumbstruck in a way I've never once seen him. Finfolk aren't supposed to attack this close to land. And whatever's under the water—

The fog barrels out from the horizon, spreading across before pouring into the bay toward us. Dark figures streak out from it as a tail shoots from the water—not a whale's tail; it's long and thin, eel-like—and slams down on another boat. One of the men is caught beneath. His scream lasts a second, then is horribly extinguished.

Panic rips across the harbor like an oil spill catching fire. A few yards away in another boat, Mance heaves a rifle over his shoulder and starts firing straight into the sea, blasts echoing across the water. Others take aim with lances and harpoons. More grab for their oars instead, wheeling their boats toward shore.

Not us though. August wanted to humiliate Silas, to force him to use his power only to bring us out to the whales. Meaning we don't have oars. We are dead in the water as waves buffet us, as projectiles fly, as gunfire and whale clicks batter our ears.

"Get down!" Silas cries.

I duck down the instant before a lance whistles over my head. I feel fear but it's muffled somehow, distant. Kit and Lydia and the others are imprisoned onshore, safe from this. Silas might survive a finfolk attack. Let the finfolk wipe the rest of us out, it would probably be for the good.

"Call the tide!" August roars at Silas. He's still behind me, knife in hand, unsteady in the rocking boat. "You wretch! Get us to shore!"

Abruptly, he shoves me aside and lurches toward Silas, knife raised.

Instinct seizes me and I slam my body into August's knees as hard as I can, knocking his feet out from under him. The breath leaves him with an *oof*. He grabs at my hair but misses, pitches into the water as I catch myself with tied hands against the side of the boat.

Later I will wonder if this saved his life. He surfaces; for an instant our eyes lock together, his full of hatred, then he kicks out and starts swimming for shore.

Just as fingers long as legs, fingers with too many joints, close over the sides of our boat.

I curl my legs to me just in time to avoid losing them as the boat snaps in two, Silas on one end, me on the other. Hands still tied, I topple backward into freezing darkness. Shocking cold. The noise of the world suddenly deadened.

Silas's arms find me, wrap around me. For just a moment, silence.

Then a barrage of clicks pummels my eardrums, rattles my bones. The being beneath blinks up at us, haloed in sinking pieces of boat like falling snow.

A woman's shape, vaguely, but of a scale with the whales that surround us. Greenish-gray skin, spine and arms and legs edged with rippling fins. Fins flaring out from a breath-stealing lovely face, black depthless eyes like a shark, wide lipless mouth.

As I watch, that mouth stretches and unleashes another blast of hideous clicks, like the whales', but somehow even louder. Silas's arms tighten around me but he can't shield us; for a moment I'm sure our teeth will fall out, our bones judder apart.

The queen's eyes—for I know with deep, instinctive certainty she must be the queen—glitter with intelligence. As the clicks echo and dissipate through the water, I have the feeling that every part of me has been perceived, inside and out. From my numb fingertips to my ragged heart.

HELLO, LITTLE ONE, says a voice in my head that is not mine, resonant and unearthly. *I'VE BEEN WAITING*.

Silas kicks up; my head breaks the surface. He shouts something to me, but I can't make sense of the words; my skull feels like a church bell just struck. Everything is noise and chaos and indistinct shapes—men shouting, weapons blasting, boats rushing past us in the fog. Pale and dark finfolk faces tip up toward us, unearthly eyes travel over us. Some of them sound like they're singing in thin voices, haunting music that winds up to the sky like smoke.

Even as some of the whalers reach shore, the finfolk still give chase. They mean to continue onto land, I realize with a stab of terror. Like in the old stories. They're going to destroy Kielstraat. Kielstraat where my siblings and the *Whistler* crew are still imprisoned.

Debris surfaces with us, seaweed and waterlogged wood and white bones. It coalesces and takes the shape of a finfolk rowboat bearing up under Silas and me, pitching in the waves. He unties my hands, then pulls me to him in the boat, wrapping his arms around me, both of us shaking with cold.

My mind is still a jumbled mess, but a flash of bright red catches my eye, focuses my attention. Curled against Silas's chest, I blink until my vision clears a little. I see that his bone pendant has slipped from the collar of his shirt and is no longer blank. Not one or two but three red dots cluster at its heart.

"Silas," I croak, lifting my hand to touch the pendant as fog wraps around our boat like a shroud, muffling all other sights and sounds. "Your favors."

An unsettling feeling inches over me as he looks down, eyes flaring wide. Just a few days ago, his pendant was blank, his favors undone. Now all at once he's done three.

And his face—he's gone pale, lips parted, shock and fear playing through his eyes. What did the finfolk ask of him? Or did he somehow complete the favors without knowing it, as his expression suggests?

"No," he whispers, as the sea bubbles off to the side of our boat and the crown of a great head rises.

WELL DONE, CHILD, that unearthly voice sounds again in my head. Yet there's warmth in it too, a kind of affection somehow, and it makes me understand she's not addressing me. *YOU HAVE RETURNED TO US.*

Not me at all, but Silas.

The pendant slips from Silas's trembling hands as the queen surfaces. Not all of her, just the top half of her head with its crown of fins, her black eyes. The fog circles us. Beyond it, I can hear the muffled sounds of battle, more gunfire and screams and eerie finfolk song. I have to get back to shore before they make landfall. I have to get my siblings away from here. But I know in my bones that if I leaped from this boat, the queen would strike me down like an insect.

"My queen," Silas whispers. His voice is barely audible even to me, but there's no doubt in my mind that the queen can hear. "I had planned to come to you in Drekja."

His arms loosen around me and the suspicion grows in me that something is happening here that I don't understand. Something is irretrievably wrong.

WE COULDN'T LET THE HUMANS' SLAUGHTER GO UNPUNISHED. She drifts up right next to the boat. Lays one great fingertip delicately over its edge, tilting the boat slightly down so she can see us. Panic speeds my heart; I brace my legs against the side of the boat to stop myself from sliding in. Screams float over the water from shore. *Kit. Lydia.*

Silas lets go of me and turns to face the queen. He's pale, breathing fast. He lifts the pendant from around his neck and holds it out to her. "I'm sorry," he says. The pendant dances, hanging from trembling fingers. "I can't fulfill our bargain."

Fogged, semitranslucent eyelids sink slowly down over the black eyes and then rise up again. The fins sprouting from her head twitch and shiver inquisitively. *BUT YOU HAVE BROUGHT WHAT WE ASKED FOR.*

"I can't give them to you," Silas whispers.

"Silas," I say, voice scraping out; I feel like my chest is still half full of water. "Silas, what is she—"

"Please." He's not talking to me, he doesn't look at me, I'm not sure if he even hears me. The pendant slips from his fingers and disappears into the sea. "I accept the curse. Or we can make a new bargain. I'll do anything you ask."

THE BARGAIN IS BINDING.

"Silas?" My voice comes out high and frightened. He turns toward me and his eyes are anguished.

"I made a mistake," he says, shoulders hunching inward. "I promised what wasn't mine to give."

A strange sound rises from the water, like the chattering of dolphins mixed with the strings of a harp breaking. Laughter, I realize with a bolt of dread. The queen is laughing.

SHOW HER.

A thin layer of water washes over the boat, surrounding Silas and me in an icy tide. When it recedes, a seashell lies there at our feet. Silas and I both grab for it at once, but I get there first, his hand coming down on top of mine, and I am plunged into memories not my own.

The secret chamber beneath the Spout in Abbonheim. Silas floats alone in the pool, and I see the ceiling through his eyes, the glowing water casting strange dancing patterns on the stone walls. The nightmares are getting worse, spilling over the boundaries of sleep to haunt him in the daytime. He's exhausted, making greenhands' mistakes on the Whistler, *losing minutes at a time when he's plunged back to the sinking* Volyar.

The icy water grasping at his legs, the screams of his dying crew all around him, the merciless shapes of the finfolk silhouetted against the dusk, just watching, just waiting.

And then there are the visions of things that haven't happened yet. Abbonheim in flames, Abbonheim crumbling, the sky choked with smoke, human blood and finfolk blood staining anew the cobblestones that have already absorbed so much Livyati blood. Flames racing across the oil-soaked water of the harbor, eating up ships and people like so much kindling.

It's intolerable. He closes his eyes, willing the visions to come that will tell him how to end it.

And they come.

He sees a little boy curled in a hammock belowdecks in a ship, consulting a map with the utmost seriousness, never mind that it's upside down.

He sees a laughing girl in a yellow dress seated at a grand piano, playing an idle melody with one hand while she holds a flute of champagne in the other.

He sees me dancing with him on the beach by the light of a bonfire, flushed and grinning, and he wants to draw me closer—but—

He is standing outside Fairfax Manor, the night dark and cold, contrasting the music and laughter coming from inside, the windows lit up in celebration. He looks down at the bone pendant, held in the palm of his hand as if it's a compass pointed toward our home, toward us.

Chapter 25

The shell shatters between our pressed-together hands, pieces slicing into my palm as I yank back from Silas. He lunges after me and grabs my wrists, holding both of us down on our knees.

I was wrong to think the finfolk didn't favor him.

All along, when the rest of us had to guess what favors might please the finfolk enough to lift our curses, he knew. They told him exactly what he had to do, had to give.

He's saying my name, over and over again with increasing desperation, but his voice sounds muffled, his face blurred by the tears in my eyes. As though I'm underwater, I'm sinking down, away. I'm still dimly aware of the finfolk queen watching us, trailing us, our boat drifting gently toward shore. But none of it seems to matter.

"You lied to me," I hear myself say. I try to pull away, but his grip on me is iron, even as his voice breaks. My whole body shakes, paralyzed by a world that is suddenly overwhelming in every sense. I can hear my own skin tearing as the scales erupt all over. I can see the tiny veins in Silas's eyes. Hear the sounds of battle raging onshore and the mournful clicking of whales in the far deep water.

"I'm sorry," he says desperately, his breath coming fast. "I'm so sorry." Behind him, the queen watches us, her head tilted and her eyes shining with something like curiosity, or maybe hunger. Flames reflect in them. Past the dissipating fog, Kielstraat is burning.

"You—" I break off with a gasp as pain surges through me, a tide of needles rolling through my limbs. My hands twitch violently in the circle of Silas's hold. The events of the past weeks warp and splinter in my memory—the night of the shareholders' meeting, the shape of him in the doorway of my room. How strange it seemed that he would risk everything to take me to Drekja, with nothing but a promise in return.

My chest aches. Physically aches, like someone has cold fingers in my ribs and is prying me apart. I know this feeling. I had it when my parents died and then again when I learned August meant to kill me. Everything is coming apart.

"You never believed I could end whaling," I say, speaking the realization out loud. My voice sounds distant. "You never meant for me to come back to Abbonheim—"

Silas gasps and at first I think it's because of the words, until I smell the blood. I look down to where our forearms are clasped together. Blood wells up where my nails have sunk through his skin.

"It's different now," he pleads, staring into my eyes. His breath hisses out through his teeth as I sink the claws into him, but he doesn't let go. The monster in me stretches, scenting the air. Whispers to me to let it out, that it's time.

"Why? Why is it different?" My pulse charges in my veins, every slamming heartbeat sending a burning sensation through me, gathering in my fingertips, underneath my skin. A monstrous queen wants me for unknown purposes. Whalers and finfolk clash on the beach of Kielstraat as the settlement burns behind them. Silas has been lying to me this whole time.

Before when my heart started to break, I told myself Kit and Lydia needed me. When I learned about August, I told myself it was a trick. Now I'm all out of lies to tell myself. Maybe I need to be a monster to survive this.

His lips move soundlessly for a moment before the words form, a pained whisper. "I just wanted silence." Tears track down his cheeks; I can smell the salt of them. His grip remains painfully tight, pinning me in place though I struggle. "I wanted sleep. I didn't know I could want anything else."

"And now you want me," I spit. "Is that it?"

He flinches, the truth in my words hitting him like a blow.

Because whether or not he changed his mind at some point, everything Silas has done is perfectly in line with his bargain. Moving my siblings and me like pieces on a chessboard so that we would end up here, alone in the far north, dependent on him for survival as the other humans scream and scatter and our enterprise burns down.

"I trusted you," I say uselessly. Another tidal wave of pain breaks through me, bringing tears to my eyes. "We all trusted you." Finally I manage to wrench away and scramble to my feet in the little boat, stumbling back from him. But I can't get far enough. The smell of his blood is dizzying.

"Annie," Silas whispers. He shifts slowly from crouching to standing, keeping his eyes on me all the while. Wide, unblinking, fearful eyes.

He's afraid of me.

I'm afraid of me.

All of us cursed are the same, I think bitterly. Faced with a fate we cannot accept, we'll do whatever we must to escape. Rats chewing off our own tails to get out of a trap, even if it means bleeding to death. And Silas is no better. All his noble talk about accepting the visions, of living with the nightmares, it was all a bluff. He wanted to escape his curse just like anyone else.

What did it matter if it cost the lives of three people he hated? What will happen when our boat hits the beach, looming ever larger in front of us? Will he go find Kit and Lydia himself?

He takes a step toward me, off-balance.

"Don't," I snarl, stopping him in his tracks as a wave of pain sweeps over me, washing my vision in red. My hands twitch with the desire to tear into something, anything. I turn to the queen and shout as loud as I can, "What do you want with us?"

She turns to look directly at me for the first time, and it takes everything in me not to flinch away.

The force of that voice directed at me is bone-shaking. *YOU ARE THEIR LEADER, ARE YOU NOT, LITTLE ONE?* she intones, a pleased curl to her voice somehow. *IF I HAVE YOU, I HAVE POWER OVER THE WHALERS.*

I howl a desperate laugh. "They don't care about me!" The wind steals my words away. "They don't need us." I fling my arm out to point at the beach. The whalers of Kielstraat are abandoning the burning settlement, sprinting for the ships tied at dock. "Look, they're leaving us behind!"

Those black eyes rest impassively on me, and I realize with a swell of dread—she doesn't believe me. I think of the whale we killed and its calf. How the hunter's motives are always inscrutable to the prey. I could just as well ask Mance to explain to the whales why we need their magic as I could convince the finfolk queen that we Fairfaxes are useless to her. That the whalers won't trade anything for us.

The world moves slowly around me, fear slipping away in the face of something darker and colder. On shore, the buildings are in flames and the small shapes of men sprint for the docks as the finfolk stream after them, fluid as smoke on the wind.

"Give me another bargain," Silas begs the queen, dodging her giant hand as our boat comes up on the beach where we butchered the whale, sliding between the spindly shapes of docks. "Please, anything."

BE STILL. BE HEALED. The queen's words, bracketed with bone-jarring clicks, slice the air. I can hear the frustration in them. *IF YOU WILL NOT, I'LL TAKE THE FAIRFAX CHILDREN FIRST AND COME BACK FOR YOU.*

Horror sinks into my stomach as the finfolk queen turns from us and rises out of the water, gliding toward Kielstraat, toward my siblings. Water streams off her body, shiny and supple like a seal or a shark, as she unfolds herself to her full height.

Taller than any of the flames devouring Kielstraat. Tall as a whale is long. Her limbs move in a rhythmic lurch over the beach. Tendrils of water wreathe her feet, her arms and legs and hands. They move with her and expand and contract as she breathes. The sailors on shore scream and scatter, falling over themselves to get away and get to the docks. She ignores them. She will find Kit and Lydia and take us all, to what end I don't want to think.

Silas's task was to deliver us three Fairfaxes to her. In return, she promised to lift his curse. A promise she said was binding.

The finfolk abide by their bargains. That's what Mama always said. If the queen is unable to lift Silas's curse, if her side of the bargain goes unfulfilled, will she let us go?

The monster uncurls inside me. I can't physically stop the queen. The only thing I can do is make it impossible to lift Silas's curse. And the only way to make sure of that—

The spindly shadows of the docks, outlined in flame, play over Silas's face as he looks at me and seems to read my thoughts even as they turn and click into place. His eyes fly wide. "Annie, please—"

The bloodlust in me rears up hotter and higher than ever, finally given a purpose, as he spins and leaps from the boat. My clouded mind turns red as I spring after him, the enchanted boat disintegrating under me.

It's him or us. It was always him or us.

"Cast off ropes!" a man yells as I hit the water, from above on the deck of the *Heralder*. Mance—I distantly recognize the harsh, rough voice. "Shove off!"

The *Heralder* creaks and groans as I chase Silas through the shallow water. Ships aren't meant to move from stationary to full speed ahead, and it lurches jerkily forward as the just-dropped sails catch the wind.

Not everyone makes it. One woman is on the gangplank when the ship decouples from the dock; the gangplank clatters into the sea, and she with it. Two more men launch themselves off the end of the dock as the *Heralder* pulls away; one catches himself on a stray rope and clings to the hull; the other falls short and starts swimming, but the ship leaves him behind.

And there's a glimmer of red-gold on deck: August leaving me behind too.

My senses register all of it, each sound and smell and color impossibly sharp and clear, but none of it matters. All that matters is Silas stumbling out of the waves.

He betrayed us. Turned us over to the finfolk.

It's him or us.

He gets a few steps up the beach before I catch him, claws tearing at his shirt and skin and bringing us both down together. I land heavily on his back, bracing my legs on top of his, the tide licking at our heels. Hang on tight as he heaves beneath me, trying to throw me off. He's taller, heavier, but the monster coils through my veins and gives me strength. I feel high, victorious, entranced by the smell of his blood.

"Annie," he gasps as I sink fingers into his hair and wrench his head back, exposing his throat. "Please."

Him or us.

My other hand pins his wrists down in the sand, but I'll open his throat with my teeth if I have to. I bend down to press my mouth to his neck, red raging in my head—

"Annie! Stop!" This second voice isn't Silas's, and it's familiar enough to freeze me where I am, looking up for its source.

Lydia sprints full tilt from the burning settlement to the beach, Kit and the rest of the *Whistler* crew at her heels. She hardly even seems to notice the finfolk queen looming a short distance away, or the *Heralder* fighting the tides to abandon us. Her anguished voice wakes up something in me, shame and grief. *They can't see me like this.*

Silas takes advantage of my moment of hesitation, bucking me off him and twisting to shove me away hard. The breath is knocked out of me and I sprawl backward in the sand, rage lighting up my insides and pushing away the doubt.

"Get away from here!" he yells at the others as he scrambles to his feet. I don't know if he's warning them away from the queen, or me. "Run!"

Up the beach, the others falter, but it doesn't matter where they run as long as Silas draws breath. The only way to save my siblings is to nullify the queen's bargain. I tense my muscles, gathering strength to spring at him again, when a *boom* from behind me jars my focus.

Kit screams, the sound cutting through me, cold awareness flooding me in its wake. Silas staggers forward.

At first, I don't understand what I'm seeing. Metal sprouting from his right shoulder blade. The smell of gunpowder and blood. A quivering rope stretched across my field of vision.

As Silas goes to his knees, I turn around, following with my eyes the rope, sagging with slack, that rises all the way up from the harpoon in Silas's back to the deck of the *Heralder*.

August stands at the gunwale, easing the harpoon rifle off his shoulder. Each movement twitches the rope as he braces it in the railing, smiling. I stare up at him, disoriented. After everything, is he trying to help me?

Then Mance hands him another rifle as the *Heralder* churns forward through the unnatural tide.

The second harpoon misses my head by inches; I feel the displaced air on my cheek as it flies past. August's eyes meet mine, full of malice, as the rope tethering Silas goes taut.

The monster is still hotly alive under my skin, it still wants Silas dead, but his choked cry as he's pulled backward shreds something in me. He scrabbles to brace the rope with one hand, leaving a bloody furrow in the sand. But the ship pulls him inexorably toward the water.

Fire and ice fill my veins, my head full of fog. The others sprint toward us, yelling, but they're too far away to stop this. I can't move, immobilized by the fight raging in my head between me and the monster.

A bolt of lightning forks down to the *Heralder*'s mainmast, setting the sail ablaze. Thunder booms, and a chorus of screams rises from deck. The queen erupts to her full height, fog flanking her and lightning crackling at her fingertips.

Another bolt strikes between the beach and the *Heralder*,

incinerating the rope tethering Silas. The thunder echos as he collapses in the tide. The queen's shout shakes the earth, a wordless scream of rage. The *Heralder*'s flaming sail shudders with it; people clap hands over their ears.

FLEE TO YOUR SHORES, LITTLE CREATURES, the queen shrieks into the burning dark. A wave rises up all along the bay and trembles there as if held up by strings before washing outward from land, tipping the *Heralder* dangerously on its side as the ship is shoved out to sea. With my sharpened vision, I see sailors lose their feet and grab for the rigging as the mast dips so close to the water that the leaping waves put out the fire.

TELL THE HUMANS TO LAY DOWN THEIR BLADES, the queen screams as they flee, *UNLESS YOU WISH FOR YOUR GREAT CITIES TO BURN TOO.*

Chapter 26

The afterimage of the lightning hangs in my vision as I finally find my feet and run toward the water, the monster and me grappling for control of my limbs. The *Heralder* has righted herself and limps toward the horizon, smoke rising from the destroyed mast. I see the flailing shapes of a few bodies in the water, gone overboard in the onslaught of waves, but the *Heralder* doesn't return for her fallen. She sails onward toward the drowning moon.

The night wind whips cold against my raw skin, ruffling the fresh scales. Heartbreak burns my chest and pours bloodlust into my veins while my conscious mind screams in protest. I reach Silas just as he pushes onto his knees, the harpoon still embedded in his shoulder. Blood and sand cover his front, his lips.

He sways and I step close to him, my whole body twitching with battling impulses—to comfort him, to tear into him. He clutches my coat to stay upright. Presses his face into the front of my thighs, trembling with the effort. My chest and throat tighten as my hands sink down to frame his face, claws brushing his cheeks, threading into his hair. I feel like I'm watching us both from above, waiting to see what part of me will win out.

It would be so easy to do what I wanted to do moments ago. End him so the finfolk queen can never lift his curse. The monster inside me whispers to do it. I have never killed so much as a chicken but I can imagine what it would feel like, the exact amount of force it would take to break his neck, how his body would go rigid, then slump against me.

The other part of me wants to scream for help. Find enough whaleblood to heal him, even if I have to slaughter a Livyatan with my bare hands and drag it to shore. Everything has happened so fast. Less than an hour ago Silas and I danced on the beach. Now heartbreak swallows me as he bleeds out into the tide.

The *Whistler* crew finally overtakes us, Ezra and Teuila grabbing my arms and hauling me back as the others fall in around Silas. The monster twists in rage, but the part of me that's still me understands. Even feels relief to be caught. At least until Kit and Lydia, a few steps behind the others, approach slowly.

Frantic words fly in every direction. *Need whaleblood. Punctured lung. Supplies are gone. It all burned.*

With my heightened senses, I can see my siblings' eyes track over me, the scales, the blood. Smell the fear coming off them, mixed in with their sweat. Kit makes to step toward me and Lydia grabs him, holds him back.

Shame and grief twist through me as I remember reaching through the bars toward Cousin Mary. How Papa had pulled me back in just the same way. "I'm sorry," I try to say, but my voice comes out a hiss; I don't think they understand.

There's movement from up the beach, slower and wetter than

the ongoing crackle of flames, and everyone goes still at once, faces tilting up.

I see with a thrill of fear that the queen is approaching, carried by a bank of fog and water and seaweed that writhes beneath her. The smell of petrichor edges out the smell of blood in the air. Ezra and Teuila shudder, though their grip on me doesn't slacken.

Kit and Lydia turn toward her too, Lydia stepping in front of Kit. My chest aches for them. I want to tell them to run, but where could they go? Nothing is left of Kielstraat but burning ruins. I've doomed us all here.

SUSANNAH FAIRFAX. The queen looms over us, her tendrils slithering out to encircle us all together. Lydia flinches; Kit covers his ears. Those black eyes find me as she plucks the second harpoon—the one August shot at me—from where it buried itself in the sand. *YOUR OWN KIND HUNTS YOU.*

"I told you," I whisper. I'm surprised I can still form words, though they come out clumsy and slow. "They don't care about me or my siblings. They left us behind." Ezra and Teuila still hold my arms—though I can feel them trembling—so I use my chin to point out toward the ocean, where the *Heralder* is just a small shape on the horizon.

The queen sighs with apparent displeasure, the sound rattling like a hurricane gale, and turns her attention to Silas next. Josephine and Zimri, faces pale with fear, shift into protective postures around him, though they must know he is past protecting.

The queen's words descend like blows. *YOU GAVE ME A WORTHLESS BARGAIN.*

Silas, on hands and knees, lifts his head. "I'm sorry," he whispers with blue-tinged lips, and I don't know if he's apologizing to me and my siblings, or the queen, or all of us. His glassy eyes travel over each face as the crew trades confused glances. "I meant to turn the Fairfaxes over to the finfolk. To be taken to Drekja and used as bargaining chips." Each word sounds like it costs him, his breath a weak rattle. "They were my three gifts to stop my visions."

The color drains from Lydia's face and the *Whistler* crew goes quiet, staring at their captain. I can't tell what they're thinking. If this seems like an acceptable price.

A small voice breaks the silence. "I'll go to Drekja."

My stomach flips over as everyone turns to Kit. *No. No.*

WILL YOU?

As the finfolk queen swivels in their direction, Lydia tries to shove Kit behind her, but he resists, plants his feet. His eyes are moon-wide, and his voice trembles, but I can tell he's trying to sound confident when he speaks again, narrow shoulders squared.

"I've read about finfolk bargains," he goes on. "If you heal Captain Silas and lift Annie's curse, I'll come with you to Drekja."

Lydia lets out a choked gasp, gripping Kit's hand tight. I expect her to protest, but instead she says, "Me too. I'll go with you."

Josephine steps toward them, but a tangle of seaweed from the queen's train rears up like a snake, warns her back. Inside me, the monster and the small voice I think is myself scream in unison to be set free.

CLEVER CHILDREN. The queen addresses Kit and Lydia, her mouth curling up into a smile full of sharp teeth. *BUT THE BARGAIN IS TILTED IN YOUR FAVOR. SHELTERING IN DREKJA WOULD BE A BOON TO YOU.* She looks around pointedly at the smoldering ruins of Kielstraat, the icy landscape beyond, the sea with no boats. *WHERE ELSE DO YOU HAVE TO GO?*

Above me, Ezra draws a ragged breath. "We'll tell you everything we know about whaling," he calls.

"And the human ships," Josephine adds, lifting her chin. My breath catches, love and pain swelling in my chest as the rest of the crew add their voices to the chorus.

For Silas—for me, even—they will let the finfolk take them to a place they've never seen, a place I'm half convinced isn't real. After they've traveled all this way to heal their own curses and resume normal lives, they're ready to put that aside, give themselves over to fate and the finfolk's mercy.

I want to call out, to protest. But the queen is right. Where else is there to go? The *Heralder* is gone, Kielstraat is destroyed, and we're hundreds of miles from any shelter or sustenance.

The queen lets their offers wash over her, quite still. I can't tell if she is pleased. Finally the great finned head sinks in a nod. *I ACCEPT THESE TERMS. I WILL HEAL THE BOY.*

"What about Annie?" Lydia whispers.

SHE MUST STRIKE HER OWN BARGAIN, IF SHE STILL CAN.

The words gust through the hollow shell of me, extinguishing the small spark of hope. Still—my siblings and the crew will remain, if not safe, at least alive in Drekja. And Silas will live. It's more than I could have asked for. I try to hold my head up, to be brave as she turns toward me. "I have nothing to bargain with," I say.

I can hear my words come out as a garbled twist, but the queen seems to understand.

WE'LL SEE, she replies. *GO, CHILDREN, AND MAKE READY. BOATS WILL ARRIVE FOR YOU SOON.*

A petrichor-scented gust of wind sweeps the beach suddenly,

almost swallowing Silas's pained gasp. The others reel back in shock as the harpoon still stuck in his shoulder dissolves into ashes, spilling down his chest and leaving a ragged wound. He doubles over as fog flows swiftly over him, hiding him from view.

Then after a moment that seems to last hours, the fog dissipates, leaving Silas huddled face down like a penitent. Slowly, so slowly, he unfolds and sits upright. He is pale and shaking and still covered in blood and sand, but the harpoon wound is gone, a new scar in its place showing through his torn shirt. He blinks, storm-cloud eyes clear.

Relief swims up through the haze of heartbreak, but I scarcely have time to feel it before the queen's seaweed vines shoot out and seize me. Teuila cries out as I'm torn from her grip. Hands reach for me, shouts of "Annie!" rise up. But they're too slow, too late to stop the queen from dragging me behind her into the sea.

The scales and the heartbreak don't shield me from the ocean's chill; it spears into me, freezing my lungs as we dive. I scream, bubbles rushing uselessly from my lips, and flail and strike at the slimy vines holding me with my claws. But all this accomplishes is more vines wrapping around me, lashing me up like a spider's prey as we go deeper and deeper, the water getting darker and colder around us.

DON'T BE AFRAID, LITTLE FAIRFAX, she clicks at me as we descend. *ALL WILL BE WELL.*

I decide not to waste air on a reply, but I'm running out anyway, lungs aching and head going fuzzy, a heavy feeling of resignation seeping into my limbs. I don't understand why the queen didn't just strike me down on the beach if she wanted me dead, why she's going to the trouble to drown me.

Maybe it's better this way. This way Kit and Lydia won't have to deal with my warped, curse-ravaged body. I close my eyes and wait for an end that doesn't come.

Instead, just as black is starting to wash over my vision, we surface. The seaweed vines drop me onto hard, damp stone. I splutter and writhe, my whole body aching as cold, musty air flows into my lungs.

I'm lying on an outcropping of rock in what seems to be an underground cave, the queen standing a few feet away. To her back is a narrow slash of an opening that must lead to the ocean, and before us, a great pool of water stretches out.

It's bounded by sharp boulders, and more rocks rise up from its surface. The walls and ceiling are stone too, as high overhead as the peaked eaves of the Seaman's Bethel; I don't see the end of the water, just a maw of darkness on the other side. And the only reason I can see anything at all—the water glows faintly green when it ripples, like the chamber beneath the Spout tavern where a lifetime ago Silas asked me to end whaling. It casts eerie, shimmering light over the queen as she slips into the glowing water and lifts herself onto a nearby boulder, the better to watch me.

"How can all be well?" I ask her, surprising myself as I push myself shakily to my feet.

IT IS SO IF YOU LOOK OUTSIDE YOURSELF, she says. She seems more comfortable down here somehow; her voice isn't as harsh and jarring. The cave swallows its echoes and renders it almost lovely. *IN A HUNDRED SHORT YEARS, YOU WILL BE GONE AND FEEL PAIN NO LONGER. IN A THOUSAND YEARS, MAN WILL BE NO LONGER AND THE EARTH AND SEA WILL BE AS THEY WERE.*

The words shouldn't be reassuring, but somehow they are. I feel my heart go quiet, like I felt as a child when my mother pulled the covers up over me, kissed my forehead, and blew her candle out.

The hazy bloodlust of the heartbreak seems to recede down here with no one to target. My words still come out in a harsh, hissing croak, but the queen seems to understand when I speak. "You said I could offer a bargain to be healed."

I SAID YOU CAN TRY, she says. *THE CURSE ON YOUR BLOODLINE IS OLD, BUT THE WILD ONES HAVE GIVEN ME THE POWER TO BREAK ITS BONDS.*

"The Wild Ones?" I ask distantly, too tired and afraid to feel much curiosity.

PRAY YOU NEVER HAVE TO TROUBLE YOURSELF ABOUT THEM, LITTLE ONE. NOW, THE PRICE.

That flicker of hope bubbles up in me again. I try not to look directly at it, not to let it grow too strong. "Name it and it's yours, anything except the people I love," I whisper. "Anything in my power to give." Which is precious little right now, but maybe there's something I can do for her, some favor.

DO YOU THINK YOU DESERVE FOR THE CURSE TO BE LIFTED FROM YOU?

My breath catches, but I don't have to think about my answer; the truth spills out automatically. "No. I have too much blood on my hands."

Guilt feels far beyond me now, and I'm almost grateful for it. More and more as the heartbreak takes hold, it seems the monster has three states of being—anger, fear, and a kind of coiled anticipation in between moments of anger and fear. It renders me more animal than human, but also shields me from what I distantly sense would be a crushing weight of shame.

I wait for her to react, and when she doesn't, I go on. "But it's not for me that I ask to be healed. It's for my brother and sister. I'm meant to care for them." I pick my words carefully, hoping to choose the right combination that will convince her, if such a thing is possible. "If I lose my humanity, they will have no one. They're innocent. Even if I don't deserve healing, they deserve a protector, and that's why I'm asking for your help."

The queen slips from her boulder and slides into the water without a splash, just a ripple. I faintly see the silvery shape of her moving through the water, then she surfaces very close to me, straightening to a standing position in the water. To be so confronted by her full height makes a lump of fear rise in my chest again.

YOUR CANDOR AND YOUR BOLDNESS PLEASE ME, she says at length. *SO HERE IS YOUR PRICE. IN EXCHANGE FOR LIFTING THE HEARTBREAK CURSE FROM YOU, I WILL TAKE YOUR LOVE.*

I blink, not following. "My love? What does that mean?"

I HAVE LIVED A LONG TIME, MINNOW, AND EMOTIONS ARE TO ME NOW AS RAINDROPS ON MY FACE. THEY LAND GENTLY AND ROLL OFF IN AN INSTANT. Her voice sounds more and more like a song the more she speaks, yet a creeping dread steals over me as I process her words. *ON THE WHOLE, I THINK THIS A MUCH PREFERABLE STATE OF BEING. YET ONE DOES MISS THE HIGHS AND LOWS OF FEELING. LIKE SALT, JUST A FEW GRAINS OF IT MAKE A FISH MORE DELICIOUS.*

My heart speeds as I consider this. "And when you take love from a person, they stop feeling it? And they wouldn't remember the person they loved anymore?"

NOT QUITE. The fins around her face flare and wave as if ruffled by a nonexistent breeze. *THEY WOULD KEEP THE MEMORIES OF THEIR BELOVED, ONLY STRIPPED OF ALL WARM EMOTION TOWARD THEM. THEY WOULD REMEMBER EVERYTHING, BUT FEEL NOTHING.*

I swallow, my mind suddenly full of memories of Silas. The longing in his eyes when we danced together, the shuddering weight of him in the tide. "And I can choose who to stop loving?" Remember everything. Feel nothing. It sounds like peace.

OH, MINNOW. Somehow it sounds like there is genuine pity in the queen's unearthly voice. *THIS IS A PRICE FOR YOU TO PAY, NOT A REWARD FOR YOU TO REAP. COME HERE.*

A deep-running prey instinct tells me not to get any closer to her, but her voice is too commanding not to obey. I move forward, dragging my boots against the rock, and the ice-cold water moves farther up my calves. My feet are numb with cold and dread, yet still I move until I'm within arm's length of the queen.

YOUR LOVE, MINNOW, AND ALL THAT GOES ALONG WITH IT, WILL REMAIN YOURS TO BEAR. She reaches out, lays the tip of one sharp finger against my chest. *I WANT THE LOVE THE OTHERS HAVE FOR YOU. WHEN YOU TOUCH THEM NEXT THEIR LOVE WILL BE TAKEN. YOUR BROTHER.*

My stomach drops.

Her fingers skim along the top of the water, beckoning. *YOUR SISTER.*

"No," I croak.

AND SILAS PRICE.

Tears start running down my cheeks. "I said I would only pay the price if it didn't bring harm to my siblings."

IT WILL NOT. She smiles serenely at me as my breathing quickens. *WE WILL KEEP THEM SAFE IN DREKJA, ALONG WITH THE REST OF YOUR HUMAN FRIENDS. THEY SHALL NOT BE HARMED.*

She leans closer. *THEY DON'T NEED YOU. YOUR SISTER IS NEARLY A WOMAN NOW. SHE CAN MANAGE*

WITHOUT YOU. YOU MUST REALIZE THAT THE PERSON PUTTING THEM IN DANGER HAS BEEN YOU THIS WHOLE TIME.

"My siblings wouldn't agree that this is harmless," I say through tears.

FORGET NOT THAT I CAN SEE YOUR HEART, she says, each word falling on me like a blade. *YOU ANTAGONIZED THE HARGREAVE BOY KNOWING IT WOULD PUT THEM AT RISK. YOU LET THEM STAY ABOARD THE* HERALDER *BECAUSE YOU COULDN'T BEAR TO BE WITHOUT THEM. YOU ENDANGERED YOUR FRIENDS THOUGH YOU KNOW YOUR SIBLINGS CARE FOR THEM TOO.* She pulls me in closer. *DO YOU THINK, MINNOW, THAT THEY'LL BE SORRY TO SEVER WHATEVER LITTLE BOND WITH YOU REMAINS?*

"No," I gasp again, but the terrible thing is, it's true.

Kit and Lydia would be safer without me. I put them in harm's way trying to keep both August and the company. It was me who kept pushing and grasping and trying to take what I thought was mine, no matter what. Still—"We're family."

THIS IS THE PRICE. She lets me go, and, unprepared, I lose my balance and fall back, landing in the knee-deep water. The cold grips me like a vise, and the stone seafloor is slimy under my stinging palms. My whole body shakes as I heave myself backward onto the dry rock ledge and pull my knees to my chest.

"Why did you lay this curse on us?" I ask miserably.

WE DIDN'T, she says simply. *DEAR CREATURE, THERE ARE OLDER AND WILDER THINGS IN THE WORLD THAN THE FINFOLK. SOON I THINK WE SHALL BE THE ONLY ONES STANDING IN THEIR WAY.*

I know I should be curious what she means, what those older

and wilder things are, but I'm too numb and distraught to care. I will live. I should be glad. But thinking about my future stripped of Kit and Lydia—and even Silas—all makes me feel like I'm in a rowboat that's slowly taking on water. It's slow, the sinking, but I can't fix it, and there's no shore in sight. Nowhere to go except down.

"It won't work on Silas," I say numbly once I've caught my breath. Yes, there was a pull between us, but if it ever amounted to love—it must be gone now, after I attacked him and left him for dead.

YOU MUST KNOW THAT HATE AND LOVE CAN BE INTERTWINED IN A SINGLE SOUL. AND THE MORE CONFLICTED AND FRACTIOUS A LOVE, THE MORE SAVORY IT IS TO ME.

"Please," I say dully. My tears feel burning hot on my icy, numb cheeks. "Please don't make me do this."

WOULD YOU CHOOSE TO TAKE ON SUFFERING YOURSELF IN ORDER TO SPARE THEM? IS THAT NOT WHAT FAMILY IS MEANT TO DO? Throughout our entire exchange, this is the closest the queen has sounded to irritated, and suddenly she's terrifying again. *LITTLE ONE, I WOULDN'T TRY TO ASK ANY MORE OF ME IF I WERE YOU. YOU'LL LIVE, AND THE PEOPLE YOU LOVE WILL BE UNBURDENED OF YOU. IT'S ALREADY MORE THAN YOU DESERVE, AFTER WHAT YOU'VE DONE. AND MORE, ONCE I HEAL YOU, YOU'LL BE IMMUNE FOREVER. NO ONE WILL EVER BREAK YOUR HEART AGAIN.*

That stops my breath. I hadn't thought to wonder about that. Being invulnerable. I'll lose everything, but my heart will never break again. And for once, I'm determined to do what's best for Kit and Lydia, what's truly best for them.

Even if it means losing them.

I step forward with a nod of assent and close my eyes as the queen reaches for me. Her fingers close around me and I hear her voice in my head again, an old, old language, as cleansing fire spills through my veins.

Chapter 27

By the time I crawl out of the sea, the others have retreated up the beach. They've rebuilt the bonfire inside the Livyatan's rib cage, five small figures huddling around it. I recognize the silhouettes of Silas, Kit and Lydia, Ezra and Josephine; meanwhile, Teuila and Zimri are a little ways off, digging a hole in the earth. None of them notice me at first as I straighten up and start to pick my way toward them.

Though it must be close to dawn by now, it's still dark, thanks to heavy, low-hanging clouds that roll ponderously by overhead, spilling intermittent bursts of drizzle and occasionally revealing slivers of a red-tinged sky. The world seems changed around me; colors are sharper, scents more muted. I can't smell blood anymore, though plenty must have soaked into the beach. Just salt water and smoke.

The cold wind bites at my face, scrapes my bare arms. The fires of Kielstraat have gone out, the embers hissing in the rain, sending plumes of smoke to join the clouds. When I get closer, I see three dark shapes lying on the sand near where Teuila digs and realize what they're doing; shock and grief roll through me.

Of course not everyone survived the skirmish with the finfolk on the beach. Certainly there are more bodies out in the bay—the sailors killed when the queen snatched the boats from the surface, or those who drowned swimming after the fleeing *Heralder*. But it hasn't sunk in before this.

Every whaler on every voyage knows they might not return, I remind myself, but it feels hollow.

Silas, of course, is the first one to notice me when I'm some ten yards away. He stands, still unsteady on his feet, his gaze finding mine.

Then Kit shouts my name, and before I can think, he's running down the beach toward me, Lydia at his heels. Even in the dark I can see the joy and relief on their faces. They must have thought I was gone, I realize with a pang.

Then another thought follows: the queen said that Kit, Lydia, and Silas's love would be taken the first time I touched them. I'm not ready for that yet. I stumble back and hold up my hands in a *stop* gesture before Kit can barrel into me.

He skids to a halt, brow furrowing in confusion. The others have risen to follow, but they stop too. Over my siblings' heads, I meet Silas's eyes again and somehow, mercifully, he seems to understand what I need. He motions for the *Whistler* crew to return to the fire, leaving just my siblings in front of me.

I swallow, looking back at Kit and Lydia as they take me in. "The queen took away my curse," I say softly.

Kit's face lights up, but Lydia looks wary, eyes skimming over my body. Being healed didn't cause the scales to fall away or the claws to retract. But they have lost their greenish-gray sheen, turning a cracked, dead white. I lift my arm and run my right palm down my left wrist, causing a shower of dead scales to fall away on the breeze.

All I want is for the three of us to be able to sit by the fire too, warm up and finally rest. But I can't rest yet. I've been healed, but I still have to pay the cost. "Walk with me?" I ask them.

A long moment passes before Lydia nods and steps forward. Throat tight, I turn and stride ahead of them toward the ruins of Kielstraat, not wanting to be observed by the others, not letting myself walk beside them lest Kit go in for a hug. Even so, walking with them is almost like we're back in Kirkrell, heading to church on a cold Seventh Day morning, except for the smell of smoke and the piercing grief in my heart.

I lead them a little ways into the settlement, until the ruin of what used to be the dining hall shields us from view of the *Whistler* crew. The light of the embers paints my siblings' faces, their wide, curious eyes. I know they must have so many questions, but I can't bear the thought of answering them. Not now, when it doesn't matter anymore.

Finally, I hold out my hand to Kit, inviting him in. He blinks in confusion but doesn't hesitate, taking my hand and letting me draw him in for a hug. He's warm and smells like the bonfire, his arms coming up around me just like always, as I bend down and kiss the top of his head. I can almost hear the questions vibrating inside him, but he doesn't voice them. Just lets me hug him.

Nothing happens until I finally make myself let go and step away. He grins at me, drawing breath, I'm sure, to finally unleash the torrent of questions—but then he freezes, blinking, the smile slipping away.

My own breath catches as a deep tremor runs through my brother, head to toe. When it ceases, he stands perfectly still, eyes blank, not moving except for the faintest rising and falling of his chest. Fear of a magic I don't understand fills me, and my heartbeat pounds in my chest.

"Annie." Lydia's voice beside me is low and fearful. "What is this? What's happening?"

She makes to step toward Kit but I throw out an arm in front of her, keeping her where she is.

"Everything will be okay," I tell her, tears thickening my voice. "I promise."

It starts slowly. A faint light appears over Kit's chest—no, not over it, I realize with a shock, but inside him. Before the heartbreak and the claws, I'd sometimes hold my hand up to the sun to see the pink light through my fingertips. It looks like that now, but through Kit's whole body. It grows bigger and brighter, lighting the map of his blood vessels from the inside, and then rises through his face, making him look like a little saint in a stained glass window.

As I stand there, rooted to the ground, the light reverses course, flowing down into the ground and branching out under our feet in the direction of the sea. I feel the heat of it through the soles of my shoes. I squeeze my eyes shut as a roaring sound fills my ears.

"Annie?"

I'm terrified that I'll find that the light has burned him up. But Kit's soft, sleepy voice sounds like it always has. When I open my eyes, there's nothing different about my brother as he blinks at me and Lydia. Not at first.

His expression when he looks at Lydia is normal, full of affection and admiration. But when he turns to me, those feelings drain away, leaving confusion in their wake. Like something is strange about me. Something is missing.

"You look different," he says eventually.

I feel the burn of tears behind my eyes, but they don't come to the surface. Maybe I've used them all up. "I'm not different," I tell him, softly and with conviction. "I'm your sister. I've loved you since the very first time I saw you, and I always will."

Kit blinks up at me. This is the part where he will tell me he loves me too, and he always will. That's what I pray for, to the Maker and the Wild Ones and every other deity I've ever heard of.

"I'm cold," he says uncertainly after a moment. "I'm going to go back to the fire."

He turns and trots back toward the whale skeleton, toward the crew. I wish I could sink and vanish into the earth like the light did. The queen said I'd be immune to heartbreak now, but without the curse, the pain of grief almost feels worse, unmediated by the fog of bloodlust. Now there is only loss.

"Annie?" Lydia's voice is soft and frightened. "What was that? Is Kit okay?"

Knowing what's going to happen next doesn't lessen the dread. I swallow a sob and turn to look at my sister, really look at her. She's almost as tall as me now; in a few years she'll probably be taller. She's fine-boned, but has Papa's strong chin and Mama's stubborn way of tilting it that should tell anyone not to get in her way.

After the cavern and the queen, swimming back to Kielstraat, I thought maybe taking her love would be easier than with Kit, because my relationship with Lydia has always been more prickly and complicated. But if anything, looking at her now, it feels harder. She's the person who knows me best in all the world, and the one who's most like me, yet she's so different too. Kinder, good to the core. And I won't get to fix things with us, and she'll probably never understand why I've done what I've done. I want to say something, but I can't think what.

The queen was right. Lydia is almost a woman, and more than

that, she doesn't need me. Whatever happens next, wherever they go, she'll survive, and she'll make sure Kit does too.

I reach out both my hands for Lydia's. She tilts her head at me, concerned, but takes them and wraps her fingers around mine, heedless of the claws.

With Kit, his love didn't drain away until after I stopped touching him. So I stay in that pose, holding Lydia's hands for too long, longer than makes sense, hoping she can't feel me shake. I try to memorize the feeling of her warmth, the sound of her breathing.

But it can't last forever. Eventually I have to let her go.

She looks confused as she releases my hands, and then goes still, that same shudder moving through her. Her eyes go wide and unfocused, and her hands slowly fall to her sides, fingers twitching as though with aftershocks.

Again that light wells up from inside her, but she's aware of it in a way that Kit wasn't. She looks down at herself, breath coming fast as the light rises through her chest, illuminating her face for one blindingly beautiful moment before draining into the ground and flowing toward the sea.

"What—?" she whispers, voice high and cracked. "What are you doing?"

"It's okay," I say, as reassuringly as I can. I look on as the stillness breaks and Lydia stumbles back. A moment passes and she hasn't met my eyes. She is breathing hard.

"What did you do?" she asks, looking up at me. I brace myself, expecting the absence of love to lead to a sharpening of anger and disappointment. But that's not what I see. Instead there's just . . . detachment.

"Annie," she says, but it sounds like a question.

"I spoke with the fae queen," I say. I step back and I'm not sure if it's to give her space or to preemptively protect myself from her judgment. "She agreed to heal me, but for a price. I have to give her the love that other people have for me."

I think she'll be angry, but Lydia has no expression at all. Or more accurately, I can't read her expression. "What does that mean?" Lydia asks.

I look into her eyes. "Do you love me?"

"Of course . . . you're my sister," she says. But her eyes slide down from me to focus on the ground. I hear the hollowness of her words.

"It's okay," I tell her after I catch my breath, all out of tears. "It's better this way."

I stand there in the rain and the smoking embers for a long time after Lydia walks away, trying to find the strength to go and fetch Silas.

I think about what I will say to him. I think about how he has suffered on my account enough, probably, to atone for his lies. I wonder how I can ensure he'll walk away from all this as unscathed as possible, as unburdened.

In the end, I don't have to find him. He appears silently amid the smoking rubble and pads toward me, unspoken things heavy between us. Even though the queen healed him, he still looks like a broken ghost of the boy I danced with hours ago, pale and bruised with sand in his hair and blood on his clothes. The embers cast deep shadows in the hollows of his face.

"I heard what you told your sister," he says. His voice is quiet and hoarse like it's been scraped over rocks. "I've heard stories about it. Trading love away." He stops a few steps from me, drawing his coat—too big, it must be borrowed or scavenged—tightly around himself. "But the finfolk usually ask for three things. Three tasks or favors or gifts."

I can't bring myself to say more than: "She did." I hold his gaze, willing him to understand.

He does. His eyes go haunted and he looks away, his throat bobbing as he swallows. "How . . . how does it work?"

I bite the inside of my cheek, rehearsing in my head the words I decided on before he appeared. After I take his love, I want him to be free of any guilt. And that will be easier, surely, if he thinks that our connection has been severed on both sides. I don't want him to know that my feelings for him remain.

So I weave just one small lie into what the queen told me.

"I'll touch you," I tell him, "and after that, our l—our feelings for each other will fade." I stumble over the word. "Our memories won't disappear, we won't forget anything that's happened. It's just that the emotions about all of it will be gone." *For you, at least.* Not me. But he doesn't need to know that. I swallow and reiterate the lie once more for good measure. "For both of us."

He sways just slightly toward me, hands coming out, and I can't tell if it's the lingering effects of blood loss or an aborted movement to pull me into him. In any case, he rights himself, lips pressed together and eyes shadowed. "What will you do after?" he asks at length.

Here is the part I haven't thought about. I try to sound confident, not wanting him to be afraid for me, even if soon it won't matter. "Go back to Kirkrell, I think. I don't expect a hero's welcome, but there must still be something I can do to stop whaling. Stop the war." *If it's not too late.*

"You won't be safe there," Silas says quietly, grief roughening his voice.

"I won't be safe anywhere. But I have to try." I open and close my fists to stop myself from reaching out for him, scales flaking off as I do. "Look after Kit and Lydia in Drekja?" I add softly. "None of this is their fault."

His breath catches; his eyes spark with hurt. "I know that."

"Yes, but I want you to remember. After." It weighs on me, the possibility that in the absence of love, the hatred he once carried for me will return. I know he wouldn't take it out on my siblings, whatever he felt for me. But I want to say it anyway.

His jaw works. "They're as good as *Whistler* crew now."

Bittersweet relief fills me. I know he'd protect any of his crew with his life, and for Kit and Lydia to be drawn into that circle assuages my fear for them. "Thank you."

There's so much else I want to say, but none of it will change what has to happen next. So I bite back the words and reach my hand out toward Silas, palm up.

Dread passes over his face; he draws breath, lips moving like he's trying to form words. Then he steps past my outstretched hand and cups my face instead, bringing our bodies close together. My breath vanishes as he looks down at me, eyes wide and dark, a silent plea. *Just once.*

I know—I know even as my hands slip under his coat that this will only make things worse. But I'm so cold and tired and lost and there's nothing left in me that can resist the gravity of him. I rise onto my toes so I can lift my face to his, just once.

He gasps softly when our lips touch, his hands threading into my hair still damp with seawater. Moves in so our bodies are pressed together, keeping each other warm as the cold wind blows smoke around us. The kiss is careful at first, both of us aware the circumstances aren't ideal. There's the taste of blood on his lips; dried blood stiffens his shirt where I clutch at him. Scales flake from my skin as we move together, and I still smell like the cavern beneath the sea that I crawled from minutes ago.

But then he drops one hand to my waist and pulls me against him, both of us swaying a little. My breath hitches, my lips parting beneath his, and Silas's control seems to fray. His grip tightens as the tip of his tongue flickers over my lips.

"Remember this too," he says against my mouth, low and ragged. "I didn't want anyone else's whole heart. I wanted the broken scraps of yours. Whatever you saw fit to give me."

Sorrow spears through the desire in me like two currents meeting to form an undertow. It takes me down, sweeping away what remains of my judgment.

I pull his face back to mine, pushing my body into his hands. He staggers but keeps us upright, our mouths pressed hard together. I can feel the desperation in him, his body unyielding even as he pulls me tighter against him, crushing the breath out of both of us. I tangle my hands in his hair, kissing his lips and his cheek and his jaw, trying to tell him how I feel without words, how much he deserves. He shudders as I catch his bottom lip between mine.

"I'm sorry," I whisper as he lowers his mouth to my throat. "So sorry." I hope he remembers that too.

His movements slow, his mouth on my neck stilling to a chaste closemouthed kiss, and then no kiss at all, just holding me tight as we breathe together. Me lifted half off my feet, him trembling with his face tucked into my shoulder.

I would ask if he's ready, but I know he's not. I'm not either, but there's no choice. I keep hold of him as he sets me on my feet and moves his hands to mine. I try to commit his eyes to memory—blown-wide pupils, wet lashes, emotion roiling under the surface.

"Keep your eyes closed until I say," I tell him softly. I don't want him to see how the light moves through him but not me.

He holds my gaze for a moment longer, then lets his eyes flutter closed. He steps back still holding my hands; they stay twined together until they can't, wrists and palms and then finally fingertips slipping apart.

As he shudders and goes still, I shut my eyes too. I didn't intend to, but I can't watch the love leave him. Still I see the brightness through my closed eyelids, feel the heat of it traveling down and dissipating under my feet.

When I finally open my eyes again, he's already looking at me. It's like the world has cycled through the seasons in the space of a moment, summer storm clouds freezing over. The warmth that had filled me after the kiss recedes, my skin chilling under his gaze.

"Silas?" I whisper.

He looks at me for a long moment, then takes something out of his coat pocket. Another seashell, mottled purple and gray, the kind the finfolk enchant to hold memories.

"This was on the beach when I went in after you," he says. His voice sounds the same on the surface, but there's a remoteness underneath, something brittle and sharp. "I knew then you'd come back. I knew I was meant to show you."

He holds his hand out with the seashell inside. I stare at him, willing myself not to shake. I don't want to know what's in that shell. Not when the last one shattered everything between us.

But I suppose that means there's nothing more to break.

With his expectant eyes on me, I put my hand over his, the shell caught between our palms.

Immediately I cry out and try to pull away, but Silas's other hand clamps down around my wrist, keeping me in place. Behind my eyes, Kirkrell falls to the finfolk.

The sea has burst the bounds of the harbor and rages through the streets I've walked my whole life, rendering them unrecognizable. Black boats slide over waters filthy with oil and rubbish and bodies. Too-tall figures wreathed in shadows fit long fingers beneath windowsills, loom over beds. Men with rifles and knives clatter toward the harbor, chased by billows of smoke and distant screams.

"This is what I was running from." Silas's icy voice cuts through the visions, but I can't see him though my eyes are open. The real world around me is gone, washed away in fire and flood.

"Why?" I gasp through tears. A horrible idea surfaces; it doesn't make sense, but maybe, maybe he hates me this much. "Are you cursing me now?"

"No." Silas grips my hand hard enough for the sharp ridges of the shell to cut both our palms, but the pain barely registers, blinded as I am by the images of war. "This is a warning."

"*I know the war will come*," I say in anguish. "You don't have to show me—"

My words die in choked silence, my breath seeming to turn to stone in my lungs. Because behind my eyes hangs another face, familiar and pale and impossibly still, eyes wide and sightless.

My knees give out beneath me. Whip-quick, Silas grabs my upper arms, holding me up while the shell falls and rolls away in the ashes. The echoing screams cease, but the lifeless face remains, burned into my memory.

When I look at Silas, tears blur my vision, but I can still feel the iciness of his regard.

"Please," I beg in a whisper. "How do I stop it?"

Much later, shivering awake in my own bed deep into the night, I will turn his next words over and over in my mind.

It's as if he knew. Knew that after a few days of stumbling south down the coast with scavenged food and blankets, my fingertips blue with frostbite, a Nunak fishing boat would find me. That we would cross paths with a ship bound for Kirkrell. That I'd return home.

That trading Silas, Kit, and Lydia's love to the finfolk queen would be only one in a string of terrible bargains I'd yet to strike.

But right now, all that is still far away. Silas settles me on my feet and his hands leave me; he steps back from me.

His voice is so cold as he tells me: "Start walking."

Acknowledgments

Break Wide the Sea was a strange, unruly book to write, my most difficult and most favorite so far. I'm so proud of how it turned out and could never have gotten it on the page without the support of my people. The debt of gratitude I owe all of you can't be captured in words, but I will try! A million thank-yous to:

Pete Knapp, Stuti Telidevara, Danielle Barthel, Olivia Valcarce, Kat Toolan, and the whole team at Park, Fine & Brower Literary Management. Pete, your brainstorming was invaluable in finding the heart of this story and shaping it into a book. I knew we were on the same wavelength when you suggested adding whales to an early draft, not even knowing that they are my absolute favorite animals. Some (fictional) whales were harmed in the making of this book, but I promise they'll get their revenge in Book 2.

The crew at Wednesday Books: Sara Goodman, Tiffany Shelton, Ashley Quintana, Cassie Gutman, Kerri Resnick, Michelle McMillian, Merilee Croft, Lena Shekhter, Daisy Glasgow, Brant Janeway, Zoe Miller, Angela Tabor, and especially my fearless editor Mara Delgado Sánchez. Thank you for believing in me and this story even when I didn't believe in myself. And for being so patient with me when I had to rewrite the book a few times to figure out what it was about.

Thanks too to Leo Teti and the whole Urano team—you all are wonderful!

Visits to the New Bedford Whaling Museum, Mystic Seaport Museum, South Street Seaport Museum, and the website for UHI Archaeology/Orkneyjar, as well as the writings of Philip Hoare, Skip Finley, and Eric Jay Dolin (among others) were all extremely helpful for both research and inspiration. Too, I'd be remiss not to mention *Our Flag Means Death*, which cemented my love of the sea and emboldened me to tell the story I wanted to tell. Any errors/omissions/oversights/liberties taken with regard to ship terminology, Orkney folklore, commercial whaling, nautical distances, or how to sail are, of course, my own.

My friends have been listening to me talk about this book for way too long now, but their enthusiasm and support has never ever flagged. Shout-out to Patrice, Brent, Arvin, Celine, Liz, Ronnie, the Cake Night crew, and anyone else who has ever listened to me ramble about #whalefacts or why everyone should read *Moby-Dick*. (I promise it's weirder and gayer than you think!)

My family is my rock, truly. Thank you to Mom, Dad, Rachel, Ben, Hannah, and my grandparents for being my first and most important fans.

Finally, dear reader, thank you for picking up *Break Wide the Sea* and spending some time with me, Annie, and the crew. I hope these characters have found a place in your heart like they have mine!

ABOUT THE AUTHOR

Sylvie Rosokoff

Sara Holland is the author of *Havenfall* and the *New York Times* bestsellers *Everless* and *Evermore*. She grew up in small-town Minnesota and has held jobs in a tea shop, a dentist's office, and a state capitol building, to name a few. She now lives in New York, where she can be found exploring bookstores or finding new ways to get caffeine into her bloodstream.